BURNING EMBERS

AN O'BRIEN TALE

STACEY REYNOLDS

Published October 12, 2020 by Stacey Reynolds

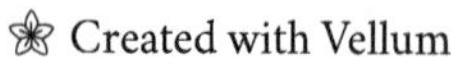

OTHER BOOKS BY THE AUTHOR

The O'Brien Tales & Novellas

Raven of the Sea:An O'Brien Tale

A Lantern in the Dark: An O'Brien Tale

Shadow Guardian: An O'Brien Tale

Fio: An O'Brien Novella

River Angels: An O'Brien Tale

The Wishing Bridge: An O'Brien Tale

The Irish Midwife: An O'Brien Tale (prequel)

Dark Irish: An O'Brien Novella

Other Books

His Wild Irish Rose: De Clare Legacy

CHARACTERS FROM THE O'BRIEN TALES SERIES

Sean O'Brien- Married to Sorcha (Mullen), father to Aidan, Michael, Brigid, Patrick, Liam, Seany (Sean Jr.), brother of William (deceased) and Maeve, son of Aoife and David. Retired and Reserve Garda Officer. Native to Doolin, Co. Clare, Ireland.

Sorcha (Mullen) O'Brien- Daughter of Michael and Edith Mullen. Sister of John (deceased). Native to Belfast, Northern Ireland. Married to Sean O'Brien with whom she has six children and eight grandchildren. A nurse midwife for over thirty years.

Brigid (O'Brien) Murphy- Daughter of Sean and Sorcha, Michael's twin, married to Finn Murphy. Mother to Cora, Colin, and Declan.

Finn Murphy- Husband to Brigid. Father of Cora, Colin, and Declan. I.T. expert who works in Ennis but does consulting work with the Garda on occasion.

Cora Murphy- Daughter of Brigid and Finn. Has emerging gifts of pre-cognition and other psychic abilities. Oldest grandchild of Sean and Sorcha.

Michael O'Brien- Son of Sean and Sorcha, married to Branna (O'Mara), three children: Brian, Halley, and Ian. Rescue swimmer for the Irish Coast Guard. Twin to Brigid.

Branna (O'Mara) O'Brien- American, married to Michael. Orphaned when her father was killed in the Second Battle of Fallujah (Major Brian O'Mara, USMC) and then lost her mother, Meghan (Kelly) O'Mara to breast cancer six years later. Mother to Brian, Halley, and Ian. Real Estate investor.

Captain Aidan O'Brien, Royal Irish Regiment- Son and eldest child of Sean and Sorcha O'Brien. Married to Alanna (Falk). Father of two children, David (Davey) and Isla. Serves active duty in the Royal Irish Regiment and currently living in Belfast, Northern Ireland

Alanna (Falk) O'Brien- American, married to Aidan, daughter of Hans Falk and Felicity Richards (divorced). Stepdaughter of Doctor Mary Flynn of Co. Clare. Mother to Davey and Isla. Best friend to Branna. Clinical Psychologist working with British military families battling PTSD and traumatic brain injuries.

Patrick O'Brien- Son of Sean and Sorcha. Married to Caitlyn (Nagle). Father to Estela, Patrick, and Orla. Currently residing in Doolin working as a Garda Officer. Serving on the National Security Surveillance Unit on the Armed Response Team in Shannon.

Caitlyn (Nagle) O'Brien- Daughter of Ronan and Bernadette Nagle, sister to Madeline and Mary. Married to Patrick. Mother to Estela, Patrick, and Orla. Early education teacher. English as a second language teacher for small children. Native to Co. Clare.

Estela O'Brien- native to Manaus, Brazil. Adopted daughter of Patrick and Caitlyn O'Brien.

Patrick O'Brien Jr.- Born in Dublin, Ireland. Adopted son of Patrick and Caitlyn O'Brien.

Orla O'Brien- daughter of Patrick and Caitlyn O'Brien.

Dr. Liam O'Brien- Second youngest child of Sean and Sorcha. Internal medicine and infectious disease specialist. Married to Dr. Izzy Collier.

Dr. Isolde *"Izzy"* (Collier) O'Brien- Doctor/Surgeon, prior United States Navy. Married to Dr. Liam O'Brien. Born in Wilcox, Arizona. Close friend to Alanna O'Brien. Daughter of Rhys and Donna Collier.

Sean *"Seany"* O'Brien Jr.- Youngest child of Sean and Sorcha.

Serving with the fire services in Dublin. Trained paramedic and fireman. Unmarried and no children.

Tadgh O'Brien- Only son of William (deceased) and Katie (Donoghue) O'Brien. Special Detectives Unit of the Garda. Married to Charlie Ryan.

Charlotte *"Charlie"* (Ryan) O'Brien- American FBI Agent with the International Human Rights Crime Division. Married to Tadgh. Sister to Josh. Currently working in Europe as the liaison to Interpol.

Josh O'Brien- Formerly Joshua Albert Ryan. Brother of Charlie. Studying Maritime Studies and Lighthouse Maintenance and living with Sean Jr.

Dr. Mary (Flynn) Falk- Retired M.D., wife of Hans Falk. Stepmother to Alanna O'Brien and Captain Erik Falk, USMC.

Sgt. Major Hans Falk, USMC Ret.- American, father of Alanna and Erik. Married to Doc Mary. Retired from the United States Marine Corps.

Maeve (O'Brien) Carrington- Daughter of David and Aoife. Wife to Nolan, mother to Cian and Cormac. Sister of Sean Sr.

Katie (Donoghue) O'Brien- Native to Inis Oirr, Aran Islands. Widow of William O'Brien. Mother of Tadgh O'Brien.

David O'Brien- Husband of Aoife, father of Sean, William, and Maeve. The oldest living patriarch of the O'Brien family.

Aoife (Kerr) O'Brien- Wife of David O'Brien, mother of Sean, William, and Maeve. Originally from Co. Donegal.

Michael Mullen- Native to Belfast, Northern Ireland, married to Edith (Kavanagh). Father of Sorcha and John.

Edith (Kavanagh) Mullen- Married to Michael Mullen, mother of Sorcha and John.

Madeline Nagle- Caitlyn and Mary's sister, daughter to Ronan and Bernadette Nagle.

Mary Nagle- Caitlyn and Madeline's sister, daughter to Ronan and Bernadette Nagle.

Jenny- Daytime barmaid at Gus O'Connor's Pub.

Dr. Seamus O'Keefe- OB-GYN who met Liam and Izzy in Brazil.

Nelson McBride-Seany's partner in the Dublin Fire Brigade.
Kamala McBride-Nelson's wife.

This book is dedicated to my father. Living without you is going to be really hard, Daddy. I hope I made you proud.

Clifford Gerald Clayton

June 25, 1938-March 19, 2020

PROLOGUE

Topsail Island, NC

Seven years earlier

Seany O'Brien hadn't dated all that much. Even so, at fifteen, he'd had a few lasses catch his eye. He'd even spent time with them, going to the cinema or meeting them in town for a burger. He'd kissed a few of them. Done more than kissed, actually. But none of them had ever stirred his heart as much as they'd stirred his loins. Lust was like breathing to a lad his age, but he'd never felt anything more than fondness for them, to be truthful. Not until now. Now, there was Moe. He'd spent the last weeks walking on sandy beaches, stealing kisses under the beach house or at the base of a sand dune. They'd talked about everything. He'd never talked so much to a girl in his life, other than family.

He had his group of friends at school, both male and female. His sister-in-law Caitlyn had two younger sisters that were in his tight circle of friends. Two pretty girls. Smart, too. But they'd never felt more than friendship for each other. It figures that the first time he'd ever felt a deep connection to a girl, both physical and emotional, she was a Yank. What was it with his brothers and American women? He saw the appeal, though. He'd been half in love with Branna, his new sister-in-law, when Michael had started the long and rocky path to his mate. And now Aidan with Alanna. He looked at Moe, with her Mona Lisa smile and her smart, serious eyes, and he finally understood. *Mate.* Could fate be that cruel? To gift him this wonderful love at this young age? Because it was love. He wouldn't let anyone lecture him about hormones or teenage crushes. He'd fallen in love this summer. With a bloody Yank that lived an ocean away. Suddenly, he had to touch her. He palmed the back of her head and pulled her mouth to his. He moaned against her mouth. "I don't want this to end. It can't be over."

He kissed her and felt the wetness of her tears. She whispered, "I don't want it to end either. This is killing me, Seany. My heart…" her voice broke and he took her palm, placing it over his own heart.

"This is yours," he said. Fighting his own tears. "We'll make it work, a chuisle. And when we are older, I'll come to you. Or you'll come to me. Promise me. This can't be the end."

"I promise," she said, kissing him hard. A rare treat, because she was the more timid one when it came to their physical passion. "I promise I won't let you go."

10 MONTHS later

Magnolia, Texas

"Of course you think that. You can't possibly fathom that I might have real feelings. A real relationship. I'm a child, right? Unless you need me to be an adult. Need me to drive or cook dinner or tutor Emmie. Then I'm responsible and such a blessing to this family. But when it comes to something I want or need, you dismiss me. Dismiss anything that doesn't fit into this household!"

Her words stung her mother, and she knew it. She couldn't take them back. They were true. But she saw the bags under her mother's eyes and the guilt in her father's eyes, and suddenly she was ashamed. She burst into tears, which was a rare thing for her.

"I know that we ask a lot of you, Moe. Too much. And I'm so sorry for that. It's the hand we all were dealt," her mother said.

Her father spoke finally. "We don't dismiss your feelings. I know how you feel about that boy. About Seany," he amended, because she hated when they called him *that boy*. He had a name. "And I'm going to be very frank with you, for the first time since this all started."

Moe folded her arms over her chest after a sweep under her eyes. "Please, enlighten me, Daddy. Tell me why it is so hard for you to see me grow up. To be happy. I'm sixteen years old. I'm creeping up on seventeen. Why is it that every other girl my age can date, can have boyfriends, and you can't let me have this?"

"Because of the way you look at each other," he said simply. "Because I don't know if you are ready for everything that is in your eyes and in your heart. You are only sixteen. How do you think this is going to play out, Moe? I'm going to put you on a plane and let you spend unsupervised time in another country with him? That his parents are just going to let him fly here for the summer? He's going to be here in this house with everything that's going on? Because I'm ashamed to admit, we are struggling to keep everything afloat. Your mom can't work because I'm a burden right now." His voice was hoarse, and Moe suddenly didn't want him to talk anymore. His pride was taking a hit even more than hers was. "Back and forth to the doctors and therapists while you spend the summer resenting that you can't just go be with your boyfriend. That he's going to feel as trapped in this house as you obviously do?"

"Daddy, don't say that! I never said I felt trapped. I just..." she put her face in her hands. "I don't know how to make you understand. I'm being torn in two."

"I know, baby. And I wish I could spare you this, but I can't. Your place is here. Right now, you're feeling a lot for the first time, but it won't be the last. I promise you. This tug of war has to end, and you're the one who has to do it. One side has to let go. We are your family, so we can't. He'll have to do it. You'll have to make him do it. Then, Moe, maybe you'll have a shot at something real. Someone who is here. Someone who can take you to your prom and graduate with you and be a true, present friend to you. I know that you'll grow up and leave us someday. Some man is going to steal your heart and that'll be it. But it cannot be now. The kindest thing you can do for both of you is to let him go. Let him meet someone who can be there for him. Someone he can take to the movies and kiss goodnight. You both deserve it. It was a summer romance, my sweet girl, and that summer is long over."

* * *

MOE LOOKED at Seany's pixelated face and wanted to die. How could she do it? But how could she not? "Moe, you don't have to do this! It won't be forever! Another year and a half and we'll be eighteen. You can fly by yourself. I can come to you."

"Seany, think about what you're saying. I know you don't want to hear it, but this can't continue. It's tearing me apart. You'll find someone else, and someday you will thank me for this. Please, my mind is made up."

"This is your parents…"

She put her hand up to stop him. "This was my decision, Seany. Mine alone. It's over. I care for you. I really do. But this is not sustainable. I will always care for you, but it's over. I'm so sorry." Her voice trembled as the tears started up again. "Please, don't make this any harder."

"Don't hang up, Moe. I love you. Don't you know that?" There, he'd said it. Surely, she wouldn't go through with it now. He'd said the words. "This is wrong. I can't stand the thought of not talking to you again. Clean break be damned. Just sleep tonight and call me tomorrow. Please, Moe."

But she didn't call. She sent a letter. And that was the end of it.

CHAPTER 1

Just to Hear again the ripple of the trout stream The women in the meadow making hay
And to sit beside a turf fire in the cabin
And see the sun go down on Galway Bay.-Arthur Colahan

Seven Years Later
Dublin, Ireland

Seany O'Brien drove his old, hand-me-down car back to Dublin with a heavy heart. It had been an eventful month. With the move, the transfer delay, and the local tragedy on the water, the pull toward that western coast was as strong as ever. He was happy with the choice of residence that he and Josh had made. The cottage was cheap and convenient to the city. It was also half the drive to his family seat in County Clare. Doolin was the O'Brien hub, so to speak. Both historically and in the literal sense. His parents lived just outside the main town. Brigid, Michael, and Patrick were within ten minutes of each other. He had nieces and nephews to spare, and it was nice to be a part of their lives with greater frequency. And then there was Josh.

Josh O'Brien, formerly Joshua Albert Ryan, was Tadgh's brother-in-law. Charlie's battle for her brother's freedom had been a victory for the whole family. Rescuing him from their abusive childhood, Charlie had brought him to Ireland on a student visa. Josh may have been born a Ryan, but the O'Brien clan had made him their own. He'd changed his name, shedding the last tie to the father who had never loved him and only caused him pain. Josh was an O'Brien through and through. Blood didn't always matter. Hell, look at Patrick's family. Estela and Patrick, Jr. were not children of Patrick and Caitlyn's bodies, but they were the children of their hearts. Soul children whom they loved just as deeply as their new baby girl, Orla.

Seany loved seeing their family expand, whether from adoption or birth. Orla looked like an angel. A dusting of auburn hair and blue green eyes that had begun overtaking the slate blue of every newborn. She grasped his finger or rooted on anything that might resemble a breast. He was used to it now. Newborns trying to gnaw on his arm or through his shirt, needing passing-off to their mothers for another feeding. Yes, it would be good to be home…or at least closer to home. His mam worked in Galway on occasion, when one of her expectant mothers needed more care than the birthing center could offer.

They needed more family around them. Josh needed it. His new family member and unlikely friend was imported from Cleveland, Ohio. Josh was younger than he was by a couple years, but he was an old soul. Seany thought about the laceration that marred his scalp. The shaven side of his sandy colored hair making a military style cut a necessity. Stitches from an assault with a beer bottle.

Justine. That psycho, little pub rat who didn't have it in her to give Josh what he needed. Safety, love, and tenderness. Seany thought about another woman. The beautiful, kind, intelligent woman who was Justine's opposite in every way. If Seany had his way, they'd be seeing a lot more of Madeline Nagle. Josh was lying low after the daring rescue that had saved more than one life. His work on the Royal National Lifeboat had placed him right where he needed to be, and he and Madeline would forever be bound to one another due to that dark evening in the stormy, open sea.

He put in a wireless call to Maddie, and once it was finished he went on his way to work. Josh was going to get a visitor whether he liked it or not.

* * *

Magnolia, Texas, U.S.A.

Maureen Rogers walked through the side door of her parents' house, only to be set upon by two fiends. Her dog Haunches and her baby brother. "Hello, Sammy. Oh, and I see you too, Haunches. Calm down." The dog really was adorable, like a pup, even at his advanced age. He was a mixed breed of Queensland Blue Heeler and Border Collie, which made him look rather silly. But he'd been a good herder in his younger years.

Her little sister said, "Hey, Moe." She watched her breeze by… a pre-teen and embracing the role. Sullen one minute, giggly the next. Moe was splitting her time between her parents' house and a sublet room in her classmate's apartment. The woman lived near the university stables, and she gave Moe the space for very little compensation. With her schedule during her last year at school, sometimes it was easier to crash close to work. But she always came home at least four days out of the week, both to see her family and her horse.

Moe threw an arm around her sister. "Hey, Em. Where's Daddy?" She knew her mother was at work. Today was a therapy day for her father, and she liked to check on him afterward.

"He's taking a nap. I need to go feed the horses. Can you watch Sammy?"

Moe said, "Why don't we all go? Sammy is old enough to help." Moe plucked her brother off the stool of their breakfast bar, forcing him to abandon his iPad.

The three left through the back door, heading to the barn after sliding into some practical boots. Moe smiled as the smells from the barn started to enter her nose. Fresh bedding, manure, and the unique smell of horses. Their three horses shuffled their hooves, growing restless as they sensed their humans coming into their space.

Artemis was an American Quarter Horse. She was the horse that Moe rode more than any and she considered the mare to be hers. Five years ago, the family had acquired her as a one-year-old filly. She was a dun with a dark dorsal stripe and white sock markings on her left hind leg. Although her body was gold, her tail and mane were almost black. She was beautiful and athletic, and the apple of Moe's eye. "Good morning, Artemis. Are you ready for something tasty?" A pang of guilt hit her in the gut. She didn't get to the barn often enough. School kept her busy. "Then maybe a ride?" The horse snorted, nuzzling her under the arm. "Okay, okay. Food first."

She went to the next stall. The grey was a little less zealous in the morning. Another American Quarter Horse, Gramps had some striping and had originally been named Tucker. He was older and starting to lose weight. "And some mash for you, old boy. You need to eat more. Maybe Em can take you out for a ride?" They fed him a high calorie mash, attempting to put some weight on him. He was gentle and still quite handsome.

Her brother piped up. "What about me? Why can't I take him? Tear Gas is too ornery." Tear Gas was her father's horse. He was a stinker in more ways than one, as he didn't listen to anyone but her father. He also had a very active GI tract, and you didn't want to ride behind him after a meal. Hence his name.

"Sammy, you can ride Gramps. Use the adult saddle and you can both fit," Moe said.

Sammy put his fists on his hips. He looked so much like their mother; it almost made her giggle. "I'm big enough to ride my own horse."

"I know you are, so you'll be up front. You can hold the reins and take Em for a ride." He seemed to consider that, eventually concluding that he could live with it. Em wisely kept quiet.

* * *

Moe traveled the meadow, loving how the grass swayed around the edge of the well-worn trail. Her mother's kitchen garden had gone to seed, the autumn changes evident in the landscape. Em said, "Mom said you were looking for a job for school credits."

Moe answered, "An internship, yes. It would start in January and go through the summer, until I graduate." She loved this moment. Out with her siblings in the late morning sunlight. The horse shifted smoothly under her, like they were one being. She patted Artemis's thick neck, feeling her soft hair and the powdery dander that came with it, no matter how many times she was brushed. She was warm and soft, and Moe suspected the horse liked this ride as much as she did.

Her sister said, "Will you go away?" It was a simple question, and Moe didn't know how to answer it. "Sometimes people leave and go to other places when they get a job. My friend Lilia's sister moved to Colorado."

"Let's not borrow trouble. I don't even know where my internship will be. There are a lot of choices, and they have to pick me, too. Let's just think about today." She smiled at her sister, then looked ahead. This was her favorite spot. "Can you handle Gramps?"

Her sister sighed. "Go ahead. Artemis is about ready to jump out of her skin with excitement."

She was right. This was Artemis's favorite spot as well. Wide open and even. Moe urged her mount forward, settling into an easy trot, but she could tell it wasn't enough. "All right girl, let's get it." She applied the pressure that signaled her horse faster, then she felt Artemis engage at a full gallop, giving the horse her head. She felt her cheeks stretch with a smile she couldn't contain. The wind in her hair was crisp and sweet from the drying grasses around her. She heard the children squeal as the unmistakable sound of horse hooves came behind her. She knew that Em would never endanger her brother by trying to follow. And Gramps was more of a moseying type of mount than a galloping. She risked a glance behind her to see her father on Tear Gas, grinning like mad as he closed the distance. She hunched down, squeezing Artemis to signal the race. She didn't need to, really. Artemis liked a challenge. Tear Gas was smaller and stockier than Artemis, but he was deceptively athletic. And under her father, he was something to see. By the time they reached the stream that bordered their property, they were neck and neck. Her father winked at her. "Nice run. You almost beat me."

She laughed, leaning in. "I did beat you, old man. And that stinky partner of yours."

He conceded. Moe and Artemis were hard to beat, even if she hadn't had a head start. Her father said, "Mom called. She's going to be late. Dinner is on us."

"Not an issue. I saw a pot roast in the fridge. I wish she didn't work so much."

"Yeah, well it's good for her. She needs her own thing, you know? She stayed home with me for two years."

"Yeah, I know. I get it." Moe understood. Until they'd gotten a handle on her father's seizures, he hadn't been allowed to drive. She thought about that accident he'd gotten into with her and Em in the car. Em had been a little girl. She thought of the panic of that night, looking around for her sister. Then she'd seen him…she'd seen Seany for the first time. He'd been holding her sister off at a safe distance, because she'd wandered off in the confusion. Protecting her while they assessed her father. Her throat tightened the way it always did when she thought about him. Seany O'Brien was the male to which she compared every other young man she'd met. None of them held a candle to the young Irishman who had bewitched her body and soul. She shook herself. "Time to head back. Gramps will eat himself sick on the sweet grass."

"Therapy was rough." It was more than he usually shared. Her dad was a joker. Never got too serious.

Moe said, "I'm sorry. Sometimes it has to be rough to get better. Right?"

"Yeah, I know. I guess it did help." Their pace was slower as they retraced the path back to Em and Sammy. "So, any ideas on the internship?"

"Equine studies are complicated. And around here, there is a lot of competition. I was thinking I'd branch out. I mean, I don't want to leave you a man short, so to speak, but…"

"We are going to be just fine, baby girl. You go wherever you want. You spread those beautiful wings. We're not going anywhere, and you'll always have a home here, but there is nothing wrong with going on an adventure. Hell, when I was your age, I was finishing Officer Candidate School and getting my orders to Okinawa. I can hardly tell you to stay home and tend the hearth."

She smiled at that. "Thanks, Daddy. I'll think on it. I have to admit, I get that itch every couple of years." He knew all about that itch. When you were a military family, you moved a lot. Moving around every two or three years felt normal. At the two-and-a-half-year mark, you started itching for the next adventure. She didn't know where she'd end up during the months spanning January to June, but she felt like something momentous was ahead.

CHAPTER 2

Dolphins Barn Fire Station
Dublin, Ireland

"O'Brien! Get your ass in here! It's your day to do the clean up!" Nelson McBride had a big mouth. His order boomed through the station. Seany was just finishing up with the inventory check and uniform inspection. He was hoping to find a spare turnout coat in his size. No joy, though. The only one had spider sacks in the collar and was roughly a size to fit his sister.

The safety strap on his left sleeve was ripped, and he needed to take it in for repair. The problem was that he needed the damn coat. Oh, well. What was the chance of it being a problem before the weekend was over? He'd make do until the boss's secretary was back, and she could help him find a loaner from another station. As he processed what McBride said, he bristled. He was not on rotation to clean up after meals. McBride had the cook's duties today, and the nasty bastard usually sloshed food everywhere and dirtied every pot in the cupboard.

Seany said, "You can bite my balls, McBride. I'm not on clean-up duty. Check the roster again." He came forward, toward the kitchen and dining area. The dry erase board was above the dining table, in plain view. McBride was slipping. Probably sleep deprivation from the new baby. He walked through the swinging door to a crowd of male voices booming toward him. His heart squeezed as he took in the spread. A cake, pizzas, American style wings, crisps of every kind. A bachelor's potluck.

"We couldn't put you out to pasture without a sendoff." McBride smiled broadly as he grabbed Seany in a hug. They'd been partnered up when Seany had received his first assignment.

"Galway is hardly out to pasture. Thanks, lads. Truly. And some American hot wings. You really went all out."

"Fried them up myself. That buffalo sauce is a bit much for my delicate system, but I know you got hooked on them when you went to the States."

"Yes, fried and spicy. There is nothing better, my friend. Worth the heartburn to be sure." Seany grabbed a wing while he read the cake. *You'll be missed, Junior!* He was the youngest at the station. One of twenty full-time firefighters instead of a retained squad. It was a coveted position, being on salary. His dual training as an EMT had been the clincher. His colleagues disagreed on what actually sealed the deal for his full-time hire. The word was out that his familial connections had influenced the Lord Mayor to speak on his behalf. His father, brother, cousins, as well as his sister-in-law, had been involved in a high-profile case involving a terrorist plot in Dublin. The Mayor and Prime Minister had given them awards. No matter how many times Seany pointed out that the current Lord Mayor and Prime Minister were both new to their offices, hence no affiliation or connections, they continued to rib him about being one of the Dublin golden boys. He loved these guys, but he was ready to forge his own path in a new town.

He'd taken one bite of his spicy chicken wing when the alarms went off. They all sprang into action as the call came over the loudspeaker. "Warehouse fire in The Liberties. Abandoned and supposed to be unoccupied. Two floor involvement, six floor structure. Elevators inoperable."

They all knew what the word *supposed* implied. The homeless problem in Dublin was increasing. These derelict buildings often had people sleeping rough in them. Some areas had little colonies of rough sleepers occupying old buildings and even entire alleys. Gardai could only do so much. He was assigned to Truck #2 and he began suiting up with the rest of the men. The ambulance and other truck were prepared and loaded with the entire shift. The retained firefighters were paged. Warehouse fires could get out of control very easily. The Liberties, a historic area of Dublin, was in the midst of a rebirth. The whiskey distilleries had abandoned Dublin for a time, but the district was beginning to thrive again. The problem with fires in a distillery area was obvious. They didn't want the flames to spread out of the derelict area and turn into a cataclysmic event.

The trucks screamed down the streets, following the coil of black smoke was visible from miles away, no doubt. McBride was next to Seany in the truck. "We couldn't send you off without a proper blaze to remember. The wings will have to wait."

"I do appreciate it, McBride. I know you think I'm bailing, but I have my reasons. I'm grateful for everything you taught me."

"Don't get sappy, lad. I'm envious. The wife has been nagging at me to move out of the city. Maybe I'll follow you out West. Get a little cottage by the sea."

"Aye, now you're talking. I'll keep my ears open. And I'll come back for a visit to see the babes and that pretty wife of yours."

"Watch it, boy. She's only got eyes for me."

"Aye, I can tell. Four kids under the age of twelve. She must like ye fine," Sean said with a cheeky grin. McBride laughed as they turned the corner and switched their minds to work. The fire had spread to a third floor on the west side of the building.

"Junior is with me. We'll enter from the east stairwell and check for occupants. Donny and Carter, come in ahead on the hose and move down the first floor. McDaniels and Foster, I want you to start on the central entrance with another hose on the second level. Jenson, you are on the ladder with Tierny." He continued to call out assignments for those who'd clear the floors for survivors and the men assigned to the hoses. Then they were in it.

* * *

Magnolia, Texas

Moe shot up from her bed, gasping for breath. She was covered in sweat, her heart racing. "Moe, you okay?" her sister said with concern. Moe shook off the feeling of dread that had washed over her. Her dream had been a free flow of horrible scenes. Starting in the thick of the hurricane that had ravaged this area three years ago. Her memories were vivid, but her sleeping brain played cruel tricks on her. Adding bits from her subconscious mind. Floating logs turning into the bodies of people she loved. She shook off the dream, answering her sister.

"I'm okay. I must have had a weird dream. Too much pot roast." She looked around the room, seeing the silhouette of Thai and Korean furniture; part of an eclectic collection of bazaar purchases they'd made in their years overseas. Dragonflies embroidered the thin sheer panels on the windows. The moonlight illuminated them, and she could see the embroidery clearly as if they flew in the night sky.

She'd shared a room with Emmy ever since they'd bought the ranch. After Daddy had medically retired, they came back to Texas to be near her grandparents, who owned a small cattle ranch. Moe had always loved being around the animals in her younger years. There were always horses around, used for moving cattle to different pastures when it was needed. Some of the horses were for sport, as her father had tried his hand at the rodeo before joining the Marines.

Moe had been born to ride. They'd taken their horses with them when they moved. Their last duty station had been Camp Lejeune, North Carolina. The base stables were nice, and she'd been right down the street in family housing. Her father's career as a Marine Officer had taken the family to a lot of places. When they'd done a tour in Japan before Em was born, they'd left the horses with her grandparents. She'd cried for days. But after a few weeks, she'd embraced her new surroundings and had fond memories of her parents backpacking with her through bamboo forests, and visiting pagodas, castles, and Shinto shrines. Making friends at her Japanese preschool had been surprisingly easy, with them learning her language as she learned Japanese. The Japanese children were so obedient and orderly in their school environment. She'd always been a mild-mannered child, and so she'd fit right in with the Japanese children.

Even now, she was teased by her peers for her constant composure, her even temperament. One particular idiot had even used the word passionless. Her first year of school when she'd had a mind to study performing arts, she'd dated one of her classmates. He hadn't understood her. He'd been from a very liberal, anti-military family. So, it had ended. She was mild mannered to a point, until you started disparaging her daddy. Those were fighting words. That course of study had lasted a semester. The students and teachers in the performing arts wing were nice enough. They just weren't her tribe. The music productions she'd had so much fun with in high school had been designated to hobby status. She still played around with it, using her software to do mashups. But her passion, albeit a quiet one, was horses. Equine Studies with a minor in Equine Therapy had become her new journey. She'd hung out in the Animal Studies and Agriculture divisions for the duration of her time at Texas A&M, and now she was ready for her internship. It was that, more than anything, which kept her up at night. There was one assignment in particular that spoke to her wandering spirit.

She got up and walked to the bathroom in the hall, one of two in the house. Some people retired in big houses near a beach or in their hometowns. This home had been all about the land and the outbuildings. A pristine six horse stable, fenced arenas for the horses, and plenty of pastureland. She approved. She didn't give one iota about sharing a room and the lack of an en suite bathroom. Talk about first world problems. She'd make an apartment above the stables if she wanted her own space. Her mind niggled back to that new opening for an intern that was taking exchange students. A semester abroad....

and a dream job, really. The question was, did she have the guts to do it? She thought of her dream. Of seeing Seany O'Brien hanging from a log, trying to pull her father out of the current. Of both men going under, her screams radiating through the flooded streets of Houston. It wasn't real, of course. She just couldn't help wondering if her subconscious was pushing her in a certain direction.

CHAPTER 3

Fire that's closest kept burns most of all...William Shakespeare

The Liberties- Dublin, Ireland

The engines parked at the front of the old building. The fire was significant, and they hurried to get the hoses running and get the pairs of men into the building to search for anyone who may be in there. Seany patted his breast, directly over his heart. He carried two pictures with him. There was one of his parents on the interior of his helmet. There was another inside his jacket. One no one knew about, except his partner who had seen it accidentally. He hadn't pressed Seany for details, which was one of the reasons he was a good partner. The old photo was a sort of talisman, and proof that he was a pathetic sap and prone to self-torture. His gesture didn't go unnoticed by his partner as they went into the building, but he just smirked and gave a tap to his head. He carried a picture of Kamala and his children inside his own helmet. Then they readied themselves to go into the heart of the beast.

Seany walked behind his partner, the smoke getting thicker. They had their Scott Air-Paks™ in place, breathing the compressed air for their own safety and survival. They'd found one man hovered in the stairwell and radioed down to the ground men, confirming they'd taken him out when he reached the bottom. They were on the third floor now, and when McBride opened the door leading out of the stairwell, thick smoke poured out. It was warm, but the fire was still mostly on the east side of the building, perhaps due to the wind. They were working from the ladder to quell the flames, but this was no walk in the garden. These old warehouses had all sorts of unknown factors. Flammable waste that was abandoned, rotted flooring, combative squatters. Lots of fun to be had without the luxury of law enforcement.

McBride yelled over his shoulder, "It's heating up. Stay tight, Junior!" They'd turned on their headlamps because the dark interior of the warehouse was made more so by the smoke. The warehouse's third floor wasn't like the third floor of a hotel. The first floor was fifty feet high with bay doors and old scaffolding. The abandoned distillery had old platforms where the copper kettles had been, long removed and sold off to the highest bidder. The third floor had obviously been the offices. There was bedding and other signs that more than one person was sleeping rough in this area. Seany heard another team come over the radio, and the words made his blood go cold.

It was McDaniels from the second floor. They were on a hose. The radio squawked, and he yelled, "We've got some sort of metal tanks up here! Maybe empty propane tanks!"

McBride answered swiftly, "You can't know for certain those are empty. Get the hell out of there!" They both knew how close the flames were to the center of the building. They made their way through slowly, scanning for any other homeless people overcome with smoke. McBride yelled back, "Junior, watch your footing. This floor is rotten. Move closer to the wall. After we check these last two offices, we'll head out. We're getting closer to those tanks than is wise." Over the radio, he heard the men say they'd exited the area, and Seany felt McBride's relief.

Just as they took the first step to the side, an explosion rocked the building. They heard the carnage as the force of it ripped through the third floor. The blast was east of their location, but they felt a radiating heat that sounded like rolling thunder as the floor beneath them shook. "Back up, O'Brien! To the stairwell, now!" But as he said it, Seany watched in horror as the rotted floor gave way underneath his partner. Seany dove toward him, grabbing the fabric of his turnout coat on his right arm. Seany hit the floor, the impact ringing his bell as he held McBride by the arm, dangling over a chasm in the floor that went all the way to ground level. His partner latched his arm around Seany's, securing the hold. Seany spoke into the mic, barking a sharp command.

"I need backup! Center of the western wing, third floor, 80 meters from the stairwell. Floor collapse. I've got McBride by the coat so move your fucking asses!" Then he used his second arm to reach for his partner's collar on the other side. His shoulder was shredded, as McBride's fall toward the ground had jolted Seany's whole body, wrenching his bicep and shoulder socket. He was suddenly grateful for every push-up he'd ever done. He said calmly, "Can you get footing on anything?"

McBride's face was stoic. "I'm dangling like a fish on a line, brother. If you can pull me up to the edge, maybe I can get an elbow over. If I try to use you for leverage, I'll pull us both over." His words were strained, and Seany's heart lurched as he saw the fire taking a foothold on the west side of the first and second floors. McBride looked down and uttered a juicy curse.

Seany's voice was calm. "I'm here. I will not leave this building without you. Now, I'm going to let go of your collar and grab the harness on your back. I'm going to pull you upward and grab it, if I can. You could have laid off the fucking pizza, by the way." McBride gave a chuckle, a gallows humor moment in the middle of the chaos, but it was all they had in the way of motivation and stress relief.

Seany knew he only had one good shot at this. His shoulder was spent, as was his left grip. He grabbed with his non-dominant hand and caught McBride's right arm. Right now, he had a death grip, and that was the only thing keeping McBride where he was. McBride had his free hand on the lip of the jagged hole. "On three," Seany said. McBride nodded. On three, he pulled up using both arms with a big heave, then disengaged the right hand to grab his partner's Scott-Pak™ harness. He got the coat instead, but he readjusted, methodically moving down to grip the strong metal harness. That's when he felt the sleeve strap on his turncoat finally give, revealing his bare wrist.

No matter. He dug his boots in and pulled back, trying to get far enough for McBride to get a shoulder over the edge. He was so heavy and Seany didn't have anything stationary to hook his feet for leverage. McBride was only a little shorter than Seany and solidly built. And his equipment weighed a ton. He felt his buddy start to shake, and then a growl came out of the man. Seany was so focused on his task, he didn't see the progression of the fire. The explosion gave the flames a little nudge after opening a chasm between the floors. McBride groaned as if in pain. His face was flushed, and his mouth was tight.

Seany looked straight ahead as the flames coiled up the south wall and overhead. They were utterly fucked if he couldn't get McBride up and over. Once he got him stabilized, he could hitch his personal escape rope to McBride's belt. Then anchor him to something as Seany got him the rest of the way out. He scrambled, ignoring the roar and the cracking of old wood overhead and under him. The heat around him was searing.

The building was old, probably built at the turn of the century using no steel beams. The distillery that pulled out in the seventies had been the last occupant. He got a burst of strength and pulled again, gaining some ground. He was sweating so badly it ran into his eyes. But he saw his partner's face. A halo of orange light shining from beneath him. Seany felt the hair singe on his exposed strip of arm, felt the burning heat, and wondered how hot it must be at his partner's feet.

He croaked, "They're coming, brother. Just hang on." And they were. Donny and Carter had been on the second floor with the hose and were fighting beneath them to keep the fire from spreading. The truck had moved its efforts west, trying from the outside to keep the fire away from them, but it was like a living hunter. The flames seeking them out. Hungry for them.

McDaniels and his partner had fled the second floor, following McBride's final command. They'd been spared certain death by leaving the area where the propane tanks were exposed to flame. They were currently making their way up the west stairs. Another station arrived to offer backup. Seany heard it all unfolding on his radio. This was good. They weren't alone. He just had to get his buddy's body off the barbecue, and all would be well. The beams above him shifted. McBride's face was resigned as he said, "I'm sorry to put this on you, Junior. Tell my wife I love her."

Seany pulled him up a few more inches, the pain in his shoulder almost unbearable. The edges of the floor were crumbling where his partner hung. Dry rot having taken over in this old, abandoned dwelling. McBride's words just kept him more focused, more determined. "No! You fucking tell her yourself!" He got McBride up just enough to help him clear his elbows over the floor. His shoulders lifting him up a few inches as Seany guided him up. Then he went to work with his escape system. Most of the guys didn't have one, but Seany's father had purchased it for him when he graduated from the academy. He latched the one end to McBride's harness and then started looking around. There was so much smoke, he could barely see, but there was an exposed water line near the stairway. An iron pipe would do. He just had to get to it. Fire raged on two sides of him now licking overhead as the ceiling burned. He backed up, holding the rope. "Don't let go, brother."

They heard the men clearing the stairwell door,shouting to them just as the part of the ceiling came down across Seany's shoulders and striking McBride on the top of the head. Seany felt the impact and the incredible heat, then there was nothing.

* * *

Magnolia, Texas

"Maureen Rogers, a 3.92 GPA, member of the Student Equine Society, and a blue-ribbon barrel racer. You are also volunteering at the local chapter of the Autism Society, where you train in hippotherapy. Not bad, Ms. Rogers. I think you've got some promising prospects for your internship. There is the non-profit route, some big ranching corporations…"

"What would you think about me studying a semester abroad?" Moe said softly and confidently.

"Hmm, well let me look a minute. Yes, there are some opportunities. How's your Spanish?"

"Passable. I get by," Moe said with little enthusiasm.

"I've got something in central England. It's not your riding style, if this resume is anything to go by."

"I trained from age ten to fifteen in English style. From six to ten years old was beginner level Dressage. I've been around due to the military. We couldn't get Western lessons in most of our duty stations. I also live on a small family ranch. I know horses, ma'am. Don't worry with regard to versatility."

"This is interesting. Have you seen this one?" She pointed on the screen.

Moe flushed, then cleared her throat. "Yes, I have seen that opening. I'd like to talk about it."

* * *

Doolin. Co. Clare, Ireland

Sean O'Brien rubbed the back of his neck, feeling twitchy as hell while he sat with his wife and daughter over some evening tea. Chamomile due to the late hour. The wee ones, Declan and Colin, were passed out on the sofa. Only Cora was missing. He started rubbing his chest, feeling a tightness there that he couldn't explain.

"Sean O'Brien, I told you not to have that second helping. You've got indigestion." His wife was a pushy little peahen.

"And how do ye know I'm not over here dying of a heart attack? You'll be pecking at me over my corpse."

She narrowed her eyes at him, a hint of amusement showing at the corner of her mouth. "Because you don't have my permission to die for another fifty years at least. And you run with that fat-headed son of yours three times a week. And ye lift weights twice a week with our dear son-in-law. You're going to outlive us all, my love. Unless you don't listen to me about the second helping, that is."

Brigid shook her head, always loving the way her parents sparred. It was done out of pure affection on her father's part, and pure mischief on her mother's. She rose, "I've got to get home, but I'll see you tomorrow." She kissed her father on the head, and her mother walked her out. "Get him to bed, but give him some Tums or something. He's off tonight."

Sorcha walked back into the house, taking antacids out of the cupboard. Sean said, "Would you quit pecking at me, woman. I don't have indigestion." But he took the Tums. "It's more of a feeling. Unsettled is the only way to describe it."

He helped his wife wash up the teacups, him drying them and placing them in the cupboard. "We should call Tadgh and Charlie in the morning. Check on the new babe. Do you remember what it was like when we had our first?"

"Aye, I do. Aidan wanted fed every half hour. Then the twins!" She said with a wave of her hand. "We didn't sleep for months. It's like they were tag teaming."

They were startled out of their nostalgia by the shrill ringing of the house phone. Sean stiffened. "Who the hell would be calling the house phone at this hour?" He jumped up, ignoring the site of his wife crossing herself. "Easy love. I'll get it."

The O'Briens had a brood of grown children who gave them grey hair on a daily basis. Military, police, fireman, doctors. A judge in Dublin had once compared them to the Avengers. And then there were aging parents.

Sean answered politely, then his face blanched. "I understand. You can tell me the rest on the road. You have my mobile? Yes, now which hospital?"

When he rang off, Sorcha was standing stiff and pale. "Who is it, Sean? Which one?" She choked the words out.

"It's Seany. There was a warehouse fire. It's bad enough that two of them had to be airlifted to the trauma center in Dublin. Get your purse and coat." Then he rang Brigid, telling her what happened. "I hate to do this, but you are going to have to call your siblings and grandparents. I will get the details to you as soon as I possibly can. I promise." She let out a sob over the phone that sent a wave of fear through him. He wanted to start sobbing himself. "He's alive, mo leanbh. That's enough for now." When he rang off, Sorcha was standing so stock still, it was as if she'd turned to marble. Then she started to shake. He grabbed her, pulling her to him. "He's alive, Sorcha. The rest we can handle." But it occurred to him what that pain had been in his chest. One of his children had been in danger.

* * *

BELFAST, Northern Ireland

Captain Aidan O'Brien slid into his shoes without tying them, running into the kitchen to grab his keys. His wife, Alanna, was hot on his heels. "Aidan, my love. I'm so sorry. Please, don't go without me. Let me settle the children. You can't drive when you're upset like this!" A knock came at the front door. "There she is. That's Kennedy from down the road. She can watch them overnight and all day tomorrow as well. Give me five minutes. Aidan!" She shouted it and finally snapped him out of his trance. She put her hands on his face. So stoic, but she saw through him like no one else. He was in hell right now. *Oh, Seany.* "Five minutes," she said again, fighting her tears.

He pressed his forehead to hers, and she felt a shudder go through him. "We go together," he said softly.

* * *

Furbogh, Co. Galway, Ireland

Josh grabbed his mobile and answered on a oner. It was Charlie. She was obviously very upset, and the baby was crying in the background. Something was wrong, and his mind raced at the possibilities. "Honey, I have some bad news, so I need you to sit down. First of all, he's alive. He's hurt, but he's alive. Seany has been injured in a warehouse fire."

Josh got tunnel vision, a wave of panic going through him. "How bad, Charlie?"

"We don't know yet. We are starting a group text to get information out quickly once we get updated. You have Katie's car, right? Okay, Patrick and Tadgh are leaving work. Ned Kelly and his daughter are taking all the children and watching them at Sorcha's home. I think Seamus and Jenny are taking a shift as well. And Cora will help. I'm taking William with me since he's still nursing. It's all hands on deck."

"I'm out the door as we speak, Charlie. But you need to keep me posted. I'm going to go pick up Katie. I do have her car."

"Katie's on the island. Just go, honey. If he comes around, he's going to want his best friend there."

Josh swallowed a sob, "I'm in the car. Call me with the updates, Charlie. I can't be texting and driving."

Charlie answered, "I will. We're almost to the hospital. I love you, Josh. Please be safe."

* * *

Doolin, Co. Clare, Ireland

Mary Nagle drove out of town and toward Dublin as an eerie silence fell over the car. Her sister, Caitlyn, was staring out the window, her fist pressed tight against her mouth, her face wet with tears. Madeline was in the back, relaying the texts coming through on Caitlyn's phone. Seany. *Jesus, please help us. Please help him. This poor family has been through enough.*

* * *

MICHAEL O'BRIEN HELD his wife's hand across the seat, only letting go long enough to shift gears. Branna wiped her tears as she scanned the screen of her phone. She hated the text thing, but when you had this many people involved, all needing updates, it was the easiest solution. "Tadgh is talking to Liam right now. Izzy is in with the trauma team. She can't be his doctor since they're related, but they are letting her assist. Something to do with his shoulder, impact injuries, and first, second, and third-degree burns." She put her hand over her mouth.

Michael revved the engine, picking up speed. "What the fuck happened? Was he wearing all of his safety gear?"

Branna said, "There is more coming through, Michael. Just mind the road."

"I can't lose a brother. I can't, Branna. I won't survive it." His hands were tight on the steering wheel now. His voice stopped in gasps and tremors. Tears misted his eyes. She put a shaking hand on his neck. His teeth were actually starting to chatter.

"Easy. You won't lose him, mo chuisle. He's strong, healthy, and he's an O'Brien. You all aren't so easy to keep down."

* * *

BRIGID RANG OFF with the last of the family. "Gran is in pieces."

Granny Aoife was next to her, Grandda David and Finn in the front seat. "She and Grandda Michael are leaving now." She'd called everyone according to location. She'd first called the Dublin crew, then those who had to drive the farthest were called first. They wanted Izzy and Liam on the front lines, and Charlie and Tadgh could talk to the fire crew and Gardai to get answers. After that, everyone needed to farm out their childcare duties and head to the hospital.

"I don't know what to do with myself now that it's done." She put her face in her hands and wept.

Granny Aoife put an arm around her. "You pray. Your Grandda

will read the updates. In a few minutes, I'll call and check on your mam and da.

* * *

St. James Hospital- Dublin, Ireland

Liam O'Brien walked down the hall, searching for his wife. He was reaching full panic. Like a nightmare that seemed to end when you woke up, but then started up again when you drifted back to sleep. He couldn't lose one of them. Six O'Brien children…seven counting Tadgh, of course. He couldn't lose one of them. Not after Eve. Not after almost losing Izzy. He practically ran into her. Then he grabbed her and lifted her off her feet. "Please, God. Izzy, if you have bad news I'm going to lay down on this floor and die." He wasn't kidding.

"He's alive. His major burns are to the left arm, just at the wrist. More minor to his shoulders because they cleared the debris off him really quickly. First degree, which is unbelievable given what happened. He had some sort of burn proof undergarments."

Liam interrupted. "He got them from Aidan. They issue them in the Army because of the IEDs and fires. Guys had their under layer of clothing melting to them in an explosion. Jesus, thank God Aidan thought to pass along a set."

Izzy said, "You should tell Aidan. Tell him that other than a sliver at the wrist from a uniform failure, he's going to be okay. He should know that he did something to protect him. Given Aidan's history, this is going to trigger all kinds of shit." Liam rubbed a hand down her hair. She was prior military and she was also a fantastic surgeon. She knew what she was talking about. She continued, "He'll be in the burn unit for a few days until they come up with a long-term treatment plan. It will scar, but it isn't life threatening. My concern is that he was hit on the head pretty hard. I requested an MRI. I'm worried about a fracture or a bleed. The X-rays don't show everything."

"You hate not being in charge of this, don't you? Requesting instead of ordering must have been hard," Liam said with a weak smile. It was all he could muster. This wasn't just any patient for them.

"It gave me the scratch on just about every level, but the rule is a good one. He hasn't woken up yet. Another signal that something is going on upstairs. But he's alive, Liam. And he's going to recover. It'll be hard, but he will. All things considered, he's a miracle, Liam."

"Tell me about the tendon and muscle tearing."

Izzy said, "The tendon tears are in his left bicep and shoulder. He also has a fractured left scapula from the rubble falling on him. He dislocated his right elbow because he twisted the rope around and then lost McBride off the ledge again. So, he's injured on both sides. I don't know how in the hell he kept hanging on. Especially when the guy fell again and was dangling. You're talking about two hundred and fifty pounds, with all that gear, practically jerking his arm out of the socket. And I'm worried he hasn't woken up yet. The pain is going to be bad between the burns and the other injuries. They'll heavily drug him, but we need him to wake up first. They need to assess a possible TBI."

Liam was looking down as he listened, nodding and looking like he was ready to lose his shit. "Okay." He paused, not sure what to do next. "How is his partner?"

Izzy shook her head. "I'm not going to lie. His chances aren't good."

* * *

TADGH SAT in the waiting room area, across from the Lieutenant from Seany's station. "There is a thick strip of his arm that got exposed. A uniform strap didn't hold, perhaps. That is the only area that seems to have a full-thickness, third-degree burn. The ceiling came in on him while he was attempting to save his partner from a floor collapse. There were propane tanks abandoned on the property. Some of the tanks still had gas in them. The explosion destabilized the structure and spread the fire to the western portion of the building, where your brother and Nelson McBride were. The Scott Pak™ took a lot of the blow for Junior, but the debris was fully consumed. He has a head injury, but I don't know how severe. His helmet is dented in the back.

He's got first degree burns through his uniform. His helmet and face mask protected his face and head, but the impact was significant. He's most likely concussed. He probably has a break in the scapular area, and they'll have to check his pelvis and vertebrae. He has severe tendon tears in his left bicep and rotator cuff from catching and holding his partner."

Tadgh felt like he was going to pass out. Their little Seany had grown up to be a fierce young man. Brave and strong and so very good down to his core. He had to be okay. And Tadgh knew firsthand what it was like to almost lose a partner. He was scared to even ask. "And his partner? How is McBride?" Tadgh knew him. He'd had Seany and McBride over for a meal after shift. The guy had a big family.

The man in front of him sank into himself, his eyes getting teary. "Junior never let go. He was unconscious, but his body just wouldn't drop that goddamn line. They pulled McBride out of the belly of the beast, passed out from a beam coming straight down on his head. He'd fallen back down, off the ledge, but Junior had latched him to a rescue line. He had it wound around his arm and he kept hold of it, even when the ceiling caved in on him and his back was burning. It's by the grace of Saint Barbara and the Almighty that McBride is alive. And it's mostly due to the will of that lad in the hospital bed."

He cleared his throat, overcome with emotion. "But he's bad. His injuries are catastrophic. Third degree burns on his feet and legs. The top layer of skin just peeled off him when they cut the uniform off." He stopped and held back a swell of nausea. "And they are doing a cervical MRI. He may have a skull fracture and a broken neck. We just don't know. The rest of him is burned and swollen, but not so severe. The uniform will do its job up until a certain temperature and only for a certain amount of time. If he's running through a room that's on fire, it's not the same as hanging there with the constant exposure for several minutes. It's like being cooked slowly. That fire just came up under him. Old wood burns hot and spreads fast, especially given the alcohol absorption over decades of distilling. Whoever left those feckin' tanks in that old building should be drawn and quartered."

Tadgh felt ruined. "Will he live? McBride, I mean. I know Seany will live. He has to. We can't discuss otherwise. But McBride..."

"I don't know, Detective. He's hanging on by will alone. And he's a tough bastard. I just don't know."

* * *

ALANNA WATCHED as her husband approached Seany's bed. He'd been in a blind panic when Brigid rang him. Seany was his darling boy. His little brother. His best man. He just had to be okay, because this family couldn't lose their baby boy. It would kill all of them. When Aidan sank down into the chair beside the bed, he took Seany's right hand. The other was bandaged. He was gentle. Aidan was surprisingly gentle, given his size and profession.

Alanna looked over her shoulder as Josh came into the room. How the hell he'd beaten the County Clare gang was a mystery, but it likely had to do with him not having any children or a spouse. She turned back to her husband, worried for him and for Seany.

"Mo dhearthái r," Aidan croaked. Then he laid his head on Seany's still figure and wept inconsolably.

Josh was silent, unable to look away from the gut-wrenching display. He had seen a lot of anger and abuse in his family, but he and Charlie cared for each other with a deep and loyal love that could only come from a sibling. Alanna rubbed Aidan's back, whispering soothing words to him as he let himself openly weep. Something he would have never done seven years ago, or so Seany had led him to believe. The way Seany told it, Alanna had been his salvation.

Alanna said, "It's okay to let it out, sweetheart. But remember he's going to be okay, Aidan. And you'll be together and teasing that sister of yours like old times. I promise you."

A nurse motioned to her, and she left the room to speak to her. The nurse said, "There is a paramedic here asking for a family member."

Alanna followed her out into the nurses' station where there was an older man standing there in an EMT uniform. "Are you the one who brought him here?"

"I am, Miss. One of them, anyway. I was cleaning the rig and found something that must have fallen out of his clothing when we cut it off him."

He put a hand out, holding an old photo. Alanna didn't recognize it at first. Then her throat seized up. The man said, "She must be special if he carries her with him always. I know he'd not want to lose it. Could you make sure he gets it back?"

Alanna wiped a single tear away. She rubbed her thumb over the picture of a pretty, slender young girl. A shot taken on the beach near her old house in North Carolina. *Oh, Seany. You never got over her, did you?*

CHAPTER 4

***Come Fairies, take me out of this dull world, for I would ride with you upon the wind and dance upon the mountains like a flame!* William Butler Yeats**

Seany sat on a bench, looking out over his mother's garden. He was sad, because not only had winter taken its colorful hues away, but someone had burned it. Charred shrubs and blackened earth were all that remained. He had an overwhelming urge to see his mother. To see all of them. But he couldn't take his eyes off of those burned rose bushes and the brown, leafy remains of cabbages turned ashen at the edges like burnt paper.

"Hello, Uncle." He knew the voice. An ache came into his throat. He often wondered if tears really came from the deep recesses of one's throat, instead of tear ducts. The pain seemed to well upward painfully, stretching the jaw and burning the nose, until sobs threatened to escape, and the tears leaked out of his eyes. Surely those small ducts couldn't contain the whole of his grief. There had to be a deeper well, which held those tears that were made for the deepest of sorrows. He croaked, "Cora, love. Come here, lass."

She walked to him. She was in her flannel nightgown, looking like a wee angel. She cupped his face in her hands. "Such sadness, Uncle. I'm so sorry."

The tears spilled down his face and hers. "Am I dead?"

"No, dear Uncle. Ye live. And you must wake up. I know it grieves you, but you must wake. We need you."

"No one needs me. Not really. But someone did, and I think I failed him. I don't want to wake. What if he's gone?" He bent his head, "What if I failed him?"

"You are needed. When one bleeds, we all bleed. That's the curse of the O'Briens. My mother weeps as if the world is ending. We all do. You must come back home, Uncle Seany. Please don't leave us."

Seany felt the hot burning pain in his left arm, then the ripping pain in his upper body. The dull pain in his back and legs. He was a swirling storm of physical pain. "Oh, God. It hurts. Christ, why do I hurt?" He couldn't remember. What had happened? Why did his misery go soul deep? Not just of flesh and bone, but into the spirit of him? It was too much.

* * *

Cora woke on the sofa of her living room. Jenny came toward her. "Lass, why are you out of bed. Are ye unwell?"

Cora realized she was heaving in great, racking sobs. "Oh, Jenny. He's in such pain. His body and soul suffer together, like the world is ending. Oh, God please help him!"

Jenny held her and rocked her as Seamus O'Keefe entered the front door. He'd agreed to take a shift with the children after work. She met his eyes, then looked away. She said softly, "It's okay, love. It was just a dream." But Jenny knew better. She'd been friends with the O'Brien family since she was in nappies. She'd fallen in love with each and every brother, watching them come and then go into the arms of their mates. She loved them all like family. And if she knew one thing for certain, Cora Murphy's dreams were never just dreams. Tears welled in her eyes as she rocked the sweet girl. Seamus sat next to them.

He said, "I spoke with Liam. He's alive. He's strong and healthy. Take heart, girls. He's alive."

Jenny had kept it all business, this co-work of a sort. The idea of babysitting with Seamus O'Keefe was putting her ovaries on a hair trigger. Her instincts told her he was good with children. She finally met his eyes, and she hoped he saw gratitude instead of all of the other things she was feeling.

* * *

SORCHA KISSED her son's hand so gently. An image of his chubby, little baby hand flashed through her mind, and her chest jerked and convulsed as she tried to hold back the sobs. Her husband, always so strong and reasonable, shuddered next to her. He put an arm across his son's thighs, the only spot free of bandages and tubes. He rolled his face into the blanket and shook with thc cffort of not completely breaking down. His tears seeped into the loose cotton weave as he took a moment to inhale.

He raised his head and said, "I can't smell him. His hair smells like smoke and the hospital things are so sterile. I just want to hold him in my arms like I did when he was a wee thing. I want to smell him…my strong, beautiful lad." His throat convulsed. "I can't lose one of them, Sorcha. Not after William. It's too much for a man to bear in a lifetime. I can't lose my baby boy."

And just like that, Sorcha took the lead. Sean was always the strong one. Always held her up, kept her calm and hopeful. Managed to pull her back from hysterics or rages, when no one else could. It was her turn to be someone like that for him. "Now you listen to me, Sean O'Brien. This lad of ours is going to be fine. He's going to wake up. He's just…taking a moment. His body has been put through hell, and he's going to wake up when he's good and ready. But he will come back to us." She took his face in her hands and made him look at her. "He's going to be okay. I vow it on my own life."

* * *

A STREAM of O'Briens came and went as the hours continued. They brought the family priest in, with a vial of water from St. Brigid's holy well in Co. Clare. After visiting and praying over Seany, he visited his partner and did the same for him. It could hardly hurt. McBride was hanging on, but his respiratory system was failing. The spinal cord injury was significant on its own, but the angle of his head as the beam came down had made the brain injury catastrophic. The base of his skull had been driven into the top of his breathing system. A heavy tank below, a burning piece of construction above, and his head between. Yet he hung on because he had a lot to live for. His family shared the waiting room with the O'Brien family. Kamala was a beautiful young mother. She always had at least one of her four children with her, gorgeous and dark haired like their mother, with their father's easy smile and amber colored eyes.

Sorcha or Aoife or one of the other O'Brien's would watch them during the short times when she could go into the ICU Burn Unit and see her husband. Children were not allowed. Kamala said, "He wouldn't want them to see him like this. Once he's up and about, they can go into the room. It would only scare them." But eventually, the hospital would let them in...to say goodbye. He wasn't in any pain. He was paralyzed, so he didn't feel the burns. His face was almost normal. His eyes would roll around and then fix on his wife. That's all. Just an acknowledgement. His eyes said, *I see you. I know you are with me.*

Izzy did bend the rules and get her in to see Seany as well. And as she watched the dark, serious young women next to Seany's bed, it almost broke her heart. *He's doing better, Junior. I can tell. And if he could talk, I know he'd want to see you. You should wake and see your mother. You've scared her something terrible.* Her tone was clipped with her melodious Hindi accent, and chiding him like an older sister, but her eyes welled with unshed tears. *Please, Junior. Who's going to keep him out of trouble if you lie around all day?* She took his hand, and she kissed his pale face. So drained of color in his unending sleep. Kamala turned to Izzy. "Why won't he wake? Is it the blow to the head?"

"He has a serious concussion. Not as serious as your husband's, but he got his clock cleaned badly. The truth is, I don't know why he won't wake. He stirs, but then it never happens." Izzy thought about what Cora had told her. "I think he's grieving. I think he's afraid to wake up. That's not a medical answer, it's a sister answer. A little over a year ago, I was on a medical mission. I almost lost my partner. We were alone and wounded. We made our way through the rainforest on foot, and I thought he was going to die. It damn near killed me. I would have given him everything I had. Every drop of my blood. I was single. I had no kids. He had a wife and children depending on him. He was a good man. The best. I would have given everything to have him be the one who survived." She exhaled. "Yeah, I think Seany gave everything and is afraid it still wasn't enough. I think his body is protecting him by staying unconscious."

Kamala thought about that. She turned back to Seany. Bare chested, bandaged, and bruised all over. And yet so beautiful, it hurt the eyes to look at him. She took his hand. "Oh Junior. No one could have done more. They told me everything." She squeezed his hand. "And if..." she choked on the words... "If he dies, then he was lucky to have had you as a partner. And I will never blame you, you silly boy. Come home to us. And hold his hand, Junior. I think he wants to see your face. He doesn't know much right now, but he feels the absence of you."

She looked up into Izzy's tear-soaked face. "Thank you, Dr. O'Brien. I needed to see him. I needed to try." She looked back to Seany. "Did his mother have a difficult birth?"

Izzy tilted her head, "I think she did. She said Aidan was the biggest, but Seany was the hardest. He was sunny side-up and didn't want to descend. It's the only child of six that almost ended in a c-section. How did you know?"

"In India, some believe that the harder a mother suffers in child-birth, the more of the child's karma she takes onto herself. She takes the bad karma from the child through her suffering, and then he or she lives a blessed life. Seany always had a light around him. He's going to be okay."

Izzy was afraid to ask if Kamala's husband had been a difficult birth. Had he been like Seany? But Kamala answered her without the question being spoken. "My husband's mother had him within three hours. He was the easiest of the three." She said nothing else and walked out of the room.

* * *

As Alanna lie abed in the spare room at Liam and Izzy's apartment, sleep eluded her. Aidan was at the hospital again. Seany still hadn't woken up. What would it take to bring him out of this self-induced coma? It had been three days since the accident. He should be awake, despite the head injury. She was afraid. She'd promised Aidan that he'd be okay. She thought back to when she'd met Seany. What a worthy young man he'd been. Brave and loyal and quick with a smile. He'd been a flirt of the first order, too. Suddenly she shot up in bed, memories flooding back to her. That time in her life had been one of the most magical. She'd fallen in love. She'd also suffered a terrible ordeal. Kidnapped and abused and eventually rescued.

But Seany had gone on his own adventure, and she knew that he'd fallen in love that summer as well. Yes, he'd been young. People often dismissed the feelings of the young. But, Seany had loved, and he'd lost. Since Maureen Rogers, he'd never fallen again. She thought about that picture he'd kept tucked in his uniform.

She grabbed her phone, hoping she still had the contact for the Rogers family. She wasn't sure what made her do it, but she felt strongly that it should be done. Love was love, after all, regardless of age or distance or even time, in some cases. And deep down, they all knew that Seany still carried a torch for the young American girl he'd met that summer seven years ago. She had a feeling that Maureen would want to know, even if she'd moved on and was in a relationship. They'd kept in touch for about three years, and then she'd reached out when Hurricane Harvey hit Houston. It had been a while, but yes! She had the number. Before she thought better of it or lost her nerve, she made the call.

* * *

HILDEBRAND EQUINE COMPLEX

Texas A & M University

College Station, Texas, USA

Moe walked from her last class toward the student parking that was shared with the veterinary school. She stopped short in her tracks when she saw him. He was a sight to see in his Levi's and Army t-shirt. Still a looker, damn him. "Mason, it's been awhile. How are you?"

The corner of his mouth turned up. "Polite as always, Moe. I'm fine. Just finishing up the last class of the day."

He'd been a veterinary tech in the Army and was using his G.I. Bill for large animal veterinarian medicine. He wasn't local. He'd grown up in Austin. He'd been her first real relationship. Her first adult one, anyway. But he'd had a lot on his plate. So had she. It wasn't a strong enough connection to suffer the storm, so to speak. And after Harvey, she hadn't been able to look at him the same. She didn't resent him. She just didn't see eye to eye with him on some fundamental truths.

"I miss you," he said simply.

"Don't, Mason. Don't do this. It's been three years. You need to move on." She wasn't worried about being alone with him. He was genuinely a very good man. A veteran like her father. Four years older than she, they'd been ill-matched from the start. After her failed attempt at dating a few artistic types, she'd agreed to go out with him. They were both freshmen, although he'd done four years in the Army. She approached him, giving him a warm smile. "I'm okay with how things ended. You should be, too. I know you've seen other women. It's not that big of a campus. Why are you really here, Mason?"

"I've been seeing a therapist. Just some unfinished business from my Army days. You get it, I know." She did. Her father was much older and wiser, and he saw a therapist twice a month. "You keep coming up. Missed opportunity and love lost. All that sappy nonsense." He gave a boyish grin, and she remembered why she'd been attracted to him. And she understood about missed opportunities and love lost. The problem was, he wasn't her lost love like she was to him. She'd cared for him. She'd tried to love him. But her heart wasn't free. Things had been going south even before the hurricane. He continued. "I know you didn't understand at the time, about the stance I took. Maybe I was wrong. I am willing to concede that maybe I was wrong."

"It wasn't just about that, Mason."

"I know. It was about you not letting yourself truly commit to me. Not letting go of some girlhood infatuation."

She bristled. That had been the beginning of the end for them. He'd asked her if she'd ever been in love. She had foolishly told him. "Listen, there is no need to go through all of that again. I want you to be happy."

He moved in, enough to allow her to pull away if she wanted. They hadn't been together that long and had broken up three years ago, but the hum of sexual attraction hadn't completely faded. "I'd be happy with you," he said.

Moe's phone went off just in time. He'd been getting ready to kiss her. And she was just lonely enough to let him, even though she'd never loved him. She liked him well enough, but he wasn't the one. She was willing to accept that maybe someday there would be another Seany O'Brien. Someone who made her heart sing and her body come alive. It just wasn't Mason. She backed away, looking at the screen on her phone. An international call. She didn't want to be rude, so she put it back in her pocket. It was probably some viral robo-call from China or Russia.

"I'm sorry, I really am. But I need to go, Mason. I wish you well with your studies. I'll be doing an internship next semester. It'll be some separation time where we won't run into each other. You can focus on something new or someone new. I'll do the same."

He touched her face. The phone went off in her pocket. He sighed.

This time it was her home phone. "This is home, so I need to get it. Goodbye, Mason." She kissed his cheek, and then walked out of the shelter of his body.

* * *

Moe was ignoring her mother as she threw items into a carry-on bag. The sight of her clothing was blurred with tears. "My passport? Is it still in the safe?"

"Moe, listen to reason. You can't just leave half-cocked. You haven't even seen this boy in seven years! It's terrible what's happened, but you can't do this!"

"Thanksgiving is next weekend. I don't have classes for over a week. I can do this. I'm going to do this."

"Do you have any idea how much it's going to cost to fly to Ireland?"

"Captain O'Brien just sent me a ticket. It's done, Momma. There is no Thanksgiving in Ireland. It's the off season. This is happening!" She threw up her hands, irritated by the mere fact that she was having to explain herself.

A voice came from behind them. "Let her go, babe. She knows her own mind, and she should go do this with our blessing."

Moe knew how much it cost him to go against her mother on this. They were always, without question, a united front. Until now. But she wasn't a child anymore. Her mother meant well, but she was a next level she-bear. "Mom, you can't protect me from this. You had your reasons when I was fifteen, but I'm not a girl anymore. I need to see him. I need to see for myself that he's okay. It's a roundtrip ticket, woman. I'm not being shipped off with a dowry and hope chest."

Moe's mother had never been able to keep a straight face when her children called her *woman.* It had started as a form of mockery more aimed at their father, who often referred to her as *woman* when he was trying to talk some sense into her. Moe hadn't just gotten her stubborn streak from her daddy. Her mother had stubbornness in spades. Her mother's mouth turned up at one corner.

"Let her go, Honey. She needs to have the freedom to see this through. Finally." Moe gave him a grateful look, wiping the tears from her face. They'd forbidden her to visit Seany in Ireland that first year that they had tried to keep a long-distance relationship together. Ever the dutiful daughter, she'd broken it off with Seany when they'd pressed her. She'd done it the only way she could. She'd video called him so that it was face-to-face. Then she'd sent him a letter, telling him that she was closing all of her social media accounts. A clean break was best, so that they ended things swiftly and in the long run, less painfully. She hadn't dated the rest of high school. Hadn't even gone to prom. The act of obedience had shattered her, and they all knew it.

Once she started college, she'd dated a couple of guys who were just looking for a 2 A.M. hook-up. Not her style, thank you. So, the first dates had been the last. Then there had been Mason. Since him, there had been no one for almost three years. She'd thrown herself into her work and had been happier for it. She loved the career path she'd chosen. She loved the horses and the clients in the therapeutic riding program. She went to school through the summers as well, and now all that was left after Christmas was an internship.

She'd suffered the loss of Seany in her life that whole time but had kept the loss at bay by working her ass off. But this...she swallowed down her panic. The thought of him injured on the job pierced her heart anew. And it was time to go to him and face her past transgressions. To see if she could make a difference. Maybe he would wake up and yell at her. A thing she'd denied him when she'd cut him out of her life. *I'm coming, Seany. Whether you want to see me or not.*

CHAPTER 5

Dublin Airport

Aidan pulled into the arrivals area of Dublin Airport with his wife riding shotgun. "She's by the Aer Lingus sign, just ahead. There!" She pointed, and Aidan saw her. Tall and lean and looking very tired. Her hair was pulled back in a braid that slung around one shoulder. She was in jeans and boots and a completely insufficient coat. It was past midnight, and she'd taken the plane ride from hell. Three stops with long layovers. One in Atlanta, one in Toronto, then the final insult of Heathrow Airport. Singly the worst feckin' airport in all of Christendom. He stopped, and Alanna flew out of the car. He watched with an overwhelming sense of déjà vu as the two women embraced, crying and laughing in equal measure. He wasn't sure this was a good idea, but anything done with love couldn't be bad. And his beautiful wife loved big. She was smart, too. Smarter than he was in a million different ways. She was a therapist, and matters of the heart were her domain.

He took Moe's bag, sliding it into the boot, and then turned to the lovely young woman with the serious, grey-blue eyes. "Maureen, it's good of you to come." She shifted in her boots, her face pained, until he opened his arms. She ran into them and broke down, again, crying and apologizing. But he understood it all. He had a daughter. And Seany and Maureen had been way too young for the feelings that developed between them. Maybe it was time. "Thank you, love. We need something to shake that dolt of a brother out of this Sleeping Beauty routine."

Moe hiccupped on a laugh, bringing both the O'Briens in for a hug. "I've missed you both. My parents send their love."

"Should we get you to the hostel?" They'd tried to put her up in a proper hotel since Liam and Tadgh's homes were stuffed to bursting with family, but she'd refused. They'd provided the plane ticket. She'd pay for her lodging. Besides, she had a week to do some intel of another sort. Something that would take her up to a remote area in the hills of Connemara.

"Take me to him. I know I look a fright, but I need to go now."

Aidan smiled sadly, rubbing a hand over her hair. "You look much the same. A little taller, maybe. But he'll be a surprise, despite his condition. He's a big lad. Strong and fit."

Alanna slapped him on the arm. "No spoilers! Let her see for herself." He laughed. This wasn't some reunion on Oprah. This was serious. But his darling wife was a hopeless romantic. This was the reunion she'd been waiting seven years for. Admittedly, him too. When they got to the hospital, she was taken to the ICU under the guise of being a cousin. Aidan and Alanna needed to get back to their children, who were sleeping in one of the brother's apartments. Besides, Alanna was pregnant. She needed her rest. Moe had assured them that she'd take a cab to the hostel. It was late, and she knew they'd pulled strings to get her in to see him.

The nurse led her toward the room, chatting about a sister who'd moved to the states. Moe was so nervous, she barely heard her. She wasn't ready. She should have slept first. What was she doing? Then she was in the doorway, and just like that he was in front of her. She choked down a sob, swallowing it and closing her eyes for a moment. Then she stepped inside. He was so still, so quiet, so heartbreakingly beautiful. The bandages and IV sent a jolt of pure panic through her.

When she heard a male voice behind her, she almost jumped out of her skin.

He was a young man, probably her age or a little younger. It couldn't be a brother. Seany was the youngest. A cousin, maybe? He introduced himself. She spoke words that didn't even register, and he invited her to sit down. Her heart rate was on the ceiling, now. She couldn't do this in front of an audience. He undoubtedly had more right to be here than she did. Then he said four words that almost sent her running for the exit. "You're her. You're Moe." She looked at Seany and took in the broad shoulders, the perfect face. His hair was short, now. But she remembered how soft it was. Remembered his kisses and that silky hair of his brushing against her face. He started to stir, and she just panicked.

Josh looked down at his roommate and tried to register what had just happened. He pushed the button for the nurse, and she was there in a flash. "He almost woke up. I mean, he settled again, but he responded to…" *Her voice. He'd heard her voice.*

The nurse checked his vitals and read the heart monitor. "Steady now, but we had a spike about two minutes ago. Did he open his eyes?" she asked.

"No, but he moved a little. The most I've seen. I need to call his parents." Josh had his phone out before she could protest and remind him about the no cell phone rule.

The nurse said, "It's a good sign. Don't give them false hope, but it's a very good sign. Obviously, his cousin got through to him. Did she leave already?"

Moe sat on the edge of her bunk in the youth hostel and wept. There had been one other woman in the room, but she'd left just as Moe was coming in. She was alone, and she just let it rip. She was such a coward! She needed to go back and face whatever was going to happen. It was just such a shock to realize that her feelings for him were just as strong now as the day they'd said goodbye. And Seany O'Brien had grown into quite a man. The boyish softness all but gone from his face. He was a man…and she wasn't a girl anymore. This was a powder keg on a good day. At least on her end. What would he think of her? She'd changed. Sure, she was the same height. A little more padding in the rump and the chest. She'd been all knees and elbows at fifteen.

Moe shook herself. She was insane, clearly. He was laid up in a hospital bed and she was wondering what he'd think of her boobs? She was a terrible person. Why had she come? She wiped away the tears, weighing her options. She should probably get a little sleep and go back to the hospital. The urge to flee was strong, but Aidan had flown her here for Seany. Not to go backpacking across Ireland. Her phone buzzed and she answered it, recognizing Alanna's new contact information. "Alanna, is everything okay?"

"He almost woke up! Josh called and the whole family is buzzing. He heard your voice, Moe. Holy shit…it worked! Why did you leave, for God's sake?"

Moe's voice was a raspy, gravelly mess. "I wasn't ready for it. For him. I just panicked, Alanna. He's so…"

"Beautiful," Alanna said simply. "I know. He looks so much like Aidan and his father when they were young. Especially now that his hair is short. He's beautiful," she said again. "And you still have feelings for him? It hasn't diminished, has it?"

Alanna O'Brien could be relentless when she put her mind to something. As she heard the pain and longing in Moe's voice, she understood everything as plain as day. This hadn't just been a teenage crush. Moe was a woman, now. And she was in love with Sean Jr. The question was, did he feel the same? He was young, but he'd always been an old soul. Was Moe the one? Alanna had her on speaker phone, and Aidan had come into the room right after they'd begun talking. She rang off, agreeing that Moe needed at least a couple of hours of uninterrupted sleep and some food. She stared at her phone, then looked at her husband.

Aidan raised a brow. "Things are going to get interesting."

She laughed. "Aidan, Honey, this family can't seem to muster a boring month. Y'all are going to drive me to drink."

MOE WOKE to the sound of some backpackers checking into the room next door. She looked at her phone. It was five in the morning, Dublin time. She'd slept about two and a half hours, and it was time to get a shower and go back to the hospital. She'd packed in such a hurry; she was really hoping she had everything she needed.

Given the hour, there was no line for the shower. She made it quick but took time to dry her hair. She'd grown it out again, intending to donate it. She took in her reflection. No makeup, just tinted moisturizer with sunscreen and lip balm. She didn't really do makeup. On hot days, it melted off. Given her work with the horses, she'd just have a layer of cosmetics under a layer of dust and dirt. Her hair was unremarkably brown, her clothes nothing to write home about. She snorted, adjusting the shark tooth necklace that she rarely took off. Then she tucked it into her shirt.

What kind of life had he lived? Did he have a lover? Multiple lovers? She put her hands over her face. "Stop it." The truth was it wasn't her outward appearance she worried about. She'd changed on the inside as well. Life had done that to her. The first couple of years in Texas had been hard. Until her father was stabilized, her mother had been overwhelmed with therapies and doctors' appointments at the V.A. She'd practically raised her siblings. As soon as she could drive, she'd taken on a caregiver role to alleviate some of the stress on her mother. She was stronger, now. She'd had to mature quickly. And they'd gifted her service to the family by educating her at one of the best agricultural schools in the country. For that, she was eternally grateful. She'd found a purpose in the halls and green spaces and horse stalls of that university. She straightened her shoulders and took one more look. She'd changed, yes. But she thought that it was for the better.

She was dressed simply in a pair of jeans and a lavender sweater. She was wearing her well-worn boots, because they were warmer than the pair of slip-ons she'd brought as an alternative. The climate was different in Texas. She put on her all-weather navy blue jacket and grabbed her purse. After a couple of hours sleeping like the dead, she was ready to do this. She was going to walk into that hospital and wake that stubborn jackass out of his slumber. If she had to shake him, she would. She shoved the thought of the prince waking Sleeping Beauty with a kiss firmly out of her mind. It was the fourth day since the accident, and she'd bet her life his family was in pieces. They wanted to see him open those baby blues even more than she did.

CHAPTER 6

St. James Hospital-Dublin

It was about quarter after six when she arrived. She hoped he was alone, but she doubted it. The O'Briens were a force. As she walked toward the unit where Seany was admitted, she saw the younger O'Brien...what was his name? Josh? Yes, that was it. He caught sight of her and slowed, just raising one brow. She cleared her throat. "How is he?"

"Still out cold. But he stirred for a moment. I thought he was coming out of it." He tilted his head, assessing her. "He seemed to respond to your voice."

"I don't know why. I haven't talked to him in seven years. I don't know why I'm here."

He stiffened a bit. "Then why come back?"

She shut her eyes. "That came out wrong. I want to be here. I always..." She stopped, not finishing her thought. She cleared her throat, and he could tell she was suppressing tears. "Alanna thought it might help. I don't know why, is all I meant. He likely hasn't thought of me in years. I would do anything to help, but I'm not sure I can."

Josh shrugged, "Alanna is wicked smart. If she and Aidan brought you here, they had their reasons." He turned to walk away, then stopped. "And he did, by the way."

"Did what?" she asked, tilting her head in question.

"Think of you," he said simply.

* * *

Moe walked into the room, knowing she had a small window before his brother Liam came in to sit with him. His shift started at ten, so he was taking a couple hours before his shift to sit with his brother. She'd spoken to Alanna, who'd filled her in on the neverending rotation that would continue until Seany was home and whole. She passed through his doorway and was still blown back by the sight of him. For seven years she'd dreamed of him, yet nothing had prepared her for the sight of him now. Her dreams were about a young, blue-eyed boy with gentle hands and untried passions. What lay before her was a man. So beautiful it hurt her to look at him. And seeing him injured and unmoving in his bed gutted her as much as it had when she'd watched her father wounded and diminished. She wanted to crawl in the bed with him. To smell him and pull him to her. He'd been so very alive during their time together. She wouldn't be a coward this time.

She approached the bed, saddened by the IV, catheter, and monitors that told her all she needed to know. He wasn't doing well. *Wake up, Seany.* Moe sank down in the chair next to the bed, but she paused before she took his hand. She hated that of all the scenarios she'd ever dreamed up in her head about their reunion…about that first touch… that it had come to this. To him being helpless in a hospital bed. "It's me, Seany. It's Moe. I'm…" she swallowed, not sure what to say. Her throat ached from suppressed emotions. "I'm so sorry this happened to you. I'm sorry about your partner." She took his hand and saw her own were shaking. "I know it's hard, Seany, but there are so many people here that are waiting for you to open your eyes. Please," she croaked. "Oh, God. I have so much to say. Please, Seany." That's when the tears came. "I stayed away. Maybe too long." She cleared her throat and said softly, "Definitely too long. But I thought about you. And even if you don't want to see me, there are people here waiting for you."

She put her face against his hand, careful of all of the IVs and monitors. Then she gently kissed it. His left arm was a mess, and it startled her to see they'd put something that looked like scales over the burned area.

A voice came from behind her. "It's sterilized tilapia skins. I learned about it during my time in Brazil. It's effective, and it replaces the need for skin grafts." She jumped when he spoke, then turned to see a doctor that could only be Liam O'Brien. She remembered that Seany's brother had been in medical school. It was startling to see the resemblance, especially with his shoulder length hair, long like Seany's had been at fifteen. He was a bit harder looking than Seany. Like he'd seen a lot. Suffered. She stood, letting go of Seany's hand.

"I'm sorry, Dr. O'Brien. I don't want to be in the way if you need..." Liam ignored her, coming to the other side of the bed to look at the monitor. Then he looked at his brother, who had begun to stir.

"Jesus Christ, he's responding again. His heart sped up and he moved." His voice was almost hysterical. She looked down and saw what he saw. "He's trying to wake up. I saw him move!"

Liam fought back the wave of emotion as he watched his brother. He remembered all too well what it was like to watch Izzy struggle to come back from the brink. "Talk to him, lass. Please. And take his hand again."

She sat again, reaching out for his hand. But instead, she kept going to place her hand on his face. She ran soft fingers along his jaw. "Wake up, Seany. You are needed here." Liam was on the other side, whispering to him. Words of love that only a brother could express to another brother.

The nurse came to the door. "Dr. O'Brien, something is going on. His vitals..."

"I know. Call his doctor, please. I think he's waking up."

Moe said, "I should go. I feel like I shouldn't be the first face he sees." Liam was crying now, and she wasn't sure he'd even heard her.

He had his forehead on Seany's, then he was kissing his forehead and speaking to him in Gaelic. She mumbled, "I should go."

And as she saw his eyes crack open, the sight of his blue irises pierced her soul. Liam was openly weeping now. Seany's head was turned to him. He croaked, "Liam…"

Then she stood and slipped out the door.

* * *

ALANNA JUMPED on the group text as soon as she rang off with Maureen. She looked at Aidan and he said, "It worked. You are brilliant, a mhuirnín." He ran his fingers through his hair, his face in a sort of dazed shock. "It worked. She brought him back to us."

She sighed, "Yes. Then she ran for cover. But you know what this means, Aidan. You do know, don't you?"

Aidan's eyes gleamed with relief and unshed tears. "It means she's his mate. I'd wondered, now and again. He never got over her. Not really. But they were so young. Jesus, Alanna. She's Seany's mate."

* * *

MAUREEN ROGERS WAS NOT one prone to grand shows of emotion. But as she sat in the ladies' room down the hall from Seany's room, she sobbed until she shook with it for the second time in a twelve-hour span. How in the hell was she going to let him go twice? He likely resented the hell out of her. Worse yet, he'd moved on and she was a faint, boyhood memory. This was too much. He was too much. The feelings he brought out in her were too overwhelming. Always had been.

Minutes went by, and she thought she heard some loud voices going down the hall toward Seany's room. Probably family. He'd had funny stories about his sister Brigid. Part of her wanted to run down there and join the celebration. She wiped her face with a paper towel, looked down the hallway, and left down the nearby stairway.

Exiting the hospital, she took out the map Alanna had given her that first night. She was in Dublin. Finally, she was in Ireland, and the city was cold, grey, and humming with activity. She needed a warmer jacket, but this one would have to do. She decided to take the long way around. It was about a forty-five-minute walk to Trinity or St. Stephen's Green. She could use a long walk. It was early, and many things weren't open, but there was a Spar Mart that boasted decent coffee. She went into the store, and the young man behind the counter smiled at her. "Are ye just making your way back from Temple Bar or are you an early riser?" he asked.

She smiled at that, and when he met her eyes it was obvious, he could tell she'd been crying. She could only imagine what she looked like. "I was just visiting a friend at the hospital. Could I get one large coffee to go?"

"Ah, I'm sorry about your friend. One take-away coffee." She paid him and he pointed to the self-serve coffee area. "Where ye headed?"

"I was thinking St. Stephen's Green for a start. I like green spaces." The young man looked down at her cowboy boots.

"That's quite a walk, love. You're going to need that hot coffee. Where are you from in America?"

"Texas, near Houston. I don't live in the city, though. My parents have a small ranch."

He put his hand on his heart. "A Yank and a real cowgirl. You're killing me, girl. Jaysus."

She smiled again. "Well, I'll get started on that walk. Thanks for the coffee." She left, feeling a little lighter than she had. A cowgirl. It was funny to realize that was exactly how someone would see her. When she'd been younger, she'd loved music and dancing and had even produced her own show. That's when she'd first started to fall hard for Seany. He'd brought flowers. Oh, he'd had Alanna hand them to her, but she'd found a way to let her know just who'd picked them out. Bells of Ireland were still her favorite flowers.

She'd left behind thoughts of Broadway lights with the shedding of her girlhood. Then she'd replaced those fanciful dreams with the smell of the stables and horse sweat. The feel of soft leather tack and well-worn boots. Of Texas sunsets, rolling fields of wheat and corn, and herds of longhorns shifting in vast pastures. She supposed she was a cowgirl at heart, even if she'd come home to it later in life. Her childhood had been spent moving from base to base, but the life she'd found in Texas had healed her family. She'd grown into womanhood there. And she was ready to stand on her own, whatever came next.

* * *

SEANY FELT like he was drowning in sensation. He heard something in the bleak fog of his subconscious that called to him. Was he dying? Was this the heavenly choir which sang as you entered heaven? He didn't think so. Mainly because of the pain. He knew he wasn't headed for hell. He'd had his moments as a youth, but he certainly hadn't earned that fate. The pain was intense, spreading through his chest and shoulders. His left arm lit up like a Christmas tree. Then there was a burst of light as he emerged from the fog.

For a moment, he thought he'd seen the impossible. Then the fear that he was indeed dead spiked through his chest. But it couldn't be her. They were an ocean apart. Then he turned his head and saw his brother's face. Intense blue eyes filled with tears. He was crying and talking to him.

He was home. He knew instinctively that he'd taken a journey, but he'd come home, and he was alive. "Liam."

He floated in and out of awareness as the physical pain settled into his body. He heard his brother say, "Give him something, for God's sake. Can't you see he is in agony?"

"Liam, tell me…" he was cut off as he clenched his teeth. Raw nerve pain radiated up his arm and across his back. "Jesus, Liam. What's wrong with me? What happened?"

Liam brushed his hair back. "How much do you remember?"

He thought back, tried to retrace his steps. He'd been at work. He was leaving to transfer to Galway. They got him a cake. "There was a fire. A warehouse fire in The Liberties." The memory of those final moments came back in a rush. He tried to sit up, sending a burst of pain through his entire torso. "McBride. Jesus, where is McBride? I think I fucked up. Liam, where is he? Did I kill him?"

"No, brother. You saved him. We will talk about it all in time, but I need you to calm down, Seany. Please. You have a lot of injuries."

"I don't remember getting treated. How long have I been out?"

Liam's face was grim. "Four days. You sustained a head injury. Everyone is here. Even Aidan. You've scared the whole lot of us half to death, brother. Jesus, it's good to see your eyes open." His voice broke as he stifled a sob.

Liam's emotional display was interrupted, however, as Seany became more lucid. He looked at the arm that was causing so much discomfort. "What the hell is wrong with my arm? I look like a fucking lizard! Holy shit, why does everything hurt? Why am I growing scales?" It was the morphine, of course. It dulled the pain and the wits.

But he calmed as the nurse finally administered fresh pain meds into his IV. As he started to drift off, he looked wistfully at his brother. He said softly, "I dreamed of her. She was even more beautiful than I remember."

* * *

SEAN ANSWERED his phone on the first ring. "It's Liam!" he yelled through the apartment. They were staying at Liam and Izzy's apartment, and Sorcha was making breakfast before they headed back to the hospital. She put the skillet off the burner and wiped her hands, suddenly at full attention. Sean covered his eyes, overcome with emotion.

"What is it?" she said shortly, suddenly terrified.

Sean had tears in his eyes. "He's awake. Oh, God. He's come back to us." Sorcha sobbed in his arms. This near miss making them dread the unthinkable. It felt like waking from a four-day nightmare that finally ended with the new day's sun.

CHAPTER 7

Only people who are capable of loving strongly can also suffer great sorrow, but this same necessity of loving serves to counteract their grief and heals them.-Leo Tolstoy

St. James Hospital, Dublin

Seany's nurse put a hand on his chest to keep him in bed, giving him her sternest look. "You can't see Mr. McBride. It's family only. I'm sorry. You may as well cooperate and stay in bed."

"No one is telling me anything. You talk about family? He is my partner. My brother. I need to see him!" His voice was suddenly weak and tight. "Please, just let me see him."

The nurse sighed. "I'll see what I can do. Maybe if his wife agrees, we can bend the rules."

Brigid and Sorcha had walked in during this little battle of wills, and Sorcha gave her a grateful look. "Stay calm, lad. You need to lie back and let yourself rest. Your body has been through so much." They could only come in two at a time. Hospital rules. Initially they'd rotated in, each weeping with joy to see him awake and alive. Now she and Brigid were returning to take a longer shift at his bedside.

Sorcha pushed his hair off his face. He needed a haircut. "Your surgery is this afternoon. Did they tell you?" They had. He hated the thought of going under. Of being asleep again. As if reading his thoughts, she said, "They won't have you under any longer than necessary. This needs to be done. Your shoulder tendons need to be repaired before you don't heal correctly."

"I just want out of here. I want to see McBride." Sorcha wasn't so sure that was a good idea. She changed the subject. "Your da is on his way from Tadgh's house. He just called. Josh is making up some time at work. He was beside himself that he wasn't here when you woke. He's been here as much as any of us."

"He's a good man. The best. I only wish he knew it."

Brigid sat next to him and touched his hand. "So are you. You were so brave. Foolishly so."

"How could I do any less? He's got a family. Children and a wife. And in the end, it didn't matter. It wasn't enough." His eyes misted.

Brigid said fiercely. "Ye may not have a wife yet, lad, but you have a family. You are everything to us. You have to outlive me, dammit! I would die right alongside you, Seany!" Her tears came steadily as he turned his head more fully toward her.

"I always thought of myself as the annoying little brother." He smiled as he said it.

"You are annoying!" she bit out. Then she softened. "But you're my babe." Her voice caught at the end. "You were a wee tot when Mam got sick. All the treatments. Chemo and radiation. Christ, it drained the life out of her. We were so scared, despite how strong she tried to seem. It was like watching someone being slowly poisoned to death. We all saw it, especially the older ones. You were like a burst of energy running through the house. The best part of each day. I was the only girl. Granny was there during the day, and Gran came from Belfast when she could. Da did what he could, but he had to work, and he took care of Mam when he wasn't at work. The older boys would rotate cleaning and cooking." She whispered the next words. "But you were my babe. I was a teenager, but I knew how to take care of you. I'd helped with Liam and Patrick and when Maeve would bring the boys. I knew how, so I did. You'd cry and come to my room. None of the boys were allowed into my room but you. You'd come snuggle up with me, nappy soaked because you started wetting again when Mam got sick. Started needing a night nappy again. I'd change you and clean your little bum. Then you'd put your cold, fat feet on me and twist your fingers in my hair."

Seany took a strand of her hair in his fingers, red like his mothers'. She looked like a younger version of their mam, and he'd likely found her the closest thing when he needed a mother. He said, "I never knew that."

"Well, you wouldn't have. You weren't even in school yet." She wiped her face and then looked at her mother. Sorcha was weeping silently, not wanting to interrupt. "Then she was well. The fight was over, and I had to give ye back to your mammy. Ye loved her best of all, of course. But ye'd still come sneak in my room every now and again." She cleared her throat. "So ye see...you were mine too. My first baby. Ye can't go before me, lad. Even in a blaze of glory. I wouldn't live through it. None of us would."

Sorcha walked over to the other side of the bed and held her only daughter to her chest. "I didn't know either. You never told me how much you did. I should have paid closer attention. No wonder you are such a wonderful mother." She smoothed her hands down Brigid's hair. "What are we going to do with this boy of ours?"

Brigid smiled through her tears. "I'll tell you what I'm going to do. I'm going to put a fecking boot up his arse if he ever pulls anything like this again." Sorcha shook her head and looked at Seany. His face was sad as he watched them, but that coaxed a laugh. He was pale and his face was tight, and she knew he was hurting. The burns on his back were minor, but the arm was severe, even with the morphine. The muscle and tendon pulls and tears were probably as painful if not more so, and he had three fractures to his scapula and ribs. He had a healing contusion on the back of his head. He was lucky, she knew. His partner's condition could testify to that.

* * *

LIAM HANDED a cup of coffee to each of his brothers, his father, and grandfathers. The women were scattered between visiting Seany and seeing the children. He'd taken the entire pot out of the nurses' station with their permission, saving himself some time. "I think he's out of the woods. The burn looks good. The head injury might cause some headaches and dizziness for a little while. We'll watch it. But he's out of any major danger. This surgery isn't going to be a long one. He's going to be just fine." He was talking so rationally that his father put his hand on his arm.

"Sit, lad. He's okay." Liam realized the pot was empty and he was still trying to pour cups of coffee. He was shaking. "Have you slept, son?"

Liam put the pot down and sat, exhaling. "I can't lose a brother, Da. I can't. Why do they all have to do these dangerous fucking jobs? I will not survive the loss of one of them!"

"You would survive it. There would be days you'd wish you hadn't, but you'd survive it." His father's words were wise and so very sad that it caught Liam right in the gut.

"Oh Christ, Da. I wasn't thinking. I'm sorry." His father lost his only brother William when Liam was a small boy. He relived it every year at that grave site. He looked at his Grandda David, "I'm sorry, Grandda." Because he'd lost a son. This had to be bringing up all sorts of flashbacks for them.

Sean said, "Don't apologize for loving your brothers. And you've been through more than most. I love you, Liam. I'm proud of you. Of all of you." He clapped a hand on his shoulder and pulled him in for a hug. "But every single one of you is giving me grey hairs. You're making me old before my time." Then each of the men joined them, wrapping themselves in a big huddle. There was safety in numbers. One of them finally said what they'd all been thinking for the last day. Patrick said, "We have to tell him. We have to tell him why he finally came out of it. He should know that she came for him."

"What if she just leaves him again? What if she doesn't stay?" Finn said. Something that had occurred to them all.

Sean said, "She told Josh not to tell him that she'd been there. We should respect her wishes. At least for now. Once he's out of surgery and we see what happens with his partner, we'll tell him. She didn't want him to know, which makes me feel like she isn't staying."

Aidan said, "She's in love with him. Alanna knows it. I think we've both always known it. They needed time, and they've had it. I don't think she'll be able to walk away again now that she's in the position to choose for herself. But it's not for us to interfere. We have to trust the process, like Grandda David is always saying." He nodded at his grandda, who returned the nod with a knowing smile.

Sean sighed. "They're young."

David snorted. "No younger than you and Sorcha or Katie and William. No younger than your mother and I were. Just trust me on this, lads. It'll all be grand in the end."

* * *

Galway City, Co. Galway

Josh cleared the last table of dishes and wiped it down. He was exhausted. Between the three jobs and driving to see Seany, he didn't know how he was still upright. He heard the bell ding at the door of The Pie Maker, and he stifled a groan. "We're closed, sorry. If you'd like one of the take away pies, I can do that."

"I'm not here for pie." He almost jumped out of his size twelves. Then he turned.

"Hello, Madeline. What brings you here?" He shook himself, realizing that it was a rude question. He walked to her and started to hug her. Her eyes took in his shorn hair and the nasty, healing gash that had only recently had been shed of its stitches. Instead of hugging him, she smoothed a hand over his head. She wanted to kiss his wound. Soothe him. But it was too familiar, and she lacked the courage.

Josh was horrified when he saw tears in her eyes. "It doesn't hurt," he said stupidly.

She stiffened. "Some things hurt in other ways, Joshua." She bit back her harsh tone. "I'm sorry this happened to you. I don't understand it, but it's none of my business, I suppose. But Seany's worried about you. So is Charlie."

She was so beautiful it hurt his soul to be with her. She was dressed simply. Jeans, a cashmere sweater, a pair of leather boots. Her coat was practical. Nothing out of the ordinary. She had her ashen blonde, silky locks wrapped up in a messy bun. Little wisps caressing her neck. Smooth, pale skin, mauve lips, and those beautiful grey-green eyes.

Her voice was deeper than her sisters' voices, but she had a lovely lilt. Instead of *things* it came out sounding more like *tings.* And the few times she'd spoken Gaelic in front of him, it had washed over him like a love song. She was bilingual in the truest sense. She spoke one as easily as the other, slipping between the two languages sometimes. He envied Seany for being able to talk to her like that. He took her hand away from his head, kissing the tips of her fingers. "You don't need to worry about me. It looks worse than it is."

"You deserve so much more than this, Joshua. I hope you know that." He shrugged noncommittally.

"Tell me about Seany," he said, evading her stare.

"I saw him for about five minutes. He's doing better. Do you know about the woman? His woman?"

"I don't think she's his. He hadn't seen her in seven years. He doesn't even know she was there, most likely."

"Some things just are, whether they're acknowledged or not. Especially when it comes to love." Her words made him thrum with warmth and need. There was a moment when their eyes met that sizzled with everything he wouldn't or couldn't say. "She came for him. That's a beginning, isn't it?"

He shrugged. "I wouldn't know. My parents didn't exactly have a healthy marriage, and I've never been loved like that. I'm not sure I'd know what to do with it."

"But you've seen your sister. The way she is with Tadgh is an inspiration. Maybe Seany has a chance at that sort of love as well. Has she been back?"

Josh said, "No. Alanna said she checked out of the hostel. They seemed to think she was headed up this way. Aidan bought a return ticket for five days from now. Not sure why she bolted, but she'd been asking about the horses. You know, the ones in the mountains."

"The Connemara ponies? I wonder why? Is she into horses?" Maddie asked.

"Yes. She's from a rural part of Texas. Real cowboy country. Alanna said she's studying horses, so I guess she wants to check out your ponies."

"Interesting. Well, she's headed to the right place. Although, I wish she'd stayed. Seems a bit cowardly to just run off like that if she really loves him. Why run?"

Josh shrugged, "Excellent question. And I'd like to find out."

"You're going to go up there? You should let me go with you. I speak the Irish, and some of those mountain folks can be a little clannish. It's not like the tourist areas. Let's head out tomorrow. It's Saturday."

"You don't have to do this," Josh said.

She put her hands on her hips. "He has been my friend since you were in nappies, Josh O'Brien. The hell I don't. And someone may as well get their happily ever after. Seany is a good man. If you don't take me, I'll just start up there on my own."

He snorted. "You're pushier than you first appear. You're all quiet and polite, but scratch beneath the surface and you're a pushy little peahen just like my sister and those O'Brien women." He threw that O'Brien-ism *peahen* in there just to get her hackles up. "See, your feathers are getting all ruffled. Peahen." He grinned as he said it, almost taunting her. He turned the last light off, walking close to her. He looked down into those grey-green eyes. "Meet me at the cottage at seven. Extra points if your mother has any of those lemon cakes lying around." He smiled.

She looked at his abdomen, her belly doing a little jump. "I don't know where you put it. This is a perk of being male. If I even look at those damn lemon cakes, I put on a half stone."

You are perfection, he wanted to say. "Seven o'clock. Don't be late. I'll call Alanna and get Moe's phone number."

He walked her to her car, then turned to leave. She said, "Josh, wait." He turned to her and before she lost her courage, she palmed his neck. She pulled him down and pressed a soft kiss to the scar he'd received from a terrible woman. "There, now," she crooned, like soothing a baby. She felt a tremor go through him. Then she got into her car and left.

CHAPTER 8

St. James Hospital-Dublin

Seany felt like hell. The surgery went well, and the orthopedic surgeon assured him the tendon tear and muscle pulls would heal. He'd have to watch his left shoulder and try not to dislocate it again. It could become a chronic problem. The broken bones would heal as well. One fracture to the scapula and two broken ribs. The burns on his back were barely noticeable anymore. Like a sunburn. The undergarments Aidan gave him did their job. Just that four-inch-wide band around his arm. Third-degree burns that turned to second-degree burns at the clothing line. He still hated looking at the fish skin. But in a week, they'd peel it off and take a look at the damage. He'd also been stepped down to a regular floor and out of the intensive care burn unit.

He thought about the cake he'd received at the station, before the fire. Pizza, wings, and cake. It had probably gone to waste. Would the Galway City fire station even take him now? He'd be on paid sick leave until he healed and could do his job again. The question was, would Galway go through with the transfer? Dammit, why was he thinking about this when his partner might never see the outside of this hospital again. As if on cue, Kamala said, "You're woolgathering. Anything you want to talk about?"

She was wheeling him down to the severe burn unit. He palmed her hand as she pushed. "Just thinking about that day. Was the cake his idea?"

"Who else? You know he thinks of any reason to make a cake." Seany snorted at that. His boy did like cake. Especially chocolate.

He squeezed again and she stopped. Then she knelt in front of him. She said, "This is going to be hard. I won't lie to you. Are you ready? If you aren't, we'll try again tomorrow."

He closed his eyes. "I tried. God, I tried but it wasn't enough." He felt a tear escape the corner of his eye and he felt like a rotter. He should be supporting her, not the other way around.

She cupped his face. "Look at me, Junior." He did, and his eyes were bright and red. "You did everything you could. You are letting your guilt affect how you see things, but I know. Everyone knows. Now all you need to do is show him you are still here. That you're okay. That you aren't going to leave him. You need this as much as he does. He likely will not say anything, but he'll see you."

They went into the room and he was on the bed. Bandages encased his lower legs, and he was in a halo brace designed to keep his neck and head from moving. He had edema in his face and hands, and portions of his knees and thighs were covered with the tilapia skin. Apparently, the higher areas hadn't sustained such serious burns.

"He doesn't feel the pain. A blessing, maybe. He broke his C2 and C3 and damaged the spinal cord. They don't know if the paralysis is permanent until the swelling subsides and they stabilize him for more testing. The spinal surgeon is afraid to do surgery before he's in better shape. He has a level 3 traumatic brain injury. That may be why he hasn't spoken."

But his eyes lit on Seany's and stayed. Seany approached the bed with Kamala pushing the wheelchair to position him next to it. "I'm here, brother. I came as soon as they let me. I told you I wouldn't leave that building without you."

Seany watched in amazement as his partner blinked once, and he heard Kamala swallow a sob. "I see you, brother. We're going to get through this. You and I."

The man just stared, then finally he blinked twice. Twice.

* * *

Seany left with a nurse, as Kamala wanted to stay with her husband. He said to the young man, "He's not going to live, is he?"

"I don't know. I think it's in God's hands now. I'm sorry. You're his partner?" he asked.

"Aye, and not a very good one, apparently."

"We'll have to disagree on that one, Mr. O'Brien. Every single one of your injuries could have been avoided if you'd left him. Don't belittle what you did. Don't rob him or her of the right to thank you for it. The only way you could have avoided his injuries is if you'd let go and let the fire take him. So enough of that talk."

Seany turned to him. "You're a bit of a hard ass, Nurse Betty."

The man didn't take offense. He shrugged. "Six years in the Army. I did a stint in Africa during the Ebola epidemic. I've learned how to deal with feeling helpless, or like my efforts have been futile. You'll do the same. Remember your partner as he was."

"Popping shit and eating the last donut?" Seany said, unable to keep the smile from his face.

"Exactly."

It just wasn't that easy. He was so medicated; it was hard to pull together all of the details of that day. But he needed to remember. He could have done something better or quicker. Something that could have made a difference. Something that would have been enough. The pain rippled through him, and he felt the sweat on his brow. "You've been up too long. We need to get you horizontal, lizard man. You need to manage your pain."

He wheeled Seany into his room, where he found his father and Aidan waiting. Once he was situated, he just looked at them both, not sure how to start. He took the paper cup of pills from the nurse and a cup of water. Once he was hooked back up to the monitors, he met his father's eyes. He was in control again. "I want to thank you both."

"Whatever for?" his father asked.

He said to Aidan, "The reason that I'm barely burned is because of that fireproof undergarment you bought me from the Army supplies. And for the personal rescue rope you got me, Da. I had it on me. I tethered McBride to it. I was trying to get to an iron pipe to secure him, but I didn't make it. I held on, though. Maybe if I'd gotten him tied up sooner. If I'd managed to get it out sooner...I don't know. I was barely hanging on, but if I'd thought of it sooner." He shook himself. "Anyway, thank you. A lot of the lads don't have that equipment. You'd think they'd issue it, but there isn't funding. More than one of my mates coveted my new equipment." He looked down at the burned part of his arm. "Except my topcoat. That had a torn safety strap. Hence the fish skin treatment." The topcoat was never going to be a problem again, since they'd apparently cut the thing off him.

"Does it pain you terribly?" Aidan asked sadly.

"It does hurt like hell. Raw nerve pain. And my chest, back, and shoulders feel like they've been through the shredder. But I'm alive and whole." He looked down at the blanket, not focusing. "Sometimes I don't know how I feel about that. I was afraid to wake up, I think. Afraid he'd died on my watch. He still might. He probably will, in fact. Yeah, I don't mean to sound ungrateful, but I really don't know how to feel. He was mine to protect. My partner."

Aidan took his hand, and his father put a hand on his thigh. "We understand, lad. Both of us understand. When I lost Willie, I felt a lot of guilt. Especially because of Tadgh and Katie. And I think Aidan understands all about the guilt that comes with surviving. It's normal. But your heart is lying to you. You have no reason to feel guilty. And in time, you'll understand that."

Seany wasn't too sure about that, so he said nothing.

* * *

County Galway

Maureen cursed as she tried to get the tiny car into second gear. She could drive a manual transmission, but she'd never done it in a vehicle this small, or on the other side of the damn car. And don't even get her started about the roads. How did two full size cars even pass each other on these country roads? Her mother would have a heart attack if she saw her right now. They knew she was going to be in Dublin to see Seany, but they hadn't gotten into the specifics about her checking out a potential internship in County Galway. Her phone was buzzing, so she found a petrol station to pull over. She answered on the fifth ring. "Hello? Alanna?" It was a local number, not from the US, so it had to be her.

"Hello, Maureen Rogers? This is Madeline Nagle. I'm a friend of the O'Brien family."

A shot of pure panic went through her. "Is he okay? Has something happened?"

Madeline said, "No! Sorry, nothing is the matter. I'm sorry to give you a fright. It's just that I'm in the Galway area and I wanted to know if you'd like to meet up? Anywhere is fine. You left Dublin so suddenly, and you've never been to Ireland. I just thought…well, that you could use a friend."

Moe found herself suddenly close to tears. She was an idiot. "Is he really okay?"

"Yes, he is. He is awake and talking. He's eating and he just came out of surgery. I'd love to meet up and tell you everything. Where are you headed exactly?"

Moe grabbed the sheet of paper she'd brought from home. "Letterfrack? It's in Connemara. I need to be there by four o'clock. I was going to stop for lunch, but I'm not sure where I am. I think I'm northeast of Galway City?" She told her the road she was on, and Madeline knew of a good cafe to stop and have a bite to eat. Moe put the address into her map program.

"I'm not far at all. I have a friend with me. I hope you don't mind. Then we can help you map out the best way to get through the hills and to Letterfrack."

"I really appreciate this. I have to fly back in a couple of days, so I need to make this…um…appointment."

"Appointment, huh? Well, now. You are a mystery woman. I'll see you at about half eleven." Madeline said, and ended the call.

Madeline turned to Josh. "She has an appointment at four in Letterfrack. Interesting." She smiled as she slid her mobile into her purse.

Josh shook his head. "You are pretty slick, Madeline Nagle. She probably would have hung up on me. She seems very skittish. I still don't feel right about not telling Seany. He should know."

"In good time. His father is right. It's better to learn her intentions before we tell him. She didn't want him to know. There is more to the story, and I think we're going to find out over lunch. But he's kind of a mess right now. Injuries aside, his partner is hanging on by a thread. I don't think he needs anymore heartache right now."

Josh drove as she talked, and it was so comfortable. He drove through dense, green countryside, admiring the patches of dried heath and damp moss. The presence of the woman beside him caused a hum of awareness throughout his whole body. They were going to work together playing matchmaker for his best friend. If he couldn't have the woman he wanted, at least Seany could have a second chance with his Moe.

MOE SAT at the small pub table, looking through the menu. She heard the front door open as a sliver of light pierced the darker interior of the pub. She saw the young woman first, who seemed to be scanning the room. Their eyes met just as another person came through the door behind her. "Oh, shiitake mushrooms," she said under her breath. The code word to replace cursing that she'd adopted due to her younger siblings.

She stood just as they made their way to the table. The pretty young woman stuck out her hand. "Maddie. You must be Maureen."

She had a lovely voice, deep but feminine with a lovely lilt. She rolled her R's and it reminded her so much of the way Seany had said her name. Those long walks on the beach. Stolen kisses under the beach house. So innocent and so absolutely mad for each other. "And I think you've met Josh, Seany's roommate."

Double shiitake mushrooms. "It's good to hear Seany is doing better. I'm so very happy for your family." She felt awkward. "I waited to order. Let's sit down and you can tell me why you really wanted to meet."

Maddie wasn't put off in the least. "Smart lass. Now, let's see." She opened the menu. "Word of advice, avoid the lamb. It's tough and muttony, not worth the price. The brie wedges are excellent and worth every calorie, as are the curry chips."

Moe smiled, "No lamb, got it."

Josh ordered the bangers and mash, and Madeline ordered the curry chips. Moe said, "I'll give you a brie wedge if you let me sample those curry fries."

Madeline beamed. "You and I are going to be friends."

Josh said, "Can I be in your club if I get a banoffee pie with three spoons, or is this a sisters before misters moment?"

"I can absolutely be bribed with dessert," Moe said with a subtle smile. She liked these two, despite the urge to flee. She wouldn't, however. Not if she could get just a glimpse into Seany's life. His friends and family. So, they settled in for their meal.

After ordering and getting a pot of tea, Maddie said, "You are the reason he woke. You do know that, don't you?"

Moe busied herself, stirring her tea. "I don't think so. He barely remembers me. It was seven years ago. I don't deserve the credit, despite what his brother said." She took a sip of the aromatic tea, honey and milk swirling with the earthy drink and coating her throat. The tea was just better here, made with an expert hand instead of in a microwave. She didn't want to think about what they were telling her. It hurt too much.

Summoning her from her thoughts, Josh said, "We'll have to agree to disagree on that one. I saw him respond to your voice. He remembers you, Maureen. And I'd wager he never forgot that summer you had together."

The waitress brought their food, with the promise of pie when they were finished. Madeline said smoothly, "So, why don't we dispense with the bull and you can tell me why you're up here in Galway instead of down there trying to get a peak under Seany's hospital Johnny?"

Josh spit out a mouthful of tea as Moe choked on her brown bread and brie. Josh's mouth dropped open. "You think you know a girl..."

Madeline just winked at him. She was usually pretty shy, but she was trying on her sister's blunt ways for the afternoon. Mary always came right out with it, and Madeline didn't have time to mince words. Mary had pumped her up the night before. *Make an impression early and don't give her time to run for the door.* Mary should work for a dating service. As far as Maddie was concerned, she was speed dating for a friend and a potential happily ever-after for one of her oldest friends.

"I'm not sure how to respond to that," Moe said, not meeting their eyes. Madeline reached across the table and took her hand.

"I'm sorry, that was rather blunt. Not my normal tactic, but I'm afraid you'll run off again. Please, you are safe here. Tell me...tell us what this is all about. Are you really just up here to see horses?"

Moe took a steadying breath and looked up. "No. I mean, yes and no. I'm here to visit a horse ranch. It's in Connemara, just along the national forest. They work with the local ponies mostly, but they have a few rescues as well. They are trying to get up and running as an equine therapy and hippotherapy center. My degree is in equine studies and hippotherapy. It's a great fit and they are looking for interns because they are cheap. It's no money, practically. Room and board and slave wages, really, but they've opened it up to international students. Apparently the two big universities that have equine studies are in Limerick and Dublin. It's far and remote for bad wages."

Josh pointed out the obvious. "Even farther for you. And you'd have to get yourself here. So, what's the draw?" Madeline elbowed him. "I'm sorry if that's rude, but you did take off as soon as he was awake...for the second time in a few hours. You told me not to tell him you'd been here. You can see what a position this puts us all in, can't you? So, are you planning on even telling him you're here?"

"I don't know!" she shot back. Then she closed her eyes. "I don't know. I just saw the opening, even before the phone call about him being hurt. I considered all these places in Texas, and then I started looking out a little farther. Colorado, Northern California, Virginia. Then I saw it, and his face just popped up in my mind..." She put her head down and fought the tears.

Josh felt like a horrible bastard. "Oh, Jesus. I'm sorry, Maureen. You didn't ask for any of this. I should be thanking you for jumping on that plane and instead, I'm being a dick. I'm so sorry, please don't cry."

She met his eyes, "I knew you were a big softy." She exchanged a knowing glance with Madeline, wiping her face. She really was turning into a weepy sissy. "Look, I'm sailing without a rudder right now. Alanna called and I just came. And the idea of coming here to study suddenly didn't seem so out of the question. I just wanted to come up here and see the place. Give the family some space. This isn't the Maureen Rogers show. Seany needs to heal and to see his partner. He needs to be with his family. They almost lost him. No one needs this kind of drama right now. I'm glad I could help, if that's what I did. So, I snuck out the back door and came up here for a last-minute interview."

Madeline squeezed her hand. "Then I wish you luck, Maureen Rogers. And I hope that we'll see each other again. I'd like to be friends. I'm starting my thesis work this summer. It'll take me two semesters. I'll be checking in with my advisor, of course, who delights in making my life difficult."

Moe smiled at that. "I'd like to hear about that sometime. Your studies and your thesis." But they didn't have time. She had an interview and they needed to eat. They kept the conversation light. When the meal was over, Josh took the check. "Neither of you are paying." He went up to pay the bill, and Madeline watched him walk to the cashier.

"You aren't together." Moe said. Not a question. "But you'd like to be." Madeline's eyes bugged out. "Don't worry. I won't say anything. You keep my secret and I'll keep yours."

Madeline smiled at that. "It's a deal, Maureen. And I hope to see you again in January."

* * *

St. James Hospital-Dublin

Liam walked down to his brother's room, Izzy beside him. "I'll tell him, Liam. It doesn't always have to be you."

"He's my brother."

"And he's my brother! Or isn't that my fucking ring on your finger?"

He stopped, hands fisted at his hips. "Do you always have to be such a hard ass?"

"Only when you are being a dumb ass," she said pissily. "He's my brother and my patient, so let me talk to him. You are too close to this and you've had the emotional shit beat out of you for days, Liam. Let me bear this for you. Please. I'm even saying please."

Liam closed his eyes, "Okay."

They walked hand in hand into Seany's room. When he saw their faces, he pushed his food tray aside. "Something is wrong. What? Is it me or is it him?"

Izzy sat down as Sorcha came into the room. She stilled, knowing something was wrong. Izzy said, "It's your partner, Seany. His wife is with him, but she said we could talk to you. He has pneumonia. Normally in a man his age and as healthy as he was, it wouldn't be a huge deal, but with the burns and the injuries, it's bad. It's a complication they tried like hell to avoid, but it's happened. They had to put him on a ventilator. He's fighting, still. He's tough. It just got a whole lot more complicated."

Seany's jaw was tight, his face full of some intense emotion that Liam couldn't put a name to. Izzy said, "Was I wrong to tell you?"

Seany's eyes shot to hers. "No! Jesus, lass. Of course not."

"Because you look like you're ready to implode with guilt and self-loathing, and I just cured your brother of that affliction a year or so ago. Kamala needs you, Seany. Your station guys need you to be okay. They need for one of you to be okay. So, pull it together before you see Kamala. Please. She's barely sane right now."

He sat up and winced. "I'm okay. I want to see him."

"I'm sorry. Only his wife. He is very ill and susceptible to infection even more so now than before. Just Kamala for now."

That's when Sorcha spoke, finally. "I have someone who has been waiting to see you, though. She's fit to be tied that it's taken so long." The door opened behind his mother and Cora came through it and ran to his bedside. Sorcha spoke hurriedly, "Careful, lass. He's injured."

But Cora had already pushed Liam aside and was crawling in beside him before anyone could stop her. She almost shouted her first words. "I'm getting tired of everyone ending up in the bloody hospital! Don't you ever do that to me again!" And it was more than the hospital stay. He remembered the dream. He remembered her. "You tried to leave me." Her voice was hoarse.

"Ah, sweet Cora. I didn't want to leave you. I was just lost and afraid. Afraid of what I'd find when I woke. But you found me, dear girl. And you reminded me of what else was waiting for me when I came back home."

She lifted her head and met his eyes. The tears broke his heart. "Did I really help?"

"You did, love. You really did."

CHAPTER 9

There are only two emotions that belong in the saddle; one is a sense of humor, and the other is patience...a horse proverb

Letterfrack, Co. Galway

Moe arrived at the old horse sanctuary a half-hour early. She'd driven the most direct route but had decided to take a scenic, slower drive on the way back to Dublin. She would take her time, spend the night in Letterfrack to look at the accommodations. Then she would start east. That would leave a couple days in Dublin, battling the temptation to go see Seany.

The drive here from Galway was filled with beautiful scenery. Taking her away from the sea, she'd driven past rocky hills, lush forests, and stunning, tranquil lakes. As she looked at the estate before her, she laughed at her choice of word. This "estate" was more like a hobbit shire, if you plunked it down between a lake and a forest. The house was a small stone cottage. One story, white-washed, with a slate roof with patches of moss growing along the shingles. The horses looked healthy, which relieved her. The fencing was old, and several slats looked like they needed replacing. The corrals needed fresh dirt. The packed earth had dips where water was collecting.

She got out of her car just in time to hear a horse vs. human altercation. She didn't think twice about running into the barn. She found herself wishing she'd worn her old boots, because horse business was always messy. She ran through the open doors to see one of the most beautiful horses she'd ever laid eyes upon giving an elderly woman a ration of shit. He reared up on his back legs as she hit the ground. He hadn't kicked her, but she'd lost her footing when she tried to back up too fast. Moe didn't think. She just scooped the woman up by the armpits and dragged her away just as the horse came back down to earth. Then it was her turn to dance. She walked closer to the gorgeous specimen and calmly made eye contact. She didn't wave her arms; she didn't yell or command. He tossed his mane, snorting. His ears were back, and he stomped his hooves. She decided getting him in one of the indoor stalls was not going to happen. She said over her shoulder, "The stone stables outside…are they vacant?"

The woman was cleaning off her jeans. "The first one is empty. He was in that one after he tried to bite my last interviewee as he walked by the stall. He's a bloody menace. I'm tempted to make dog food out of him!"

The woman's voice was gruff, and she had a thick accent. She swore at the beast in Gaelic and he shook his head, the muscles twitching down his shoulders and back loin. Moe continued to watch him, giving him just enough attention to be aware of her, but not indulging the ungentlemanly behavior. She waited…and waited. Finally, he exhaled, and the ears perked up. She approached him, saying calmly, "What is your name, big fellah? You are handsome. I bet you know it, too; don't you?" She took the reins, humming softly. He nuzzled her a little more roughly than was necessary. "Yes, I see you. You're a big tough guy. You've made your point. Now let's get you where you belong, although you seem hellbent on resisting this nice warm stall." She walked him inside and noticed the woman's eyes tracked them both. One side of her mouth tipped up.

The first stall was extra wide, and she smiled as a soft, white and gray head poked out of the neighboring stall to say hello. "This is for a mare and her foal. I hope you haven't put out a mother and child due to your tantrums." Her voice was chiding but soothing. She rubbed him along his flank as she settled him in the stall.

The voice behind her held some grudging respect. "The mare and foal are inside where he should be. The temperature is going to drop tonight." She tilted her head, eyeing Moe. "Am I to assume you are Maureen Rogers? The Yank from Texas A & M?"

Moe rubbed her hands together, seriously regretting the tailored trousers and sweater. She put it out then, shaking the woman's hand. "Yes ma'am. And you must be the ranch owner, Moira Burke."

"The one and only. Thanks for the assistance. You know your way around horses. What can you tell me about him?"

This was a quiz, and she hoped she was up to snuff. "He's not a Connemara. Not quite beefy enough to be a draught horse, although he has the height. I'd say Irish Sport. About four years old, and…" She cocked her head, assessing him. "Maybe seventeen hands. He's a big boy." She looked under the horse and he shifted. "Settle down, buddy. I'm just having a look at your business end." She turned to her interviewer. "He's a stallion. Are you planning to breed him?"

"I considered it. He's a lot of trouble, but his bloodlines are excellent. It would be a pity to let prime seed go to waste, but I'll have to see how the temperament ripens now that he's settled. I rescued him about three weeks ago. He wasn't quite so pretty. I have managed to get him to submit to grooming. He was nasty, too. The owner was in over his head." She walked out of the stall, letting Maureen close and latch the door. "I know the feeling," she said absently. She shook herself. "Well, now. Since you've been kind enough to drag my bum out of the line of fire, I suppose I should put the kettle on. There are fresh biscuits in the kitchen."

Moe followed her, settling herself at a small kitchen table as the woman prepared tea. "The paperwork said you were taking on interns to help get a non-profit up and running. Besides the big guy, how many head do you have?"

"Fourteen others. I breed Connemaras and sell them. Or at least I did. They are valuable horses, as I'm sure you know. But I'm getting old, and I have all the money I need. I want to do something else. I like the idea of a therapeutic riding center. My friend's great grandson is autistic, and he really loves the horses. Connemara ponies are gentle, rarely sick, and a good beginner ride."

Moe smiled at that. "How old is he? The boy, I mean."

"He's six. He's been riding for about a year. We started him out on our only mini horse. Useless thing, but he's a hit with the kids. He's calm and gentle. The other thirteen include one mule and one thoroughbred stallion that was bred for racing but he never really took to it. He's fast, so you better watch he doesn't get out. He's also randy as hell, so I have to watch him around my mares." Moe smiled at that. She continued, "And eleven Connemara ponies. One of those was just born in the spring. We have another mare, Sadie, who's carrying. That will likely be the last one, and I'll probably sell the foal. I already have a buyer. She's due in March."

"I would love to see them all. I'm staying in town tonight, so if you'd rather rest and do this interview in the morning, I can get out of your hair."

"Getting knocked on my bum by a horse is not an uncommon occurrence, I'm afraid. I'm a bit short on patience as I age. But I think I can manage an interview."

The woman had to be at least seventy years old. "Surely you have a staff?"

"Yes, of course. I have two grooms who rotate on the weekends and work together during the week. A part-time trainer as well. You'll meet Devlin after I get a cup or two of tea in my belly. He's the head groom. The other two employees have gone for the day. I'll have to hire more, of course, but if I can get some patrons through a non-profit, it won't be coming out of my own wallet. And I can get a volunteer team. My intention is to get a full-time trainer who can run the therapeutic program as well as a hippotherapy program. The two internship openings are for equine studies, specifically to work with the regional ponies, and help get the therapeutic riding program up and running. I need help getting this place ready for inspection and getting the horses trained. I can't pay much, but I can house the interns and feed them. I also have a spare car if there is a need. It'll be long hours."

"I understand. Do you mind if I ask how many you've interviewed?"

She gave a wry smile, "I had a list of twenty-two candidates." Moe's heart sank. Locals, no doubt. "Three international students, including yourself, and nineteen from various Limerick, Cork, and Dublin universities. I video conferenced a woman from Colorado State University and an Aussie lad from Queensland University. Out of the Irish students, ten decided it was too remote or didn't pay enough. So that leaves an even dozen to choose from."

Moe held in a sigh, then lifted her head. "What would you like to know about my qualifications?"

"Your qualifications are all in your resume packet. Tell me something I don't know. How did you learn to handle a horse like our ill-mannered friend?"

So, Moe told her. She told her about her grandparents' ranch. About growing up as a military child and taking their horses with them when they were stateside. About learning to adapt and overcome.

"And is your father retired? Or will you move again?"

She cleared her throat, not sure where to start. "He's medically retired. He was injured in Iraq. The head injury caused seizures. But the one goal he had, even before being able to drive again, was to be able to sit a horse. He has an ornery Appaloosa on our small ranch. We only have three horses. It's nothing like this spread."

"Aye, well this spread has seen better days. I've let it get away from me a bit. I had a distant relative come and try to help, but he was worse than useless. He wanted me to bequeath the place to him and had just been trying to sweeten me up."

"I'm sorry. Family should help with no strings attached. He sounds like a rotter."

The woman laughed. “You’ve been hanging with the locals, I see.”

Moe smiled at that, shrugging. “I have some friends here in Clare and Belfast. And I met a couple of new friends in Galway, actually. It’s been a while, but I do have some connections.”

“You’ve had a brief look at my farm. Tell me what you see. And don’t hold back, because I’d have you speak plainly.”

Moe had already compiled a list in her head. “You need fresh dirt brought in for the corral areas and you need a few able-bodied people to help you spread it evenly and fill in the areas that are making puddles. The fence needs repaired and even replaced in a few spots. The barn looks good, and what I’ve seen of the horses tells me that they are well cared for. You need someone to organize that tack room. You also have a leaky faucet outside of the east corral that is making the ground soft. I’d have a plumber come and have a look.”

Moira smiled, “Very good. All on my list of things to do this autumn before we get any snow. Except for the tack room. Neat and tidy was never my strong suit. I also have to replace a few of the heaters in the barn and get the cottages ready for the interns.” She poured them both some more tea. “So, a military brat, eh? It explains the lack of a Texas accent. My expectations for a drawl were too high, I suppose. Well, Maureen Rogers. When can you start? It’ll be hard work. You are going to get your hands dirty. You might work fifty hours a week. But I will never be cruel to you. You’ll be safe and cared for like my own kin.”

Moe started to stutter like an idiot. “I got the position? Really?”

“Yes, my dear. Now, let’s go over these other resumes and you can give me your opinions. Then, I’ll show you the cottage by the lough-side pasture. It is small, so you won’t have a lot of room, but you’ll have your own space. The other apartment is connected to my house. You can choose which one suits you, and the second intern will get the other.” Maureen was torn between being near the horses or near the lake. She’d just have to see them for herself. She couldn’t wait to start.

* * *

MOE DROVE into the village of Letterfrack to the National Park Hostel. She parked her rental in the car park next to the building. She entered the old building and was greeted by a friendly innkeeper. "Sure, we've got a few rooms open. Do you need private accommodations or just a girl's bunk?"

"The bunk will do just fine, ma'am. Thank you. Is there anywhere around here to get some supper? I had lunch at noon and I'm starving." It was already seven o'clock.

"We've got a few places to choose from. There may be a trad session goin' at Veldon's or there is The Lodge. Otherwise, you'll have to drive to Clifden or Tullycross. How long are you staying?"

"Just tonight. I had an interview at the Burke Stables. I'm going to be doing an internship in two months."

"Ah, how is old Moira? Still trying to do everything herself?" the woman asked. Moe just returned her smile and introduced herself. "I'm Patti. If you need anything tonight, you just let me know."

Moe went to her room and found it blissfully empty. She called her parents and got the third degree before she dropped the news on them. Her internship started January 10. Her mother hit the ceiling. When her father went out on the porch for some fresh air, he said quietly. "I guess it's time for your adventure. Good for you, baby."

This brought tears to her eyes. "Thanks, Dad."

"So, you really didn't stick around to see him after the Prince Charming routine you pulled? Dang, baby girl. I never pegged you for a coward."

And how the hell was she going to argue with that?

SEANY STARED OUT HIS WINDOW, barely registering that someone had knocked. He looked up to see Mary and Madeline Nagle were standing there. Charlie was next to them, holding his little cousin William. "Three beautiful lasses. You travel in style, William." He smiled slightly, but it didn't reach his eyes. Like flirting was just a reflex. Both of the Nagle sisters came to his bed, kissing him on the cheek. Charlie leaned down, planting one on the lips. He rubbed his lips on William's soft head, thinking about McBride's baby. A little girl. She might never know her father. His eyes burned and he looked away. "Any news on the fire investigation? Was it arson?"

Charlie sighed. "They haven't released the report yet. The illegal dumping of the propane may not be related to the fire."

"What do you think?" He met her eyes.

Charlie said, "This isn't my expertise, Seany. If I had to take a guess, I would say that the homeless population was responsible for the fire. It's getting pretty cold at night. And someone who didn't want to pay to dump old propane could have left them there. Or maybe that little village of rough sleepers got them out of a dump. Maybe they were going to use them for cooking? It's all a guess. They scattered when the fire happened, but there were probably at least twenty people living in that old building. Maybe I'm wrong. Your arson investigators would probably know more. They work with the Gardai. When Tadgh knows something, he'll tell you all of it. He won't hold back."

Mary and Madeline had been quiet during the conversation, just listening. He hadn't even noticed that Mary had cleared away his tray and Madeline was setting down a vase full of flowers. Bells of Ireland. He closed his eyes as an old pain washed through him. Those were the flowers they'd given Moe after her big show debut. She'd been so touched. A blush and that Mona Lisa smile gracing her beautiful face.

"Are you in pain, love?" Madeline's voice was deep and melodious as she smoothed his hair back.

Yes. "No, I'm okay. Just tired of being in this bed. And they won't let me see McBride. It's a bullshit rule."

Madeline said, "I'm sorry. From what I know about burns, infection is a big concern. Add pneumonia and he's very vulnerable. I'm sorry for it, though. It must be murder not being able to see him."

Seany said, "If he dies, how am I going to live with it." His voice was soft as he stared out his window at the pouring rain.

It was Charlie who took his hand. "You'll live with it because it wasn't your fault. Everyone knows that but you, Seany."

He shook himself, changing the subject. "How is Josh? Did you make sure he got the rent?"

She said, "He got it. Don't worry about that kind of stuff, Seany. Just get better. You have a new life waiting for you. He is upset he hasn't had more time to come to Dublin, but he's working the three jobs. He loves the lighthouse gig, though."

Seany gave a weak smile. "It seems he was born to it. I can't imagine every man could take to it like he has."

Madeline said, "I don't know. I think it would be a peaceful life. Just imagine when they were all manned 24-7. Before they became automatic. They lived right there on the shore, keeping the lights going. It's rather romantic, I think. Especially the really remote lighthouses."

Seany watched the minute something clicked in Charlie's mind. She really looked at Madeline. Charlie said, "Yes, I agree. The keeper and his wife all alone for months at a time? It is romantic. Maybe my brother will find someone of a like mind. Someone who will appreciate what a pure soul he has. He deserves that."

Madeline was blushing now, and Seany exchanged glances with Mary. She winked at him and he worked hard at suppressing a smile. He loved Josh and Maddie, but they were both idiots.

* * *

Letterfrack, Co. Galway

After a hearty breakfast, Moe found herself back on the road out of the village and toward the horse ranch. Did they call it a ranch in Ireland? She'd have to ask. She couldn't get the place out of her mind. The urge to just dig in and start working was overwhelming. It was going to be a challenge. But she really liked Moira. She didn't seem to have much family, but the people at the ranch seemed to be a good substitute, and the horses were like her children. It was a great thing she was trying to do. There weren't enough therapy centers in America. She assumed it was the same in Ireland. It was a big undertaking. They'd need a team of volunteers. Using interns for cheap labor was a genius move. Professionals who would work for little or nothing because they needed the work for their degree. Needed to pay their dues before heading out into the workforce. But she had to go home. Had to finish the semester, for one thing.

That large Irish Sport horse was still on her mind. He was magnificent. He was also a handful, and a liability if they didn't get a handle on him. He was beautiful, though. And as with humans, being good looking usually meant you got some breaks in life.

Moira didn't look surprised when she pulled into the drive. She got out, and the woman whistled toward the barn. That's when a tall, strong man about her dad's age came out to greet her. The head groom, Devlin, had been out in the far pasture yesterday, so she hadn't met him. Quick to follow was a younger man, about twenty-five years old. "This young man is Rory. He is our other groom and the farrier. He's just starting out in the trade, but he's very good. And last but not least is our lovely trainer Penelope." Moe shook her hand. She was petite and dark haired, with deep brown eyes and long lashes.

"You can call me Penny. We are so glad you'll be joining us. As you can see, I'll be out of commission soon." She patted her little baby bump, and Moe warmed at the sight of it. She'd always felt pregnant women were so beautiful. They really did glow.

"It's so nice to meet everyone. I just couldn't resist coming back out before I left for Dublin. I will finish out the semester and be back here ready to work by the second week in January."

Devlin smiled with a twinkle of mischief in his eye. "Work, aye… but can she ride?"

Moe raised a brow. "I'm a Texan. I was raised in the saddle."

"Oh, a cowgirl is it? Well, now. I'm not sure we've got one of those fancy saddles. Care to try one of our mares on for size? I won't subject you to the beast again today."

"What is his name? Surely, it's not *the beast,* although, he'd earn the nickname."

"His name is Balor. It's from Irish mythology. It's a good, strong name for a troublemaking horse. I'm assuming those boots aren't just for show, so I'll put you on Skadi today. Come meet the whole group. Everyone is still in the stables. We'll ride out to see the pastureland, get the full tour. Moira, are you coming?"

"Not this morning. I've got to call the other candidate today."

Moe asked, "Who did you go with, if you don't mind me being a bit nosy?"

"Not at all. I took your advice and am going to try for the Aussie."

Moe nodded. "That sounds promising. I wouldn't rule out the woman from Colorado either. It's an amazing school. She had an impressive resume. A lot more experience than our man from down under."

"Aye, she did. I'll keep her in mind. I just need someone to make a commitment through June. She may not be able to do that if she has a home and family, so I'm going to get a better feel for it when I call them both."

"Well, you've got me locked in until June for sure, and after that, we'll see. Now, I know I came unannounced. I'll get out of your hair and go meet the horses. Thank you, Moira. This is going to be a great opportunity. I know I can learn a lot from you."

They walked into the barn and the smell of sweet, fresh hay was in the air. She loved the shuffling hooves and noises the horses made. She noticed that they'd gotten the troublemaker in an indoor stall. She approached him, and his ears went back. "Don't get your feathers ruffled, Balor. I'm just saying hello." She rubbed his thick, warm neck and he settled a little.

"He's calm around you. Moira said you had the touch. Now, Balor, you can't be greedy with her time. There are others to meet." Devlin made a clicking sound, and from the stable where he'd opened the door came a chestnut colored mini horse. "Maureen, meet War Hammer."

Maureen cracked off an unladylike laugh. "Well, hello there mighty War Hammer." He was so small; it was like looking at an overstuffed toy. He was friendly, pushing his nose into her thigh like a Golden retriever and begging for love. “You are adorable. How about showing me the rest of your friends?”

The mule was next. Franklin was actually sleek and black, with a shiny coat. Then she met the aforementioned randy thoroughbred, Cassanova. *Too right,* she thought. Then she met the first Connemara. “This is your mount today. Skadi, the Norse goddess of winter.”

Moe thought it was the perfect name for her. She opened the stall and approached her. “Oh, my dear. You are lovely, aren’t you? Absolutely stunning.” And she was stunning. A blue-eyed cremello, she was creamy white all over. A perfect example of the species. She had a long, well kept, white mane. She could have been one of those movie star horses you saw on *Game of Thrones* or *Lord of the Rings*. She suspected the mare was the cream of the crop, and they honored her with this mount.

Devlin said, “She is a beauty, for all the good it does us.”

“What do you mean?” Maureen couldn’t understand how this horse could be found wanting.

“Blue-eyed creams can’t be bred, or shouldn’t be is more accurate. It’s the blue eyes. It’s considered a genetic flaw. They are o’er sensitive to the sun and can have vision problems. Breed standards demand that she not reproduce, because that double-dilute gene will contaminate a new generation. She’s decorative, but Moira got her for a song because serious breeders don’t have much use for her sort. We didn’t want her falling into the wrong hands, so we brought her home with us the same day we were acquiring that liver chestnut two stalls down.”

“That’s terrible. Who could ever see this beautiful creature as flawed?”

“It’s no hardship on the girl. There is a solid reason not to breed her, given the eye problems they can develop. Responsible breeding is important. She’s well fed and cared for. She loves people. Connemaras are just about the most even-tempered ponies you’ll ever come across. This new venture of Moira’s is going to work because of that fact. They are perfect horses for beginner riders. They are athletic and stable. Kind to children. You're going to fall in love, Maureen. You won't want to go home."

The words were meant for the horses, but the hair raised up on her arms, nonetheless.

She kissed the sweet, docile horse's velvety muzzle, then went to meet the rest. A few were the silvery, dappled gray that she saw in a lot of the books on Connemara ponies. There was a dun, with black mane and tail and black legs. There was a sooty buckskin and another cremello, although not as well made as Skadi, that had brown, soulful eyes. The second one to win the beauty contest was a solid gray. No distinguishing marks other than the tail and mane being darker. It was a stallion and a champion breeder. The dominant white would have been a handsome fellow, but apparently he had an affinity for mud.

Devlin said, "We can't keep him clean for more than ten minutes. He's still young and wants to play." His voice held genuine affection, and she found that she liked the man tremendously. You could tell a lot about a person by how they interacted with animals.

After some quick lessons on the saddle she'd be using, she found herself astride Skadi, and she knew she was grinning like an idiot. "My Artemis would be very jealous right now. She's an American Quarter Horse."

"And the apple of your eye, no doubt." She and Devlin rode at an easy pace. Skadi was sleek and graceful. A perfect lady, so to speak. She told him about Texas and their small horse ranch and farm.

"So, I'm curious. We all are. Did you just fly here to do the interview, or did you have another reason? Seems like you'd have used video conference like many of the others did." Her hands paused on the reins. "I mean, it's not my business, of course, if you'd rather not say."

"No, it's okay. I had originally considered the internship and was going to reach out for a video interview, then something happened." So, she told him. Not so much about the nature of her relationship to the O'Briens or Seany, but the basics.

"I saw the news report on the tele. They say the one lad is still critical. Your fella is out of intensive care, though. It's been all over the media. They're calling for better equipment and more firefighters."

All she said to that was, "He's not my fella."

"If you say so," he said simply. Then they continued the tour of the property.

CHAPTER 10

Moe drove the country roads back to Dublin, just stopping at a Spar Mart for a coffee. Moira had packed a bagged supper for her to take with her after stuffing her with an early lunch. When she finally made it to Dublin, it was dark. She dropped off her car rental and took a cab back to the hostel. She checked her texts on the way and noticed her mother had sent two, her little sister three, Madeline one, and Alanna one. Inviting her to have dinner with the family. There was no way in hell she was going to have dinner with Seany's family while he was laid up in the hospital. He supposedly didn't even know she was here. This is not how it needed to get back to him. She had no idea what he was like now. What his life was like now. She'd be the worst sort of intruder showing up for Sunday dinner. Besides, it was late. It was almost eight, and she was tired. She sent her regrets, then shut her phone down. Her battery was on two percent.

She didn't check it again until the morning. She was at the same hostel she'd stayed in before, and now there were some rowdy German kids bunking in with her. She didn't mind the noise. She had little siblings and shared a room. And the Germans were fun. About her age and game to party. Some of them had been out all night and had just stumbled in for the complimentary breakfast.

She nibbled on some toast and checked her emails, but then she heard a familiar voice. She looked up and saw Alanna talking to the hostel manager. She waved her over and the two women hugged. Alanna was still drop dead gorgeous. Pregnant with her third child, she had the softness and glowing radiance of impending motherhood. Her bright green eyes and long blonde hair just screamed Victoria Secret model, but she didn't really seem to understand how beautiful she was. She'd been there for Moe's family at a very dark time in their lives. When Alanna sat down to talk, Moe asked her. "Are you still a counselor?"

"I am, part time. We lived in England up until recently. Now we're back in Belfast. We have a little house outside the city, where the schools are better. It was Aidan's grandparents' house, and now my sister-in-law Branna owns it. We rent from her. Real estate is kind of her thing. I'm less busy now, because most of the Royal Irish Soldiers are in the Reserves, unlike Aidan. It's good, considering the man has kept me knocked up for the last five years."

Moe smiled at that. "Is this a boy or a girl? You have one of each, right?"

"Yes, Davey and Isla. We don't know what this one is. Given the family record, it's likely a boy. He'll be named Keeghan. If it's a girl, she'll be Baby Girl O'Brien because we can't settle on a name." She stole a toast point off of Moe's plate. "Enough about me. Did you get the internship?"

Moe's mouth dropped. "Did Madeline tell you?"

"No but remind me to smack her a good one for not telling me. Your mother told me. She's fit to be tied. You know how they get when they figure out you don't need their permission for everything. Every parent struggles with it, so don't be too hard on her. I'm sure I'll be just as nosy and pushy. You should meet Seany's mother. Talk about a she-bear. So, did you get it? You did, didn't you?"

"Why don't you wait and ask my mother?" Moe said with an arched brow.

"Don't make me call her, girl. I need details. I'm in a delicate condition. You can't be stressing me out."

Moe never got tired of that southern accent of hers. She really was adorable. "Yes, I got it."

The squeal that came out of her shot through the breakfast room, and a couple of Germans on the starting end of a hangover winced at the pitch. "Sorry," she whispered. "You should come to the hospital. He's out of ICU. They may let him come home in a few more days. You don't fly out until after midnight tomorrow. I still haven't forgiven you for taking off like that."

"Alanna, I can't. I'm not ready and it would be a huge intrusion right now. Your family needs to be with him. They don't need some teenage drama rerun interfering with the family rallying around Seany. The news online said his partner is still bad off."

Alanna's face fell. "He's got pneumonia. It's not good, given his other injuries."

Moe's eyes closed. She hurt for Seany. Hurt for his partner and his family. "I'm so sorry for everyone. He has children?"

"Four," Alanna said sadly. "Three boys and a baby girl." Alanna's throat was rough with emotion. "We've been there, haven't we? With our own daddies." She took Moe's hand. "What are you doing for the rest of your time? And when are you coming back?"

"I'm going to Trinity, maybe to Christ Church or St. Patrick's Cathedral. I may try to go on standby for an earlier flight tomorrow."

"I wish you didn't feel like you had to stay away." Alanna's voice was sad, but Moe knew she understood.

"It can't happen like this. If it even does happen. I'm going to be up in those hills working my butt off. I may not even see him when I get back."

"Is that what you want? It doesn't seem like it. Or else why get on that plane?" Alanna cocked a brow, daring Moe to argue with her.

"I don't know what I want, and..." she swallowed hard and continued, "he may not want to see me. It's not just about my feelings. I hurt him. Now that he's grown and it's in the past, maybe it should stay there."

Alanna snorted. She whispered something like, *trust the process.* Which made no sense to Moe at all.

* * *

32 Hours Later

Seany saw her so clearly. Her beautiful, serious eyes. Her secret smile. But she was fading. Why was she fading? He woke with a start, his chest heaving and his brow sweaty. It was dark in his room. He'd sent his family home. His parents wouldn't leave Dublin until he was released, but at least they could get some sleep at Liam's place. He took a sip from his hospital pitcher and wished he could shake off the dream. She came to him now and again. The ethereal creature of his boyhood fantasies. But this time had been different. She was different. He didn't understand it. Probably fever dreams from pain and medication. He thought about his partner and it was like another knife to the heart. *Please don't leave us. Don't leave Kamala and the kids.*

He played those moments leading up to his injuries over and over again. Maybe if he'd gotten the rope out sooner. If he'd left him and hooked the system to something before he attached it to McBride. Or if he'd let go and held him with one arm and… He punched the mattress. It was so disjointed. What had seemed like hours had only been a few minutes. At least that is what they'd told him based on the radio communication.

That damn fire had spread so fast. Maybe if they hadn't checked that last bit of building. If he'd told McBride to…to what? McBride was a smart, competent fireman. Seany looked to him for guidance, not the other way around. But there had to have been something he could have done differently. Something that would have changed the outcome. His arm was humming with nerve pain and the stitches from his surgery were pulling at the shoulder every time he moved his upper body. He hurt everywhere, but especially in his heart. And there was no medication for that.

* * *

MAUREEN FELT the plane lift off the ground and she felt like her heart was ripping in two. Leaving Seany in that hospital bed went against something very primitive in her nature. Tears fell silently as she pictured that youthful, flirtatious young buck with the long hair. Strumming the guitar or with the North Carolina sunset lighting up his sandy colored hair. Those untried kisses and embraces. He'd made her feel beautiful and wanted for the first time in her life. But it was more than that. He'd seen her. Really seen to the heart of her.

Then she remembered that virile man in the hospital bed. Diminished by his injuries, yes. Pale and still. But he was breathtaking with a broad chest and muscled arms. Long, strong legs. He was Seany magnified. She'd only caught a glimpse of those dusty blue eyes, so much like his brother's. They'd burned for her once, a long time ago. She would be back in less than two months. And she wasn't sure if she had the courage to look him in the eyes again. Afraid of seeing that the flame had extinguished. Afraid that not even an ember had survived between them.

CHAPTER 11

St. James Hospital-Dublin

Seany shook with the effort of not breaking down. He was aware of every sound. The beeps and wheezes of the machines taking McBride's vitals, the nurses talking at the nurse's station, footsteps in the hall, the ventilator giving McBride what he needed. Seany felt sick. His upper lip and forehead were sweating, his chest was tight, and he felt trapped. He wanted to run out of there and hide from this. He wanted to scream at God.

Kamala wanted him here. The children had come in briefly. The family and nurses had cleaned him up, and Seany saw that even in the destroyed state of McBride's body, he'd rallied to appear better than he was. To put up a front for his kids. The older two were crying, because they understood. The other was a wee boy, barely out of nappies. Then there was the baby, blissfully unaware and cooing in his gran's arms. It was brutal altogether. Kamala's parents said their goodbyes and took the children out. All that was left was Kamala, Nelson's parents, and his older sister and brother. Nelson Sr. held his wife as she sobbed silently. The siblings sat close, his sister wiping away a steady stream of tears. Seany felt like an intruder, but Kamala was convinced that he should be here. That McBride would want him here. She said, "Junior, come sit by me. Please, come closer." He looked at the McBride's.

The father said, "We've said our goodbyes, Junior. It's all right. Go to him. You both need it, I think." The use of his station name by Nelson's parents gutted him. He'd had dinner at their house. He'd shared the cookies from Mrs. McBride and Nelson's grandmother. It was a big family, like his own.

He wheeled himself over. He was following nurse's orders on the wheelchair, but it was better since there were no chairs left. She took his hand and he shuddered with the weight of his grief. Then he met his buddy's eyes. Barely focused and weary. "Junior, he sees you. He knows you're here." He saw her throat working, trying to stave off the tears. They fell silently, despite her efforts.

Seany reached his less battered arm across the bed and pushed his partner's hair off his forehead. The other arm was bound to his chest in a sling and Velcro band. His hair had grown in the two weeks he'd been in here. They both needed a haircut. He just said, "I love you, brother. And I'd take your place if I could. I swear it. Please forgive me." His voice broke and he swallowed hard, trying to keep his composure. Nelson's family was on the other side, each with a hand on him. "I'm so sorry." He said the words again, and they sounded completely useless, even to him.

McBride shut his eyes and opened them. An acknowledgement of sorts. Seany looked at his monitors, barely reading them through the unshed tears. His blood pressure was in the basement. His oxygen levels were barely in range, even with the ventilator at the highest level. Jesus, this was really happening.

Out of nowhere, Kamala said, "Sing something to him, Seany. He said you could sing. That you did the trad sessions back home. I think he'd like it." She turned around and her eyes pleaded with him. "Please." That's when he saw it. The despair so deep that she was barely standing. She was losing her mate, and she knew it. Her throat worked as she choked back another plea.

So, he did. His voice was rough at first, but then he settled into an even baritone. *The Parting Glass,* smooth and sweet enough to slice him to the bone. Tears came down Kamala's face, but she was smiling as she rubbed her husband's arm. Seany's voice trembled as he managed to get out the words. He put his hand on his buddy's chest, meeting his eyes as he sang. And just like that, his partner drifted away.

* * *

Glasnevin Cemetery, Dublin, Ireland

Seany practically hummed with grief and physical pain. He'd refused to use any sort of wheelchair. His only concession was the sling that kept him from using his one arm. He could salute, though. His uniform was noticeably loose on him. He'd lost weight in the hospital. His cheeks were sunken and pale from not eating enough and being indoors. He watched as six men from his station carried McBride's casket. He should be there, holding his partner up for the last time. As if reading his thoughts, his brother put a hand on his shoulder. His whole family was here, but it was Aidan who stayed the closest.

Seany looked across the gravesite to McBride's widow and children. Jesus, they were so small. Three boys with no da. A little baby girl who wouldn't even remember him. A tremor went through Seany as he thought of his smiling, energetic friend. How could it be over? It should have been him. That thought rolled over and over again in his head. Why hadn't God taken him? No one needed him. They'd mourn him, but they didn't need him. He didn't realize how tight his body was until they rang the brass bell for the first time. He jolted and Aidan moved closer, trying to support him without smothering him. Three rings, three times, and Seany could hear the sniffles and sobs throughout the crowd. He looked at Kamala again and her chin was up. Her jet-black hair was smoothed down her back. Her long, black lashes were coated in tears. Streams of tears flowed down her cheeks as she silently wept. She was a rock. One of the grandparents held the oldest boy, who wept openly because he fully understood that he wasn't going to see his father again. At least not in this life.

The casket was draped with their firehouse flag. His helmet was displayed on an altar to the right. At the conclusion of the flag folding, it was given to Kamala and she hugged it to her body like a life preserver. He wanted to fall at her feet and beg for forgiveness. They'd found no fault with his actions. They actually planned to give him a medal. But he didn't want it. He wanted Kamala to have her husband again. As they finished with a prayer, Seany couldn't muster an amen. God had gotten it wrong this time. He looked at that little baby girl again, swaddled against the cold in a little pink blanket. Dead wrong.

CHAPTER 12

Six Weeks Later

Shannon Airport-Shannon, Ireland

Moe headed to the baggage claim area, keeping an eye out for Devlin. She stood at the carousel, her carry-on bag biting into her shoulder. The trip here from Texas had been a little better than the one in November, but she was still exhausted. She always had trouble sleeping on planes. When she saw her big suitcase, she grabbed the handle. Then she hooked her carry-on over the handle and wheeled it all over to oversized baggage. There were skis, a surfboard, and then... there it was. Her saddle. She got some odd looks from the locals, but it just made her smile to herself. A saddle was a very personal thing. And she had some ideas about how to handle Balor. They'd had no luck with him, and time wasn't on their side. They needed to break him of his bad habits early on, and they'd already had him two months. He was defiant just for the sake of being defiant, and it had to stop. If they had any hope of being able to keep him, he had to learn to channel that energy into something positive.

She was just about to pay a few euro for a luggage trolly when she spotted Devlin. He smirked as he took her saddle in both hands. "Well, you've come prepared to make a statement. Tell me you've brought your chaps and spurs, or I'll be disappointed."

"I would never use spurs on a horse, but as for the chaps, of course. Don't you wear them?" She smiled as she said it.

"Aye, but they're not as decorative as the western style. I've been tellin' the neighbors we have a real cowgirl coming. Ye can't go making me out to be a liar."

She fixed her ball cap and pulled her long ponytail through the hole in the back. "My ten-gallon hat wouldn't fit. Sorry."

* * *

SHE SLEPT ALMOST the whole way. When she woke, it was dark and the road was surrounded by trees. "We're just up the road, lass. We've got a nice warm bed waiting for you."

Moe stretched and said, "Sorry, Devlin. I sleep better in cars than on planes." He returned a smile. "The suspense is killing me. Who did she pick for the last intern?"

"She gave a second interview. Dug deeper, so to speak. The Aussie's parents wouldn't pay the fare. Another bloke failed his nutrition class and has to repeat it."

She shook her head. "That is a class that can make or break you, depending on the teacher and how heavy a class load you scheduled. I don't envy him. People think nutrition is going to be an easy class, but it's not. At least not for horses. You can make a horse ill, or even kill it, if you don't know how and when and what to feed it. I'm not telling you anything you don't know. That's rotten luck, but if he can't pass that class, he shouldn't be caring for your horses. So, who's it going to be?"

"The young woman from Colorado State University. Michele something or other. She'll be here in a few days. She was at the top of the list, but the second interview sealed it. She's quite impressive."

"I remember her. Michele Kane, prior military. I really liked the look of her resume. And she volunteers at a therapeutic riding center. She's perfect."

Devlin said, "Well, I just got severely outnumbered. Not that Rory is going to mind. He's not likely to complain about two pretty American girls staying with us for the next six months." He turned down a dirt road that looked familiar, and within seconds, she was looking at the horse barn, lit by the headlights of the ranch's Land Cruiser. She hopped out, suddenly wide awake. When she began unloading her stuff, he said, "Just the saddle. I'll drive the rest over."

"How far is the cottage?"

"It's a good walk, but you'll be glad for it. Ye've got more room than the other one. Michele will be just there." He pointed to the big house. "There is an addition in the back. Its got it's own entrance and a nice bath, but it's not quite the getaway you'll be enjoying."

"I don't mind either way," Moe suddenly felt selfish for taking the nicer place.

"Michele is interested in the business aspect more so than you, and you are going to be working with Penelope to take over the training when she has the baby. Michele will need to be closer to Moira so she can utilize her office and learn the ropes. Besides, ye came in person to interview. That tips the odds in your favor. Now, take that to the tack room. Moira has prepared a nice spread for your first night."

"Yes, I guess it's only seven-thirty. Or half seven, as you all put it. I could definitely eat, but I'll get some groceries for the cottage tomorrow. I can fend for myself."

"Moira likes a full table. Don't worry yourself over imposing. She's a woman. Ye've got to give her someone to spoil and peck at."

Moe was surprised that someone as successful as Moira had no husband, kids or grandkids. Not that these things defined a woman, but it was unconventional. Especially in her peer group. Then again, Moe was assuming a lot. Just because she wasn't married now, doesn't mean she'd never married. And some people couldn't have kids. It was obvious that Moira considered the people here her family. That was a nice thought. Moe guessed that made her a foster kid. She'd called her parents on the trip from the airport, so that was done. She put her saddle on a rack in the tack room, liking how it looked resting up there with the others. She wished the sun was still up, because she'd have liked to get a look at the progress they'd made in getting the place up to snuff.

She smoothed her hand over the soft leather, well-worn with years of use. She'd always been taught to care for the leather, because a good saddle was a costly thing. She looked down the long row of stalls, wondering who was put where. She'd met all of the horses, of course. She wondered what Moira had in store for her. Michele would be doing office work and helping train the horses. What would she be doing? She knew she'd step in to replace Penelope, but she was excited to hear all about the different classes.

"Woolgathering, are ye?" Devlin smiled as she shook herself out of her thoughts.

"Sorry, I'm sure dinner is waiting. Just getting used to everything. It's a long time to be…somewhere else," Moe said with a slight shrug. Hoping he understood.

"Yes well, I think you'll get on just grand."

They walked to the house, and Maureen took in the peaceful hum of nightfall in the country. The sounds were a little different, but it was nice. There were no traffic sounds nearby. Just a whinny from the stables and some shuffling from inside the house. When Devlin opened the door, the smell of something heavenly wafted out.

Her stomach let out a howl, finally waking up. Moira was standing by the stove in a pair of comfortable looking denim trousers and a loose sweater. Her long silver braid was around one shoulder. Her face held the heavy lines of a woman who'd spent her life outdoors, but her eyes were sharp and intelligent. The first time she'd met her, she'd been trying to take on Balor in a foul mood. Her hair had been in a loose bun at her nape, wisps flying everywhere from her efforts. There was an easy grace to Moira. Not fussy, but formidable and attractive in a way that seemed effortless. She'd likely been a real beauty in her youth as well. Her eyes were amber, like whiskey. Her smile was crooked and mischievous. "There she is. It's good to see you again, Maureen Rogers."

"My family calls me Moe. I go by that or Maureen."

"Which do you prefer?" she asked, brow raised.

Moe thought about it. "I don't really know. Dealer's choice, I suppose."

Just as she made herself all the way into the room, Rory came in the back door behind them. They exchanged niceties. Moe looked around the warm kitchen. The largest window was over the sink and looked out over the barn. She noticed how much smaller the appliances were than in America. It was homey, though. A nook was off to the right, with a table and four chairs. Moira said, "It's small, but it works. Do ye come from a large home?"

"Not at all. Every military base house we ever lived in was tiny. The ranch has a three-bedroom house with two bathrooms. There are five of us, so you've got room to spare in this house. I commuted to school for the first six semesters. I couldn't see the sense in paying for the dorms when I was so close. It was less than an hour to most of my classes and the equine center. I sublet a room in someone's townhouse last semester, because my hours at the stables were so long, as well as my classes. It was a busy few months, so I'm glad it's over."

"Well, I know you graduate in May. I appreciate the fact that you were willing to extend over the summer. I just don't want to break in another student if everyone is happy. Will you miss your ceremony?"

Moe shrugged. "It's okay. It's the work that's important. I'm not going to bail on you just for a ten-minute walk and to hear my name said over a microphone. I'm happy to be here, Moira. Thank you for this opportunity."

She sat between Rory and Devlin and across from Moira as they said the blessing and began heaping mounds of food on her plate. "Do you like mashed spuds? I hope so because I serve a lot of them." Moe loved potatoes in every form, and she said so. There was roast beef, baked mushrooms, some sort of seeded bread, and peas.

When Moe took a bite of the potatoes, she almost moaned. "What did you put in these potatoes?"

"Fresh cream and butter from a local farm in Galway. Since Kerry seems to be sending all their butter to the Yanks, we had to look closer to home," she winked at Moe as she said it. She wasn't wrong. American's loved their Kerrygold.

"Do you have beef cattle around here?" she asked. "Because you haven't lived until you've had proper Texas brisket."

"Well, now. Anytime you want to commandeer my little cooker or the barbecue, I will gladly pass over my apron, lass." Moira raised her glass of lemonade. "A toast, to new friends and new purpose."

They all raised their glasses, clinking them together. It was a good night.

* * *

DEVLIN DROPPED Moe off at the lake cottage and she was so tired she was ready to strip right in front of him. He carried her bags inside the door and left without delay. But part of her needed to just go out onto the small patio and soak in the night air, just for a minute. It was past ten, and the moon and stars were shining over the lake. Or lough, as Moira called it. It made her think of Loch Ness and prehistoric monsters when she heard it. This lough was tranquil and smelled like stone and fresh water. She wished it was warmer so she could go for a dip. Then again, it would be a good pick me up in the morning to jump in.

After a few minutes, she went in to get a better look at the place she'd call home for the next six months. The sitting room and kitchen were all open floor plan with a small table, a tiny sofa, a rocker, and a proper hearth. The furniture was worn, but clean and soft to the touch. There were baseboard heaters in the main room as well as the water closet. She had a shower stall with no tub, but it was clean and well kept. The double bed had fresh linen and a decent mattress. She'd even bought new pillows. Moe was tempted to just crash, but she put her clothing away in the small chest of drawers and wardrobe. She set her toiletries up in the bathroom. When she went into the kitchen to get a glass of water, she found that Moira had stocked some necessities in the fridge and cupboard. Butter, milk, eggs, bread, cheese, apples, tea, and instant coffee. She looked in the freezer, found some ice, and filled a glass for her nightstand. After a quick shower, she settled herself into bed. Tomorrow was the start of everything.

CHAPTER 13

Galway City, Ireland

Beads of sweat gathered on Seany's forehead as he used the rubber therapy bands for resistance. His physical therapist stopped him with a gentle hand. "You're overdoing it. This is not a time to push into the pain. You are still healing. Now, use this band instead. It's more flexible. Come across your chest, that's it."

"I should be lifting weights and doing push-ups and pull-ups. I'm never going to get back on rotation at this pace. I can push harder."

"If you don't let this tendon heal, you'll be back in the O.R. instead of in a fire truck. Stop being such a bloody caveman and do as you're told. Now, get on the table over the heated pad and I will rub you down."

"I'll bet you say that to all the boys." Seany dodged a swipe. Amy was twice his age and a very good therapist. She also didn't take any cheek. He stretched out on the therapy table and she went to work on him. Stretching and rubbing almost to the point of pain, but not quite. He couldn't help but surrender to it. She worked the incision scar tissue, trying to keep adhesions from taking root. "When will I be ready to go back? They've held the position for me, but they won't do it forever."

"I'll talk to your physician. He's the one who has to clear you. You are doing really well. You are healing faster than predicted. But the shoulder isn't your only problem. Have you seen the shrink?"

"I don't need a bloody shrink."

"You had a concussion. You were out for several days. You also lost your partner. If you didn't need a shrink, it would be a surprise. They just want to make sure you're ready, O'Brien. The more you fight them, the longer it's going to take to get cleared for duty."

He sighed, his jaw tightening at the thought of seeing some stupid shrink. "What happened sucked. I don't think a feckin' rehash is going to do me any good. I just want to work."

"Listen, love. I'm no mental health therapist. I only handle external pain. But I see it in your eyes. The hurt, the anger, and the guilt. If you don't take care of it, it will ruin a lot of good things you have ahead of you."

* * *

SEANY CAME in to find Josh sleeping on the kitchen table. He had a book on lighthouse maintenance opened. His coffee was cold. "Wake up, princess. You have to get back to work."

Josh stretched, his hair sticking up at odd angles. He'd been growing it out, to Seany's surprise. He spent a lot of time outdoors, and it was thick and streaked with highlights. It grew fast, and it was obvious the scar across his scalp was what had motivated his change in style. "Sorry. I was going to make lunch, but I passed out." He looked at his phone. "Shit, I have a shift at the ferry in two hours. I need to eat and shower."

Seany motioned toward the lav. "Go shower. I'll make something and have it ready."

"Thanks, babycakes," Josh said as Seany threw a dish towel at him.

Seany stirred the tin of beef stew, watching the congealed muck warm into something edible. He missed his mother's cooking at times like this. They weren't too far, and he'd expect a visit from his parents soon. His mother worked in a women's clinic as a midwife, but she found her way to the hospital in Galway on occasion. His father was retired from the Gardai, and was in the reserve unit for County Clare. Unlike some military and first responders who retired young, he never picked up a second career. When Seany's mam was fighting breast cancer, he'd had to juggle work, caregiving, and being a parent. After retirement, he decided that he would never take this time with his wife for granted. They were financially comfortable and his mother was working again. So, his da spent time between his grown children, his grandchildren, two sets of aging parents, and being the very best husband he could be. As if summoned from his thoughts, Seany's cell phone gave a shout. "Hey, Da. What's the craic?"

"I thought I'd stop by. Your mother has been batch cooking and baking with your grandmother. I keep reminding her that our children are adults and no longer living with us, but you know how she gets."

Seany smiled. "I was heating something out of a tin and missing the old days. Your timing is perfect. Josh has been working like a dog."

"I'll be there by half two." That was in twenty minutes. A sneak attack, no doubt, to check on his welfare. Like he was going to hang himself in the shower or something. Then the other shoe dropped. "Alanna is with me."

He loved his sister-in-law. He treasured her like his own blood, because he'd watched her transform his brother. Brought him back from his own personal hell. And they'd almost lost her. He'd been there for all of it. He watched her brought out of the scrub of some North Carolina barrier island, bruised and abused. He loved her almost as much as his brother did. However, she was a mental health therapist. Specializing in PTSD and traumatic brain injuries. There is only one reason she'd be coming all the way to Furbogh from Belfast. A little in-house head shrinking. He shouldn't be surprised or even put out. He'd given her permission to speak to his superiors and his doctor. He thought it would be easiest to get the required head shrinking done by the family expert. She'd visit, check the box, and he'd be back on duty in a flash.

He gave a shout to Josh, warning him to not be prancing around bare-assed. Then he began straightening up the place. Sweaty gym socks and dirty teacups stashed in their proper place. He opened the door and there she was. Like the sun at midday, bright and warm. He hugged her, feeling the pain shoot through his shoulder. She was gentle, unlike her regular squeeze, and it made him feel a little bit angry. Not at her. At himself. At his body. "Hello, Blondie." He kissed her hair and then took another restrained hug from his father. He felt distant, like he was in a glass case screaming to get out. He didn't like feeling fragile.

Alanna joined him on the sofa, and she took his hand. "You're in pain."

"It's not so bad. Not anymore. The doc said it takes time."

"Yes, he's right. How are the headaches?"

He stood and said briskly, "They aren't as often. How about some tea?"

Alanna knew when to back off. It was her specialty. Seany's father walked to the electric kettle. "I'll get it. Just sit and visit."

"I can lift a kettle, Da. I'm not an invalid." His tone was sharper than he'd meant. Josh made an appearance out of the bathroom.

Josh said, "He gets testy after PT. Just punch him in his bad shoulder if he gives you too much lip."

Sean Sr. cracked off a laugh and raised a brow at Seany. "I'll forgive the cheek. Now sit down and relax. Humor your old Da and give me something to do." He fired up the kettle, using the boiling time to put some homemade meals away in the fridge. He took out a couple of ancient takeaway containers, sniffed, reared back in disgust, and chucked them in the bin. "You lads are going to perish from food poisoning." But Seany had barely taken in the statement. He was focused on Alanna's face, and it didn't bode well.

"What's wrong? They didn't go for it?" he asked.

"Actually, there was a compromise. I can't be your therapist. For one, I'm not licensed in Ireland. I practice in the UK. First Shropshire, then Belfast. Secondly, I'm family, so I can't treat you. I'm sorry, but I'm not surprised. It's frowned upon in every branch of medicine and mental health practice."

"Mam delivered your babies. How is that any different?"

"She had an attending physician," she explained, starting to get irritated.

"Yes, your stepmother! Do these rules only apply for me? Don't tell me you don't still work with Aidan."

Sean Sr. almost intervened, but Alanna put up a hand, silencing him. This was between Seany and her. "She wasn't my stepmother yet. And yes, I work with Aidan. But he doesn't need to be medically and mentally cleared for duty. It's informal. And he's a willing participant. I suppose you just thought you'd sweeten me up and I'd sign off without putting you through the regular paces. Tell me I'm wrong." She wasn't, and she knew it.

Suddenly Sean Sr. and Josh needed to check the oil in the automobiles, and they left without a word. Alanna lifted her chin. "What I do is important. And it works. I wish I could be your therapist, because I am used to dealing with pigheaded men who don't think they need my help. And believe me Sean David O'Brien, Jr., I could have you on the mat and pinned to the floor within two sessions. I would not go easy on you because you're my little brother. But I can't treat you. Not officially. You have to look into a different therapist or type of therapy if you want cleared. That said, you know I'm here for you unofficially with all of the love in my heart. I will treat you on the sly. But don't sass me, brother. I will eat your lunch."

Seany's face had been tight during this whole set down, but at that, one corner of his mouth twitched. "I'm starting to remember why my brother couldn't resist you."

She narrowed her eyes at him. "Don't you forget it, big guy."

"So, what is the compromise you came to with the powers that be?" he asked.

"Alternative and unorthodox therapies," she hedged.

"What, like meditation and a vision quest?" he said smartly.

She kept a completely straight face, innocent as a spring lamb, when she said, "Equine therapy. There is a place not too far from here in the Connemara Mountains."

* * *

Letterfrack, Co. Galway

Moe stood before the beautiful Irish Sport like a soldier ready for war. He really was being a total dick. She meant that in the sweetest way. She liked Balor. She really did. But he tried her patience like no other horse she'd ever met. Today was going to be different. Balor was an athlete. A naughty one. As for why he was naughty? She didn't know. Everyone, including horses, had a backstory. So, she only knew what she knew. Nicety-nice wasn't working with him, so she was going full Texas. If he didn't want to run the standard paces that she ran with the other horses, then she was going to start getting creative. She set the barrels up at the appropriate distance apart.

Devlin shook his head, but Penelope just sat on the fence line, grinning ear to ear. She screamed, "Well done, girl! Show that little shite who's boss!"

When she kicked her heels, he shot across the corral, but she didn't let him indulge himself. She cut over, pulling him right and trying to make the turn. It didn't work. He bucked, but she'd been ready for it. "Huh! Easy boy!" She muscled him back under control. Backing him up until he was ready to try again. She shot toward the barrel, willing him to submit and round the barrel. Not only did he refuse, but she got tossed for good measure. *Shit. This is going to hurt.* The air shot out of her as she landed.

Devlin yelled as Penelope screeched. They ran into the ring as Moe got tossed from the saddle. Moe rolled under the fence, completely covered in dirt. "I'm okay!"

Devlin was by her side and rolling her on her back before the words were out of her mouth. "I'm okay. I just need a minute." She sat up. It wasn't her first time being knocked on her ass, but she was only one fall away from a big injury. And Balor was a tall horse. She dusted herself off. "I'm okay. This is between him me." She went back into the ring, cool as a cucumber. Balor reared and shook his head, trying to show her who was boss. She spread her arms. "Are you done yet? Because I'm getting paid by the hour, smart ass."

Devlin barked out a laugh, nodding at Penelope. "I like this one."

* * *

THEY ALL SAT around the kitchen table, eating the lunch Moira had made for everyone. "We have a temporary certificate as a non-profit. They did the preliminary inspection a few days before you came. There will be another more formal inspection of our paper trail, our business plan, and my financial records this week, and a government inspection of the facility in three weeks."

Devlin said something in Irish that Moe didn't understand. *An Roinn Talmhaíochta, Bia agus Mara.* He often switched back and forth between the two languages. Penelope smiled at her. "That would be the Department of Agriculture, Food, and the Marine. Like your USDA."

"Ah, gotcha. Are we ready for that inspection? What are we worried about? How can I help?"

"Manpower is my big concern. It affects safety. I've started a list of locals who are interested in volunteering. I have some commitments from patrons for cash flow. I've been doing fine on my own, but if I'm going to hire speech and occupational therapists and start looking into another trainer, I need to have income to pay them. I also need three more board members. I'm afraid my distant cousin, Hugo, is going to bulldoze over the current members if I let him onto the board. I need smart people who can respect each other and have our best interest at heart. They don't even have to be local. As long as they could make the board meetings four times a year, I'd take a blow-in."

"A blow-in?" Moe asked.

"Someone who hasn't lived in this area since God was a boy. The only two that aren't blow-ins are Moira and Devlin. Rory is from Kildare, originally. I'm from Sligo. You're a Yank, and we've got another coming in from Colorado."

"Thank you for the slang lesson, Penelope. We'll have to teach her as we go. Now, about Balor…I'm worried this whole thing was a mistake. Not your part, Maureen. You've been great. I'm questioning my own judgment."

Moe said, "He is a fine horse, Moira. He's going to take a firm hand. I know I seem inexperienced, but I grew up around horses. My daddy has a strong-willed horse. You haven't met stubborn until you've worked with an Appaloosa. Tear Gas was a downright stinker, and I helped break him. He was half wild when my father bid on him at an auction. Everyone thought he was crazy."

"Tear Gas?" Rory asked. So, she explained the name, which had him and Devlin in complete hysterics.

Penelope rolled her eyes. "Why do men act like wee boys whenever the subject of passing wind comes up?"

Moe smiled at that, then said, "My point is, I really think he's going to come around. For demonstration purposes, if nothing else. I'm not sure I'd put an inexperienced rider on him. Maybe never. But if we hosted community open houses for the public, in order to get some revenue coming in, I think he'd be an asset. He's a handsome devil, and barrel racing isn't an Irish sport. We have our beautiful local ponies, but we also have Cassanova, who you admitted likes to run. And we have Balor. You have Skadi, who is Dressage trained, and a couple of really impressive jumpers. The older, gentler horses could do pony rides and parades. We can do face painting on the kids and let them decorate a couple of the horses with body paint. I've been to these sorts of events before. They bring in clients, donors, and potential volunteers."

Moira was watching Moe as she became excited and animated. "It's all well and good as long as you can get that bloody-minded animal under control. The rest is brilliant, Maureen. Truly."

Moe beamed at the praise. "So, now that we have the temporary status, when do we start taking applicants for those jobs? And when is the first class for equine therapy? And are we going to look into a physical therapist for hippotherapy?"

"We'll walk before we run. We don't have the equipment for

hippotherapy yet. We need a lift and we need some adjustments made to a couple of our saddles. I have a grant pending, and now that we've gained our non-profit status. I think we'll get it. As for the speech and occupational therapy, I have interviews happening today and tomorrow. Two speech and three occupational therapists in all. I need one of each four days a week for six hours once we start with the children. Fridays are going to be for training, maintenance, and paperwork. Saturdays are going to be for trail rides for our advanced riders. Sundays we are closed. I have another trainer coming in the next month or so. He worked with the mounted Garda. He's retired as of last year, and he's very good. I think he'll be a good fit with helping you train, Maureen. This one is getting ready to drop." She pointed to Penny.

Penny scowled, rubbing her protruding belly. "I've got two weeks, Moira."

"No, what you mean is that you are full term at thirty-eight weeks and not close to a hospital. You can work another week, if your doctor signs off on it, but then you are to go home and not come back until the little fiend is at least eight weeks old." She smiled. "And maybe we'll get a local girl to come in and watch the baby so you can bring her with you to work."

Moe squealed. "It's a girl? I love baby girls!"

Devlin looked at Rory and said, "Jaysus, we can't get a break with all of these females."

Penny smacked him. Rory said, "I wouldn't say that again, or you're going to be packing your tea from home."

Moira stood. "That said, lads get the dishes." Both men groaned as the women left to return to their work. Moira followed Moe and Penelope out to the barn. "The first applicants for equine therapy are already coming in. We have a children's class that will start next month on Tuesdays and Thursdays. Once we get another trainer in here full time, we will start the second class in the afternoons. Mondays and Wednesdays are going to be adult sessions. I have a veterans group set up for two weeks from today. There are going to be some private adult sessions as well, until we get a bigger reach and the weather improves. The end of the month and February are going to be slow because it's cold. The beginner classes won't start in the saddle right away anyway. There is a lot to be covered before they sit on a horse. Maureen, you have a small group session starting next Monday, just to get our feet wet. I have one man confirmed. PTSD, TBI, and an injury in the line of duty. Some sort of first responder situation."

That squeezed her heart. Her father had really gotten something out of working with horses. Even before he could ride again, he loved the ritual of caring for them and taking them out to the pasture. She said, "I thought I'd borrow Devlin again. I want to go over the rest of the property. And I have a lot of questions about the Connemaras."

"Absolutely. I'll tell him to finish up by half three and you can get a good ride in before it's dark."

Maureen went back to Balor's outdoor stall, ready to start again. "Are you ready to be nice?"

He actually greeted her with a nuzzle. "Awe, buddy. Every time I get ready to give up on you, you start being sweet. I wish I knew what happened to make you so angry." She patted his soft neck. "I'm not going to give up on you. I promise. Just remember we are on the same team, okay?" He made an endearing rumble, then followed her out of the stall without an argument.

* * *

Belfast, Northern Ireland

Alanna had been home for a full twenty-four hours before her conscience started getting to her. It wasn't as if it was unprofessional. She wasn't treating him. Not really. But she'd offered to treat him in an unofficial capacity, just like she did her husband. And she was setting him up for a big shock. Aidan looked at her, brow raised. "So, we're finally going to tell him?"

"I think we have to, Aidan. He shouldn't go into this therapeutic situation and get blind-sided. I was just so eager to get him to agree. Equine therapy is a great alternative to traditional therapy. He'll have to attend two sessions with a department designated psychologist, and in between he has to do equine therapy for eight weeks. That's how long the program is for a new client. They can extend if they like, but eight weeks is the minimum. I just feel like he might walk out on the whole thing if I don't come clean."

He narrowed his eyes. "Alanna O'Brien. You are a shameless deceiver. This is all about you getting him together with Maureen. If you'd pressed him, he would have gone to a regular therapist. He loves his job. You have orchestrated this entire thing to play matchmaker."

She put her hands on her hips, ready to give him a tongue lashing, and he wanted to tackle her onto the bed. Bad idea since she was past her due date for their third child by two days. She said, "I am not!" Then she softened. "Well, maybe I am. I need to tell him in person. I'm going to drive there in the morning. Edith is coming to watch the kids."

"You cannot go on that long ride again this far into your pregnancy. The only reason I was okay with it this past week was because Mam drove you there and Da drove you back. No way in hell, woman!"

She raised a brow, rearing back. "Listen to me, Captain O'Brien. It's not your job to tell me what I can and can't do. I went over my due date with the other two. I had them both at 41 weeks. I'm fine. I will go, spend the night, and come back the next day. It's not that long of a drive. Furbogh is not even four hours. I told Seany I was coming." She walked to Aidan and pulled him down for a kiss. "The hospital is fifteen minutes away in Galway."

"But it's not your hospital. And what if you pop on the way there?"

"I won't. Just relax, Aidan. If I feel something, I'll call your mother. I promise."

Furbogh, Co. Galway

"Did she say why she was coming back so soon?" Josh asked. "What did you guys talk about when she was here? I thought she couldn't be your therapist." Josh was mashing potatoes for dinner. A staple in the household. He'd picked up some fresh fish from the fishmonger near his lighthouse.

"She can't officially treat me. I saw that therapist yesterday. I check in again in a month. My other therapy starts Monday. Alanna got the department head to sign off on equine therapy. Can you believe it? Instead of talking about my feelings, I get to ride a horse in the Connemara mountains."

Josh froze. *Oh, shit.*

"And she didn't say why she was coming again. I'm surprised Aidan is letting her make the drive, as far along as she is. She's spending the night, so I'll be on the couch."

"No, you won't. I'll be on the couch. You need to be comfortable with that shoulder. I can sleep anywhere. Do you know how many times I've crashed on other people's couches because I didn't want to deal with my dad?"

That made Seany incredibly sad. "Thanks, brother. You're closer to the bathroom. That's good for a pregnant woman."

Josh asked, "So, what do you know about this equine therapy?"

"Nothing. I mean, other than it being good for children with disabilities. My friend Tim's son is autistic. They live in Virginia and his boy does equine therapy. Not sure what it has to do with me, but I'm not going to argue. The department is going to keep me on as an EMT until I get cleared by the physical therapist and surgeon. No fires, but it's better than nothing. I start back next week. I'm on a modified schedule to accommodate therapy sessions and PT. Once I'm back on rotation with the firefighters, I'll be three days on, four days off like before.

Josh knew why Alanna was on her way. She obviously hadn't told him who was working as an intern at the therapeutic riding center. And no one has clued Seany in about the circumstance surrounding his first week in the ICU. He didn't know why he'd woken up. Should he tell him? "When does Alanna get here?"

Seany said, "She said she'd be here around ten. Why?"

"Just curious. I work at the lighthouse tomorrow morning, but I'll get home around half eleven. Then I don't work at the Pie Maker until six. I'll have a little time to visit." He was going to text Alanna and tell her to wait for him. Seany needed to know everything. He'd kept quiet, per the family's request. He'd felt rotten about it, but they had some solid reasons. Now Moe was back. The question was, did she know about Seany's therapy? Something told him she didn't know. Maddie was supposed to contact him if she heard anything from Moe. She hadn't heard from her, but he thought that Moe's start date was some time in mid-January. It was well into the latter half of January. He hoped to hell that Alanna knew what she was doing.

"So, I'm surprised at the dry spell with the ladies recently. You dated a lot in Dublin. After Justine, I may never date again, but you were on a winning streak."

Seany stretched like a big lion. "Yes, well. I am quite the charmer. I just…want to focus on getting healed up. And I don't know…it was getting old. I'm no saint, but that whole Dublin singles scene was heavy on the hook-up, light on the emotional connection. It scratches after a while. Does that make me sound like a pussy?"

"No, no. I get it. I mean, look at your brothers. When you see that sort of connection, it's hard to settle, I suppose. Have you ever been close to that? I mean, there hasn't been anyone serious since I've known you."

"Once, for a short time. I was young. It was just a summer romance, really. I barely remember it now."

Liar, Josh thought. He continued making dinner, watching Seany do his shoulder exercises. Alanna was lucky she was so adorable. He had a feeling Sean O'Brien, Jr. was going to be pissed at this family-wide gag order. They were all lucky, because he had to live with the guy.

* * *

SEANY HUGGED HIS SISTER-IN-LAW, taking her bag from out of the boot. "This is a lot for one night."

She gave him a dry look. "Aidan made me bring my hospital bag in case I dropped this baby on your doorstep." She rubbed her back, feeling really happy to be out of the driver's seat.

"Come, love. Just have a lie down in Josh's room." She obliged, sliding her swollen feet out of her shoes. He put a pillow under her knees.

She took his hand as he set down a glass of ice water. "You're a good man, Seany. Some woman is going to be very lucky someday."

He just smiled at that. How could he explain to her that for the first time since he'd experience his first cockstand, women were the last thing on his mind. He just couldn't get out of his own head enough to give something to someone else. He just said, "Rest up and I'll make some lunch. Josh should be home any minute."

Alanna watched her brother-in-law leave and close the door. She suddenly felt nervous. He wasn't a boy anymore. He was grown. He'd always been mature for his age. She closed her eyes, trying to rest her body, but she felt like the baby was trying to kick into her chest cavity. She rolled, putting the pillow between her knees. She rubbed her back as she thought about how the hell she was going to tell Seany about Moe. Then, she was probably going to have to tell Moe about Seany.

A tapping knock came ten minutes later. "Josh is here. Are you hungry?" He came into the room, noticing that she was slow to get up. "Let me help you, love. I know the mattress isn't that great."

"No, it's not that, Sweetie. This is the last stage of pregnancy. The baby is big and is probably pressing on a nerve." She waddled into the kitchen behind him, giving Josh a look that told him exactly how much she was dreading this little chat.

They sat down to eat and she stirred her soup nervously as Seany tucked into his. He froze with his second spoonful headed to his mouth. "You're both staring at me. Did I miss something?"

Alanna put her spoon down. "We have to talk, Seany. It's past time, really."

His brows were furrowed. "About what?" He looked at Josh. "It's obviously something you both know about. Spill it."

Alanna said, "It's probably best if we start from the beginning, when you were in the ICU. You weren't waking up and we'd tried everything. Priests, family, even Kamala came in and talked to you. So…I made a phone call. It was on a whim, really. I hadn't slept and we were so desperate. I didn't even actually think it would work. I mean, I hoped it would, but before I had a chance to think too much about it my phone was in my hand."

"Christ, lass. I'm not following. I remember waking up with Liam over me. I mean…" A prickling feeling started at the back of his neck. "What did you do, Alanna? Out with it."

Seany listened to the entirety of her story, up until the part where he woke up. His face blanched. Holy God. He had seen her. It'd been real, not a dream. Then she'd fled. Twice, actually. Once when Josh was in the room and once when Liam was there. He'd woken up and she'd fled. Again. No phone call, no visit, no nothing since then.

His jaw was tight, a sudden anger gripping his gut. "Thank you for telling me. I'm not sure why the fuck the whole family decided to keep it a secret, but…." Then it dawned on him. "She didn't want me to know she'd been there, did she? Jesus, she is something else," he said with a sneer. "You guilted her into coming, then she swore you to silence. Well, you can tell her I'm not going to harass her. I don't know why she even came. It's not like she's reached out in the last how many years? It's not like she gives a shit. She got a free plane ticket. That's something. I hope she enjoyed the sights!"

Josh spoke over Alanna's protests, silencing her. "She does care, Seany. You are wrong. I saw her and so did Liam. She was completely wrecked. Liam said she sobbed over your bed. She said she was sorry and that she shouldn't have stayed away so long."

Seany shook his head, "This is bullshit! She feckin' bolted without even a hello or goodbye. I don't want to hear any more of this. She's gone, and she didn't want me to know. "

"She's not," Alanna said.

"She's not what?" he said, with a little more anger than he should be expressing with his sister-in-law.

She and Josh said it at the same time. "Gone." She repeated. "She's not gone."

"I'm sorry, Alanna, but I'm not following. Are you telling me she's been here for all this time?"

"No, she just got back last week. After the hospital, she went to an interview for a study abroad internship. She got the position…and she's back."

"Internship? Where? What kind of bloody internship?"

Alanna's smile was made of glass. "Um…as a therapeutic riding instructor in Connemara?" She trailed the sentence off like a question, keeping that smile in place.

"What!" Seany jumped up out of his seat. Josh did the same. Josh said, "Maddie and I met with her before the interview. It's a good job for her, but I really think she's here for more than that job. I mean, Texas has plenty of ranches. She didn't need to come to Ireland."

"You knew about this, too?" The betrayal in Seany's eyes just gutted Josh.

"Brother, I'm sorry. The family told me not to say anything. I hated it, but I was outnumbered big time. I'm so sorry."

"I can't talk to you two right now. Alanna, you weren't going to tell me at first, were you? You were just going to let me show up and…" He gritted his teeth. "I'm not doing it. Screw this whole thing." He tried to leave and Alanna jumped up out of her seat. She cried out as pain radiated through her lower back.

Seany forgot everything and cursed as he went to her. She was bent over the table and he started rubbing her lower back. "Easy, love. Jesus, you shouldn't have made this trip, Alanna."

"When did the contractions start?" Josh asked.

She said through clenched teeth, "It's not contractions. It's my back. It's too much car time over the last week."

"Alanna, it could be back labor. Charlie had it. It radiates through your back instead of your abdomen."

"I'm not in labor!" she said testily. "Rub lower, Seany. Along my left buttcheek. Ach!" Seany hesitated for a minute, wondering if Aidan was going to kill him for rubbing his wife's ass. "Do it!" Her southern belle accent was pronounced.

"I'm calling Aunt Sorcha," Josh said.

"I don't need you to call Sorcha. Everyone just calm down. I think it's passing." She exhaled and Seany let go of her left ass cheek like it was on fire. She put her head up, sweating but with a smile. "I'm okay, thank you Seany." She arched her back, stretching. Then a gush of water came out, soaking her leggings, shoes, and the floor underneath her.

* * *

SORCHA GOT IN THE CAR, heading for Galway within a minute. "Seany, I need you to get her to the hospital."

She heard Seany say, "Josh, go start her car. She's got a roomier backseat. Take the booster seat out."

They worked efficiently, guiding her into the backseat. Seany took the passenger seat and Josh drove. They had Sorcha on speaker. "Boys, move fast. Back labor can be tricky. She's possibly been in labor for hours and hasn't known what it was. And third babies can come fast." Just as she said it Alanna let out a howl. They were only one minute into the drive.

Alanna screamed, "Sorcha, something is wrong. I feel like I have to push already!"

Sorcha said, "Seany, I need you to get in the backseat, lay her flat, and take her trousers off."

Seany went into full EMT mode. He was worried, and Alanna's modesty was going to have to take a backseat, so to speak. He put her bag under her head. Then he nodded at her, helping her with her leggings and knickers. "Oh, Jaysus. Mom, I see a head," he said grimly. They were well and truly in it.

"Alright, darling. There is an ambulance just leaving University Hospital. You are all doing great. Josh, I'm going to ask you to pull over, okay? We don't need you getting into a car crash with those two unbuckled. The ambulance is fifteen minutes away. Alanna, my sweeting, how are you doing?"

Alanna was shaking, covered in sweat. "I'm trying to hold on, but I can feel the contractions now. Jesus, they came on hard and fast." She groaned, trying not to cry out.

"It's probably because the baby shifted after you had a lie down," Sorcha said calmly.

Seany took over. As he cleaned his hands with hand sanitizer, he wished to God he'd grabbed some rubber gloves. "Okay love, you're going to breathe little breaths, and try to calm your mind. The next contraction, you are going to push."

He heard the tears in his mother's voice. "Very good, Seany. You're doing great. You know just what to do. Remember your training."

He directed Josh to get into the backseat on the other side and let Alanna sit between his legs. He cradled her, wiping her hair away from her face. Josh said, "I've got you, sweetheart. No worries. You've done this twice before."

Seany had been taking her pulse. He held a hand on her abdomen, and he felt the tightening of her womb through her belly, starting another contraction. "Okay, Momma. Let's roll."

Alanna sat up and, without invitation, put her left foot on Seany's shoulder. He suppressed a laugh because the poor thing was in a lot of pain. She clenched her jaw, pushing with everything she had. She ground her molars, growling like a she-bear. Seany said, "Great, now let Josh hold you, darlin'. Rest a minute. I don't think this is going to take long. This baby is ready to meet you."

Suddenly she was crying. "Aidan's going to kill me! He told me this would happen! He should be here! He's going to kill me!"

Seany chuckled. "He'll do no such thing, girl. He'll certainly hit you with a few *I told you so's* but he's going to be so happy to see you and the baby safe. He'll forget all about it." He was trying to keep her mind occupied as her body geared up for another contraction. "Take a breath, Alanna. A big one. Hold it. Push!"

Alanna fell back against Josh, completely spent. Seany said, "Mam, the head is almost out!"

"Okay Alanna, make this a good one," Sorcha said encouragingly.

Alanna growled a scream, low in her throat as the head cleared the birth canal. Seany said calmly, "We have a nuchal cord, Mam." The cord was wrapped around the baby's neck, which wasn't uncommon and usually not life threatening.

"You know what to do, Seany. Gently use your finger to unwrap it. It's not tight, is it?" It wasn't, so she said to Alanna, "Then one more push from Mammy, my dear. We need to clear the shoulders and get this baby untangled."

Alanna needed no direction as the last contraction tackled her. She grabbed her knees and screamed as she pushed her baby boy into the world and into the hands of his Uncle Seany. The first quick action was to handle the nuchal cord. Seany gently slipped a finger between the baby's neck and the pulsing cord and it slipped off without resistance. "It's a boy!" He yelled the words, more excited than he'd ever been in his life. Keeghan O'Brien gave a howl as Seany cleared his mouth. He whispered Gaelic endearments to the squiggly little parcel, feeling the sting of hot tears as he stared at the living miracle he'd witnessed. Aidan's flesh and blood. His too, he supposed.

He pushed thoughts of McBride's little baby girl out of his mind, shutting it out before it derailed him completely. He wrapped his nephew in a clean receiving blanket from Alanna's hospital bag, the one Aidan had insisted she bring with her. His brother was too smart by half. "Mam, I'm going to leave the cord alone. I can hear the ambulance."

Sorcha said, "That's exactly right. She'll pass the placenta in a few minutes, most likely. Just keep them warm and comfortable. They'll take care of the cord in the ambulance. Good lads. All three of you, well done." Her voice was thick with emotion. "Aidan is on his way to the hospital. Your father has been relaying everything to him."

Alanna wept tears of joy as her mucky, bloody, screeching baby boy rubbed his mouth along her cheek. "Thank you, Seany. And Josh. Thank you so much. I'm such an idiot!"

Seany said, "You are an idiot, but we'll talk about that later. I'm inclined to cut you a small break in light of the situation."

She laughed and then groaned as her belly gave a howl. She was bleeding, but he didn't think it was an abnormal amount. He couldn't believe he'd just delivered Aidan's baby. Looking down, Alanna said, "I'm really going to need this car detailed after this."

Then it was the boys' turn to laugh as the EMTs stared at them through the car windows.

* * *

SEANY STOOD as Aidan came in the room. Finally. He was exhausted, both mentally and physically. After the drama had simmered down, and he'd seen Alanna safely to the hospital, he was left with his thoughts. Josh had taken Alanna's car home to try cleaning it up. Luckily she had seat protectors in the back, from dealing with two small children. Aidan's eyes never left his wife's. She was nodding off, trying to nurse their son. When he came up next to her, she jolted awake. Then she burst into tears. He took the baby, cradling it as he kissed her on the head.

"Darlin', if I got mad at you every time you didn't listen to me, we'd be fighting every day. Everything turned out just grand. And look what you did...what you both did." His eyes misted with tears as he looked at Seany, but Alanna was not going to be placated.

She wailed, "And he could have DIED! The cord was around his neck! And Seany saved him!" Aidan's eyes shot to Seany's and he shook his head, reassuring him that this was not as dramatic as it probably seemed to Alanna. She continued, not noticing. "Because I'm stupid! And, and, and..." She hiccupped the words as she screeched, "And Seany saw my vaginaaaaa!"

Seany turned beat red and Aidan choked on a laugh. Seany said, "I didn't. I was looking at the baby's head. That's all I saw."

She flung her hands up in the air, "Yeah! The baby's head that was coming out of my vagina! How am I supposed to look at you over the Thanksgiving turkey now?"

"Luckily we don't have Thanksgiving, so it's no bother," Aidan shrugged.

She pointed at him. "Stop laughing at me! You, you, pigheaded know-it-all," she went on and on with her insults and Seany looked at

Aidan, almost scared. Aidan smiled at him and mouthed, *hormones.* "I saw that Aidan O'Brien!" she yelled.

He laughed again. "She gets like this every time. It's only the first day. Their hormones take a huge turn after the birth. Mam says it's normal. Although, it's not usually this bad. It's probably because you saw her vagina."

Her crying reached a slow crescendo at that reminder, wailing with tears pouring down her face. That was until little Keegan started crying like it was a competition. She snapped right out of it. "Give him to me!" Then she started crooning like the sweetest little mommy who ever drew breath. "Yes, that's Mommy's big boy. You wanted to see me so badly, you messed up Daddy's backseat."

Aidan said dryly, "I had her take my car. It has new tires and a recent brake job. Now I'm regretting it."

"It's not so bad. Ye had those protectors over the seats," Seany said. "Josh is hosing it down as we speak."

"I'm starting to think those things were the best Father's Day present I've ever received," Aidan said. He looked down at his son, nursing like a little champ. "Three kids. Two sons and a daughter. Seven years ago, I'd have never thought this was possible. Yet here I am, with a new babe and a beautiful wife. I guess I was a late bloomer." He gave Seany a crooked grin. "Why don't we let them have their tea, and I'll see if someone can drive you home. We'll worry about the other car later."

They left the room and walked next to each other in silence for a few moments. "Do you know why Alanna came?" Seany asked.

"Aye, I do. I hope you weren't too hard on her. We kind of forced the gag order on the women. And Josh. He wanted to tell you. We wanted to see what she was going to do before we opened that can of worms."

"That wasn't your call to make," Seany said sharply.

"You're right. It was Maureen's. She came all the way here. She dropped everything and was on a plane within twelve hours of Alanna making that call. So, she had a right to do things her way. She said she didn't want to take the focus away from you and your family. That she didn't want to intrude. This wasn't easy on any of us. Especially you, Seany. You could have died, and then where would we be? She brought you back to us. You responded to her voice, Seany. When nothing else worked. When no one else worked. Remember that. You're going to need that information someday."

"I should have been told."

"You've had enough to deal with. And Alanna knew it was time. Especially given that you are headed up to Connemara next week."

Seany shook his head. "The hell I am. No feckin' way."

Seany tried to dismiss the idea, but then he saw Aidan reach into his wallet. "We've been meaning to give this to you. It just never seemed like the right time with all the family swarming around you. I wasn't sure you'd want to answer their questions." He recognized what Aidan held out to him. "The paramedics found it. It fell out of your coat in the ambulance. They wanted to make sure you got it back. They figured she must be something special if you carried it. Were they right?"

Seany took the photo from Aidan, bent to fit in his small breast pocket. He'd thought he lost it in the fire. Aidan said simply, "You'll go. Some things you can't run from, Seany. I know that better than anyone."

CHAPTER 14

Letterfrack, Co. Galway

Moe was freshly showered and in bed after a full day of work. Her shoulders ached from the rein work with Balor. Her rump was sore from her Dressage work with Skadi, and she was glad the other intern would be taking over her training. She was a stunner, her moves so beautiful as her silky, well-kept mane and tail blew in tendrils around her body. She'd be a stunning addition to the open house demonstrations.

She really loved this place. The landscape was so different from Texas. Of course, she'd traveled with her family, and even lived overseas. But in the wake of her father's injury, they seemed to have been cocooned from the military community and the rest of the world. Horses had been her refuge. It was odd, really. Music had been an escape for her as a youth. Still was, to a degree, and reading, come to think. But horses were different. In a way that a mother can take solace in the raising and loving of children, horses gave that to her. Their warm, strong bodies. Their gentle, soulful eyes. Their smell and the way they moved. It was so beautiful to her. And they were smart and teachable creatures.

This journey…the Connemara journey, was not just about these beautiful creatures. It was about the landscape… the sea and the loughs, the plant life diverse and nourishing for the ponies, the rocks and moss and breathtaking forests. She knew that she was living a rare opportunity, being here to learn. She'd gone to one of the most well-respected Agricultural colleges in the world. But Ireland was going to teach her something unique and wonderful; something that couldn't be transplanted. These horses were the way they were because of where they lived. Hearty and not prone to illness. Strong and gentle. Even-tempered with small children. It could never be recreated in a genetics lab. These horses were some of the old Celts. And like its' people, still a bit wild. Needing their own land to flourish.

The people on this ranch were much the same. She couldn't imagine them living outside of Ireland. They were educated and friendly. But they were the best part of their native culture, and likely wouldn't flourish in another land. Like the O'Briens.

Every time she heard the melodious speech patterns and rolling *r*'s, she thought of him. Seany. As beautiful as she remembered, but with a man's honed features. She closed her eyes, remembering those sunny days and balmy evenings together. They'd been strictly supervised, as was the agreement with Alanna and her parents. But Alanna and Aidan had trusted them enough to allow them some privacy. They'd had their own rules. There were nights, from the comfort of Seany's arms, that she'd been ready to throw those rules out the window. But he'd cupped her face. *We can't take this too far, because I have to leave you. It wouldn't be fair to me or you. If it's meant to be, Moe, then we'll come together again. We just have to see if this thing between us can withstand the separation. If it can't…* He'd shrugged. *Don't think I don't want you, a chéadsearc.*

She hadn't known what it meant. Neither had Alanna. Maybe she'd ask Moira or Penny tomorrow. They both spoke the Irish. She hadn't asked him…feeling that if he'd wanted to, he would have said it in English. She didn't want to embarrass him or break the spell that his words had cast over her.

How many times had she replayed that first kiss…and the last.

He'd been the most wonderful kisser. Even at the young age of fifteen, he'd been masterful with his lips. At least, she'd thought so. He'd been her first kiss, and to this day she'd never met his equal. The last kisses had been tender, desperate, and heartbreaking. Even with their promises to keep in touch, they were both old enough to understand that the last night together that summer could well be their last night forever. She'd taken his hand from her waist as they laid intertwined. Smoothed it along her hip. That had been more than he could resist. He'd rolled on top of her, cupping her bottom as he rolled his hips. She'd been close enough to feel his arousal through his clothes before, but it was different horizontally. So much different with him cradled between her thighs as he'd rocked against her. She had panted against his mouth, had been starved for what was happening. But he'd been the one to stop it, thank God. If she'd been with him, she'd have never recovered from the loss.

A wave of longing, bone deep, moved through her soul. She couldn't understand it. She'd been fifteen, almost sixteen when they'd met. It had been a brief summer romance. But Seany O'Brien was the sort of person that stuck with you. He'd held nothing back. He was kind and brave and every young girl's fantasy. Every grown woman's, too. She felt foolish as tears leaked down her temples and into her hair. She'd thought that once she got to Ireland, she'd be able to go and face him. But she was afraid, as much as it chaffed to admit it. Because when she thought about that broad chested, beautiful man she'd seen in the hospital, she knew that she was still, as always, out of her league with Seany O'Brien.

Furbogh, Co. Galway

He couldn't sleep. It wasn't the shoulder pain. It wasn't the unbelievably bizarre experience of helping Alanna give birth. It was her. Maureen Rogers. His chéadsearc. His first love. The Maureen Rogers who had ghosted him a year after his return to Ireland. The girl who had taught him about yearning. Not just of the body, but of the heart.

Then she'd broken his heart without a second thought. At least she'd done it face to face. Or as much as she could, given the geography. Break-up by video call was a kick in the nuts, because he'd had to see her face…and her tears. But she'd done what she said she would. She'd closed all of her social media accounts. She'd changed her cell phone number. Like he was some sort of stray dog that would just keep coming around if she didn't burn her house down and leave the neighborhood. It still angered him. He'd cared for her. Deeply. And she'd treated him like some sort of needy stalker who had to be cut off completely.

He couldn't believe she'd come. And to add insult to injury, she'd made his family agree not to tell him. Humiliating, to say the least. And they didn't see it that way, which was maddening. They thought he'd woken up because of her. *Yay, Moe. Hero of the day.* He'd been so out of it and medicated that he'd thought seeing her face had been a dream. It wouldn't have been the first time. He'd dreamt of her off and on for years. Woken up sweating, and panting, his balls aching.

He'd been with a few women since those young, innocent days of his youth. He hadn't loved any of them anymore than they'd loved him. It had been recreational. Sowing his oats, as Patrick had called it. But none of those more experienced, eager lovers had ever come close to the experience of holding Maureen Rogers against him. She'd been so innocent. Never even been kissed. But she'd come alive in his arms, moving and exploring that newfound passion. Kissing him like he was keeping her alive.

His body stirred as he remembered the one and only time they'd broken their stand-up rule. It was a rule that told him just how innocent they'd been. The rule was that they'd never kiss unless they were standing up, so they wouldn't take things too far. He smiled at the thought of that. Neither of them understanding that you could make love standing up, with a little practice. The thought of Moe pressed against the wall, legs apart, while he took her from behind assaulted his brain. No. He was not going to get all juiced up over some girl he'd known in secondary school. It was beneath him…really. He looked down below his waist, trying to come up with another explanation for why his cock looked like a cricket bat underneath his sheets.

That last night together had fed his teenage fantasies long after Moe had dumped him. Pulling her hips up to meet him as he ground his body to hers. Fully clothed, but torturous and so arousing. He ran a hand up her rib cage and teased the bottom of her breast with his thumb. Grazed it over her nipple, which was stiff under her shirt. Her hips had jerked under him and he'd been ready to just put them both out of their misery. He'd pulled her shirt aside, kissing the mound of her breast. She'd curled her fingers in his hair which had emboldened him. When he'd exposed her delicate, pink nipple, he'd sworn to just have a taste. He circled his tongue around it, and she'd moaned like nothing he'd ever heard before. He'd rocked his hips against her heat, going on pure instinct. That friction through her jeans and the draws he took on her nipple had caused her to arch her back and cry out. He'd given himself an orgasm by fifteen, so he'd known what was happening to her. She had not, however. Maybe in theory. But as she came down from that explosion, she'd shook in his arms. His cock had been at full salute, but he hadn't dared to take it any further. The fact that he'd finally known the joy of giving a female pleasure was enough to keep him reeling for a lifetime. She'd trusted him enough to let go, and to this day, he treasured that sexual experience above all others. Funny, given the fact that they'd kept their clothes on. With an edgy lust dogging him under the sheets, his trip down memory lane swung to anger, as it always did. Would he ever be free of her?

* * *

Letterfrack, Co. Galway

Moe really hated this guy. The distant relative of Moira's was here. He was the son of her second cousin, whatever that made him. His name was Hugo, and he was a real piece of work. He was currently demanding to know the cost of all of the repairs and improvements Moira had made to the property. He wasn't asking Moira, of course. He wouldn't dare. He'd cornered her in the tack room and was trying to give her the third degree. He was also unabashedly giving her the once over.

"She can't possibly afford all of these improvements. She's going to be retiring." He was such a prick.

Moe said calmly, "That's news to me, sir. The retiring, that is. She hasn't mentioned it. As for her finances, that is none of my business and I would never ask. She's a grown woman. A very intelligent, business savvy woman. Which begs the question, if you need to pry into her finances, why don't you ask her?"

He leaned in, "Watch your mouth, girl. I can have you back on a plane to America tonight. I'm taking a bigger role here, and you don't want to get on my bad side. She's too old to be chasing these ponies around anymore. Now, let me ask again..."

"Not too old to turn you over my knee, Hugo." He froze as he turned to face his *Auntie Moira,* as he called her.

"Oh, Auntie. No offense, love. I'm just worried about you. And I don't appreciate getting cheek from the help." Moe stiffened at that. Moira gave her an apologetic look, holding up a hand to stop her retort.

"That's so kind of you. However, I won't have you harassing my intern or anyone else on my staff. And Ms. Rogers was spot on. It's no one's business how much money I spend or retain. As for taking a bigger role in the stable business..." She smiled so beatifically that Moe was almost afraid he'd spoken the truth. "There is about a snowball's chance in hell that you'll be taking any sort of role in this enterprise, unless you fill out a volunteer application. And given your complete ignorance and inexperience with horses, I doubt even that would happen."

He stuttered over his defense. "Save it, Hugo." She sighed. "Listen, you are family. I loved your mother like a wee sister. If you want to come for Sunday roast, you are more than welcome. But this is my home. These are my stables, my horses, and my affairs. You need to stick to your own business deals and not worry your head about mine."

She looked to Moe. "Maureen, can I see you for a moment?" Then she gave Hugo a dismissive look and he huffed off toward the house.

She mumbled under her breath. "Jaysus, he is such a tosser. He's just like his da." Moe stifled a laugh. "The best thing my cousin ever did was divorce that bastard. He was always running some sort of get-rich-quick scheme or hitting the track and casinos. He burned through her entire inheritance before she'd caught on. I had hoped, due to her influence, that Hugo had come out all right. I guess not."

"I'm sorry. You should be able to depend on family. Do you have any nieces or nephews? You said you didn't have kids or grandkids."

Moira smiled sadly, "No, I married young. Our one child died at eighteen in an automobile collision. It was a drunk driver." Moe covered her mouth. Moira smiled at her, putting a hand on her shoulder. "I still think about her every day. But it happened twenty-five years ago, and I've learned to live with it. The loss killed what was left of my marriage. He wasn't what you'd call a faithful sort. So, once Abigail was gone, I decided I could let go of the lie. Which brings me back to Hugo. He is under the delusion that I'm leaving all I have to him because we share blood. I have a couple more extended cousin types. The others don't even know I'm still alive, I'd wager. And that's okay, as the relation is distant. There is an honesty to the lack of contact. Hugo, on the other hand, is sniffing around hoping I'm going to die so he can cash in on my ponies. They're valuable and so is my land."

Moe had stayed quiet up until now. "So, is that why you've started the non-profit? So that it all stays intact?"

"No. I started the non-profit because it's needed. The rest will sort itself out in time. I'm just wondering when the tosser," she pointed a thumb in Hugo's direction, "is going to get it through his fat head that I'm not going to be his meal ticket. Do you know the eejit actually asked to move in with me? So he could look after me, or so he said. Ha! I'd like to see him try." She shook herself. "But that's enough of that. I'm sorry he was trying to bully you. Feel free to kick him in the ass with those pointy boots if he tries again."

"I'll remember that you gave me your permission. Now, I just finished organizing the tack room. Care to take a look?" She waved her all the way into the room, and Moira gasped.

"Well, well. You have worked a miracle, dear Maureen. Now, you better lay down the law with Rory and Devlin. They are good lads but they aren't one for putting things back in the same place twice. Especially Rory."

"I heard that!" Rory said as he walked into the barn. He kissed Moira on the cheek, then whistled at the sight of the clean tack room. "It looks grand, Maureen. Truly. Now, who's going to help me work with the beast?"

"Time for Balor's mani-pedi," Moira said dryly. "Maureen, would you like to assist?"

Behind them came Devlin's rough voice. "She can't. I need her. Actually, I need them both. I've got some fence down in the eastern pasture, where it borders the park land."

"That fencing was just replaced!" Moira shouted.

"Aye, I know. It looks like someone may have hit it with their car or something. It's along that park access road. No one goes back there other than the rangers. I called, and they don't know anything about it. I have to move the stallions to the small pasture by the lake before they find the hole."

Moira sighed, rubbing her head. "Okay, I'll ride Skadi out and grab Primrose. She's in season. I don't want the boys having a go at her. She needs to wait another year before I decide whether to breed her."

"Aye, we'll drive the Land Cruiser over and block the downed fence until we move the others. She's the only one we need to worry about?"

"Yes, and take pictures of that fence. I want the rangers to keep an eye on that road and see if there is anyone with damage to their car coming in and out."

* * *

MAUREEN GOT out of the vehicle, taking a good look at the damage. "Something isn't right."

Devlin said, "What do you mean?"

"It seems…staged?" She showed him. "The damaged pieces are inside the fence line, but look. These logs all have the rounded part facing the road. Now, look at how these pieces are splintered. If you forget about where you found them and think about how they were broken…" She put the wooden pieces back together. "And look at the posts. They've been pushed inward a little, but look at the mud where they were leaned significantly outward and shifted the top of the opening."

Devlin whistled. "I'll be damned. They were pulled, not crashed into. Someone used something to pull the fence down. Then they threw the debris inside the fence line."

"Or someone else coming down the road just cleared it and threw it over here so they could get by," Rory said, shrugging.

Moe nodded, "Yes, you're right. I didn't think about that. Either way, you can see that it was pulled that way until it broke. Probably with chains or something. I think Moira needs to file a police report. I can't say for sure, but this looks deliberate."

CHAPTER 15

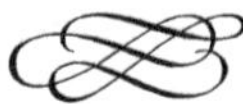

***"Riding a horse is not a gentle hobby, to be picked up and laid down like a game of solitaire. It is a grand passion."* —Ralph Waldo Emerson**

Seany got out of the car, walking up the drive to his old partner's house. He'd come straight after physical therapy, and the dull pain in his shoulder was making him sweat, even with the cold temperatures. He'd gotten what he asked for in that she'd intensified the strength training. At the time, it had been good to feel the pain. It felt like progress. Now it just hummed in the aftermath, making him rethink his earlier cockiness. He was greeted at the door by McBride's oldest son. Only nine years old, he was all elbows and knees. His face lit up at the sight of Seany, which was like a kick in the nuts. He had Kamala's coloring, but for the eyes. The eyes were McBride's through and through.

"Junior!" He leaped forward and let Seany catch him up in an embrace. He felt the burn in the left shoulder but ignored it. Then there were two smaller boys, each hugging a leg and sitting their bums on each of his feet.

Kamala said from behind him, "Boys, please. Junior is still recovering." But Seany put the skinny nine-year-old under his good arm like he was carrying a pigskin. He roared as he stepped one foot in front of the other. The giggling boys hung on to his legs for dear life.

"Fee Fi Fo Fum....I smell the blood of three monkeys!" They squealed as he fell onto the couch, taking them all with him.

Kamala shook her head. "What would your therapist say?"

He gave her a look, and she returned it with a look of understanding. The three boys didn't have their da to wrestle with anymore. Let him do this small thing for them.

After the three lads had settled in front of their video game, Seany sat with Kamala and had a cup of tea. She made it with those aromatic spices and honey powder. "Lots of milk, just how you like it."

Seany smiled at that, feeling a pang of tenderness so deep for this woman, he almost teared up. "It's perfect. Thank you, Kamala." He looked around. "Where's the baby?"

She reached over to her laptop and wiggled her finger on the touchpad to wake it up. A wireless baby monitor showing him that little Nellie was asleep in her crib. Nellie...named after her father Nelson. Then he did tear up. "Junior," her tone was so comforting as she put a hand over his.

He shook himself. "I should be comforting you, not the other way around."

"I have others who do that for me. My parents and his parents. My brother and sister and even my children, in their own way. Who do you let comfort you, Junior?"

She never used his given name. It was always his station call sign. Junior. Not just from the suffix his name carried, but because he'd been the youngest one ever to be hired on full-time. "I have family," he evaded.

"But do you let them in? I spoke to your cousin, Tadgh. He knew Nelson pretty well, and he called to check on the family. When I asked him about you, he said that no one really knew how you were doing. That you didn't talk about anything other than your physical injuries."

"There is nothing to talk about. I failed. Now little Nellie's father is dead, and I can't take it back. So I must live with it." He took a long pull on his tea and asked, talking over her. "How are the boys?

Did they catch up from the school they missed? Do they need anything?"

"They are caught up," she answered, knowing that he didn't want to be pushed. "They are smart like their mother." Seany barked out a laugh, and the tension of the moment eased.

"It's been two months. Have they sorted out the survivor benefits? Do you need money, Kamala?"

She sighed, "Junior, you barely make a living wage. Are you actually offering to support me and these children?"

He looked at her dead seriously, "Yes. Forever, if I could. I'm serious, Kamala."

She squeezed his hand. "I know you are, Junior. But I'm a little old for you. I mean, that was a proposal, right? I don't even think my wedding garment would fit me, but I can try…"

The corner of his mouth twitched. He narrowed his eyes at her. "Yer makin' fun of me now. Yer a heartless, little harpy. But aye, try it on. I'll call the priest. Don't think I won't do it, just to get the better of you."

Kamala cocked her head. "Well, now. My mommy-and-me group would be jealous. Hot twenty-two year old. This idea is growing on me. Do you change diapers?" Then she smacked him. "You're an idiot, Junior. Yes, I have sorted out his benefits. And I'm going to go back to work. I don't need a pity marriage, thank you." She knew that the marriage thing had been a joke, but it was easier than her saying outright that she wouldn't take his charity.

"Nellie is so small, still," he said absently.

"My sister will watch the kids. I need to work, Junior. I need the distraction. And believe it or not, I loved my career."

She'd worked off and on between the birth of her children, but this time it would be for good. "I'm sure being a chemist sounds like a horrid bore to a neanderthal like you, but I like my microscope."

"Different strokes, I suppose," he said.

"Are you seeing anyone, Seany? Nelson didn't think so, but men can be rather clueless."

"No, there is no one." He thought of Maureen Rogers and almost said something, but she beat him to the punch.

"So, tell me about Moe."

He groaned, "Who told you about that? Was it Tadgh? No, probably my sister. Nosy peahen."

She wasn't about to reveal her source. "Spill it, Junior. Give me something juicy to distract myself."

He sighed, meeting her eyes. Then he looked at the door and wondered if he made a run for it, could he make it to the car in time. She'd been on the girls' football team in school so probably not. She seemed to read his thoughts, raising a brow and giving him a look that said...*Don't make me beat it out of you.* So, he started. "It was a long time ago, when I was fifteen."

KAMALA LISTENED and asked questions for about twenty minutes. When it appeared he was done, she slapped the table. "The little coward. How dare she come in and save the day, then tuck her tail and run again. She's not a girl anymore. There is no parent telling her what to do. And she's here! She's an hour or so away from you. And she hasn't reached out? She should be lucky to be in your life again."

"I don't think she knows that I'm her new client on Monday. Apparently, I'm supposed to just fill out the paperwork when I get there."

Kamala looked at her watch. "Well, I wouldn't trust your family not to warn her, despite you threatening them to stay silent. You can't wait, Junior." She looked at her smart watch. "You need to go spring all of this..." she waved her hands in the air, motioning to all of him, "on her before she has a chance to prepare. Good for the goose, good for the gander, and all that. The tight t-shirt is perfect. She'll rue the day she ever jilted you. It's not a long drive. You go hit her from behind, Junior. Why should you be on the defensive?"

Kamala knew exactly how to get to him. If she'd made excuses for Moe or become all swoony, he'd likely go through with canceling the horse therapy. She smiled on the inside, none of her scheming showing on her face. She was going to turn his male pride against him. She may have lost her happily ever after, but Nelson would have liked the idea of Junior finding his.

* * *

Moe rode Cassanova into the ring next to the stable. While they'd moved the other stallions to a different pasture, she'd noticed Cassanova walking with an uneven gait. Moira came out to greet her, reaching for the reins. That's when she saw that Balor was out of his stall. "He threw a shoe. Maybe Rory can work on them both today." Cassanova's ears went back as he saw Balor. "Easy boy. He's just here for the snacks."

But Balor wasn't known for playing well with others. He shook his head, snorting at the other horse. "Knock it off, Balor. This ring is plenty big enough for both of you."

That's when Moe noticed the vehicle in the drive. An unfamiliar one. Cass started stepping sideways, irritated.

Seany heard her voice and had to fight the impulse to run for his car. It made him angry, this response he had to her. He had every right to be here. To check out this therapy center before he agreed to the deal. The owner of the ranch was a lovely woman. Closer to his granny's age, but athletic and sharp. He came around the corner, just as a big horse took a nip at another one. The one Maureen was riding. The sight of her knocked the breath out of him. It was a small noise he made, the exhale, but enough to set the aggressive horse's temper off. He reared up, screeching. That's when the other horse lost its shit. Seany watched in horror as the smaller, sleeker horse tried to buck Moe out of the saddle. He was in the ring before he thought better of it. The petite, older woman threw an arm up.

"Back up, lad. Let her handle him!"

Moe saw someone out of the corner of her eye, and that's all she could take in. Cassanova, the little shit, was trying to land her on her ass. "Moira, don't try to get him. He's too upset." She meant Balor, of course. "Open the gate!"

Moira did, and Moe muscled Cass into submission with a few cutting words and some rein work. "Whoa! Down, boy. Knock it off." She took him out the gate and let him ride it off for a minute. Then she steered him into the stable where she tied him off. Rory came in just as she was leaving. "He needs some tending to before you work on the shoe. Balor just tried to take a hunk out of him." Then she grabbed a length of rope and left the barn, breezing past Devlin. She didn't look at Moira or the other person. Her eyes were on Balor. He was dancing around the ring, pitching a fit. She stood right in the middle, turning with him as he circled. With each pass, she got closer to the fence, never taking her eyes off him. When he stopped and reared up, she folded her arms around her chest, not saying a word. He was losing some bravado under her intense gaze. She never spoke. She didn't scold him or try to grab him. When she took another step, he snorted at her. Then she finally took his reins. She tied him off with a rope and he was pissed. She circled as the horse ran the circumference of the ring, screeching at her like an angry toddler. She just stayed steady. She had enough rope to where he couldn't pull her over. He only had so much arena. Round and round he circled.

Seany watched in amazement as Moe wore the fiend down. Much like he remembered, she was quiet, patient, and smart. Damn her. She was going to get her neck broken. The woman next to him said, "This is our intern, Maureen. She's an American. A real cowgirl sort. She's got great instincts. She'll likely be the one working with you and the horse she chooses for you."

Seany looked out at the pair, saying nothing. He looked at the magnificent horse she was trying to bend to her will. He was big. Really big.

"She refuses to give up on Balor. He's kind of a shit, to be honest. She's trying to channel that energy and athleticism into something positive. Barrel racing, for God's sake. Apparently it's some sort of American rodeo sport."

Seany suppressed a smile. He was not going to find this at all charming or admirable. "She's going to get her fool head kicked in more likely."

Moira raised her brows at him. "Quite the optimist, aren't ye?" she said. That's when he looked back up and saw Balor finally submit, if only a little. He stopped, slumped his shoulders, and let out a huge sigh. All she said was, "Yeah, you're tired, huh? Ready to go in?"

He came toward her, ears up, slow and steady. She put a hand out, and he put his muzzle into her waiting palm. "This would be easier if you just cooperated, buddy." She took the rope off, took his reins and led him into the barn.

* * *

MOE WAS EXHAUSTED. Thirsty, too. She'd cleaned the tack room for three hours, then contended with that dickhead cousin Hugo, then had to move horses to another pasture, then mended the fence with Devlin and Rory. Just when she thought she was going to drop off that stallion to get a new shoe, and actually get a bite to eat, Balor had decided to play the fool. She was grimy, sweaty, and tired. And she was just a little dizzy from going in circles waiting for Balor to get tired. She looked up to see Moira walk in. She'd been bent over Cassanova's hoof, checking his other front shoe.

Moira said, "Nice work out there. If you aren't too knackered, I've got someone I'd like you to meet." She looked into the doorway of the barn, just as he appeared. She shot up straight and way too fast. Little sparkling diamonds started floating in front of her. Moira shouted, and the last thing Moe remembered was the sight of hay and dirt rushing toward her.

For the second time in thirty minutes, Seany's heart dropped into his shoes. He ran toward her but it was too late. The man tending to the horses was out of reach when Moe took a nosedive. Both horses started stirring. Luckily the big one wasn't near her. Moira was bent over her, but he scooted between Moe and the horse's hooves, scooping her up off the ground.

"Bring her in the house!" Moira yelled.

She was already coming around. She started batting at her face. "It's okay, lass. Calm down until I can put you down."

She wasn't much taller than she'd been. Maybe an inch. But she was curvier. She'd filled out. And he was going to stop thinking about that right now. He went in through the back door of the house, finding the first flat surface he could put her on that wasn't a countertop or table. Moe didn't stay put. Of course she didn't. She shot up and tried to stand. "Moira, some cold water would be grand," he said as he pushed her soundly down on her ass. "Sit, Maureen. For chrissakes, are you trying to hurt yourself?" He looked at Moira. "When is the last time she ate or had something to drink?" Her eyes were unfocused, so he knew it had been awhile. He gave her the water. "Slowly, girl. That's it." She drank deeply. He looked at Moira.

"She had breakfast, drank some juice and tea. She had some water out in the barn this morning, but that was..." She looked at her watch. Eight hours or more. Then she looked at Devlin. "I don't suppose you had snacks and water in the Cruiser?"

He looked sheepish. "No, sorry. I'm guessing breakfast was the last time she ate."

Seany looked at her smart watch. It had a pulse and heart monitor built in. He handed Moira the glass. "That's enough for now. Lie back, Moe. I want to get a heart rate."

She reclined again. He could tell exactly when she became fully aware. Her eyes flared and she tried to sit up. "Lie down before you fall on your ass again." He pushed her down. She bristled. "Or I swear to God I will sit on you." He leaned in as he said it. He felt her submission and had to keep the smile off his face. "Heart rate is a little fast. That might be from the shock, though."

"Why would she be shocked?" Devlin said.

But Moira's eyes were narrowed. "Ye called her Moe." Moira's simple words stopped everyone dead in their tracks. "So you're him. The one she came for in November."

He didn't answer her. Instead, he gave Moe a clinical once over. "Does your head hurt? You landed on your knee first, so the head collision wasn't so bad." He turned to Moira. "If she has trouble walking, you need to get her to Galway for some x-rays." He took the hand that was scraped up. "Does this hurt anywhere?" he asked as he probed along the bones of her hand and wrist. She just shook her head, her cheeks flaming red. He lifted her chin and turned to look at the rosy abrasion on her cheekbone. More probing. She shook him off. He was so cold, it had her close to tears. He was checking her because that's what he did. His touch wasn't warm or welcoming. She was so humiliated. Especially when he said, "The good thing about falling from a dead faint is that you don't tense up or try breaking the fall. That's when a lot of the broken bones and sprains happen."

"I didn't faint." She said pissily. "I just stood up too fast and I didn't eat enough. We had an emergency and I just went without thinking. I'm fine. Why are you here?"

He stood up, not answering. "Give her something with protein and a little sugar. Maybe a peanut butter and jam sandwich or something. She didn't hit her head too hard but watch her for signs of a concussion. And clean out the abrasions." He went for the door. "I'll be outside. Take your time." He met her eyes when he said it. He wouldn't leave until she spoke with him.

As Seany walked out into the cool winter air, he turned to see Moe sitting on the sofa, head in hands. This was not going at all like he'd envisioned.

* * *

Moe wolfed down a Nutella sandwich and a glass of milk in record time. Before Moira could question her further, she went outside and started walking toward her cottage. She couldn't do this right now. Why had he come? She knew the family wouldn't stay silent for long, but to just let him ambush her? She heard him coming from behind her and she kept up the brisk pace. He didn't catch up to her. By the sounds of his steps, he was pacing her own. It infuriated her. She hated this. Hated the coldness in his eyes. Those beautiful, dusty blue eyes. She reached her cabin, sweating despite the cool temperature. She didn't turn, didn't invite him in, didn't acknowledge him. She went straight through the main part of the one-room cabin and into the bathroom.

Slamming the door, she looked in the mirror. Her gut twisted as she took in her appearance. Not a stitch of make-up, dirt crusting her chin and cheek, all the way into her hairline. There was hay in her hair, for God's sake. She turned on the cold water, soaping up her hands. She cleaned under her fingernails and got her hands nice and clean before tending to the rest. She took a washcloth and used cold soapy water to clean her abrasions. Then she unbraided her hair, brushing out the dirt and hay as best she could. Hot tears came down her face, battling the water for dominance. She splashed the water on her face and neck, getting her t-shirt wet around the neckline. The shock of the cold down the front of her shirt was enough to snap her out of the pity roll she'd started. She took in her attire from head to toe. Her worn boots, dirty jeans, a t-shirt and a barn coat…at least her face and hands were clean. She washed the remnants of her sandwich out of her mouth and turned to leave the shelter of the bathroom. No doubt he was getting sick of waiting outside. She took a deep breath. She had no right to be prickly with him. It wasn't his fault she fainted. Nothing was his fault. And he was upright and whole. The fact that he looked like six-foot-three walking sin was not his fault either. Damn it. He'd always been out of her league in the looks department.

Seany sat calmly as he heard Moe try to wash off the dirt and the surprise of seeing him. No doubt she was in there giving herself a pep talk. The door opened, and she froze at the sight of him. She straightened, narrowing her eyes. "By all means, come in and make yourself at home."

He didn't smile or bristle. He just looked her up and down. He said coolly, "Well, you came into my temporary quarters without an invite, so I decided to return the favor."

She stood there, silent, watching as he stood. She did her own once-over before she could stop herself. Then her calm face met his eyes. It made him mental, that inner calm she could turn on at will. Like he was an unruly horse. "Nothing to say? Are you just going to turn in circles until I tire myself out?"

"That depends."

"On what, for fuck's sake?"

"On how ornery you're going to be. And I was invited…into your room, I mean. Your brother invited me."

"Aye, and now they've all got it in their heads that you somehow woke me like Sleeping Beauty. Is that what you think? That I was waiting for Princess Charming to come in and break some sort of bloody spell? I had a head injury. It took me a minute. This wasn't about you."

"I agree," she said smoothly. "I can't control what the rest of them think. I'm glad you're okay. How is your partner?"

"He's dead."

She jerked like she'd been slapped. "Oh, God. I'm sorry, Seany. I'm so sorry."

"I would have thought you knew. I mean, you and Alanna have cooked up this therapy scheme. She didn't tell you about McBride?"

Moe cocked her head. "What are you talking about? I haven't talked to Alanna since I left Dublin at the end of November."

Seany could hardly believe it. Alanna had told him as much, but he felt certain that she'd been covering up, or at the very least, had called Moe once she'd told him. "Well, then. Let me get you all caught up. I'm your Monday/Wednesday rider."

Moe's face blanched. That's when he knew for certain that she hadn't taken part in orchestrating any of this. Of course she hadn't. She ran from him every chance she got. "So, don't worry yourself. I'll drop out of the program. I see the department shrink tomorrow. This was a bad idea."

She exhaled, met his cool stare, and said, "Are you done?"

He'd been halfway through a turn toward the door. That calm tone was just a bit more than he could take. "Not even close!" he shot back. "Since when did you become so feckin' reckless? You could have broken your bloody neck on that horse! I thought you were going to study music production! Sit in front of a goddamn computer or take up the tambourine or some shit. And of all the places to do your internship, why here, Maureen?"

His change of subject almost gave her whiplash. She wouldn't let him rattle her, though. She ignored the gibe about the tambourine. "I was managing fine until you jumped into the arena like a greenhorn and spooked both horses. I can see I would have had my work cut out for me. You should definitely stick to the shrink's couch instead of equine therapy. And the reason I picked this place is none of your business, seeing as you aren't staying. If you don't want to be here, Seany, then I don't owe you an explanation."

Her comment bit at his pride. "Greenhorn? Is that some sort of Yank slang I'm unfamiliar with, or is it redneck dialect?"

"Greenhorn, in this context, refers to an arrogant jackass who doesn't know squat about handling a horse. You can see your way out." And given she had nowhere to go, she left out the front door. Walking down the short path to the shore of the lough, she waited for him to leave. Waited for the telltale crunch of hiking boots on the road leading to the main house. She stared out at the lough, wishing to God this hadn't all gone down this way. His voice made her jump.

"You've gotten really good at walking away from me without a backward glance. I heard how you fled from the hospital rather than see me awake. Tell me, Maureen. What has happened in your life to make you such a coward?"

The word stung. Her father had used the same word. "I'm not a coward. I just..." she swallowed. Her face registered regret, and that was something. "I felt like an intruder. Your family was so worried. They'd gone days without sleep. You were never alone. They waited and prayed. So, I just felt like I should let them be with you without inserting any drama. You were hurt, Seany. We were all scared. I just didn't want to add any tension."

"I'm not a lad, Maureen. You don't have to worry about hurting me. My adolescent heartache scabbed over a long time ago." Then he turned and left without another word.

* * *

SEANY REACHED his car faster this time, not taking his time as he watched Maureen Rogers walk away from him yet again. Sure, it was him who'd done the actual walking, but she'd turned her back on him in every way that mattered. She was so beautiful he had a hard time processing it. Gone was the lanky girl on the cusp of womanhood. Her hair was still thick and long. Her skin pale, despite the climate in which she lived. Those gray eyes, pools of mysterious depth. The only thing missing was the smile. That Mona Lisa smile, delicate and restrained. What had those eyes seen in the last seven years?

Moira showed herself on the porch of her small, cozy home. "Leaving? But will you be back?" she asked smoothly.

"I'll be here by ten. You have my word," he said.

"Good. We've acquired some volunteers and four more men to fill the class." Moira smiled as he seemed to take in this unexpected information. He'd been prepared to spend these sessions alone with Moe. He wasn't sure if he was relieved or not. He simply nodded, getting into his old car and heading back to Furbogh.

* * *

Furbogh, Co. Galway

Seany was tired as he came through the door. His shoulder hurt, and the nerves regenerating at the burn site were sending needling pricks of pain through his arm and what felt like electrical pulses under his skin. He hadn't taken his medicine since last night. He looked at the marred skin, expecting it to be smoldering and smoking. Then he shut out the pain and the memories of feeling the skin burn as he held on to his partner for dear life.

"Where did you disappear to, for chrissakes? Your mother has been calling every half hour," Josh said. "Don't you answer texts?"

Seany slid his keys onto the counter, sighing. "Sorry. I was driving quite a bit. I went to see Kamala and the kids. Then I drove to Connemara."

Josh froze over the plate he was drying. "Well, I guess I'm not surprised. I didn't reach out to her."

"I know you didn't. I caught her completely unaware," he said. But his words lacked bravado. "It sort of took the wind out of my sails when she dropped into a dead faint." He winced, the memory still fresh in his mind.

"Jesus, Seany. You know how to make an entrance."

"I'd like to say it was my raw manliness that gave her the vapors, but she hadn't eaten and she'd been dealing with a horse that was being a real shithead. She saw me and stood up too fast, I think."

"So of course, you went into full paramedic mode," Josh said, trying not to grin.

Seany was rubbing his neck. "Aye, I suppose I did. It's been a busy week considering I haven't gone back to work yet."

"Speaking of which, Alanna is going to stay awhile at your parents' house. She needs the help with the three of them. Aidan is taking leave. They want us there for dinner tomorrow night if you can swing it?"

"I start work next Friday. I have the equine class." He refused to call it therapy. "Monday and Wednesday, and PT alternating days. I'm going to get very busy very soon."

"It's good you're going back to work. I know you hate being benched. The rest will come with time." Josh smiled at this unlikely new best friend. More like a brother. "How are Kamala and the kids?"

"As well as can be expected. Kamala was as gracious and sweet as ever." Seany sat at the kitchen table, running his hands roughly through his short hair. "She's going to go back to work. I'd imagine she needs the wages, but I also think she wants to because it's a distraction. Being home all day will drive her insane. He's everywhere in that house."

"Those poor kids. It's kind of sickening that men like my father live long, miserable lives. He was a curse on our family. Then guys like McBride, who love their kids and take care of them get snuffed out too soon. Just like Tadgh's dad." He shook his head. "It doesn't seem fair."

Seany's heart squeezed for Josh. He was proof that you could survive just about anything and keep your soul intact. He was such a good person. He deserved a lot more than he got out of life. "You should call Maddie. She'd want an update."

Josh eyed him suspiciously. "I guess I could do that. You making Moe swoon into a faint is a juicy bit of gossip." Seany threw a piece of junk mail at him as he ducked. "I'm at the lighthouse tomorrow, bright and early. I'm hitting the rack."

"Me too. PT took a lot out of me today. Everything did. I'm wrecked."

Josh clapped him on the back. "It's going to get better, Seany. You just have to open yourself up for it."

"It's too late and I'm too tired for your impression of Dr. Phil."

Josh responded without missing a beat. Southern accent thick as he pointed a finger. *"Let it go, man. Don't be a prisoner of victim city!"*

Seany barked out a laugh. "I can't believe you have that memorized. You are grounded from screen time." Josh just wiggled his eyebrows and went into his bedroom.

He sat there for a moment, deciding whether he was going to eat. He couldn't muster any hunger for food. He closed his eyes and saw her. Strong, defiant, infuriatingly calm despite those qualities. She was an enigma. Always had been. He saw her, that fifteen-year-old-girl who had set him on fire. Serious. Protective of her siblings. A good daughter.

It wasn't that she'd dumped him. The romance had been doomed to failure, given the distance. But the finality is what hurt him. The walking away without a backward glance. She stole something precious from him. She stole their friendship. She locked it up and hid the key from him. If she hadn't done that, then maybe down the road, they would have… He shook himself, pushing the thought away. She'd made her choice. He needed this therapy to get reinstated. Riding a horse was a far better option than some head shrinker twice a week. And Maureen Rogers wasn't going to get off easy by inviting him to drop the whole idea. Greenhorn indeed. He'd ridden a horse before. More than once, in fact. He'd ridden with Moe that summer. And on Dingle Beach with his family. During Izzy and Liam's wedding in

Arizona, they'd taken a ride around her parents' farm. Moe thought she knew him, but she didn't.

The sight of her almost getting bucked off that big stallion went through his head again. He thought about his partner lying in the burn unit with a broken neck. Slowly suffocating on a ventilator. It only took a tragic moment for everything to change.

CHAPTER 16

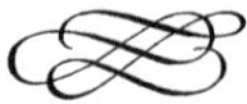

"Even a happy life cannot be without a measure of darkness, and the word 'happy' would lose its meaning if it were not balanced by sadness."
- Carl Jung

Galway City

Seany stared across the office at the stern looking woman. She'd surprised him with her American accent. She'd just shrugged, telling him that her husband was a native. It shouldn't surprise him. Three of his brothers had American wives and he told her so. "That's interesting. Was the county getting sparse for eligible women? Did your family run an ad?" The sarcasm surprised him, and he warmed to her. Not stern. Just no nonsense. "So, it appears you've thwarted tradition and figured out a way to see less of me. I'm not sure whether to be impressed or offended. Equine therapy, is it? Well, that'll be fun. And group therapy is an excellent tool."

"If ye call mucking stalls together group therapy, then I suppose so." He smiled at his own joke, until a suspicion niggled at him. "You are joking?"

"Oh, no. I mean, the horse stuff is, in itself, therapeutic. One with nature, man, and beast, all that. I highly approve. But your group will be tended to by a therapist as well. They've just secured a volunteer for at least the first few weeks. Once a week. Apparently your second session per week will be private. Your schedule is more flexible than the others, being on the 72 on 96 off schedule."

Seany was rubbing the bridge of his nose. "Oh shit."

"Well said, Mr. O'Brien. Now, why don't we get down to why you're here with me today?"

He looked up, "I don't know. Maybe so the department can cover its ass? Some sort of bullshit red tape to show I'm fit for duty and not a harm to myself? I mean, it's not like I'm in the guards and carrying a pistol."

"If you were, would you be a harm to yourself?" she said plainly. "Don't give me that look, you brought it up," she said dryly. The more he listened to her, he was placing her accent to be from New York or New Jersey.

He shook his head, "No, of course not."

She stared at him. Waiting.

"Why don't you tell me why I'm here? What exactly is the fear?" he asked, suddenly tired.

"Well, PTSD for a start. Survivor guilt. Your own lack of confidence in your ability to do your job effectively. Misplaced anger. Pushing yourself physically before you are ready to go back to full duty. Though, one could argue that working as the full-time EMT is returning to full duty. According to your records, that's what you studied in college."

"That is a long list, Doc. Why don't we start with the job? Yes, I did get my degree in EMT studies. However, I started as a firefighter and took to the work. I'd be happy to return to it. It's the job to which I made the transfer. They've been more than patient holding my position, but they won't hold it forever. Getting hired on full time as a firefighter in Ireland is not easy. It's usually an on-call type of thing. It's different here than in America."

"Yes, I'm aware. That answers one of my questions. As for the rest, I don't think you'd own up to any sort of problems, would you?"

"I lost my partner. I failed to save him in a fire. Excuse me if I needed a minute," he said, with more than a little snark.

She lifted her palms. "That's where you are seeing things differently than every other person involved. You didn't fail to save him. You indeed did save him, at your own peril. You sustained a laundry list of injuries and lay unconscious in an intensive care unit for days because of it."

"I wasn't in a coma or something. I just wouldn't wake up."

"Wouldn't or couldn't?" she asked.

He cocked his head, assessing her. "You are not going to cut me any slack, are you?"

"Not an inch. But it's done out of a genuine hope that you come out the other side whole and ready to live life again."

* * *

Doolin, Co. Clare

Seany and Josh pulled into the family homestead about an hour before dinner. Seany had been quiet during the ride from Galway. Josh had given him an easy silence. He understood what it was like to get put through the wringer by a therapist. When he'd first escaped the clutches of his abusive father, Charlie had decided to put him in therapy. Hours after the session, he'd still been rattling around in his own head. It hadn't lasted long. He'd turned eighteen and refused to let her pay for it. He didn't have an NHS card, because he was here on a student visa.

"Ready for the third degree, brother?" he asked. Seany groaned. "Don't worry. They do it because they love you. Let them fuss over you. You're a lucky man."

Seany knew this, but he wasn't looking forward to having his mother, granny, and sister all pecking at him at once.

* * *

SEANY HELD the small baby boy in his hands and could scarcely believe he'd delivered him. Well, not really. Alanna was the real hero. He looked up and met her eyes. She smiled warmly and came to sit next to him. The baby had a soft layer of fuzz on his head, and he wiggled like he could smell his mother. Seany put him in the crook of his arm, rocking him gently. "You did good, Mammy."

She put her head on his shoulder. "I don't know if I thanked you. I remember a lot of screeching and crying. Sorry," she said with a smile.

"Don't apologize. And don't be embarrassed. I'm just glad you're both okay. Da tells me Hans is flying in from Brazil."

"Yes, Mary insisted. It's such a wonderful thing they are doing at that orphanage. He's always been good with kids." The baby started crying and she took him, putting him over her shoulder. "Moe called me last night."

"I had a feeling she would," he said. And it wasn't defensive. He knew Alanna didn't have a calculating bone in her body. His sister on the other hand…

"I heard there have been all sorts of things going on with you, brother dear. None of which I'm privy to. Spill it. Or so help me God I will wrestle you to the floor." Brigid sat next to him with a bump to his hip.

"You are pregnant, sister. Again. Ye'll not be wrestling anyone."

"You just try me, Sean David O'Brien, Jr.," she said. "I have rights as your only sister!"

Alanna giggled as a liquid blast came from Keegan's diaper. "My thoughts exactly, lad," Seany said. And even Brigid had to smile a little.

Alanna stood, wincing. "Oof, Keegan. I know you need a change, but you beat mommy up in the backseat of that car." She waddled off, causing Aidan to follow her, handing off little Isla to his mother.

Brigid said, "I'm so proud of you, dearthháir."

"For what, exactly?" he asked.

"Not many men would be brave enough to stare down the gully and deliver a baby in the backseat of a car." She grinned at his laughter. "And for getting back on the job. Now, tell me what the hell has been going on, Seany."

He said, "You know about Maureen Rogers coming to the hospital, I assume. So, I won't go over the whole blatant hypocrisy of your outrage. Someone should have told me."

She narrowed her eyes. "Aye, probably. It was Da's decision, in the end. That aside, we can't dismiss what happened in the hospital room as easily as you. Liam and Josh were there. You roused to her voice the first time. The second time, when she stayed and talked with you, you woke. Nothing else worked. No one else worked. She brought you back, Seany. Whether ye like to admit it or not."

"I'd scarcely have a reason to deny it if it were actually true. It's not."

"Bollocks," she said. "Don't give me that look. It's a load of bollocks. You'd deny it because she broke your heart. And ye've pined for the lass for years. Ye'd deny it because you're afraid to admit there is still something between you. Now, what's happened since you found out? And don't leave anything out. I want to hear it all."

Brigid wasn't often quiet, but she kept her mouth shut and listened as he explained his decision to go confront her in Connemara, and the chaos that followed. It didn't last long, because soon her brow was furrowed and without warning she slapped him on his arm. "Ow! Fucking hell, Brigid. Could you at least do it on my good arm?"

"You don't have a good arm! Ye dislocated the elbow on the other side. You're burned, ripped, and cracked all over the fecking' place, and ye got that thick head of yours bashed in. That's the only reason I can understand why you'd shock the devil out of the poor lass right in the middle of her dealing with an out-of-control horse! Ye coulda gotten the poor lass killed!"

Seany jerked at the words and Brigid immediately wished she could take them back. "Hyperbole, maybe." She said more calmly. Then a small smile creeped onto her face. "So, ye made her swoon at the sight of you?"

Josh interjected. "You should have seen her face when she saw him at the hospital."

He winked at Brigid, and Seany narrowed his eyes at him. "Do tell, love. Don't hold back now!" Brigid said.

"Let's just say I'm guessing our Seany has filled out since high school."

That shouldn't have given Seany a thrill, but it did. He kept all emotion off his face, other than dry sarcasm. "Aye, I'm sure the death pallor and catheter were a real turn on." But he secretly wanted to know what Josh had seen in her eyes.

* * *

Connemara, Co. Galway

Moira handed Moe a stack of paperwork. "We aren't official yet. We need one more board member to turn our temporary status into a permanent one. And the final inspection, but I'm not worried on that account. We need to find that last board member. Here are your other applications for Monday's session. Oh, and I spoke with the mental health counselor today. She'll be here Monday to meet the lads."

Moe stopped shuffling. "Counselor?"

"Yes. It's perfect timing, really. Our first two weeks the lads will be acquainting themselves with the horses. Your Seany is the only one with riding experience."

"He's not my Seany," she said firmly. "And that won't be an issue. I'm riding with him on Wednesdays. So, what do you think? Should the group therapy come before or after? And will she ride?"

"Not likely. Or not the first couple of weeks. She just had a baby. A couple of days ago, in fact."

"She had a baby a couple of days ago and she's going to come here Monday? That seems a bit too soon, don't you think?"

"Aye, that's what I said. So, she's going to play it by ear. See how she feels Sunday night. I also told her she was welcome to bring the laddie with her. I love babies. We'll be flexible for her. I don't want to lose her as a volunteer."

"That's really forward thinking of you, Moira. American businesses can be really heartless when it comes to working parents. Good for you."

"Aye, well it's the least we can do. She's living in Belfast," Moira said. Moe froze what she was doing, a big smile coming across her face.

CHAPTER 17

Seany walked into the barn just as he heard Moe chewing some guy's ear off. "Listen, Hugo. I'm sure you mean well, but I am not going to have you micromanage what kind of feed I give the horses."

"What about this thing? He hardly qualifies as a horse. He's a waste of space! This is needless waste!" He was referring to her little buddy, War Hammer, and it pissed her off.

"He's for the children in the program and will serve other purposes once we start the hippotherapy program."

"Hippo? This isn't a zoo, for chrissakes! She can barely afford the horses!" Hugo spat. Seany stood back, wanting to listen to how she handled herself. But he actually had to put his hand over his mouth with that stupid comment.

Moe rubbed her forehead, trying to stay calm. "Just google it. There are no actual hippos involved. That aside, Moira was pretty clear that you have no business trying to tell the staff here anything. Now I have work to do, Hugo. If you have a problem, talk to Moira."

Seany heard the low grumbling of a man's voice and heard Moe shout. "Get your hand off me right now, Hugo."

Game time. He came around the corner and aggressed on the little fucker. Hugo's face registered fear as he actually got behind Moe. "Excuse me, Maureen. It sounded like you needed a little help."

"Not in the slightest," she said as she folded her arms over her chest. "Hugo was just going up to the house." He scurried like a little rodent and was gone in a flash. He mumbled something about walking dog food as he passed the horse stalls.

"Everything was fine. I didn't need any interference."

"I agree. But it was kind of fun to scare the little prat." He didn't agree, but he wasn't about to give her a hard time after she'd gone ten rounds with wonder boy. "Who's this?" Seany ran a hand over the mini-horse's mane.

"This is War Hammer," she said with a straight face.

Seany suppressed a grin and leaned down eye level with the little guy. "I'm interested to hear how you got that name. Was it all of your girlfriends who named you that…because of the size of your hammer?"

A voice came from behind him. "Oh, yes. He's a real ladies' man, aren't ye War Hammer?" Rory came in, carrying his farrier kit.

"Moe, aren't you going to introduce us proper like? Last time he was here, you fell…"

"I know what I did," she snapped. "No need to relive it. Rory, this is Seany O'Brien."

"Sean will do. Nice to meet you, Rory." Moe breezed past him. "You're early. By more than two hours. Feel free to go to the house for some tea. Moira is in there."

"I don't need tea. Thanks." He leaned on the stall, watching her.

"I wouldn't stand there," she said easily. No sooner had she said it than Balor stuck his head out and tried to nip Seany.

"You little fecker. Just wait until the hippos get here. They'll teach you a thing or two." He watched Moe for any sign of thaw. He could tell she was suppressing a grin. He'd give anything to see that Mona Lisa smile.

Rory said, "What's this about hippos?"

She went into the tack room, coming out with her western saddle. "Ask Hugo. Apparently he's a horse expert. Can you help me saddle up Balor? I want to practice with him before the group gets here."

Seany watched as they worked together. Rory was good with horses and managed to coax a few smiles out of Moe. It irritated Seany to watch them work so well together, which was completely stupid. Rory said, "I'll set up the barrels. Cassanova's going to be jealous."

"Cassanova gets enough attention. I know the type." Seany swore she glanced his way. He'd never seen barrel racing, but he didn't like the idea of Moe getting up on that huge horse.

"What's the purpose of this? I mean, besides your unhealthy, thrill-seeking tendencies?" he said to her.

Without skipping a beat, she said, "Says the man who runs into burning buildings."

"Touché. But really, explain why you came to Ireland only to shove your Texas ways down the poor lad's throat?"

Rory barked out a laugh, "Nicely said, Seany without the *y*."

"I don't want to wreck your male solidarity, boys. Balor undoubtedly appreciates it. The reason is simple. He's an overbearing, pigheaded male with an overload of testosterone. Something I'm sure you've both heard from a woman's mouth on more than one occasion. The barrel racing is to teach him discipline and work off some of the energy that tends to get him in trouble. He's got a bad history from his previous owner. They couldn't handle him, so they gave him the shove. I'm going to make him earn his keep. He's going to barrel race for the open house and then if he learns to play nice, Moira may stud him out to the other Irish hunter and thoroughbred breeders in the country. The genetics are there, but breeders may be put off if he has a bad reputation."

Seany said without thinking, "At least he'll be getting laid for his trouble." Rory choked down a laugh. "Sorry, that was uncouth. It was a bad joke." Moe was blushing, which made him feel like a rotter.

Moe said, "Well, the joke's on him. They use artificial insemination for horses nowadays. It has a way better success rate."

"Poor sod." But his words died in his throat as Moe worked her way into a pair of leather chaps. The breath shot out of him as she bent to fasten them. Rory just watched him, shaking his head. She stepped up on the stool to mount the horse. He said, "I was expecting you to jump up there like Calamity Jane."

"That pulls on him unnecessarily, and I'm a little too short for this tall a horse. Better safe than sorry. I've already fallen off him once."

And at that, she urged the horse forward and out of the barn. Seany swore under his breath. "Death wish. Jesus, Joseph, and Mary. She has a death wish."

He stood and watched as she ran Balor through several attempts. He fought more than he cooperated. At first, anyway. But soon she was getting him to round the barrels. "He seems big for this sort of sport."

Rory said, "He is. He's more suited for jumping. Irish sport horses are a crossbreed of an Irish draught and a thoroughbred. But she's not competing, so it hardly matters. She's trying to save the fiend from himself. Moira took him on in a moment of madness because she's got a big heart. He was a rescue. He was underweight, covered in filth, and half crazed when he got here, which wasn't that long ago. She's worked wonders with him, really."

They watched her in silence, and Seany wondered if Rory saw what he did. She was absolutely breathtaking. She'd always been smart and serious. Serious about family, school, and music. They'd had horses back when he'd met her. She'd taken him riding before. She was a natural, back then. She was a pro now. She didn't let that horse forget who was in charge, despite his ill-temper.

Moe was trying like hell to concentrate on Balor, but it wasn't easy. Why the hell had he come early? He'd acted like he hated her the last time he was here. And maybe he had his reasons. After a few successful runs, she cooled Balor down. She was going to get hurt if she wasn't focused. Rory was gone by the time she finished, so Devlin helped her with Balor. "Go, lass. I'll brush him down. Rest your bones and get a bite to eat before your other charges show up."

Moe slid her chaps off, hanging them in the tack room. Then she washed up in the sink. She had dust on her face, hands, and even in her mouth. She cupped her hand under the faucet. The water was so clean and pure in this wild area. She swished it around, spitting it out and then taking another gulp. She wiped her face off with a towel, and when she opened her eyes, Seany too-handsome-for-his-own-good O'Brien was standing in the doorway, watching her. She jumped. "Jesus Christ! Do you mind!"

"What? There isn't even a door. It's not like I caught you in your knickers." She growled and pushed past him. She wanted to knock the smirk off his face. "Why are you here?" she said as she stomped toward her cabin. "You said you were quitting!"

"Why are you so angry?" he said calmly.

"I'm not angry!" She was. And he couldn't be more delighted. Miss Calm U.S.A. had her back up, and it was glorious. He'd never seen her so out of sorts. She kept going, trying to speak in a more calm, dignified manner. "You come here, you spook my horse, you chew me out, say you're quitting, make sure that I know my presence at your sickbed was unappreciated."

"I wasn't sick. I was injured. You make me sound like some dying old woman," he argued as he walked behind her. She really did fill out her jeans perfectly. She got to her doorstep. "Maureen, you are being a little irrational right now."

She pointed in his face. "Get your act together before you step into the group setting or I will kick you out of my class. And what happened to Moe?"

"Moe is a girl's name. You're no girl anymore." He had a challenge in his eyes.

"Is that why you dropped the *y*, Seany?" she goaded.

"Seany is for family and friends. Everyone else can call me Sean." He spat the words, letting her know on which side of that fence he considered her to be.

She stiffened and he saw the pain his words inflicted. "I'm glad you cleared that up, Sean." She went through the door and tried to close it, but he was on her in a flash. His arms brought her back to his chest.

"I'm sorry." His mouth was against her ear. "I'm sorry, lass."

She felt a sob bubble up her throat, and she trembled with the effort of suppressing it. "I didn't come back here to hurt you, Sean."

"I know. What I don't know is why you did come." She felt the warmth and strength of him against her. His arms were looser, giving her a chance to pull away. She fought the urge to press back and into him, knowing that was exactly the wrong thing to do right now. Tensions were high. She knew he wanted an answer. Thankfully her phone saved her. She turned, taking it out of her back pocket. She spoke, but she didn't look away from his eyes. She had to look up at him, even with her boots on. "Okay, thanks Moira. We'll be right up."

Seany watched her as she rang off. "We have a problem in the hay barn. I have to go. Class starts in forty-five minutes. Help yourself if you want some coffee or tea. There are snacks in the cabinets."

"Maureen."

"I have to go. They need all hands." And she was out the door without answering his bloody question.

* * *

Moe stifled a curse as she looked under the top layer of hay. It was wet, and mold was already setting in. "How?"

Devlin said, "That's the thing. I don't know. The roof is almost new. These doors are never left open. If I'd fed this to the horses and not paid attention." She knew the answer. Sick horses.

"Is this the month's supply?"

"We have more coming in a week, but I can call him and get it out here today or tomorrow. It's curious, though. First the fence and now this. I know I didn't do this, and you don't deal with loading the hay in the tractor, so I know it wasn't you."

Rory was behind them with Moira. "Well, I sure as hell didn't do it."

Moira said, "I'm old, but senility has yet to kick in. I don't like this. I mean, there is a healthy competition around here among the breeders, but none would put the horses in harm's way."

Moe said, "Moira, I hate to even suggest it."

"No way. Hugo is a prat to be sure. But he's already trying to pinch my pennies. He certainly wouldn't ruin a hundred euros worth of hay or destroy a new fence. He wants me spending less money, not more."

"Well, I'm on limited time. Let's get this cleaned out." Moe said, shaking her head at the mess.

Devlin said, "Rory and I will handle this. Moira can help you with the horses if we aren't done. You aren't riding today, right?"

Moe answered, "Right. They'll meet the group, we'll go over safety stuff, get them acquainted with the equipment. I'll bring War Hammer out as well as Skadi. She's pretty and docile. She'll charm their socks off."

Rory smiled at that and said, "Atta girl. Tell Seany without the *y* to behave himself. I saw you two bickering the whole way back to your cottage."

She ignored the curious glances from Devlin and Moira. "Don't worry. He's been warned."

* * *

SEANY WALKED into the barn after taking an extended time-out at Moe's cottage. He'd had to, because having her pulled flush against him had his cock at full salute. Holy hell, the feel of her had been heaven. She'd grown about an inch to his five. She came to just under his chin. Her hair smelled like flowers and honey. All he could think about was his mouth being so close to her ear. He'd wanted to taste her. Tilt her head and cover her neck with kisses. He was an idiot. She hadn't reached out in over six years. Ten months after he'd left Ireland, she'd ended it. They'd both moved on in the seven years since he'd last held her in his arms. That path had gone cold and needed to remain so. He shouldn't be letting his thoughts wander in that direction. Once this internship was over, she was headed back to Texas. He'd be a fool to fall for her twice. He was shaken out of his inner turmoil by familiar voices.

He rounded the corner and had to do a double take. "Hans?" He was lifted off his feet by the big Marine to the delighted giggles of Moira and…Alanna?

Moira said, "I see you two know each other, so I'll skip the introductions. Kyle, Matthew, Owen, this is your group therapist Alanna O'Brien. This is her father, and the other participant, Hans Falk of the U.S. Marines."

Hans put out a hand. "Retired. Nice to meet you."

Moira continued. "And this is Sean O'Brien. He was with the Dublin Fire Brigade and has recently transferred to Galway." She pointed to the first guy. "Kyle is a Garda Officer in Dublin. Matthew is Coast Guard. Owen is in the Army. I'm sorry, lads. I can't remember all of your ranks. You're on your own after this." Moira had a warm, disarming way about her. Like your favorite aunt. But all Seany fully processed were the words *group therapist.* He cursed under his breath, and Hans put an arm around him. He whispered through a smile, "Don't be a dick, son. Suck it up." Seany heard the humor in his voice and he groaned. He'd been duped by his own sister-in-law. He wondered if his department-assigned psychologist had known it was his sister-in-law.

He looked past all of them to see Moe holding his new nephew. She was tickling his nose with the end of her braid. Then she leaned down and kissed his forehead. It stirred something in him to watch her. She'd always been sort of motherly to her siblings, but it gave him an odd feeling to have her here in Ireland. Not away from home where Aidan had been the only tie to home. Maureen was in Ireland and she was holding little Keegan. It was a strange feeling, and not an altogether unpleasant one. He watched her with an intensity that unnerved him.

Hans whistled through his teeth and then said, "Brother, you are in trouble."

* * *

THEY SAT IN A CIRCLE, inside the heated barn. Alanna said, "I'm so glad to be here with you all. I won't be riding. At least not at first. I just had

Keegan and I need to heal. But I wanted to be here on your first day, to get to know everyone. I think we should just start by telling a little about ourselves and if you are comfortable, why you decided that equine therapy was a good alternative for you. I'll go first, then Moira. After her, we'll go around clockwise. Does that sound good?" There was a grumble of agreement. "And please, we aren't here to pressure anyone. Share as much as you are comfortable sharing, and we won't push."

She began, "I'm a licensed mental health counselor. I studied and worked in America with the military community. My specialty was in alternative therapies for service members with TBIs and PTSD. TBI stands for traumatic brain injury. The men and women I worked with were usually in heavy combat. You all met Hans, my father and a Sergeant Major in the Marine Corps. His story isn't mine to tell, but we've grown in this journey together. I also met my husband, a handsome Irishman, during his training in North Carolina. He's a Captain in the Royal Irish Regiment and is recovering from PTSD. And finally...I'm a survivor of sexual and physical battery and kidnapping. My assailant was killed in prison, but I still dream about it. I still get scared sometimes. I, like you, am a work in progress." She swallowed a lump in her throat. "Now, Moira is the owner of this wonderful ranch. I'll let her continue."

Moira was holding Keegan now. "My name is Moira. I've never been a first responder. I'm just a horse breeder. I wanted to transition away from breeding and start this non-profit, because it is needed. I have no spouse or children. No surviving ones, anyway. I just have this place and these horses. And I want it all to mean something."

Moe was next. She cleared her throat. "My name is Maureen Rogers. I'm an intern from Texas A&M in the States. I, too, was a military child, like Alanna. My father was treated for his TBI at the same clinic where she worked. I went into equine therapy after watching the love of horses bring my father back from a very dark place. He started having seizures about seven years ago. It ended his military career. When we moved back to Texas, his loss of self-worth was... hard to watch. He didn't want to stop being a Marine. He got worse before he got better. And part of his journey was our little ranch and being able to ride again. It hasn't been easy for any of us. We were..." she shook herself, not finishing. "Anyway, I believe in this therapy. I'm here to make sure Moira's dream is fulfilled and that men like you have somewhere to go when traditional therapy doesn't appeal or has failed. I'm so glad you all are here, and I can't wait to get you up on these beautiful horses."

Seany watched Moe speak, her outward appearance calm and serious. But the little speech had taken something out of her. She'd been about to reveal something, but hadn't. Matthew spoke next. "I'm with the search and rescue unit in Donegal. I'm also a bank clerk. I came here today after an incident with the recovery of a dead child. He'd been killed beforehand. I just...can't get on with things. They didn't find his killer. I'm having dreams. And, well that's about all." He shrugged shyly. Moe squeezed his hand.

Kyle was Garda in Dublin and responded to a multiple fatality motor vehicle accident including another officer and his partner. Both dead on arrival, as well as two teenagers. Owen was a Sergeant in the Irish Army. He'd been to Africa during the Ebola epidemic. He was having a hard time processing the death and human rights atrocities he'd witnessed during his time there.

"My name is Hans. You're probably wondering how I ended up in this group, being an American and all. Well, my daughter and I both had the good sense to marry an Irish citizen. My wife is currently in Brazil doing missionary work. She's a doctor. I just came home to meet our little mascot over there, and Alanna asked me if I'd like to join the group for the next couple weeks." He looked down at his hands, collecting his thoughts. Then he spoke, meeting the other men in the eyes. "Among other combat tours, I fought in the second battle of Fallujah. During the worst of the fighting, we were clearing buildings in the heart of the city. We took sniper fire and I was hit. As was my best friend, Brian O'Mara." He met Seany's eyes as he continued. "I pulled him out of the line of fire. But he was hit in the neck. It was a once-in-a-lifetime shot. Our necks are protected to a degree, but there is this small gap." He brushed his hand, as if feeling it. "I couldn't save him. He was my friend, and I loved him and he bled out in less than a minute. I held him while he died. His last words were for his wife and daughter." He swallowed. "He died and I didn't, and I'm still having a hard time forgiving myself for that. Like the lady said, we're all a work in progress. I'm okay most days. But every once in a while, it sneaks up on me. Sometimes it's when I see his daughter and his grandkids." He shook his head. "I tried, but it wasn't enough. And it's only through a lot of love and faith and my head-shrinking daughter that I've come to realize that none of it was my fault."

Seany tore his gaze away from Hans, looking at Alanna. Her eyes were filled with tears. So were Moe's, although she hid it better. He couldn't do this. Jesus, why was he here?

"My name is Sean O'Brien. I'm a firefighter, as Moira told you. I was injured during a warehouse fire." There was a long pause. He met Alanna's gaze, and somehow she knew he wasn't going to give any more. Then he looked at Moe. There was no judgment. Just a serious intensity that he couldn't match, so he looked away.

"Okay, I'm glad you're all here. I won't be here next week, but I should be recovered enough to come the week after." She eased up out of her chair. "Daddy, I'll see you back in Doolin."

They all stood and watched the lovely, petite woman leave and walk toward the house. Moira said, "I'm going to release you all to Maureen and Devlin. I'm going to tend to the lass and see her on her way. And we've got our other intern flying in tonight. You'll all meet her next week. Another stunning Yank." The men grumbled with laughter.

Moe stood, "Now, let's talk horses. I'm going to go over some safety measures with everyone. Hans and Sean have a moderate amount of experience in the saddle. The other three of you have little or no riding experience?" They nodded shyly. "Don't worry about that. No experience means you haven't started any bad habits. I'll have you riding on your own in no time. The first thing you need to understand is that these horses are living, breathing, and precious. They require a great deal of care. While you are here, you will help us with that. I'm going to teach you today how to brush your horse, how to pick out his or her hooves, how to clean up his droppings, and the safe way to show the horse some affection. Horses have their own personalities, just like us or other domestic animals. They get tired, cranky, playful, and ornery. Some more than others. So, let's go meet your new friends. Unless there is some sort of problem, you will have the same horse the entire time you are here."

They walked down to the stalls that had horses in them. Some horses, like Balor and Cassanova, were out in the pasture. "These aren't all of our horses, but they are good, reliable mounts and excellent choices for new riders. I know they look big, but they are sweethearts."

"This is Skadi. She's a Connemara pony and I will be riding her, so don't get any ideas." As if Skadi understood, she nuzzled under Moe's chin. She giggled and rubbed her neck.

Seany loved watching her. Two beautiful creatures who obviously felt affection for one another. Moe's face was beaming. Something that didn't happen often, if memory served. She continued. "Hans, you've got the dapple grey. His name is Hercules. He's a good sturdy mount."

"Sturdy? Are you saying he's an old, fat guy mount?" Hans joked.

"Don't fish for compliments, Devil Dog. He's tall enough for those tree trunks you call legs." She smiled at him as he threw his head back and laughed.

"Hercules it is."

Seany watched her approach the next stall. "Chancellor is another cremello like Skadi, but with brown eyes. That's one of the ways you can tell them apart. Kyle, I'm going to put you on Chancellor. He's a little older. He's very kind and a good starter pony. He won't give you any problems."

Seany looked at the next pony. A dun mare with a sleek coat. "This is Frida. Matthew, you look like a ladies' man. She's a dun Connemara and I think you two will get along wonderfully. That other dun across the way is her baby boy. Not so little anymore. His name is Molasses, and Owen, you're going to ride him. And last but not least, Franklin the mule." She eyed Seany from under her lashes. There was a pregnant pause. "Franklin likes long walks in the rain and enjoys romance novels read to him in the evenings." Another pause. Then there it was. That Mona Lisa smile. "He's not getting a rider this time around." The group grumbled with laughter. "Sean, across from Franklin is Storm."

Seany looked across at the most stunning stallion he'd ever seen. Even better looking than that demon Balor. He was grey. Impossibly so. Monochromatic to the degree that he didn't seem real. His coat had a satin sheen. His tail and mane were also grey, albeit a little darker. His eyes were so dark, they were almost black. He was perfectly named. He approached, and the regal creature turned his head slightly, his eye watching Seany's approach. "You are handsome, aren't you? Hello, Storm."

Devlin, Seany found, was a likable sort. He rode a jet-black Connemara with two white socks. His name was Galileo. Seany found it interesting how the horses were named. And he was curious how they'd chosen each horse for each rider. The only man with a mare was Matthew, and he thought he knew why. She was very gentle. Despite Matthew's career as a soldier, he seemed wary of horses. Inexperience more than a genuine fear. Moe's mount, Skadi, was breathtaking. As beautiful as Storm was handsome. He wondered why she'd chosen Storm for him. He was big, like the one she'd chosen for Hans. But there was something altogether arrogant about Storm, as if he knew he was a stunner. He was, according to Devlin, their champion breeder. Award winning for his symmetry and coat. After commenting that Skadi and Storm would make interesting offspring, Devlin explained why Skadi couldn't be bred. Yet Maureen adored her. Not because of what she could offer the breeding world, but because she nuzzled her under the chin and made her smile.

* * *

EVERYONE WAS HEADED to their cars when Seany stopped to give Hans a man hug. Moe ran from the barn. She hugged Hans as well. "I'm so glad you could join us for a little while, Hans. Next week, Devlin is going to take you out during the classroom time. You too, Sean."

He suddenly hated that she kept calling him Sean. Hated that his words had made such a stinging impression. "I'll be here Wednesday if we're still going out?"

"Yes. I'll be the one to take you out, unless you prefer someone else? We have a new intern coming in or I can see if Devlin is available. Let Moira know and be here at eleven," she said, and turned without offering him any real goodbye. He could see the grin on Hans' face.

"She hugged me. You got nada, my man. You must have really stepped in it."

"What makes you think I even wanted a hug?" he said pissily. "Besides, she just has a soft spot for pensioners."

No sooner had he said it than Hans had him in a headlock. "I might be old, but I'm still fast." Both men laughed until Hans couldn't hang on anymore.

They looked up and noticed Moira was staring at them. "Boys will be boys," she said, waving as she went toward the barn.

* * *

Furbogh, Co. Galway

Seany woke from a dream. A good one for a change. He was walking through the woods with his father and grandfather. He suddenly missed them quite desperately. He looked at the time and decided to get up and make breakfast for Josh. The poor guy worked his tail off, then came home to study for his exams. Most of his testing was practical and on-the-job, but there was coursework. He was smart, just like Charlie. But there was always this urgency about him. Like he was auditioning, and he was afraid he was going to be found unworthy. That everything was going to be taken away from him.

He had the porridge ready when Josh woke. He came out of the bedroom looking exhausted. And for the first time, Seany noticed that his jeans were looser. He needed to talk to Charlie. Josh couldn't keep up this pace. All this and he'd been running back and forth to Dublin to sit at his bedside. A thickness swelled up in Seany's throat, and such brotherly affection for Josh that it almost had him tearing up. He'd been blessed with four of the best big brothers and a big sister that would walk through hell for him. It was about time he started being that for Josh. "You look tired, mo cara. Sit and eat."

"Thanks, man. Jesus, I really fell hard. I don't remember taking my clothes off or brushing my teeth. I was on autopilot."

Seany said, "You were up until at least midnight. You need to ease up a bit. Maybe cut back at the ferry?"

He shook his head. "I'm way below the salary requirement for an extended visa. I'm on a student visa now, but that's almost done."

"Surely the family can pull some strings. You have family living here, Josh. No way are they going to kick you out."

Josh shook his head. "It's hard to become a citizen in Ireland. And it's hard to stay if you aren't a citizen. I just want to do everything right. And getting a decent paying job is paramount."

"Maybe you could work remotely at some job in the States as well as the Lighthouse tech stuff?" Sean asked.

"I don't have any kind of skills that would get me a work-from-home gig. I mean, I think I make okay money for someone our age, but they may not see it that way. I have to prove I can take care of myself. And no alternate medical insurance is a hit against me. Branna made decent money when she made this move. I came here a pauper. I'm just now able to support myself."

"Don't say stuff like that. You weren't a pauper. You were a kid."

"Why not? It's true. I walked out of my parents' house with a bunch of old clothes and a borrowed suitcase."

"Well, you're self-made. Fuck the government."

Josh smiled, "Cora offered to marry me when she turned eighteen if I got tossed out. A marriage of convenience, she called it. Where does she come up with stuff like that?"

Seany said, dead serious, "You aren't my type, man, but if they try to toss you out of Ireland, I will fucking marry you. Don't laugh, you bastard. I happen to be a handsome devil!"

Josh threw his napkin across the table. "You aren't my type either, so you can forget about consummating the marriage!"

They shot insults back and forth for a while, then Seany went out to check the mail. "When is the last time you checked this, you lay about? The damn box is stuffed."

"Three days?" Josh said, shoveling in the porridge. He watched as Seany sorted. One pile of crap, one pile for him, one pile for Josh. Then he froze. "This looks like a card. It's not your birthday, is it? No, you had your birthday three months ago."

"Let's see. Maybe it's a secret admirer." When he saw the handwriting, his face blanched.

"What is it?" Seany asked.

Josh tried to shrug it off, but he knew who it was from. It was the third one he'd received. "It's probably someone trying to sell me insurance. I'll just look at it later."

Seany slapped a hand over it. "Don't bullshit me. What's amiss?"

Josh sighed. He opened it, scowled, then handed it to Seany. He knew he wasn't going to let it rest.

"It's the third one she's sent. The first two were kind of trying to play nice. They gave her probation. She wanted to start over," he said, making air quotes. "The second one was a little more desperate. Insinuating she'd hurt herself if I didn't at least call her."

"So, it's escalated. This isn't playing nice." He read it again. *Don't say I didn't warn you, you little prick. I can make real trouble for you.*

"She can't make trouble. She pled guilty in order to get probation. It'll just look like retaliation if she tries to make trouble, and she can't violate the terms of her probation. You need to turn her into the court. She's not supposed to be contacting you."

"I know. I just didn't want them putting her back in jail. It's no place for a woman, even if she is a psycho."

"But this is the third one. Call Tadgh or I will. I'm serious, Josh."

"I will. I'll call him today. I promise. He's going to be at Katie's tonight. Her parents' house, I mean. She's in from the island."

"Oh, grand. I've got PT today then I ride tomorrow, but maybe I'll go with you. I haven't seen Aunt Katie in ages."

"She came to see you in the hospital. She tried to keep the spots open for your parents and siblings, since they wouldn't let more than two in at a time, but she did come."

"No one told me. I suppose it never occurred to me to ask who came and went."

"Everyone came, Seany. Even Madeline and Mary came. They watched the kids while your siblings took turns. They watched Kamala's kids, too."

Seany's throat constricted. Josh saw it, of course. He said, "I'm sorry. I shouldn't have brought her up."

"Don't be sorry. She's in our lives. She'll always be in my life now. I can't walk away from them."

Josh said, "Of course you can't. It's not in you to be anything but a good guy. You're a real hero, Seany. If I didn't tell you that before, I should have."

"You're just sucking up to me so I'll marry you," he said with a grin.

"Piss off," Josh said, whipping a piece of junk mail at him. "And I expect my wife to clean up as well as cook, so get to those dishes. I need a shower."

He ran before Seany could catch him, slamming the bathroom door. "That's the last breakfast I make for you, you ungrateful tosser!"

CHAPTER 18

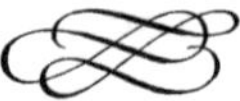

Letterfrack, Co. Galway

Maureen poured tea for the five candidates sat in the living room of Moira's home. She was interviewing occupational therapists as well as speech therapists. Eventually, with proper funding, they'd start a hippotherapy program as well. They'd need a physical therapist and more volunteers. The kids and physically disabled riders needed one-on-one adult supervision as they rode. Moe thought about the children she'd watched flourish in such programs. They used pictures, signs, and color-coded reins to help non-verbal children start to learn how to not only lead the powerful animals, but eventually use words to command. The physical bond needed no help. Autistic children were often more physical due to their lack of language. They communicated with touch and movement. Much like horses. Her favorite student had been a little boy named George. He had curly, dark hair and dancing eyes. He was sweet and quick with a giggle, and he loved the horses. He hadn't been afraid for a moment. His only adversity had been the helmet, so his family and therapists had worked with him beforehand to tolerate one. Once he'd linked getting to ride his horse with putting that helmet on, he'd never resisted again. He'd been eager to outfit himself and get in the saddle. And his gentle, old horse had loved him right back. Moe couldn't wait to get the children's therapy program off the ground.

Moe was making small talk about the non-profit to ease the tension. "We're so happy to have such a response. We have another equine specialist coming in today from Colorado. She's got an impressive resume and some experience volunteering for another riding center. Everything is coming together."

"Any advice?" one of the women asked.

"She's smart and has decades of experience. She's also fair, so just be a straight shooter." Seeing that her Texas slang was eluding them, "Just be straightforward. Tell her why you want to be here."

She set the tea thermos down on the table. "Please don't be shy. If you need more, help yourself. I think I just heard our groom pull in the drive with the new girl." Moe was out the door in seconds. Moira was behind her.

Moe was ecstatic when the new intern, Michele, dropped her bag and ran in for a hug. "Finally! I feel like I know you already!"

"Me too. Welcome to Ireland, Devil Dog!" She hugged the older woman who had served several years as an officer in the Marine Corps before going back to college. She was petite, but strong and tough looking, like most female Marines Moe had met. She had soft brown hair with golden highlights that contoured around her tanned face. She had eyes like pieces of amber.

"Thanks, Texas. I'm so glad that flight is over!"

Moe picked up her bag. "I'm sorry, Moira. I'll take this to her room, and you can greet her properly."

Devlin smiled at the display. "Moira, dear. We've been invaded by Yanks."

* * *

Golf Yank 11, Galway City Fire and Rescue Station

Seany walked into the main fire station in Galway. It was a whole-time station, unlike the retained stations scattered around the rest of the county. His stomach was doing flips both from the lingering discomfort of his PT station and the reality of his job starting. He'd be operating in the advance paramedic response unit until he was cleared for duty as a whole-time firefighter again. The good news he had to deliver was that he was on track to readiness within the month. He had in his hand the paperwork from his PT, and the department psychologist had cleared him pending the completion of his equine therapy and a final assessment.

He walked into the employee entrance, having already been there twice. This time, he was going to meet some of his co-workers on the paramedic side. He'd be working Thursday, but they wanted him today to meet his direct supervisor.

"There he is. It's about time you got off your ass and started working again." The man who greeted him was actually the station chief who'd accepted his transfer.

"Chief Braddock, good to see you again." He shook the man's hand.

"Welcome to the Eleven, lad. Come and meet your direct supervisor. He's the head of our advanced paramedic and EMT units. He can show you your response unit as well as let you meet some of the men. I want you to see the NHS ambulances, too. It's good to know what you've got on hand. Our EMTs are top notch. You're not going to want to leave, I think. The smoke eaters are a bunch of uncivilized buffoons."

"I heard that, Chief!" An older man poked his head out of an office that marked him as another high-ranking member of the fire brigade.

"That's Lieutenant Daily. You won't have to work with him, luckily. He's a terrible cook and he forgets to courtesy flush."

"Sod off!" Daily screamed, and Chief Braddock just chuckled under his breath. He went down two more doors to the office he was looking for. "Keeley, this is our new guy. Don't get attached. He's only here until he's cleared for duty."

A fit, fortyish man with red hair stood from his desk. "Aye, so I hear. I heard what happened in Dublin, lad. I'm sorry about your partner."

Chief Braddock looked uncomfortable. He said, "He's the sensitive one. I should have said something. Sorry,"

"Not at all. And thank you. It was rough. He was a great man. Now, I just want to work," Seany said simply.

Keeley said, "And we're honored to have you. Word from Dublin is that you nearly died trying to save him. They were sorry to lose you, but I suspect their loss is our gain. Chief Braddock tells me you have family on the west coast?"

Seany was relieved for the change of subject. "Aye, mostly in Doolin. A little in Galway. And some in Dublin and Belfast. Doctors and Garda, mostly."

"Word also has it you just delivered a baby in the backseat of a Peugeot 308," Keeley said. The Chief choked on his coffee, and the other man smiled. "Ye hadn't heard that one, then? Aye, his brother's child I believe."

Seany was actually blushing. "Aye, that would be the one in Belfast. He's in the Royal Irish Regiment. She went fast with the third. It wasn't ideal, but she was brilliant. She did most of the work."

"And a nuchal cord, was it?" He looked at the Chief and explained. "Cord wrapped around the child's neck."

Chief Braddock recoiled a bit. He said, "Christ, son. You're making us all look bad doing that sort of thing in your off hours. Let's leave some hero work for the rest of us."

Keeley put on his coat and they all left the office. "Come now, and I'll show you my rig. She's brand new, so if you scratch her, I'm not going to love you for it." And off they went to the bay. Suddenly Seany felt more at ease, like he was right where he was meant to be.

* * *

Letterfrack, Co. Galway

Moe was grinning from ear to ear as she helped Devlin muck the stalls. The interviews were done just in time for that idiot Hugo to show up. He'd seen the last woman leaving and had inquired to Moira about who the woman had been. She'd just shrugged and said, "Business stuff. Now, I've just put the kettle on. Feel free to come in and have a biscuit."

Now he was pestering Michele. Moe had warned her about the little shit, and she was sure Michele could hold her own. She heard her say, "I don't know how things work in Ireland, Mr…I didn't catch your name." He gave it and she continued, "But where I'm from, it is considered the height of rudeness to ask someone how much they get paid. And my assumption is that if you had any credible reason for asking, you'd already know. Now, I'm a little jet lagged, so we're just going to start over and pretend this little dance never happened."

Moe clapped her hand over her mouth as Devlin's brows shot up. Hugo sputtered all the way to Moira's back door, slamming it on his way inside the house. Michele yelled, "Enjoy your cookie!"

Devlin and Moe were leaning against the stall door holding their stomachs as Michele popped her head inside. "I don't think Little Lord Fauntleroy likes me very much."

Devlin said dryly. "His father was English. He's never spent more than a weekend at a time in England, but he plays that side up when he's trying to interrogate. I have to say… I'm starting to realize why you two beat out all of the male applicants. You Yanks don't play around."

"Marine brat and Marine officer," Moe said pointing at herself and Michele. "It's a lifestyle that crushes the weak."

"Aye, herself I can see. But you? You look all sweet and calm. Like that lough when there is no wind. But underneath you can be a tsunami." He looked at Michele, "And not just with Hugo. She lit into one of her riders. An old flame, I suspect."

"Devlin, you little gossip. I am not talking about Sean!" But Michele was already intrigued.

"Sean, is it? I thought it was Seany?" Devlin goaded.

"Oooh, he's Irish? Damn girl, you just got here. You already have an ex-Irishman? I want in! Where are you finding them?"

Devlin looked offended. "Excuse me. I'm single. I think I just suffered an insult."

Michele waved a hand. "Workplace romance. Been there, done that."

The bantering stopped suddenly as Devlin heard raised voices. He ran toward the house, the women trailing behind him.

Moira shouted. "How dare you! You think you're going to find some way to sabotage this for me? Let me tell you something, Hugo. You will never get a blade of grass or a mound of dirt out of this place. When I die, and I'm not planning on it anytime soon, you are not, nor will you ever be, mentioned in my last will and testament. Not a dime. Do you hear me? So, I don't want to see you in that barn ever again. You will park around front, you will ring the doorbell, and you will bloody well wait to be let in the house. If I am not here to answer the doorbell, you will leave!"

"You old bitch. Who the hell do ye think is going to take care of you when you get too old to do it yourself? You've got no one. Your husband left you decades ago and your daughter is six feet under. I'm all you have!"

The anger was rolling off Devlin as he stood in the doorway. Hugo hadn't seen him come in. "I'm going to say this once, you pissy little chancer. You will speak to Moira with a civil tongue and some fecking respect or I'll batter ya to within an inch of your life. And as for who will take care of her, she can bloody well take care of herself. If she needs something, there is not a person within twenty kilometers of this place who wouldn't aid her. The first on that list being me."

Moe chimed in, "And me for as long as I'm here. Hell, even after I will get on a plane if she needs me."

Rory had come in the side door. "And me. I have several tools at my disposal that will remove that foul tongue of yours, so watch it, man."

"So, dear Hugo," Moira said, her eyes burning with emotion, "You can piss off back to Mayo, and wait for an invitation before you come back. I'm not feeling very hospitable in the foreseeable future."

* * *

SEANY WAS SURPRISED to see the crowd at the Donoghue home. Katie's parents were up in years, just like his own grandparents, but they'd always been friends to the O'Brien family, even after Katie had been widowed. Tadgh and Charlie were here with the baby. William was growing like a weed. Brigid and Finn were also in attendance with their three children. Brigid wasn't even showing yet, but he always thought she was rather beautiful when she was pregnant. Her skin was youthful and glowing. He saw a flash of dark hair and Cora slammed into him. Brigid yelled, "Cora, he's still recovering."

Cora started at that. "Oh, sorry Uncle. I forgot. Ye look so strong and healthy."

He bent down, nose to nose. "Flattery will get you everywhere, my girl. Come with me, now, and tell me how you've been." He walked by Katie, who was holding her grandson. He kissed her on the top of the head. "Don't get up, Auntie. Cora's taking care of me."

She dragged him to a chair and made him sit. "I'll get ye some of Katie's warm bread and dip. It's lovely altogether."

Branna and Michael were here as well. Branna was child free. "Where are the babes?" he asked.

"They are at Caitlyn's. The twins love little Estela. Especially Haley. They're in a Barbie doll phase."

"And how is Ian? Growing like a weed? I haven't seen him in a few weeks."

"You should come home. Stay with us. We built that spare room onto the back of the cottage so that people could visit. We even upgraded the sofa bed!" She smiled, and Seany's heart swelled. Had it been almost seven years? Jesus, time flew. Eight years since Branna O'Mara had taken the O'Brien clan by storm. Michael's mate, who'd gone nose to nose with his hard ass brother in a battle for Kelly Cottage. But his twin had been the first to find love, of course. Brigid had always been competitive. And then Patrick had found Caitlyn. Their love story had been easier at the start but hadn't always been perfect. They'd lived through their own hardships. It took the rest of his brothers a little time to catch up, and it had all started with a fiery, raven-haired beauty. The next had been Aidan, then Tadgh, and finally Liam. The rest was history.

He thought about his future and couldn't see it clearly. He couldn't see past the pain and the anger. The guilt. It seemed in this moment like he'd never be happy. Never be whole. All of these children had their fathers. The McBride children… he shook himself, looking up to see Branna watching him. She took his hand. "I know all about being the one left behind, brother. Just promise me that you won't get lost in your grief. Come home and see us, Seany. We'll make a real night of it. Go to Gus's and you can dust off that guitar of yours. What's her name? Dana?"

"No, I gave Dana to Josh. He's been plucking away trying to teach himself. My new one is Scarlett. I haven't broken her in properly."

"Well, then. Perfect time to do it. Michael brought his guitar and Brigid has her fiddle."

Finn popped his head between them. "I've got my drum and Cora has her whistle."

"I don't have my guitar with me. You'll have to play without me."

Katie looked up from the baby, having listened to the back and forth. "I guess you'll be singing then. Tadgh has William's old guitar in the back bedroom. I'm going to have to insist, Seany dear. It's been ages since I've heard you all play together."

Branna shrugged. "Captured. Practice those pipes for Gus's. We'll tell Mom to expect you for Sunday roast."

Dinner was finger foods, and the Donoghues were delighted by the trad session that broke out in their sitting room. Brigid and Cora did a duet, *Sweet Afton.* Seany found himself tearing up as he watched them, one redhead, one with hair as black as the night sky. Brigid played along with her fiddle, and it was a sweet and melancholy tune. They played more lively tunes, and Seany found that he was getting back into sync with his family. They'd always had their music to bind them. After being teased about taking up a second career as a cowboy in Connemara, he delighted them all by singing *The Wild Rover.* That got the group rolling, and next was *The Hills of Connemara*. They were shocked senseless when Finn did a rare bit of vocals and sang *Wearin' the Britches.* A lighthearted instrumental with dark and disturbing lyrics about a man beating his disobedient wife. Brigid cuffed him on the side of the head, which had the entire house booming with rowdy laughter.

Seany sat on the couch, later in the evening, watching as Josh tended to Katie's parents. Katie smiled and met Seany's eyes. "He's a blessing, isn't he?"

"He is. He came along at a time when my older brothers had sort of left me behind. He couldn't be more of a brother to me if he'd been born to it."

Brigid sat, shaking her head at Cora sprawled in Seany's lap, dead to the world. "She's a little big to be rocked to sleep."

Seany kissed her dark head. "Just let me spoil her. She's e'er saving the day and growing up too fast. It's nice when she's like this."

Brigid's eyes welled. "She does love her uncles. We're headed home, though. Finn can take her."

"I'll get her to the car." Seany stood with her in his arms and felt the bite of pain shoot through his shoulder. Finn slid in gracefully and took her, pretending not to notice.

"You have to let yourself heal, Seany. It was no small injury. And your elbow on the other side. Just take it easy," Brigid said.

"I'm not an invalid," he said. Then he apologized. "Sorry, I'm a bit touchy about it I guess. I had PT today and my shoulder is fatigued. I need to head home as well. I have to be in Letterfrack at eleven."

"So, you're doing it. Equine therapy with your Texas lass."

"She's not mine."

His sister's mouth twitched. "If you say so, love."

Seany was opening his car door when he heard Cora yell his name. She was climbing out of the backseat of Finn's car.

"Uncle Sean wait. Mam says you're riding horses. I wanted to know if they let kids ride. I don't want to butt into your therapy. I just mean another time. You've got a friend there. Maybe she could take me for a ride. I love horses. It's so expensive at home because of the tourists. Can you please ask?"

How was he going to tell her no? He wasn't. "I'll ask. I'm not making any promises, okay?" She threw her arms around him. "You better check with your mam and da as well. It's a long drive up there from Doolin."

She waved a hand. "I'll handle them, don't worry on that account." And she looked so much like her grandmother in that moment that he barked out a laugh. "Go, now. They've got to get you all in bed. Ye've got school tomorrow." He waved at his brother-in-law who, having loaded his precious family, drove them home to County Clare. That's when he saw Josh, who'd disappeared early in the evening with Charlie. So, he'd told her. When Tadgh approached Seany's car, he was shaking his head. "That Justine is like a bad penny."

"I know. They shouldn't have given her probation. Josh is scarred for life both physically and mentally. If the roles had been reversed, he'd be doing a year in the gaol. I'm telling you, brother. She's got something ugly brewing. I can't fathom what it is."

Tadgh rubbed the back of his neck. "The worst thing she could do to him, other than hurting his family, is to get him kicked out of Ireland. He'd have nowhere to go."

Seany froze. "How the hell could she do that?"

"I don't know. I'm just thinking out loud. Josh is so worried about it, and I'm afraid of what he said to her when they were on good terms. If it came to that, we'd have to move to the States. There is no way we'd leave him to fend for himself."

"It won't come to that. He's got family here. It will not come to that."

* * *

Letterfrack, Co. Galway

Moe was saddling Skadi when she felt him enter the barn. He wasn't loud, but she sensed him as if he'd shouted his arrival. She didn't meet his eyes. "Moira told me that you chose not to switch instructors. Thank you for being on time. We're going to start today with showing you how to saddle Storm." She pulled a final strap on her saddle, then walked past him. "The tack room is where you get your equipment and return it. Storm is a big horse and you're tall, so I think this saddle will be a good fit."

She patted a cognac colored English saddle. He said, "Why aren't you using your fancy saddle?" She looked at her western saddle, then finally met his eye. "If I'm going to teach you to ride on an English saddle, it's easier for me to use the same. I'm familiar with both styles and Dressage. Skadi will be doing a Dressage demonstration at the open house next weekend."

"Dressage? Oh, the dancing?"

She gave him a small smile. "Sort of. She's magnificent. You should come to the open house. There will be demonstrations and then a barn dance. It's kind of a kick off to the new venture. Breeder and rescue turned into a Therapeutic Riding Center. It's next Sunday and it's open to the public. I think there will be a lot of people there if the weather holds. Do you work on Sundays?"

"No, not yet. Thursday until Saturday. I'm not cleared for the fire brigade for another month. I'm working in the advanced paramedic unit until then."

"That's really great, Sean. You've gone into a noble profession. It seems like a family tradition. Are you the first firefighter slash paramedic?"

"Aye, the first on my father's side. There was a fireman on the Mullen side back about seventy or eighty years ago. Then me." He picked up the saddle.

She put the block she was using next to Storm and Seany snorted. "I don't need a booster."

"Doctor's orders. You have a pre-existing injury and this block will position you up higher so you don't strain your shoulder."

His mouth was tight. She put her hands on her hips. "Do you want to go back to firefighting in a month?" He just glared at her. "I'll take the silence as a yes. Just get on the damn block, Sean."

He was feeling a small strain on his shoulder, but he'd never admit it. And her calling him Sean was making him mental, which was ridiculous. Plenty of people called him Sean. Only family and friends... Dammit. Why had he said that to her?

He walked up the two-tiered block and put the saddle and blanket over the horse's back. He'd gotten to know the horse on Tuesday. He was all business. He didn't nuzzle Seany the way that Skadi did Moe. Hell, that infernal Balor even gave her a nuzzle on occasion. He got off the block and moved it to the side.

"Okay, you want to make sure it's even and centered on the pad or blanket. We want him to be comfortable. Face forward and reach under his belly to grab that girth. That's it. Under the flap and buckle. Now, if this were a horse like Balor, I'd kind of warn him I was going to cinch. Push down on the saddle, pull up on the girth. You don't want to startle a horse that tends toward skittishness or ornery behavior. My dad's Appaloosa needs to be handled carefully. He's a jerk for everyone but Daddy. My horse Artemis is a lady."

"What is your dad's horse's name?" he said, smiling at how engrossed she was in horse talk.

She blushed. "Tear Gas. You don't want to be downwind from him. That's all I'll say on the matter."

Seany chuckled. "I think I understand."

She walked to a wooden stand which was shaped like a horse head. She explained how to hold the reins so that he could command the horse without making him uncomfortable. "As soon as he does what you want, let up on the tension, then return your hands to where you started."

"I have ridden before," he said, a little miffed that she was treating him like a child.

"Which is why you are getting a brief refresher and are actually allowed to ride on the trail next Wednesday. We'll do arena work first, so you and Storm can get used to each other. I've seen you ride, and I know you can do it. Those other guys can't ride until the third week."

"Why aren't they here twice a week?"

"Because your therapy is meant to get you fit for duty. They volunteered to come. We doubled up for you so you could get the green light sooner."

"Was that yer doin', Maureen?" he said softly.

His Irish lilt rolled through her body like warm silk. He rolled the *r* and made her name sound so much better than when anyone else said it. "Ah, no. Moira spoke to your doctor when he sent the health screening. Our schedule is more open since we haven't started the kids' program. She's a great lady. She was just trying to help."

"Well then, I'll have to give her my thanks."

By two hours into the day, Seany was more than a little frustrated. He'd wanted to get out into the mountains, but the red tape of places like this meant he had to have his riding assessed in the arena first. Most of that had been done by Devlin, with Moe only assisting. She was an intern, after all. As he felt the horse under him, a small part of him wanted to make a dash for the gate and fly into the expansive wilderness he knew was mere miles away.

They made their way back to the barn as the other men were leaving. Moe said to Devlin, "I think they are ready for arena work. It was a good day."

Devlin motioned, "This one is ready for a long ride. I've got no reservations. Next Wednesday, take him around the lough.

* * *

Galway City, Galway

Seany liked the men on his shift. The fire brigade was a mixed range of ages, all likable guys. His other paramedic, Joseph, was married with a four-year-old son at home. "You don't seem old enough to have a four year old." He couldn't be more than a year or two older than Seany.

"I'm cursed with a baby face. I'm twenty-seven. I got married at twenty-two, had Joey by twenty-three. My wife, Evie, works reception at the hospital. Have you got a girl?"

He paused. It was just long enough for Joseph to draw a conclusion. "You hesitated. You've got something brewing. Good luck to ye. Having a good woman is the best decision you'll ever make in your life."

"Amen to that," said a voice from the next room. It was Chief Braddock. "Make sure you stock up on the rig supplies for tomorrow. Friday nights are always busy. Fecking college kids."

"Come with me. I'll introduce you to the NHS EMTs. We'll have two staffed ambulances as support until Sunday. It usually slows down by then. This is going to be a lot quieter than what you were used to in Dublin."

"I worked fire brigade and filled in if we were short on the ambulance units. Not very often, though. It was a great station, but this is closer to home."

"Yeah, I heard what happened. Sorry. I guess you won't be with us too long, then. How are the injuries?"

"I get stronger every day. Thanks for asking." No sooner had they walked into the ambulance bay, than the alarms went off.

"Possible carbon monoxide poisoning in Grattan Park. Family of four is waiting in the garden and feeling off. The family hamster is deceased, and the resident Corgi is sluggish and unresponsive."

Seany frowned. That was the housing area where Katie's parents lived. The house number didn't sound right, though. His heart rate started to come down. Katie's household would be three and they didn't own a hamster that he knew of. They grabbed their coats and followed the engine through the city to a stretch of houses between Claddagh and Salthill. His shift had only started a half hour ago, and they already had a call. The fear that he would be bored after working in Dublin started to ease just a bit.

Seany was more than happy to let Joseph drive, as he knew the city like the back of his hand. They cut through some back streets, making it to the scene before the engine. They went directly into the garden around the back of the house.

Seany jumped out of the large ambulance, taking his medical bag with him. He saw two teenagers and a middle-aged couple in the back. The teenage girl was holding her dead hamster, crying and hoping he'd come awake with some fresh air. The brother had the Corgi's head in his lap. Seany sized up the family and immediately went to the side of the petite mother. She was the smallest and more vulnerable. The husband was rubbing her back, and Seany noticed she'd gotten sick in the grass. "Ma'am, I'm Firefighter O'Brien. I'm also a paramedic. I would like to have a look at you, if that's okay?" Seany heard the engine pull up and the firefighters enter the house. He took the woman's blood pressure. Joseph checked the two kids, who were thirteen and fifteen. He looked at the mam. "Does your blood pressure normally run low?"

She nodded. "I have a terrible headache and my stomach is off." She frantically leaned over the patio chair to get sick again.

Her husband said, "We thought it was another migraine until my girl found her hamster dead. Then the dog started stumbling around. We all felt off for the last day or two, but then I started to put the pieces together. Christ. I forgot to put new batteries in the detector. It is likely from the gas furnace. I could have killed the whole family."

"They'll find the source, sir. I promise. And depending on what you have in the house, you should have a few of them scattered about." The NHS ambulances got there right after the engine, and the EMTs were checking the other two in the family. "Which room was the hamster located?"

"My daughter's. The dog sleeps with the lad," he said.

Seany said, "We need to get you all to the hospital. Your size probably helped in your favor, but you've all been exposed." He asked the wife, "Any history of heart disease?" She shook her head. "Smoker? No, that's good. This kind EMT is going to ask you to lie down on the gurney and we'll get some fresh air in your lungs." There were sufficient staff there to take all four. Two in the larger AP unit which Seany had arrived in, as well as the two NHS ambulances. The fire team found the leak and it wasn't from the aging boiler. The new gas cooker had been installed incorrectly. A sub-officer with the firefighter unit assured the family that they'd drop the dog off at the local vet. It, in fact, ended up going in the Chief's car. Braddock had a soft spot for dogs, apparently. The father also managed to pry the hamster away from his sobbing daughter.

"We'll give him a proper burial, love. When everyone gets home. I swear it." Seany's heart squeezed. It was something his father would have said in the same situation. And the thought of his parents made a wave of panic go through him. He was going to inspect everyone's house in the family, and everyone was getting state-of-the-art carbon monoxide and smoke detectors for the next holiday. As a matter of fact, he'd be checking Moira's house, as well as the barn and both sides of that lake cottage. Jesus wept. The older he got, the more stuff he had to worry about.

* * *

THE WEEKEND FLEW by with no serious events after the carbon monoxide poisoning ambulance run. Seany decided that a visit home was overdue. He wouldn't be there for Sunday roast, as he'd promised, but the day before. There was good craic to be found on a Saturday night, and it meant he could see his parents and then head to the grand opening of the Burke Therapeutic Riding Center.

He wasn't going to tell his family about his developing relationship...or whatever the hell it was. He needed to keep it private. The only reason he'd told Josh was because he was his best mate. Everyone needed someone to talk to, and Josh was his someone. It didn't go both ways. Not really. He thought about what Kamala had asked him. *Who do you let comfort you, Junior?* He was starting to understand the importance of that question. Who did Josh let comfort him? His sister? Maybe, but never completely. He kept things from her in order to protect her newfound happiness.

He'd called Josh on his way to the house to see if he wanted to join him for an overnight trip to Doolin. Josh could be packed and ready by the time he was ready to head down to Clare. He could drop him off on the way back up the coast early Sunday morning. He undoubtedly had to work either the ferry or at The Pie Maker.

"I can't, brother. I'm on call for the Lifeboat tonight but give everyone my love. Tell Cora I hope she's dry-land training. Our flip turn session at Leisureland is next weekend."

"Will do. I'll see you in a few."

After a quick stop to grab some clean clothes, he was off in the other direction, back to his native home.

CHAPTER 19

Alanna and Hans weren't able to come to the Monday session because the baby had been up all night, so Moe ran the circle herself. She was not a therapist or trained counselor, so she kept it simple. They went around the group and talked about their week. She was surprised when Seany offered up a small nugget of information. He'd told the group about his transfer, and his first couple of days on the job. It was something, but she suspected that he was doing the bare minimum in order to get the participation trophy. It frustrated her. She tried hard to treat him like everyone else. When it came time to work with the less experienced men, she made the decision to hand Seany off to Devlin as she'd planned and let him take him in a loop around the east pasture. They were fenced and it was an easy ride, but she didn't feel like he was ready to go up into the mountains. This wasn't for sport, and he hadn't made any attempt to bond with his pony.

Seany was gritting his teeth as Moe handed him off to Devlin and went to work with the other men. She all but ignored him. Which begged the question, why the hell was she here in Ireland? Why had she come if she wanted nothing to do with him? Christ, that sounded arrogant, even to his own ears.

He liked Devlin, though. He was a smart, humble man who knew the property and every horse like the back of his hand. He tried to concentrate. Tried to learn from this man who'd worked with horses since he was ten years old. And he tried like hell not to give a second thought to Maureen Rogers.

* * *

Galway City, County Galway

"How was the riding yesterday?" his physical therapist asked. She'd been stretching his shoulder, doing some resistance training.

"It's great, actually. Better than scab picking with some shrink. And Connemara is gorgeous altogether. I hadn't really spent a lot of time in that area. The guys in the group are good sorts. Garda, Coast Guard, and Army. And my sister-in-law's da, who was a Marine in America. Then he told her about delivering Alanna's baby in the backseat.

"You're taking a piss! I always wanted something like that to happen to me. Real superhero stuff." Then he told her about the post-partum shrieking. *Hashtag, he saw my vagina.* By the end of the tale she was doubled over laughing. "So, next time you will go out on the bridle trails and into the park. That's going to be amazing. I'm so jealous, I could spit. I think I need horse therapy."

* * *

Furbogh, Co. Galway

It was late at night when Josh came into the room to find Seany sitting ramrod straight in bed. His eyes were open, but Josh wasn't sure anyone was there. "Seany, buddy, what's up? I heard you yelling."

"He's looking at me. He's telling me with his eyes. He's going to leave and it's my fault. McBride, please. Don't go."

Josh eased over. "Seany, brother, you're talking in your sleep."

As he got closer, he saw that Seany was covered in sweat. Goose bumps covered his arms and chest. "Time to go back to bed, brother. It's okay."

He urged him back down onto the pillow. "Just close your eyes. I'm not going anywhere." Then he sat on an old, crappy easy chair that was next to Seany's bed. "I won't go anywhere."

* * *

Letterfrack, Co. Galway

She wouldn't look at him, and he thought maybe she was feeling a little flustered. Calm, serious Maureen Rogers getting flustered was something to see. Just the thought of her stomping back to her cottage that first day made his loins tighten. *Down boy,* he thought. He couldn't imagine a whole lot of things that would be more uncomfortable than riding a horse with blue balls. She was just so damn beautiful. Some girls lost their luster as they aged. She'd been pretty. Now? She stole his breath, especially as she urged her mount forward and took him out of the barn. She was so natural. Like she and that beautiful white horse were an extension of each other. This was the first time she'd worked with him alone.

He settled in, feeling the horse move smoothly under him. She looked over her shoulder. "When the path widens past the fence, you can come alongside me." Absolutely. Although, the view from behind was spectacular. Better to be next to her where he was forced to pay attention. "How does it feel? He's an easy ride. I took him out last evening, just to get to know him."

"It feels good. He's warm." As he said it, he could see his breath. He had gloves on and so did she. "That coat you're wearing isn't warm enough. I hope you layered."

"I did. I'm going to have to find somewhere to shop. There is not a whole lot around here. I'm usually off Sundays, so maybe I'll drive into Galway. We have a car available if we want it."

"So, your other intern arrived safely, then?"

"Yes, she's a really neat lady. Did some time in the Marines. She went to Colorado State and studied the same thing I did. She actually took a class from Temple Grandin."

When she could tell he didn't know the name, she explained about the famous woman who'd revolutionized the cattle industry. "She's an advocate for people with autism. She has Asperger's. It's a high functioning form of autism. They made a movie about her life." She realized she was rambling. "Anyway, Michele is going to be a real asset for getting this therapy center up and running."

She pointed ahead. "We are going to cross the road, and there is a bridle path the park lets us use. It's wooded for a little ways, then it opens up to a meadow and you can see the mountains."

They were swallowed up by the forest, and Seany just soaked in the crunch of the leaves under the horses' feet. Some of the trees were bare, some not. It smelled good and he found himself truly enjoying it. As she'd said, a few minutes later the path opened up to a wide expanse of park land. He smelled the fresh stream that poured into a small lough. The earth was rocky, but there were boggy patches and dried heather. Skadi stopped, trying to nibble. "Not yet, Skadi. Take us halfway around the lake and you can have a snack."

He smiled at the way she talked to the pony. Gentle and patient. "Will we go up into the mountains?" He looked up at the far away peaks, with their snow caps and evergreen bush.

"Not this time. We'll start out with a loop around the lake. Maybe when it's not quite so chilly."

"It's never truly warm. I mean, we get the occasional heat wave, but nothing like what you're used to."

"Yes, luckily these ponies are hearty. How do you like Storm? Is he warming up to you at all?"

Seany lifted a shoulder. "He's not as sweet as your Skadi, but I like him all the same. He's not ready to give up his secrets."

"Like his rider, " she said absently.

"What does that mean?" he said defensively.

She didn't rise to meet his temper. She said calmly, "I mean during the introduction you held back. That's all."

"Excuse me if I don't feel the need to get all touchy feely with a bunch of strangers. I'm here to ride."

"This is more than just riding. At least it can be if you give it a chance, Sean."

"And stop with the Sean!" he was actually getting pissed off.

"Just enjoy your ride. Don't blow a gasket just because you don't like hearing the truth. Watch the puddle, here. Some horses don't like puddles."

She went around it, so he did as well. Storm made a grunting noise, pushing air out of his nose. "What's that supposed to mean?" he asked dryly.

Moe grinned, getting the ride back on track before Seany had a tantrum and got nothing out of it. "So, Alanna tells me she has three kids? It's crazy to think about when I remember them together in North Carolina. They work fast. A baby every other year."

"Aye, especially fast with Keegan. She dropped the lad in the backseat before we got to the hospital."

Moe halted her horse, jaw dropped. "I'm sorry. Did you just say she had him in your car?"

"No, Aidan's car. Josh was driving until things were past the point of no return. Then he pulled over and I got in back with her. She went fast. My mother was on speaker, luckily, because the cord was wrapped around his neck."

"You delivered Alanna's baby?" she asked, loudly enough that Skadi snorted and shifted nervously. She rubbed her neck absently as she shook her head. She repeated, "You delivered your nephew in the backseat of a car?"

"Aye, I did. Don't sound so surprised. I am a paramedic."

She met his eyes, which was rare today. "What was it like? I mean, wow. It must have been...magic."

He paused at that, stopping the glib comment that he'd almost let fly. "It was. She was brilliant. Tough as nails, really. She pushed him into the world, and he was there in my palms, the cord still attached. It was miraculous. I mean, you can learn about a thing, but to see it is something else altogether. I kind of understand the appeal for my mother."

She nodded, not feeling the need to say anything else, then she urged Skadi forward. They rode in silence again, because nature had its own music. The only thing she said was, "I can't wait to see this in the spring and the full bloom of summer. I've heard about the heather."

He watched her, just far enough back to see her face scan the landscape. He remembered the feel of her as he'd pulled her back against him. No, she wasn't the girl he'd loved so long ago. She was so much more.

They made their way halfway around the lough, and she stopped. "We can rest a while. Moira packed a lunch."

She took out a rolled-up blanket, spread it on the pebbly shore of the lough, and took out a bundle from her saddle bag.

"Do you need help?" she said, but he was already off the horse and leading him to a wooden post that was obviously made to tie off horses.

"It's nice that she lives next to the park. Good bridle trails are like gold in her business, I'd wager."

She nodded and said, "Yes. She's doing a good thing. She could retire very comfortably if she just sold those horses to other breeders. Connemaras are very valuable ponies and she's a very well-respected breeder. Excellent stock. Her studs are champions."

"Not a bad job, either. Too bad they take the fun out of the process."

She smirked, but he also saw a blush come to her cheeks. "Come have some tea and other things. She's been baking. I don't know what some of this stuff is, but it looks good."

He sat on the blanket and glanced at the selection. "Barmbrack, bridies, and soda farls. She's got some lemon curd and clotted cream. Holy Bride, this looks good. It's like being home."

She smiled at that. "I'm going to put on weight living at her house. Although, baling wet hay and fixing a smashed fence, on top of all of my other duties, is certainly burning the calories. So, a bridie is what, exactly? I can sort of tell what the other things are, but this is new."

"It's a hand pie stuffed with savory things. Meat, potatoes, peas, sometimes cheese. That's traditional. You'll see curry ones and vegetarian ones as well."

"Hmph, Moira would never insult me with a vegetarian dish. Texans like their beef."

"You don't sound different having been there for six years."

"I think you form your speech patterns earlier than sixteen. That's not to say when I get around my family the speech doesn't take on a little drawl," she said slowly. He just chuckled as he poured tea out of a thermos.

"What did you mean when you said Storm was like his rider?" he asked, picking at his soda bread.

She chewed, thinking about how to play this. "I don't want to argue with you. If you aren't ready or willing, then there is no point beating a dead horse. No pun intended."

"Ready or willing? For what?" he asked, letting irritation creep back into his voice.

She met his eyes, showing some steel. "To take this seriously."

"Why? Because I wouldn't bare my soul in the circle of love?"

She shot to her feet. "Jesus, when did you get so arrogant?"

"I don't know, Maureen. Maybe during the last six years when you refused to speak to me?" he said, getting to his feet.

She ignored the gibe, refusing to be derailed from the subject at hand. "You cheapen this whole thing by acting like you're above it. Jesus, the look on Hans's face." She shook her head, and the look of genuine disappointment in her eyes was enough to make him go apeshit. But she wasn't done. "The stuff Alanna said. Didn't that touch anything in you, Sean? Have you gotten so cold? Didn't it occur to you that they were there for you? I mean, Hans has how many days with Alanna and the baby before he flies back to Brazil? And he's driving two hours one way to come to therapy when he's likely put those demons to rest years ago. He came to support you and her. She'd just had a baby a week earlier and she came here for an hour. She spent four hours in the car with a newborn to come here for an hour. For you!"

"I don't need anyone's help or pity!"

She snorted. "Where have I heard that before? Jesus, you should move to America and join the Marines. Hans lost his best friend. His comrade. Brian O'Mara died in his arms. He revisited that little party for you! And you just gloss over your experience with some crap about an injury."

"I talked about my first shift. I talked about the transfer."

"But you didn't talk about why you are here, Sean. This was a mistake. This is obviously personal, and I should have never agreed to it. I should put you with Michele one-on-one and take myself out of the situation."

"Personal? Well, you want to get personal, Maureen? What about you, you bloody hypocrite? You started to say something after the bit about your father and family. You started to share something and backed out."

She gritted her teeth and hissed at him, "I'm not in therapy. Rule number one. Don't make it about you. It's about the person who is there for help. My personal baggage doesn't matter. Alanna only shared as much as she did to try and break through that armor you have on, because you were there when she was kidnapped. If the group would have all been strangers, she'd have never gone there."

"Well, then. If you think I'm going to open a vein, Maureen Rogers, you better be willing to do the same. We aren't strangers. And despite my impulse to deny it, it is personal. You show me yours and I'll show you mine."

She clenched her jaw, ready to blow her top. Then she swallowed, took a deep breath and leveled her eyes on him. "Are you going to eat, or do you want to ride back?"

He pointed. "Oh, no you don't. I have four hours and we've been at this for…" he looked at his watch. "Seventy-eight minutes. It's a half-hour ride back to the barn. You want me to submit to this head shrinking by horse, then I want answers."

She cocked her head, and the calm that had come over her made him want to dunk her in the lough. "Regarding?"

"Why did you do it? Why cut off all contact? We could have stayed friends. You scraped me off your shoe like a bad smell. Closed off your email and social media like I was some sort of stalker. Why? And why come at all? What the hell am I to you? A free plane ticket? God knows you didn't stick around after you'd kept your end of the bargain." That one stung, and she lost that calm demeanor. Grey eyes met blue and she unexpectedly launched herself at him. She shoved him. When he barely budged, she growled.

"You are such an idiot. You don't know anything!"

"Then tell me. I deserve this from you," he said. His voice was deep, and it was not a request.

"You have no idea what that took out of me." She was shaking, he saw it. "You moved on with things, no doubt. With your charm and good looks. That sacrifice for my family took something from me that you can't even fathom. Then I threw myself into my schoolwork and helped take care of my siblings. I was a second mother to my siblings at sixteen because my dad's seizures just kept getting worse with stress. He was depressed, and my mother had him back and forth to Houston three times a week to the VA. You have no idea what my life was like, so don't judge me, Sean. Don't you dare! I was fifteen when we met. I'd never even held a boy's hand. And you came along and suddenly I felt beautiful and cherished and a sort of..." She shook her head.

"Go on. Don't stop. Make me understand. A sort of what?"

She looked at him, and he saw her tears. But he would have this from her first. "Sensuality...I guess. You brought me to life and then you were gone. My parents saw it. They knew I wasn't old enough to feel what I was feeling. They weren't going to let me visit or let you come there to stay. They wore me down." Her voice was hoarse. "They teamed up and wore me down. They made me feel like a lovesick puppy and convinced me that I needed to do what I did. And you know what?" She let out a little laugh. "They were right. I was too young. We couldn't be friends. It was past that for me. I'm not like you, Sean." He tensed his jaw at her continued use of *Sean*. "You would have eventually moved on with some hot little village girl and it would have broken me. I am not like you."

He narrowed his eyes. "Do you think I let you go so easily? I spent the last few years trying to paper over your memory with other women." She winced, "Yes, it stings. I won't believe you never had someone after me. You're twenty-two years old, Maureen. The thought of you with other men makes me mental. And those women were like a stiff drink. They numbed the ache for a while, then nothing. I felt nothing."

"I don't want to hear this. I can't. I shouldn't have come. I should have taken some internship in Texas. This was so stupid!" She got on her knees on the blanket, furiously packing up the ruined picnic. The ruined ride. The ruined everything.

"Stop. Moe, stop!" He was next to her and she wouldn't look at him. The blood pounded in his ears. He pulled her up by the elbows. "Look at me. Look me in the eye before you tuck tail and run again." His accent was the thickest she'd ever heard it. A man's voice. A man's anger. She was tight against his chest. "Are ye going to run again, lass? Your mam and da aren't here to use as an excuse." He ground out the words out, and she looked at him. Then at his mouth. That was all it took. His hands were in her hair and he kissed her. A harsh, punishing kiss at first touch. But she felt a tremor go through his whole body, and he softened. Tasted. He moaned and broke the kiss. "You taste the same. Exactly the same." Then he slanted his mouth over hers and she slumped in his arms, weak at the core of herself. He didn't kiss the same. Holy hell.

CHAPTER 20

Holy hell. Seany 2.0 knew how to kiss a woman. Not a moment of hesitation. It miffed her, the effect he had on her. How many women had he bedded in order to perfect his moves? She dug her hands in his hair and he growled, pulling her hips into his. He was hard. A thick rope of arousal that scared and exhilarated her. His hips jerked away with a hiss. He pulled his mouth away, but he kept her right where she was; their mouths hovering, their breath mingling.

Seany said, "You're not leaving and you're not swapping with another instructor. Your ass is mine two days a week for the next month and a half." He was as breathless as she was, which was something. He gave her hair a measured tug and her neck arched. She throbbed between her thighs at the show of dominance. "Do you hear me, Maureen? You'll stay and see this through."

He stood, not trying to hide his arousal, thick and pressing against his jeans. He took her hand, helping her off her knees. Then he dipped his head and gave her a different sort of kiss. Lazy and thorough. "And as for this," he said huskily. "it's your choice, Maureen. Before you start something, make sure you mean it."

Seany had to put some distance between them. He hadn't meant to kiss her. And once he'd done it, he hadn't wanted to stop. *Mine.* The word pounded through his body like a war cry. When he'd pulled away, the sight of her almost had him going in for round two. She was flushed, and her grey eyes weren't calm or serious. They were stirring with passion and arousal. Her mouth was pink and wet from his kisses. His cock was throbbing to get into her. She hadn't denied that there had been lovers in her past. He wanted to roger her until he erased any trace of another man. He went to the edge of the lough, threw his coat off, squatted, and began splashing cold water on his face. "Fuck, that's cold." He murmured the words, then ran his cold, wet hands through his hair.

He turned and she had a dry cloth. Instead of just handing it to him, she dried his chin and then his hands like a child. She paused, running her thumb over the red burns that had started to scar over. The tilapia skins had done a lot, but he'd be marked forever by that awful day. A tear fell on his forearm as she bent and kissed the marred skin. Then she looked up at him. "I'll see it through."

* * *

THEY TOOK their time going back to the barn, not ready to have the privacy end. He pulled off his jumper, making her wear it under her coat. He needed to cool down before they got back, anyway. He'd have been better off dipping his cock in that cold water. Once they were back to the stables, they cooled the horses down by brushing them. He watched as Storm nuzzled Skadi. Moe met his eyes and gave him that sweet, small little smile of hers. When they finished, she noticed Michele had come into the barn.

Seany's back was to Michele and she mouthed to Moe with a look of incredulity on her face. *OH MY GOD.* Moe gave her a murderous look which made Seany turn around.

Moe cleared her throat. "Sean, this is Michele. She's the intern from Colorado State that I told you about."

Seany went to her, "Maureen has been telling me about how you've impressed everyone. And a Marine. No doubt you've had a lot to talk about." He smiled warmly at her, and Moe could tell Michele wasn't immune to him, despite being twenty years his senior.

Michele said, "Well, I'm glad you decided to give equine therapy a try. I worked with a veteran group in Colorado. I think they got a lot out of it." He gave Moe a sideways glance and she returned it with a smug one that said, *See, I told you so.*

Michele left to go help Devlin move some of the horses in from the pasture before the temperature dropped. Seany returned to Storm, jealous he'd been pushing his muzzle into Moe's palm. "Any love for me, lad?" Storm just grumbled and turned away. "Why does this horse hate me?"

"You're confusing hate with indifference. You're indifferent to him and he's likewise to you. He wants to be bromanced."

"A. That's not a thing. B. I'm not groveling to him."

"Both of you have the same problem. You're used to being worshipped. Try earning it," she said smoothly, walking Skadi into her stall. She fed her some fresh hay and took a treat out of her pocket.

"Hey, give me one of those! You're bribing her with treats! I want in!" He laughed as she tried to slip by him. He pinned her to the stall door beside Skadi's. "You cheated." He slipped a hand in her coat pocket, taking out a piece of carrot. "You're shameless, woman. You told me I shouldn't feed him."

"Not unless I say you can, and when he's done a good job. He didn't buck you off into the lake, so I'd say he earned it. Flatten your palm." He did, and Storm gummed his hand, taking the treat. Then he turned away again and heard Moe laughing.

"It's going to take more than a piece of carrot." She took Storm's reins, led him into the stall, then took off his bridle. "Good boy, Storm. You did well today," she said with genuine affection. He nuzzled her and she kissed him on the nose. Then she smugly closed the door.

Moira appeared in the barn. "Sean, love. How was your ride?"

He said, "It was gorgeous altogether. I'm rather fond of your park. Ye have a lot more trees up here than in Clare, where I grew up. It's a nice bit of ground."

She smiled at that. "It is. Stay for an early dinner. We rise early, here, so we eat early. Maureen can drive you into town for a pint and pick up some feed. I called ahead."

It wasn't a request. Seany had been around strong-willed women enough to recognize when he was being given a direct order. "That would be grand. Thank you, Moira."

Moira said, "I'm afraid there is nowhere in town to get a warmer coat. Ye can borrow one until you have time to run into Galway."

Moe blushed, knowing that Moira had noticed the humongous sweater she was wearing. "Thanks. This barn coat gets me through the winter at home. I wasn't really thinking. I just need to wash up before we drive into town."

"I can drive," Seany said. "I've seen the Yanks on the road every day since I was old enough to see over the dash. Ye don't do so well on these narrow roads."

Moira laughed, waving them off as she headed back for the house. "Dinner is in three hours. Take your time."

Seany said, "I'll drive you to the cottage. I'd like to clean up as well. I smell like horse."

"Get used to the smell if you are going to be here twice a week for the next six weeks." They took his car to her cottage and suddenly her heart was pounding. "It's only ten minutes to the feed store and back. I think there is a pub in town."

He turned off the car and looked at her. "I don't want a pint just now." Her eyes flared, but she didn't look away as she nodded. Then she opened the door, met him in front of the car, and took his hand. He hadn't paid attention the first time. Not really. The cabin was two sided. A unit on each side. He wondered why they hadn't put Michele there and he asked.

"She's helping with a lot of the admin type stuff. Moira has a guest efficiency attached to the main house. I liked it out here, so..."

They went into her side of the cottage and he was enveloped with a condensed version of her scent. Shampoo, soap, and woman. He was wondering if this was a good idea. He'd told her it was her choice. "Maureen, there is no expectation..." He didn't finish the sentence because she took his face in her hands and brought her mouth up to his. He wrapped his arms around her and pulled her to him. Just like that, heat burned anew. He took his time, exploring not just her mouth, but her body. "You feel different," he said. He ran his hands over her hips, then back up, letting his thumbs just graze the side of her breast. She blushed and she trembled a bit.

"I'm sure you were expecting that slim teenager you remembered."

"Aye, I was," he said. She stiffened, withdrawing from him in a way that wasn't physical. He narrowed his eyes. "Imagine my surprise when a woman stood where the girl had been. It shook me to my bones. I won't lie. It's why I said Moe was a girl's name. It wasn't meant to insult you. I remember Moe as a quiet, shy, young girl on the cusp of adulthood. All long, thin limbs and..." He ran his hands down the same path again and groaned. "Fewer curves. Christ, woman. I can't believe the feel of you. I dreamed of you, so often. I'd wake with my heart in my throat and my balls aching. Not knowing anything but that small taste of heaven. That last night when you let go in my arms. And now I'm not a boy anymore, and I want you just as bad. Worse, even. Much, much worse." He kissed her again, pulling her hips up and in, so that he felt her flat stomach and heated core against his cock. "Tell me to stop, Maureen. Say it and I'll go. Or I'll stay and go jump in the feckin' lough to cool off."

She was nuts. What was she doing? But he needed her. She felt it as easily as she felt his arousal. He was in a lot of pain, and she wanted him. She'd always wanted him. He was right. She wasn't a girl anymore. "I don't want you to stop, Sean."

"Call me Seany. Say it." He bit the words out as he covered her neck with hot kisses. She moaned his name and it made him crazy. He pulled her coat off, then his. Next came his jumper off her body. She was wearing a t-shirt that said *Ride it Like You Stole It.* Absolutely. A rodeo turn of phrase, but all he could think about was Maureen astride him. He scooped her up in his arms and carried her to the bed. Then he was on top of her, stretching across her body as he stared into her eyes. "You can change your mind, Moe." The sound of that endearment on his lips made up her mind.

"I'm not going to change my mind."

He eased down on top of her, cradling himself between her thighs. No need to rush things. Moira had given them plenty of rope to hang themselves with, and she'd done it with a knowing twinkle in her eye. "Let me taste your mouth, a chuisle."

She arched up and he took her mouth, pressing his hips into her. She whimpered against his lips. He put a hand at the nape of her neck and slid his tongue deep, rolling his hips and moaning as she ran her hands under his shirt.

Moe couldn't believe the feel of his muscled back. Smooth and sculpted. He let her take his shirt off and then she just stared at him. "You're beautiful. You always were, but you don't feel the same either. You're beautiful," she repeated.

He raised up the hem of her t-shirt as he feathered kisses along her stomach and up her rib cage, sipping and then nipping with his teeth. Taking his time as he tasted her skin. Then he slid the shirt over her head. Her bra was simple cotton, but it clasped in the front. His hands shook a little as he undid the clasp. This was definitely not the Moe he remembered. He just stared like an idiot.

"Is something wrong?" she asked.

He fingered the shark tooth necklace he'd made her seven years ago. They'd found it on the beach, and he'd attached it with wire and a leather cord. Now it fell between her breasts, warm from her skin. "You still have it." His words were soft, then his eyes roamed over her breasts. She tried to cover up and he pinned her wrists to the bed. "Don't you dare. You are going to let me look my fill, Maureen Rogers. I've been dreaming about these ever since I first saw you bouncing around on that damn thoroughbred." She squealed as she tried to free herself. But when he let go, it was only to cup one breast in his big palm. Her hips jerked against his cock. He took a nipple in his mouth, and she bowed off the bed, moaning as he took a deep pull on it. He looked up at her, a devilish grin on his face. "Some things haven't changed." Then he moved to the other side. Her breasts were so sensitive, it drove him mad. He knew if he shed her knickers right now, she'd be wet for him. She was close to coming already. He licked and pulled as he felt her hips roll under him, mimicking the act that would have him seated deep inside her.

He was raw and hungry. "I can't wait. I'm going to disgrace myself all over my trousers if I don't get inside you soon, lass. I've got condoms in the car somewhere, I think."

Oh, that was a cheery thought. Condoms in the car in case he hooked up on the go. She said softly, "I'm on the pill. It's okay."

A strange look flickered across his face and then it was gone. He kissed her deeply before going for her jeans. He peeled them off her like a pro. He slid her panties down a little slower, taking in every inch of her. She fought the urge to grab the blanket and cover herself. And suddenly it wasn't so strange…because of what she saw in his eyes. He thought she was beautiful.

Seany meant to go slow, but the sight of her just slayed him. He saw uncertainty at first, but then smoldering desire as she laid back on the pillow. He leaned over her and kissed her mouth. Then he ran a palm up the inside of her thigh. Her skin was smooth and soft against the rough skin of his palm. Then he slid his hand further, right where she needed him. She hissed as he made contact with a whole lot of buttery silk. He lost his bloody mind. He unzipped his jeans, freeing his cock, and wriggled out of them as he made his way between her legs. "I really can't wait. You are exquisite. You feel like warm silk, mo chuisle. I need inside you." He kissed his way down her neck to the warm spot between her breasts. He felt her heart beating like mad. He felt the slickness of her desire and had to have her. Now.

She gripped his biceps, breaking their kiss to put her face in his neck. He slid his cock inside her to the hilt, and her nails bit into his arms as she tensed all over. He stopped immediately. She was rigid under him and so tight it was almost painful. Too tight. Something was wrong. And oh, God. He really hoped it wasn't what he thought it was.

She gasped for air right after he'd entered her, just one gulp and then she exhaled. She said, "I'm okay. Don't stop." He pulled her face away from his neck and looked at the tension in her face. Pain. She was in pain, while he was buried to his balls in her body. He withdrew slowly. So carefully. Although, he'd already done the damage. She tried not to show her discomfort.

When he withdrew all the way, she looked puzzled. "What's wrong?" He put his forehead to hers, kissing her between the brows. Then a soft brush of the lips. After that, he pulled the covers between them and sat on the edge of the bed. "What did I do?" she asked, and it squeezed his heart.

He shook his head. Staring down at his cock and the evidence of her lost virginity. Holy God, what had he done? He hadn't even gone slowly. He grabbed his jeans as he stood, saying, "I need a minute. Don't get up." His voice was hoarse with emotion. Then he closed the bathroom door. She could hear the sink running, then the buckle of his leather belt as he put his pants back on. She sat up, pulling her knees to herself. She could guess why he was so rattled, but in her defense, he'd never asked.

He came out, looking like delicious sin, and the throb started between her thighs again. "Why did you stop?"

He ran a hand over his face. "Why do you think, Moe? Jesus Christ, woman. Why didn't you tell me? You said you were on the pill."

"I am on the pill." She said it so calmly that he narrowed his eyes at her.

"A lie by omission is still a lie. When I said that I knew there had been other men for you, you didn't contradict me."

"Like I was going to after you bragged about how many women you'd been with? And I have dated. I even had a boyfriend for a little while. It just didn't get that far. I didn't want him like that."

"You should have told me."

"Why? Why does it matter if you were my first?"

He said tightly, "I would have done things differently, or not at all."

She stood, blanket held up to her naked body like a goddess. Hair a mess because he'd just been inside her. His cock was on fire. That's when her tone got steely. "You'd have done things differently? Oh, so you didn't leave the other women completely unsatisfied and sexually frustrated? How nice for them. You just saved the budget menu for me? Thanks. You can leave now. I'd like to say it's been a pleasure, but," And the infernal woman just shrugged at him.

He narrowed his eyes, and that was the only warning she had before he pounced. He was on her in a flash, pinning her to the bed. He kissed the hell out of her, "Don't push me, Moe." But even as he said it, ego demanded he make her scream his name while she came. He kissed his way down to her breast, cupping her sex with his big hand. "Spread your legs. Let me feel you." His words were guttural, and she moaned as he slid a finger through her wet heat. He latched on to her breast as he found the sensitive spot and traced small circles around the center of her arousal.

Moe wasn't going to stop him. Maybe if she got him worked up enough, they'd make it back to where they'd been. That initial thrust had hurt, yes. But it had also been wonderful. It was everything she'd waited for. Why she'd never been able to be with someone else. She wanted him, and this had been just about perfect. It couldn't be over.

He teased her sex as he suckled her, and she felt that familiar climb. The moment right before he made her explode. "Seany," she shook her head back and forth, not able to handle the feelings he evoked in her. But wanting them all the same. She heard his voice, words she couldn't understand. *His native tongue,* she thought. He was crooning to her in Gaelic. And that did it.

Seany slid a finger deep inside her as she started to climax. The pulses of her orgasm gripping him as he watched her face. Her eyes were unfocused, and she opened her mouth on a moan. He kissed her, swallowing her cries and whimpers as he worked his hand against her. He was so close to spilling himself in his jeans, he shook with the effort of holding back.

She was exquisite. She sighed against his mouth as he finally pulled his hand from her body. He squeezed her hip, then stood. He slid his t-shirt over his head. His face darkened as he saw the blood on the inside of her thighs. She pulled the blanket over herself. He said, "I'll give you some privacy. Then we need to talk." He took his coat off the floor, walking out the front door.

She dressed after washing up, loving the feel of her sensitive skin.

But it hadn't been enough. For her, but especially for him. He hadn't even let her relieve him. He had to be hurting. She slid her coat on and walked out to find him sitting on the small picnic table. He dwarfed the thing, but he made room for her as he stared out at the lake. She started to explain to him. To try to make him understand. But he spoke first and shocked the hell out of her.

"Marry me," he said, finally looking away from the placid lough. His eyes were filled with emotion, but not the right emotion. Guilt. She saw guilt, and it made her a little angry. She understood him. He'd always been an honorable, stand-up guy. More arrogant now, maybe, but still good to his core. She actually let a bitter laugh escape and he stiffened. "I'm serious."

She stopped smiling. "I know you are. I'm sorry, but it's absurd. You don't want to marry me, Seany. You didn't even like me a few hours ago."

"You are so wrong about that. I don't even know where to start." His voice was so serious that it made her throat seize up. She put her mouth against his shoulder.

"You can't marry someone out of guilt. Even if you like them. And I would never let someone marry me because of it. Don't take this away from me. I wanted this. You know that. You felt how much I wanted you."

"I know you did, but it should have been different. We should have waited. I mean, I can't even say I'm upset you've never been with anyone else. I'd be lying if I said it. But it shouldn't have happened like this. I threw you down and ripped your jeans off like a barbarian."

"I like you when you're acting like a barbarian. And we didn't have to stop. We don't have to, even now. We can go right back into that cabin and make love, Seany."

He closed his eyes, as if pained. "That sounds incredible, but it's too soon. I should have slowed down. I told myself after the ride today that I would. I just needed you so desperately." The peace and warmth he'd felt with Moe in his arms was enough to make him forget everything else. He'd just needed her. It was that simple.

She put her lips to his temple. "And you have me. All of me. You don't need to marry me to have it."

"I would. I'd take you home and marry you tomorrow if I thought you'd agree to it."

She said, "But not for the right reasons. So, I'm afraid I'm going to have to turn you down. And I'm doing it because of how I feel about you. I don't want you on those terms. If we need to take it slower, then we'll do it. But I'd be remiss if I didn't point out the fact that the deed has technically already been done."

He put his face in his hands. "You should have told me, Maureen." He shook himself. "Hell woman, what's it to be? Moe or Maureen? I'm too confused to decide."

"I like when you call me Maureen. It's probably the sexy accent. You roll your *r*s and it curls my toes." His heart warmed as he watched her cheeks color, like she'd revealed more than she should.

He smiled at that. "Sexy, eh?" He pulled her across his lap. "And how about when I say *a muirnín,*" She just gave him a small smile, but her eyes burned. He took her mouth softly. "I love your smile. I've seen it in my dreams so many times." Her eyes teared up, and he kissed them, tasting the saltiness. "Don't cry, darlin'. Please. I can't bear it."

"I'm sorry I goaded you into..." She searched for the word. She closed her eyes and said, "Servicing me. That wasn't what I intended." He gave her a doubting look. "I mean, it's not all I intended. I just wanted you back. I want to finish what we started. It was a terrible thing to say to you. I'm sorry. I have no right to be jealous about other women."

She wouldn't look at him. He lifted her chin. "And are you jealous?"

She gave him a dry look. "That's a silly question given how fast I went bitch on you." He smiled, a look of pure male satisfaction on his face.

She swallowed hard, unable to stop more tears from escaping the corners of her eyes. "I'm sorry I hurt you, Seany. I mean about what happened six years ago. I'm so sorry." They'd tried for almost a year to make it work, and then she'd just ended it. That year apart had been painful, but nothing compared to the six years following, when she'd cut him out of her life completely.

"It's in the past. Let's just take it one day at a time," he said sadly. "Let's go for a drive. We'll get the feed and you can show me around."

"I'd like that," she said.

"And I'd like to meet you in Galway when you come shopping. You can even come to my cottage. You've met Josh. He lives with me. Then we can go into Galway together."

She took in his face like she was memorizing it. "It's a deal."

"I'm sorry I hurt you too, Maureen." He rubbed a hand over her belly and her body rolled before she could stop it. "Despite that, I am ready to drag you back into that cottage. The way you rouse to me," he shook his head. He leaned down and rubbed his mouth over hers so tenderly, it broke her heart.

She said, "How about we just go back in there and let me take care of your problem? You have to be hurting…and I'm not ignorant about what to do."

His cock jerked, absolutely on board with Plan B. "No, love. He's in the penalty box. I'm hurting, but I'll live. Some things are worth waiting for."

She raised her head up and caught his mouth. Just needing to be close to him again. She'd never had this. She'd never let herself have it. But she'd gone on the pill a week after she got back to Texas because she promised herself that if she ever had the chance to have it with Seany, she was going to take it.

He cradled her head in the crook of his elbow, fusing his mouth with hers. He drank her in, savoring her heat and tasting passion. They were out in the open, which is the only reason he'd allowed himself another small taste of heaven.

* * *

THE FEED WASN'T MUCH, because it was specialty food for the coming foal. Seany put it in the boot, then sat in the driver's seat. "So, what is there to do in Letterfrack?"

"We were doing it. Then you ran out of my cottage," Moe said so calmly that Seany choked on his own laugh.

Coughing, he tossed the invoice for the feed at her. "That's enough cheek out of you, Miss."

She was laughing softly, because that's how she showed her emotion most times. "I'm only half kidding. There is almost nothing here. A pub with seafood about two minutes away, but if we want a coffee shop or tea house, Clifden is fifteen minutes."

He thought for a minute and said, "Let's just go to the beach. There is a cove right near here, I think. You loved the beach if memory serves."

"I did. I still do. We drive to Galveston a lot at home. It's not too far from Magnolia," she said. "The beach is just what I need. I've been so busy I haven't had time. Lettergesh has public parking and it's about fifteen minutes the other way. We have time if we go now."

"Aye, I know. My brother is in the Coast Guard and Josh is with the Royal National Lifeboat," he said. "We had a bit of action up this way and there were search crews all over these waters." He started driving and he told her the tale of two ferry boats crashing near Galway Bay. About Josh rescuing Madeline, and with Cora's help, eventually finding a little Welsh boy who had drifted into a sea cave off the coast of Ballyconneely.

Moe listened to the story and could scarcely believe it, but she could tell that he was serious. She remembered him telling her about his little niece's gifts when they were younger. "She was only four or five when you told me about her. It seems she didn't grow out of it."

"No, she hasn't. Her gifts have developed, in fact. And her father's bloodline is the source. He'd kept it quiet. Had been taught to conceal it from a young age. His parents actually had him hypnotized and exposed him to doctors doing aversion therapy to try and train him to suppress the gifts. He hadn't been but a small child at the time. Secrets like that get buried when you're dealing with young kids. My sister was fit to be tied, though. He essentially lied to her."

"If they used pain as the aversion technique, I hope she understands now. And even adults bury unpleasant memories. It's in our nature to suppress unpleasantness."

"Yes, I suppose it is. I know you were disappointed in me for not sharing the other day," he said.

She turned to him, and he was staring at the road, not meeting her eyes. "I'm sorry. I shouldn't have pushed you."

He said nothing for a moment, then he said, "Hans is over a decade away from that tragic event. Even the other men were six months to a year distant from the events that led them to your barn. I just buried my friend. The burns are still peeling and raw. I'm still raw."

"I understand," she said. Then she put her hand on his arm as he parked the car. "I will not push you, Seany. Well…I might. But not to the degree that I did today. I know the facts, but I don't know what you went through. I don't know what's in your mind and heart. If you don't want to tell me or Alanna or anyone else in that group, then it is your choice." She paused. "But maybe you could tell Storm." He looked at her to see if she was kidding. "I'm serious. You can talk to him because he's not going to tell anyone. And even if you don't do it with words, you can do it with your body and your heart. Learn how to take care of him, how to show him your loyalty and affection. Spend time alone with him. There is a reason so many people have emotional support dogs. It's unconditional."

"I'll think about it," was all he said. Then they walked to the beach path and onto the beach. "This is gorgeous, isn't it?" Seany said, taking in the scenery. "Look at the mountain range off in the distance."

Moe burrowed into Seany's sweater and the oversized coat that Devlin had lent her. "It's beautiful. This was a really good idea. Now that I know where this is, I'll come more often."

Seany took her hand as they walked, a peaceful silence between them as they listened to the waves crest over the rocky formations and felt the ebb and flow of the cold water under their feet. He thought again about what had passed between them in that small cottage. He'd moved beyond the initial self-loathing that had come in the wake of his realization. She'd been more than willing, and that was the heart of the matter. She'd waited. She'd managed to get through her last two years of high school and four years of college with her virginity still intact. But after one afternoon alone with him, she'd offered herself freely.

She thought the matter had been settled, but it wasn't. In the last week he'd joked about marriage both with Kamala and Josh of all people. Did he want to get married? If you'd asked him a few months ago, hell, even a day ago, he would have said no. He stopped walking and pulled Maureen to him without hesitation or invitation. She yielded to him so sweetly it caused him to moan against her mouth. Not just from arousal, but from a well of emotion that had him aching to be close to her. Maureen was here. It was hard to even wrap his head around. But for how long?

CHAPTER 21

Seany was enjoying dinner immensely. Moira was a sharp, witty woman who seemed younger than her years. She didn't dress like a seventy-year-old. She was wearing jeans and a crew neck sweatshirt. Devlin was a good chap and obviously very loyal to the landowner as well as the land. He loved Moira like a mother. Rory, he determined early on, had an eye for Maureen. The interesting thing about it was that everyone saw it but Maureen. It wasn't in leering glances or suggestive comments. It was in the way he hung on her every word. Cherished her every sweet smile. Seany understood completely. He wondered about the ex-boyfriend she mentioned. Some feckin' cowboy, no doubt.

"So, Seany without the Y, when do you start work again?" Rory said, and there was no calculation in his voice. He was a nice guy, and he reminded him a little of Josh, minus the haunted eyes.

"Tomorrow, thank the Virgin. I'll be on duty until Saturday afternoon," he said.

"Is it true you take turns cooking for your shift?" Michele asked the question this time. "I think I need to marry a fireman. I hate cooking."

"Aye, we rotate cooking and cleaning up. I'll scout the station for prospective suitors and compile a list for you." He winked at her and she laughed.

"I like this guy. Keep him around. How did you like Storm?"

"He was easy to ride, to be sure. Not sure he's sold on me. Apparently, I need to talk to him." He eyed Maureen, who just grinned when Michele and Devlin both agreed wholeheartedly. "Well, now. This has been grand, but I've got an early morning. Thank you, Moira." He thanked her in Gaelic and she returned the sentiment in kind.

Moe stood. "I'll walk you out."

When they both left, Michele leaned toward Moira. "I'd like to order a hot fireman for my private sessions as well. Make him a little older, though."

* * *

Furbogh, Co. Galway

Seany got home around nine o'clock and found that Josh had just gotten home as well. "They let me out early since I worked with Pete at the crack of dawn. He drove me to Slyne Head, so we had to leave at six. I'm exhausted."

"You look knackered, brother. You should go to bed straight away."

"Not until you tell me what happened today. You look like someone beat the shit out of you and didn't leave any marks."

Seany sighed. "I don't know where to start."

"Start from the minute you saw her. My love life is a parched desert with no rain in sight. I need to live vicariously." He smiled when Seany laughed. "Seriously, what happened today? Something big, I can tell."

So, he told him. Not the details, but the important parts.

"Jesus, dude. When you do something, you don't do it halfway. So what did you do?"

"I asked her to marry me." Whatever Josh had been expecting, it hadn't been that because he started choking on a bite of frosted flakes. Seany clapped him on the back.

Josh recovered, meeting his eyes. Then he nodded. "Of course you did. That's the kind of guy you are. If I had anything to offer a woman, I'd have probably done the same. And she said no, because no woman worth anything would want to get married out of obligation. She seemed like a really good person. She is passionate about her work."

"Yes, she is. I don't know what I was thinking, and it was stupid of me to move so fast. If I'd given myself time to think about it, she's not the type to just hop into bed with someone. At least she wasn't when I knew her."

"She's twenty-two. It's not unheard of to be a virgin at her age. She must still really care for you. I mean, put aside the fact that she was here within a day after she was told you were hurt. It's obvious you mean a great deal to her. Do you still have feelings for her? Other than lust, I mean. She's beautiful, but she's quality, Seany. I hope you know what you're doing."

"I have no idea what I'm doing. All I know is that I am not going to be able to stay away from her. She's doing this internship until June. All I can do is take it a day at a time. She'll probably leave again. Her life is in America. She'll graduate and move on. But I'm going to take this time with her. I may regret it, but the course is set."

"Don't beat yourself up, Seany. She's a grown woman. What she gave you was a gift. Don't reject that gift by feeling guilty. When I lost my virginity, it was anything but romantic. A rather experienced senior jumped my ass in the basement of the house that hosted our swim team party. She called me Ryan. Not even a first name. Just...*get over here, Ryan.* And you know I went, because nowhere in the real world does a sophomore boy say no to a hot senior when she's looking for sex. Ever. But it wasn't a gift I gave her. It was embarrassingly quick and meaningless. I'd venture a guess that your first time wasn't much better."

It hadn't been. Seany hadn't thought about it in such an undiluted way. A gift. Moe had given him something very special. She'd given it to herself as well. He didn't regret stopping. How could he? There hadn't even been a lot of foreplay. A fact that shamed him, considering it hadn't even occurred to him to talk to her about sex before pouncing. *A gift.*

"I'm headed down to Mam's on Saturday after work. Da's going to change the oil in my car and they wanted me to go to the trad session. You coming?"

"I can't."

"Let me guess; you're working." Seany said, and it was a statement not a question.

* * *

Galway City, Galway

The shift was quiet the first night, but it didn't last. He'd had a fitful night. He had nerve pain at his burn site; like shots of electricity sometimes, pins and needles other times. And the shoulder was getting used to a different bed and pillow. The cots at the station were small and less comfortable than his bed at home.

Seany was helping do the lunch dishes when the alarm went off through the station. "Possible attempted suicide at the University. Room 285 in Corrib Village. The roommate came home to find a nineteen-year-old male hanging in the shower. The student on the scene and the Resident Advisor are administering CPR."

They were in the rig and howling toward the University within minutes. Seany jumped out of the ambulance, bringing the gurney into the elevator as they made their way to the second floor. There were coeds sobbing and holding up their phones as he and Joseph came down the hallway.

The Resident Advisor and the roommate were still doing CPR when they came in. The R.A. said, "I'm a nursing student. We're doing compressions, but the airway is compromised. My breaths aren't getting in!"

The man's face and neck were grotesquely swollen. Seany took the head as Joseph took over compressions. "He crushed his airway. When is the last time anyone talked to him?"

The roommate was shell shocked. "Um, I saw him around half seven this morning. I have an early class. Then he texted me at ten and told me to make sure I fed the fish. I didn't understand." The boy's voice broke. "He failed his statistics class. He was going to lose his scholarship. But I didn't think he'd…"

Seany called over his radio, telling dispatch to have the trauma chute ready to take him. "Let's get him to the hospital!"

They loaded him onto a backboard, then onto the gurney just as two of the NHS EMTs showed up. Seany straddled him on the gurney, while Joseph and one of the EMTs wheeled them back down the hall. He screamed at the students in the hall. "Put those fucking phones away!" The last thing he needed was this getting on the news before someone called the parents.

He said under his breath, "Come on, brother. Keep fighting." The other EMT bagged. If the hospital wasn't so close, they'd be intubating, but that was risky in the field. "Tell them to be ready to intubate! I've got a pulse!" Thank God. But how long had this kid gone without a heartbeat? Without oxygen? He may have just revived a dead man.

* * *

SEANY RUBBED his face as they sat in the lounge area of the station. By the time he'd gone, the kid was on a ventilator with a weak heartbeat. The question was, did he have any brain activity? Jesus, what a night. The guards were questioning the roommate now, trying to make sense of the senseless. He'd had a pretty fucking rough few months, but he'd never consider something like that. Over what? Grades? A girlfriend?

"Don't think too much on it. It'll drive you mad to be sure," Joseph said with an understanding look.

"Jaysus, I need a feckin' pint."

LETTERFRACK, Co. Galway

Moe watched Michele on Skadi's back and was mesmerized. She had a basic knowledge of Dressage but watching two competitors come together was humbling. Skadi was exquisite, and her excitement over the coming open house was matched with nervous tension.

Moira was a hell of a businesswoman. She'd been working tirelessly to promote the event. BBC Ireland was even going to make an appearance for the horse demonstrations. Tickets to the barn dance had sold out, and the weather was going to be moderate, if not brisk. Moira was going to have a food truck company come from Galway during the dinner hour. They served boxty, bangers with chips, and soft drinks. She'd opted to have an alcohol-free event. The barn dance tickets included a meal and a drink. She also intended to bake six dozen cookies. The reason they'd sold tickets was that they didn't have room for it to be a free-for-all. They couldn't keep the horses out in the stone outdoor stables and corral much past eight o'clock because they were used to the heated barn, so they'd planned the evening within those parameters. The traditional band that was playing was coming down from Sligo and had volunteered the evening session to help Moira. They were fairly well known, so it helped sell tickets to be sure.

Despite the absolute chaos of these final days, Moe was consumed with thoughts of Seany. He texted her once or twice a day but wasn't overeager. She wasn't sure if she was happy about that or not. They were both busy, and she didn't have time for a clingy man. But this wasn't just anyone. It was Seany. What if he didn't come?

The sun was low in the sky, and Michele was cooling Skadi down when Moira came out of the house cursing like a sailor. Moe ran to her. "What's wrong?"

Moira looked like her head was going to pop off. She took a cleansing breath, trying to compose coherent speech. "The music group canceled. Well, let me rephrase that. I canceled."

"What do you mean? You would never have canceled," Moe said.

"Aye, I wouldn't have. According to them, a woman claiming to be me called and told them the event had been canceled due to some electrical problem in the barn. They said she sounded older, like me, and seemed to know all about the farm. So, they took another paid venue for tomorrow night and they can't cancel on them to come here."

"Oh no! I'm so sorry! Why would someone do something like that? This is a charity event!" Moe understood her fury, now.

"I don't know, but I'm bloody well going to find out. For now, I've got to try booking another musical group. Maybe someone from Galway. No one is going to work for free, and they aren't going to drive all the way out here for a ninety-minute gig. Dammit!"

Moe's phone rang and she wasn't going to pick it up, but Moira waved her off. "Get it. I have to go try to salvage this. Hiring a band, if I can find one, is going to eat up half my ticket sales."

She walked off, muttering to herself. Moe tried to pick up the call, but it went to voicemail. She hit redial. "Sorry, Seany. Moira was having a meltdown."

"What's amiss? She doesn't strike me as the meltdown sort," Seany asked.

"She isn't. It's one thing after another around here, though, and she's reached her breaking point." She told Seany what was going on with the barn dance.

"Hold on Seany, she's back." Moira looked like death warmed over. "What's wrong, honey?"

Michele was next to them now. Moira said, "I just called the food truck owners. I had a bad feeling." Her eyes started to mist over. "Someone canceled with them a week ago. They said they'd return my deposit because of the confusion, but they can't come. They've got another event as well. Some event at the University."

"Seany, I need to call you back."

He said, "No! Moe, wait. Can you tell me what time the music is supposed to start?"

"Six-thirty. Why?" she asked.

"Let me call you back in ten minutes. Just ten. Tell her not to hire anyone!"

* * *

MOE CALLED AROUND FRANTICALLY, but no one could pull off a catering job with that short notice. Not for the price the food truck had been willing to offer. A thought started brimming in her mind. She was from Texas, by God. She could throw a hootenanny and manage to get everyone fed. That started her thinking. She dialed international. "Mom, I need your brisket recipe. Stat."

She ran into Moira's study and found her in tears. "Who would do this? I didn't think I was too old to start something new, but maybe I am. I can't deal with this shite!"

"Moira, I have an idea. Who's the local beef seller around here?"

Moira stared at her like she was dense to the situation at hand. "Hear me out. We have five ovens on the property, right? And Devlin's house has one and he lives practically next door. We can do a cowboy supper! I know it's not local food, but if we can get six decent sized briskets and get them all cooking by 8:00 A.M., I think it will work. Texas BBQ night! If we make the food ourselves, we can do this! A huge vat of beans, some sort of rolls, you've already made the cookies. Call your volunteers. They can stay by the ovens to watch the meat. I'll show Devlin how to slice it up and he can serve it hot and freshly carved. I'll make cold sides tonight. Cabbage slaw is all we really need to round out the meal. The beans can be done on the stove top. Or we could do them over a fire to make it look authentic."

Moira stopped her. "Let's not bite off more than we can chew. I like the idea. If your Seany comes through on the music, we might be able to pull this off. Let me call a cattle farmer I know who sells his beef wholesale. Beef is a bit dear in Ireland, but if he'll at least discount it, I may be able to make it work. Maybe I can get him to donate the beef altogether. Once that happens, we can run to Clifden to get the rest of the food. It's going to be a long night. I hate it, because we have such a long day tomorrow. What a mess. I advertised this event with the name of the band and the food truck details. "

Moe's phone rang and she answered it on a oner. "Seany, please tell me you have good news." She could tell he was at a pub and she hated that she'd interrupted his evening off.

"Yes, love. I have very good news. Those tossers from Sligo have nothing on the group who will be playing tomorrow night. They'll be there at half five. Some of them earlier to see the demonstrations. Now, ask me what else I sorted."

"What else did you sort?"

"I just got a group of doctors to hire The Pie Maker to deliver five dozen pies tomorrow night. Half chicken and mushroom, half beef and stout. That should be enough for everyone and the staff. They are closed tomorrow, and when he told them the situation, they agreed to do it last minute. Josh works there, so he'll be our delivery boy. He's doing it for nothing. If you whip up a green salad and get bottled drinks, I think you've got yourself a meal."

"Oh my God, you are a miracle worker! Who are these doctors?"

"You'll meet them tomorrow. Can you squeeze in a few more at the dance?"

"Of course! Seany, thank you. You just saved us from a sleepless night of cooking brisket and baked beans and shredding cabbage!"

"Brisket?"

"Never mind. If we pull this off, I will drive down to County Clare and cook it for the whole group."

"See you tomorrow, a chuisle." He said the words softly and she felt them to her toes.

Moira looked so impatient, she thought she was going to strangle her. "Out with it, for pity's sake!"

Moe told her and her eyes bugged. "The Pie Maker. That's perfect! They've got lovely food. Can they keep them hot?" She waved a hand. "Never mind. It doesn't matter. A green salad and drinks. Let's get to the store, and you can tell me about the music."

* * *

Gus O'Connor's Pub-Doolin, Co. Clare

Seany rang off with Maureen and was grinning like a lad when he looked up at Finn. Finn said, "You are a sap, brother. Look at that grin." He nudged him. "Good for you. I won't tell Brigid everything. She'll be booking a wedding photographer before the weekend is out."

"Thanks. And thanks for doing this. Driving Brigid up, I mean."

"All I know is you better get your niece up on one of those ponies sometime tomorrow or I'll never hear the end of it."

"I'll make it happen. If I can't tomorrow, I'll book a ride for the whole family."

Brigid came up and they fell silent. She narrowed her eyes. "There is more to this than you're letting on, isn't there?"

Seany said, "No. Now take this lout home and get some sleep. It's a long drive tomorrow."

"Finn's mother and father are going to watch the boys. It's good for Cora to get some one-on-one time, and it is a long drive for them."

"So that is Mam, Da, Michael, Liam, and you," Seany said.

"And you. You don't think you're getting off that easy, do you? You better have your guitar with you. Oh! And Patrick is coming with his bouzouki. I just rang him. And Liam is bringing his Fado guitar as well, just for a bit of good craic. It'll be grand altogether. Are you sure they only need us for ninety minutes?"

"They need the barn back for the horses, but I bet they wouldn't complain if you played during dinner. I really appreciate this. Moira and her staff have worked so hard."

"And who is Moira?"

"The woman who owns the ranch. She's closer to Granny's age than mine. Relax." Finn was behind her and mouthed the word *liar.* He wasn't lying. Moira was seventy. There was no way Brigid could know the whole of it. She'd be giving Moe the third degree within minutes of her arrival. She could have been KGB.

Liam and Seamus came up to the bar and Seany said, "I've got this round, lads. You didn't have to do it but thank you for doing it all the same." Izzy came up on the other side of him and planted a wet kiss on his cheek.

Liam said, "Hey! Watch it."

Seany laughed. "She kissed me, brother. I can't help my animal magnetism." He winked at Izzy. "You are all invited to participate in the dance, too. So, Seamus, I expect you to be there. If you don't have a date, you'll be at the mercy of matchmakers."

"It's a bit late notice for all that," he edged. Then Seany's eyes went across the bar to the stage area where a perky, thirty-something blonde was participating in the trad session. "I never took you for a coward, Seamus. I mean, poisonous snakes and killer spiders are fine, but you can't handle a wee village lass?"

"What are you on about? She's half my age," he rolled his eyes. "She'd never go for it."

Izzy laughed. "She is not half your age. Jeez, Seamus. She's probably about eight years younger than you. And have you seen how she looks at you?"

"She does no such thing," he said dismissively, but inside, his heart jumped a bit.

Liam and Finn did it almost in unison. They pretended to sneeze and said *pussy* under their breath. Then Seany pretended to cough and added *chickenshit.* Izzy's brows shot up. "Come on boys. Don't tease him. He's been out of the game a while. I mean, some guys just lose their mojo."

"Alright, you bastards. I'll do it if only to shut you up." Jenny had come down from the performing area and walked toward the bar.

Just as he started the approach, some tosser came from the other side of the bar. Jenny obviously knew him. Seamus did a wide left turn for the toilet just as the unknown competitor kissed Jenny on the mouth. They all cursed under their breath. Seamus came around the back way, shaking his head. "You guys suck."

"We didn't know. Jenny never let on she had a new fella. She hasn't dated in ages. I'm so sorry, Seamus. We shouldn't have pushed it," Brigid said.

"No harm done. I was just doing it to get you all off my back. She's too young for me," he said. Then he sat back on the stool and drank his pint.

* * *

Letterfrack, Co. Galway

Moe fell asleep hard, the stress of the day taking a toll. She was nervous, which would normally keep her awake, but this internship was very physical and hands on. She was asleep right after her head hit the pillow. Unfortunately, it wasn't a peaceful sleep. She'd dreamed again of the stretch of days in August of 2017. When she'd awakened, she couldn't help but relive the events in her head as she drifted between wakefulness and sleep.

Moe steered the zodiac through the water in front of another boat which was following along. She was behind the helm so the men she was with could be ready to drag someone aboard if they found someone in the water. Houston was completely underwater. So many people were stranded. She maneuvered around a box truck just near where the reservoir had poured its excess runoff into the city streets and homes. It was still raining, but she caught sight of motion. Then a woman waving frantically. "Ahead! On the right!" They pulled along just as a large piece of construction debris pushed the small car backward. The little girl screamed as the car started to move. Who the hell owned a car that small in Texas? "We're coming!" She came alongside the car and felt it push back against the boat. "Hurry! Hand me the girl!"

The mother handed the child off to one of the men, a classmate from her equine class. The other boat had another classmate and her father's friend and fellow veteran. He yelled to her, "You've got room for maybe four more. Let's check further into the borough."

They loaded the mother next, covering them both with blankets and giving them fresh water to drink. "I need Thumper! My bunny!" Moe had assumed it was a toy. She looked in the backseat where there was about four inches of space. The cage was visible, as was the matted fur and a nose and teeth bared above the water line. No movement.

"Honey, I think thumper got out of his cage. Rabbits are tricky. He probably swam until he found dry land."

The girl started struggling. "No, he was in his cage! It was closed. I want Thumper!" She knew, though. Deep down she read Moe's face. The girl turned to her mother. "I told you we needed to get him!"

"Honey, the water came up so fast. I barely got you out. I only had two arms. I'm so sorry." The wailing began, rising to a high pitch that made Moe's arms break out in gooseflesh. The little girl was mad at the world, then she screamed again, pointing.

A dead dog floated by, causing Moe's stomach to roll. The woman shielded her daughter's eyes, but it was too late to protect her from the horrors around them. "Get us out of here! Take the lead!" she yelled to the other boat.

Moe woke with her head pounding and her heart sore with old despair. She'd drifted off again at some point during the trip down memory lane and fallen into another strange and vivid dream. She saw the face, bloated and vacant. A human face. Cold limbs and torn clothing. She was sweating now, and she got up, knowing she wouldn't sleep again tonight. It was still dark, but she may as well be working. They had a big day ahead of them.

CHAPTER 22

Moe was still nervous a half hour before the first event of the day. What if no one came? They knew people were coming to the dance, but the events during the day were free and open to the public. Michele was cool as a cucumber, and Moe envied her strength and focus. Moira was buzzing around, arranging things and signing invoices for two portable johns and some rented tables and chairs for the pre-dance dinner.

"You ready, cowgirl?" Michele winked at her. "Dressage is probably pretty common around here, so your barrel racing with that barbarian horse of yours will be a draw for the locals."

"I just hope he doesn't buck me off in front of everyone. He's moody and he wouldn't eat his oats this morning."

"Hey, just between you and me..." Michele rubbed her upper lip. "I just have a bad feeling about the mix up with the caterer and the band. I mean, it doesn't sound like a mix up. It sounds like malicious sabotage."

"Yeah, about that. Some other stuff has happened."

"What other stuff?" The voice came from behind her. She turned and a warm glow spread over her flesh.

"You're here," she said with a small smile.

"Did you doubt me?"

Michele gave him a wave then said, "Maureen, why don't you fill us in on what else has happened."

She told them about the fence being pulled down and then staged to look like a car crash. Then about the hay barn being flooded. Seany said, "One of those things on its own could be explained away, but all four points to mischief of another sort. You're going to have a couple of Gardai officers here tonight. I think maybe Moira should talk to them."

"Is this the band you arranged? Singing cops and doctors?" Michele said, smiling.

"Exactly. Now, tell me what I can do."

"Nothing. Really, we're totally finished. Oh, and if you or the band don't want to use those portable toilets, Moira said you could go in the house."

"Okay then." Seany heard a screech from behind him.

Michele just said, "Incoming at your six." Seany whipped around and caught Cora up in his arms.

"Uncle Seany! I'm so excited to see the ponies. Can I go see them?"

"Well, I don't know. These ladies behind me and the big fella coming out of the barn are in charge. I'm just here to look pretty," Seany said.

Cora smirked. "Women like humility, Uncle. Look at Da. He's 'er catching the women's eyes and ye don't hear him talking about being pretty."

Finn came up just as she said it. "Aye, your mam would likely cuff me upside the head." Finn put out his hand. "Sorry to come early. The rest are coming later. Finn Murphy." He shook hands with both women. "I've got Brigid and Sorcha's fiddles and my drum. The rest will bring their own. Where will the band be setting up?"

Moe said, "Wait…who exactly is coming to play?"

Finn looked from Seany to Moe. Seany answered for him. "Only the best musicians on the Wild Atlantic Way. The O'Briens of course." Moe looked horrified.

Finn laughed. "I assure you we all play very well."

"No! It's not that at all. I mean, Alanna has told me about all of them. But you made your family drive all the way up here from Doolin? It's got to be two hours one way!"

"About two and a half," Finn said, and Seany punched him. Finn rubbed his arm. "Ow, what? It is!"

"They were happy to help. And the doctors who paid for the catering are going to be here as well. Seamus O'Keefe and Liam and Izzy O'Brien."

Michele whistled. "Nice family. All I have is a stressed out mom who raised me by herself and an eight-year-old boxer."

"Not always nice, but they are loyal and good in a crisis," he said with a wink. "They love to play, and we have a few horse enthusiasts in the group. Izzy grew up on a farm in Arizona. Her family and extended family all have horses. We rode through the estate during the week of her wedding. She might try to steal a ride if you're not careful."

Moira spoke from behind them. "Lad, your family has an open invitation to come on a less hectic weekend and we'll ride them up and down Connemara. We'll make a real day of it. I owe you all a debt. This day would have been ruined. Or so expensive the non-profit would have gone in the hole."

"I suspect it's nothing you wouldn't have done for someone else. Just enjoy the day. Once you get this non-profit up and running, maybe they'll take you up on the offer."

Moe said, "Cora, would you like to come up to the VIP benches so you can see the demonstrations better? I think you're really going to like it. I'll put you as close to the riding arena as I can get you."

Seany's heart squeezed as she took Cora's hand. Moira showed Finn where to store the instruments until the evening. Seany went to the outdoor stalls to see Storm. He approached the gate, opened and then secured it behind him, and started looking for the grey horse who needed to be bromanced.

* * *

Cora watched, spellbound as Moe stood beside the enormous horse. He was skittish, but Moe seemed to whisper to him, soothe him, then mount a saddle which looked like something out of the movies. "Why is her saddle different from the others? And her clothes?"

Moira was next to her, having liked the girl instantly. She said, "It's a western saddle. She brought it from Texas. Saddles can be like your favorite pair of shoes. Comfortable and familiar. Kind of personal. And Balor was kind of naughty and a bit of a live wire. She taught him how to barrel race because it takes a burst of strength and speed. It's a good way to get him to focus and maybe to tire him out a little. Get rid of some of that energy. She barrel raced in Texas at the rodeo."

As Moira left to move through the crowd, Cora looked at Seany and said, "So, she's a cowgirl? I want to learn to ride like her." The starting gun went off and they watched as Moe and Balor ran the course. He wasn't elegant. He was still learning. But the crowd ate it up. She did two courses and then did a trot around the ring so everyone could cheer for him. Seany noticed the men taking her in. The boot leg, rhinestone studded jeans that were low on her hips. The leather chaps hugged her thighs. The little t-shirt and hair whipping behind her. He wasn't sure he liked the male appreciation which seemed to ripple through the men in the crowd. The jealousy was ridiculous, but there you have it. He watched her lead Balor out of the riding arena and to the outdoor stalls. He noticed some of the horses were missing. He assumed they were out in the pasture if they weren't working today. He saw Maureen give Balor a small treat from her hand and kiss him on the nose. She really did love the stubborn beast. Next was Michele, who did a Dressage demonstration with Skadi. Everyone gasped at the sight of her. Skadi was storybook beautiful, and Cora couldn't take her eyes off her. "That's the pony Maureen rides when she takes me riding. She is gorgeous, isn't she?"

Cora's head was ready to pop off. "Oh Uncle, you have to take me to meet her before we go. Do you think I can pet her?"

Moe plopped down on the other side of her and said, "I'll make sure you can. She's a very sweet pony. But for now, I have a surprise for you. I'm going to take you first, and then we'll tell the rest of the kids." She whispered it. Cora nodded.

Intrigued, Seany and Finn followed. Finn shook his head as Cora ran to the pen. "Oh! He's so cute! What's his name?"

Moe smirked and said, "It's War Hammer."

Finn threw his head back and laughed. After Cora kissed and stroked him and begged her father to let her have a mini horse, Moe decided to distract her. "Would you like to walk War Hammer out into the arena? Just once while I talk about him? Then we'll bring him back to the pen and let the children line up. We have him penned so the kids don't all rush him at once. One or two at a time. You can help with that as well."

"Yes! Da, can I?"

"Of course. Your mam is going to be sad she missed it. I'll take more pictures." Then Moe put her cowboy hat on Cora and the child's hero worship was so over the top Seany said, "It's just like the carrots. You don't fight fair." And off the two ladies went.

The day was grand. Sunny and warm for the season. After some petting of War Hammer, and then some children's games in the arena, they set up two of the smaller, more docile horses to offer pony rides. Rory and Devlin handled most of it. Moira hobnobbed with local breeders and business owners, trying to secure sponsors and explain the non-profit's goals for starting a hippotherapy program in addition to the therapeutic riding. A steady stream of people visited the information table and took pamphlets and class schedules.

One woman came to fill out a raffle ticket for a free ride, all smiles and intending the prize to go to her grandchild. "You forgot your pen!" Moira yelled, but the woman didn't hear her. It was one of those free pens people made up as swag to advertise a business. Corey and Jameson Natural Resource Corporation. Moira left it by the raffle tickets, because no matter how many pens she put out, they all managed to walk off.

The O'Briens started arriving just as the day's events were done. Seany helped his family unload instruments There was a tent extending out of the barn, strewn with lights. There were tables around the garden where everyone would sit and eat. Moira had been so happy about the food being donated, she'd gone all out with not only a green salad and cookies, but platters of local cheeses and crackers and fruit trays. As everyone started checking in for the dance, Moira took their tickets and told them about the program changes. As the homemade pies from Galway far exceeded the bangers and boxty they'd been expecting, no one was going to complain. As for the band change, they'd just have to hear it to judge for themselves. Everyone was just excited for an evening out. It seemed to be all adults. Couples mostly, and some single people looking for a good mixer.

Josh nudged him. "You did good, brother. Actions matter. She won't forget what you did for her."

He shrugged, dismissing the praise. "She's been brilliant today. Truly."

"Where is she?"

"I think she and Michele wanted to shower quickly and change out of their denims. It's dirty work, horses are."

Liam approached them both. "They'll start to serve the food in ten minutes. We'll play some mellow music to get the mood right. This is good craic altogether, brother. I wish we had something like this where we live. Dublin is so fecking crowded. Ye can really hear yourself think out here where the land is a bit wild. It reminds me of St. Clare's. It was nestled in the rainforest between two rivers. We had a dance there, once. It was for the older children, not adults."

"You miss it, don't you?" Josh said. "Do you think you'll go back?" Liam fidgeted and gave them a sheepish look.

Seany's brows raised. "You are going back. When is this happening? I'm assuming it's the both of you. What does St. James Hospital say about it?"

"They'll hold our jobs for three months after we run out of vacation time. We leave at the end of April. I haven't told Mam yet."

"You should. I mean, maybe she'd want to go with you. She is a midwife, after all. Is Seamus going?"

"Am I going where?" Seamus asked as he approached.

"Manaus," Liam said.

"No, I can't leave the practice right now. I am so jealous I could spit, but I've got a kid in college. Maybe next year. You should see if your mam can go."

Seany raised a brow at Liam, "See."

"Okay, okay. I'll tell her tonight. Hans goes back next week. Maybe with him there, Da will be more at ease."

"Izzy said they have married housing units now. Maybe Da could go? He'd be extra security and he could teach music. He taught five sons how to play the guitar, for God's sake. Those kids can't be half as naughty as we were."

Liam's jaw dropped. He hadn't thought of that. They were always shorthanded at the school. "Jesus, that's an incredible idea." He started looking around. "Izzy is with them right now. She came along to see the horses. And to snoop on your woman," he added.

Seany started, "She's not..."

Liam cut him off. "Sod off, brother. Seriously?" Then his jaw dropped as he looked behind Seany.

Seamus whistled under his breath. "Now there is a fine bit of stuff. Who are the hotties?

Seany turned around and almost swallowed his tongue. Maureen was wearing a cute little dress which was swishing at mid-thigh, a jean jacket, and a pair of cowboy boots. Her legs were bare, except for a pair of thick socks which matched her dress. She also had a knit beanie that slouched around her long, silky hair. She even had on a touch of makeup. Every male head in attendance turned.

Michele had opted for some dark, stretchy jeans to hug her curvy figure and a snug sweater to contour her other attributes. Her auburn hair hung past her shoulders. Seamus said to no one in particular. "I've got the age-appropriate redhead. I call the slow dance." Like they were in tenth year at the school dance or something. Liam smacked him on the back. "Go get 'em, tiger."

Seany introduced everyone, but he couldn't stop staring at Maureen like an idiot. She blushed under his hot gaze. He really needed to get his shit together before... "Seany, love, you'll have to introduce us to your friends."

He turned to see his mother, his sister, and Izzy all standing behind him with questions dancing in their eyes. He cleared his throat. "Mam, Brigid, and Izzy, this is Michele and Maureen. They are both from America and are interns at the riding center."

Maureen shook all of their hands. His mother narrowed her eyes, taking in the girl's face. "Maureen...you look familiar." Then it hit her like someone had just zapped her in the ass with a cattle prod. "You're in some photos I've seen from Aidan's time in America. Maureen as in Moe?"

Moe blushed. "Yes, ma'am."

Sorcha grabbed her before anyone knew what was happening. Then she broke down sobbing like a lunatic.

* * *

SEANY WALKED Moe into the barn while his family was eating and playing for the dinner guests. "Sorry about my mother. She's a hugger. And apparently a loud, public crier."

All three women had hugged her and cried. "I didn't do anything, like you said before. I mean, you were probably coming out of it anyway. It was a coincidence."

Seany wasn't so sure. The pull he felt for her seemed like something supernatural. "You'll never convince them. Don't even try."

"I thought they'd all hate me," she said absently, like she hadn't meant to say it out loud. Then she shook herself. "I mean, everyone is so nice, but they probably know what happened."

"They've raised six kids, Maureen. Lots of scraped knees and broken hearts. They believe everything in life has to go through a process. There are certain things which must happen in order to get to a place where you're supposed to be. Don't worry about them judging you. We were only fifteen."

"Thanks for that. It wasn't an easy time. Nothing has been particularly easy since I was that age."

"What do you mean? Your dad's problems?"

"Yeah, and other stuff. It's not important right now. I don't know about you, but I'm hungry. Let's go get one of those pies before they're all gone." She dragged him out of the barn before he could push her for more. She was keeping something to herself that he thought was important. He needed to hear it. Even if it was about her old boyfriend.

* * *

THE DANCE WAS in full swing. Moira was flushed with exhaustion after dancing with Kyle, one of the other men in the riding program. It was good craic, to be sure. But when they started with *The Hills of Connemara,* the locals were mad for it.

A gallon for the butcher and a quart for Tom
And a bottle for the poor old Father Tom
To help the poor old dear along
In the hills of Connemara
Gather up the pots and the old tin can
And the mash, and the corn, the barley, and the bran
And then run like the devil from the excise man
Keep the smoke from rising, Barney
Now swing to the left, now swing to the right
Sure, the excise man can dance all night
He's drinkin' up the tea 'til the broad daylight
In the hills of Connemara

THE CROWD WHOOPED and hollered as they danced in the barnyard. And it occurred to Moe perhaps things weren't so different here than in Texas. Country people loved a good dance.

Cora was the only child in attendance, but she was in good

company with Izzy. Both of them loved to dance, and Cora's hair was damp at the hairline from the exertion. After forty minutes straight of jigs, reels, some amusing and fast-paced ballads, Seany watched Liam approach the mic. "We're going to slow it down a bit, so grab your sweetheart and twirl her in your arms, lads."

Seany smiled as he watched Seamus boldly approach Michele and lead her out onto the dirt and grass dance floor. The lights were twinkling in the clear night sky and Seany moved toward Maureen. "Sorry, Brigid. Third degree is over. Go find your man." Brigid relinquished Moe's attention with a gleam in her eye.

He led her toward the dance floor only to curse when Liam started playing the guitar. He knew the song. For feck sake. Ed Sheeran's *Perfect.* He was going to kill him. Moe sensed his hesitation. "We don't have to dance. If your shoulder is bothering you or something." He pulled her to him, smelling her warm scent. Honeysuckle, soap, and woman. He felt her hair against his chin and shuddered, rubbing his thumb along her back.

We were just kids when we fell in love, not knowing what it was, I will not give you up this time.

He pulled her closer and heard her sniffles. "Don't weep, love. We're together again. Even if it's just for a little while." She nuzzled the skin under his jaw. "I can't stop thinking about you. About feeling you against me. About the sight of you, bared for me."

She hissed. "Stop. Your parents are watching." She swiped at her tears, flushing like mad.

"Which is the only thing making my cock behave. I'm ready to drag you into one of these stalls so I can put my head under your skirt."

"Seany, stop." He met her eyes and she looked down, as red as he'd ever seen her.

"Have you ever…"

"No! No I have never. Now stop talking about this. You are the devil, Sean O'Brien."

"Lass, you have no idea." But she was going to find out.

* * *

THE LAST OF the horses were in the barn and everyone but Moe, Seany, and Devlin were back to their quarters or on the road. Devlin waved as he walked to his car. "Thanks for shutting everything down. It was a great night."

"Finally, everyone is gone," Seany said as Maureen closed the large barn doors and started shutting down the lights. As soon as they were shut, Seany had her pinned to the door. She sighed as he kissed down her neck. "You taste good," he said as he nibbled her ear. He ran his hands up her thighs and under her skirt. "Every time I swear I'm going to take it slow, I get my hands on you and you feel like this. Soft and smooth, and you're warm."

She was panting. She knew it. She didn't care. The feel of Seany's hands running under her skirt made her hips roll of their own accord. She was wet. Had been ever since their dance. She felt the intensity of his desire against her belly. He thumbed her nipples through her dress, and she moaned. "Seany, I want you."

"You have me. I'm right here." Just as he said it, he slipped his hand into her panties. He groaned, "You are like warm honey." She was senseless, gasping in his ear as he nibbled her through her bra.

"Seany, I'm going to explode if you don't stop." His laughter grumbled against her breast and she went off like a cannon. He helped her ride it out until she was slumped against the wood boards on the stable door. She watched him with heat sparking between her thighs as he put the fingers he'd just used against her flesh into his mouth. He actually swayed forward, his forearms landing on the door on either side of her head. "I want you against my mouth, a chuisle. Is it to be here? Because I don't think I can wait until we sneak back to your cottage. I need it now."

She shivered. "The loft, where we keep the fresh hay." *How fucking perfect.*

He watched her as she ascended the ladder. A shot of pale blue panties and perfect skin as her skirt swayed enticingly. There were blocks of hay, and also some that was loose and spread around the floor of the loft. She'd grabbed a clean blanket from the tack room, like the one they'd picnicked on. She spread it out, bending to smooth the corners. He dropped to his knees, grabbing her hips as he kissed the back of her thighs. She stood, grabbing a beam as he nibbled her bottom, her skirt rucked up over her hips. "Lie down on your back. I need to see you." She did as he asked and he climbed over her, taking her mouth deep and slow. He took his time on the buttons which started at her neckline. He unbuttoned them just far enough to spread the two halves and reveal her breasts. He unclasped her bra and took turns, licking and taking greedy pulls on her nipples. She had her hands in his hair, arching as if to beg for more. Then he lifted her skirt, watching those blue panties make another appearance.

"Should I take off my boots?" she said stupidly.

"No way. Those boots stay right where they are," he purred.

He slid her panties off over the boots, then he put one leg over his shoulder. "I am having about a hundred farmer's daughter fantasies come to life right now. Jesus, I never thought boots could be so sexy." He covered the inside of her knee with hot, wet kisses. He grazed his teeth along the soft flesh of her thigh.

At the first brush of his mouth, Moe came off the blanket with a gasp. Then he licked right up the center of her, and she arched. He smoothed both big hands up the backs of her thighs so her knees were bent and her boots were on his shoulders. He savored her, feeding off her gasps and sighs and moans. Her soft thighs nestled his head perfectly as he drank her silken heat. He moaned against her hot flesh, pressing his cock into the floor to keep himself in check. Then he focused on the swollen center, slipping his finger into her core as she clenched around him. He felt her body start to climb and he knew just how to send her through the roof. Her breasts were so sensitive. He switched his position, letting her legs fall off his shoulders as he spread her wide. He pinned her thighs open with his big shoulders as he worked her sex with his mouth and hand and reached up where her dress was spread and her round, high breasts peaked for him. Her nipples were pink and beautiful and he cupped her breast as he circled her nipple with his middle fingers. She undulated under his hands and mouth, waves of flesh that rolled and met his every touch. He fluttered his tongue right where she needed him, then sucked the little nub inside his lips as she came in crashing waves. He cupped her ass with both hands and pinned her to his mouth as she bit the blanket to stifle her screams. When she finally came back down to earth, she was completely spent. Her eyes were glassy, and she was pink with arousal. He wanted to take her. To spill inside her. But he'd rushed before and regretted it.

She raised up, her dress open and her hair in tangles. "Don't even think for one minute we are done."

A slow grin spread across his face. He'd made her come twice. He thought going for a third was a perfect plan. He started to dip his head again and she closed her knees, putting her legs to the side. "Oh no. It's my turn." She got on her knees, meeting him chest to chest. She lifted his sweater over his head, then she started to unbutton his jeans. She met his eyes. "I want to touch you. I want to see you. I barely got a chance last time." She unbuttoned his fly slowly as she covered his chest with warm, wet kisses. She grazed his nipples with her teeth, the passion flaring between them. His cock sprung from behind his fly and she looked down. Then her eyes devoured him from the base of his cock to the broad expanse of his chest. She guided him where she'd been earlier. "Lie back. I want to see you."

He looked like a fallen angel. His broad chest, his tight abs, and his proud, long sex hard and erect out of his open jeans. She climbed over him and kissed him, feeling his smooth chest and abs with her hand. "You're so beautiful." She moaned against his mouth as she took him in her hand. She had a light touch at first, running fingers over his shaft and cupping his heavy testicles. She straddled his thighs and he jerked as he felt her sex against his jeans. He wanted in her. Wanted to pull her astride him and slide her down on to his cock. Cup her ass as she rode him. But she was inexperienced, and right now he wanted her to take the lead. And did she ever. She started kissing down his chest, stopping to nibble his nipples again. Then lower. His hips jerked. He took her face in his hands, pulling her hair away from her face. The ends were tickling the tip of his cock. "You don't have to."

"I want to. Of course I do. I may not be as...skilled as you," she said shyly, "but I want to."

"Believe me when I tell you, a participation trophy is nothing to be ashamed of in this regard," he said hoarsely.

She lowered her head, taking him in her hand as she touched her tongue to the head. Then she took the tip in her mouth tentatively. "Do you like this?"

He watched her with hungry eyes. "What do you think?" he said huskily. He moaned as she took him into herself, his neck arching as he surrendered. Her hair brushed his thighs and he looked down as she dipped her head to take him all the way into her mouth.

Moe felt powerful and feminine. She didn't precisely know what she was doing, but she'd experienced the pleasures of the flesh under his mouth and had been overwhelmed by the experience. She wanted to give the same to him. She watched his beautiful body flex, his hips rolling, and she became aroused to the point of pain. The embers of her two orgasms lighting anew. As if he sensed it, he grabbed her shoulders and flipped her onto her back. "You have to stop, or I'm going to come in your mouth." His voice was harsh and edgy. Then he put the ridge of his cock against the cleft of her sex and began to rub himself. It sent her through the roof as she watched him let go. The warm jets pooling on her belly and covering her core. She'd wanted him inside her, but this was erotic and raw, so she'd take it. She put her nails in his ass, and he covered her mouth as she ground against him.

They lay exhausted and limp together, the smells of hay and horses and the noises of the barn finally permeating their senses. He kissed her cheeks, her eyes, her chin, and then her mouth again. He took her panties and cleaned her belly, and himself as best he could. But she noticed he left some of his seed on her sex, rubbing it around her tender flesh as if to mark her.

He smiled at the sight of her. She watched his body hungrily, and he thought about taking her. Just plunging into her willing body. But he'd already been hasty the first time, and a dusty hayloft was not what he wanted for their first time really making love. Although, as he looked around, then looked at her sprawled in the hay with those cute little shitkickers still on her feet, he couldn't think of anywhere more perfect. He folded the wet panties and put them in his pocket.

"Hey," she protested with a grin.

"Trophy. Sorry, they're mine now," he said with a devilish grin. Her eyes flared. They tried to make some order out of her hair and clothes. Then she picked hay out of his. They descended the ladder... and that was when Seany smelled it. The coppery tang of blood and the acrid smell of excrement.

"Maureen, stop. Something is wrong, I think." Then they heard it. An unholy heave of a sick animal. Her eyes were frantic as she checked the stalls. Balor was thumping his hoof against the stall, agitated. Then she found the problem. "Oh, God. It's Sadie. She's the pregnant mare." Moe and Seany went into the stall where the horse was frothing at the mouth and covered in diarrhea. There were other substances too, fluid and blood. "No, no. It's too soon." Sadie was a dappled gray with three black socks and white peppering her face and head. A pretty horse with a swollen abdomen. "Something is not right. Labor wouldn't cause this." She looked around frantically. "She got into something or ate something bad."

Seany looked around for anything out of place, then he saw it. He held up some discarded wild flowers. Moe looked and then her face blanched. "Lupine. Oh, Jesus. It's poisonous to horses. Check the other stalls!" Seany couldn't understand why she'd have him check the other horses, but he did as she asked. Sure enough, there were sprigs strewn around in five more stalls. Wilted stalks of the same botanical. What the hell? Had some child come in and brought them into the barn for the horses? But no...that wasn't possible. The horses had been outside, and some even out in the pasture. A chill went up his spine.

Maureen fumbled for her phone. When Moira didn't pick up, she ran to the house, leaving Seany to clear the stalls of the noxious plant life. She pounded on the door, but it was Michele who made an appearance first. "Call the vet! Get Moira up! Someone poisoned the horses!" She went into Michele's room. "I need a pair of sweats or leggings, please. And don't ask."

Michele pointed to the drawers and ran to get Moira. As soon as Moe threw some yoga pants on under her dress, she ran back to the barn barefoot. Seany had made a pile. "There were plants in five other stalls. Balor's, the mule's, War Hammer's, Skadi's, and one more of the Connemara's, Clarence was the name, I think. What is going on, Moe?"

Moira made an appearance, wearing a robe. "The vet is on her way. Tell me what has happened."

Moe pointed to the pile of plants. "It was in six of the stalls. I don't know if any of the other five ingested any but Sadie's really sick. It's lupine." The tears were pouring down her face. "Check the mini-pony. He's the smallest. And Moira, there may be other things I wouldn't recognize. Local plants." Then she called off the other four stalls where Seany had found it.

"He's asleep, but he's fine." Michele yelled over the stall wall. "Do you think maybe it was a child?"

Seany said, "It occurred to me as well, but no. These horses were all outside when the kids were here. And those flowers weren't readily noticeable. They were hidden in the straw. Sadie's been nibbling on hers, so they were up top in plain sight, but the rest had a few twigs of straw over them, hiding them from view. I think this may have been deliberate. Can't you give her something to make her vomit?"

Moe's voice was barely restrained sorrow. "Horses can't vomit. Their anatomy doesn't allow for it."

He watched as Moira took charge of Sadie. "Moe, Michele, check the other horses for any signs of dizziness, diarrhea, low heart rate, listlessness, convulsions, contracted pupils, anything out of the ordinary. And hand me my first aid kit from the tack room. I want to get a temperature and listen to the baby. I don't grow lupine on my property, so someone brought it into the barn. This is wilted, but it was fresh cut. This plant is out of season up here right now. The flowers came from a hothouse or somewhere. Someone who knew it could kill them brought it here." Her voice broke, and she took a second to rein in her emotions. "Seany, if you could go into my kitchen, there is a list of phone numbers on the wall by the phone. Call Devlin, Rory, and the Garda station."

He did, and then he called his da. He wanted to know if anyone in the family had seen someone coming in or out of the barn holding plants or dried flowers. When he came out, the veterinarian was there.

"I'm afraid I can't move her just yet. This foal is coming. The spasms and diarrhea put her into labor."

"Is it too soon?" Moe was next to them again, her face stained with tears.

"It's early, but not that early. If we get the foal out now, it's less likely to get any of the toxins. There is no antidote for lupine toxicity, but we can give her fluids and they can both be hospitalized. Thank God you were out here when she started to get sick."

No one gave her a sideways glance about her still being in the barn with Seany. Rory and Devlin came peeling in the drive almost at the same time. The vet cleaned Sadie off as best she could. The poor horse twitched with strange spasms and was wet with perspiration. "I can see the head; this is going to be fast. Come, everyone, and have a look. It's a caul birth. They are very rare. See how the amniotic sack is still over the face and head?" She grabbed the front legs and Sadie trembled, making sickening noises as she pushed her baby into the world.

Moira wrapped it in a warm blanket, wiping out its mouth and nose. "There, there. We've got a little girl, don't we? You're going to be just grand. You're going to take a ride with your mam in the trailer." She looked at the doctor. "She's small. You will take her too, right?"

The vet nodded. "Yes, she'll need to be bottle-fed until we get Mam healthy." Or if. This well could be fatal to Sadie. "You're going to have to watch the others, to make sure. I'll call my staff and have them on standby. Those horses need moved and every bit of the hay replaced."

They had a sling-type contraption which could assist them in lifting a horse, but they managed to get Sadie on her feet after she had given birth. Devlin backed the horse trailer into the stable and the vet loaded her and stayed with her in the back. "Is it a long way to the vet hospital?" Michele asked.

"No, about fifteen minutes. Maureen, stay here and speak with the

Garda officers if they manage to get here. It may not be until tomorrow. You, Michele, and Rory need to call me if any of the other horses get sick. Take them out of their stalls four at a time, tie them up, and clean out all of the straw. Put fresh stuff from the loft in there only after you've checked it. If you find more weeds or anything else suspicious, take pictures for the police report."

Seany said, "I'll stay until it's done, Moira. It'll go faster if I help."

"Thank you, lad. If you need to spend the night, I've got a guest room." Then they were gone.

* * *

MOE PASSED out around four o'clock, slumped over a table in the tack room. Michele finished her third bottle of water, tossed it in the garbage can, and waved goodnight as she headed for the house. Rory said, "I think we're in the clear with the others. It doesn't seem like they ingested any. None of those other stems were gnawed on and they'd all had a good dinner. Poor Sadie. She likes to nibble on the trail, or she did. We haven't been taking her past the west part of the pasture since we found out she was expecting." He shook his head. "The guards won't be here until after Noon tomorrow. There have been one too many incidents around here. Something isn't right."

"Moe told me about the other incidents. The hay barn and the fence. Then there was the sabotage of the open house. You're right. Someone is making more than mischief around here. This is malicious. To kill a pregnant mare is downright evil. Could it be a competitor?"

"No one I know in this business would ever do something like this. And a competitor wouldn't come after Moira in this way just as she's stopping the breeding. She's out of the competition. No, this is more personal than that, I think."

"Moe and Moira dismissed the idea of it being Hugo. He's after her to stop spending so much money, and he wouldn't want to run up vet bills and kill valuable stock from her horses."

"Yes, and he wasn't here today. He'd never have the bollocks for something like this. I would be surprised if he knew enough about horses to drop those exact flowers in their stalls. And it was a woman who called the food truck and band leader." He washed his hands in the deep sink, soaping up to his elbows as he talked. When he dried off, he nodded to Moe. "Best get her into a bed. Moira called. She's headed back home. Thanks for staying."

"Glad I could help," Seany said as he began walking toward Moe. He thought about waking her, then he just picked her up. She felt good in his hands. He noticed she'd retrieved her boots at some point. Rory opened Seany's car door. "Thanks, brother. It'll be easier to drive her over."

She woke just as he was stopping in front of her cottage. "How long have I been asleep? The horses!"

"Mother and baby are fine, love. They don't think she ate very much, thankfully. The others are resting in their stalls. Ye needed your sleep, girl." He opened the door for her, and she untangled her limbs to get out of the car. "I know you'll want a shower, but then get in bed. You have your therapy class at noon."

"So do you. You may as well stay."

"I thought I'd go up to the house. Moira offered the guest bed."

"It may be better, since I'm working. This might look unprofessional."

"But then I'm taking you home with me for the night. Maybe two. We can shop in Galway, and I'll bring you back nice and early on Wednesday for my private ride."

Moe smirked, but she looked so tired. She pointed at him, "There is a dirty joke in there somewhere, but I'm too tired to think of it."

He pulled her in for a kiss. "You can show me, once you've rested. Sweet dreams, love."

* * *

Seany woke after about six hours of sleep to the smell of sizzling rashers. He walked into Moira's kitchen rubbing the stubble from the day before. He was wearing the same clothes as well. He still had

Maureen's panties in his pocket, a little reminder of the taste of heaven they'd shared last night. Moira said, "Good morning, lad. You were dead to the world when I came in. I was letting Moe sleep, but I think her phone is dead."

Michele came in just then, holding Moe's phone. "No, she left it in the tack room. Poor thing was exhausted."

Moira said to Michele, "Best go wake her, if you don't mind. Take a cup of coffee with you. This will be done by the time you get back."

But Seany was already on it. "I'll get her. And if it's okay, I'd like to take her back to Galway after she speaks with the Garda officer. She's got the day off and I want to take her shopping. This way you won't be short a vehicle."

Moira said, "Aye, I need to go to the vet today, thank you. And I think she needs a break. She's been putting in long hours. Last night was hard on everyone."

Seany said, "If you don't mind, my da is going to call you today. He's retired Garda but he's on a reserve list in case they need him. I spoke with him last night about what's been going on around here."

"Thank you. I met your da last night. He seems a good sort. I'll take any help I can get. Now scoot. She's bound to wake up hungry," Moira said.

Seany would have normally walked the quarter mile to her cottage, but he drove to speed up the process. He knocked. When she didn't answer he opened the door. The blinds were pulled and it was dark in the cottage. He heard her, then. Thrashing and whimpering. He went to her and said, "Maureen, sweetheart, wake up." She woke up with her arms flailing and her eyes wild with panic. "Jesus Christ, Moe." He pulled her onto his lap as he soothed her. "Calm, now. That's it. You're awake now. It's okay."

Her heart was thundering. But he was here now. Instead of her parents, it was him. Warm and solid. He felt so good. "I'm okay. It's okay. I was just dreaming." She repeated her mother's words. So many times during her childhood, she'd comforted her. But Moe hadn't told her about her nightmares over the last three years. They'd passed for a time, maybe because she was here in Ireland. But seeing Sadie struggle, watching the small foal push into the world, had triggered something. "I'm okay."

She sat up, pulling away from him. "I'm okay. It's just a stress dream. I'm overly tired."

Seany watched her, eyes narrowed. "It didn't seem like you were okay. Do you dream like that often?"

"No," she lied. "I'm just worn out. But I have class today, and I can rest afterward. I'll sleep in the car."

"Okay, that's good. And we'll make it an early night. I want you to stay with me tonight, but I can sleep on the couch. Moira is finishing up breakfast, so she told me to come wake you. You left your phone in the barn."

Moe scrubbed her face. "Okay, give me a minute."

He watched as she stood, completely unaware or uncaring that she was in a skimpy tank top and panties. As if she read his mind, she looked down. "Sorry," she said.

His laughter rumbled deep in his chest. "Don't ever apologize for walking around in your knickers, love. I'm certainly grateful."

She smiled, grabbing some clean clothes and heading into her bathroom. After about five minutes, she came out dressed in a sweatshirt and jeans. She put on her barn coat and slid her boots over her jeans. "I'm ready."

He took her arm and pulled her to him. "Are you sure you're okay?"

"Positive." She said it matter-of-factly, but he didn't believe her.

* * *

BREAKFAST WAS A SOLEMN AFFAIR. Everyone was tired and emotionally drained. Seany ducked outside, to give the staff time to debrief as a group, before they had to go face the day. Maureen said, "I'm not going to go to Galway. I think it would be good to keep as many eyes on the place as possible. I don't really need a winter coat. It's not even very cold today."

"I did not hire you to work as a security guard, Moe. None of you are here in this capacity. I'll lock the barn at night. And I want you two to lock your quarters whether you are in them or not. The Garda officer should be here within the hour. Michele will cover for you when he gets here."

Then she gave her a stern, motherly look. "I can't make you go to Galway, but I can make you take some time off. I don't want to see you in the barn after this afternoon until Wednesday at ten. Understood?" She lifted a hand. "That is final. You need a break."

Hans and Alanna were the first to arrive. He hugged Seany. "Sorry about last week. New baby and all. I just couldn't leave them. Aidan has got him now, and Sorcha and the other family will help."

Alanna yawned, and Seany thought about what Moe had said. "I want to thank you both for coming all this way. It means a lot. I know you did this for me."

Hans put a hand on his shoulder. "I've run this particular crucible. I know where you're at, son. And if you want to talk, you do some kind of video call and I will make the time. You hear?"

"Thanks. I will."

"And you never get too old to talk to your dad. Sean buried his brother. That's about as bad as it gets. So, if you think no one understands, I want you to remember the two old guys in your life who've got your back. Copy that?"

"Yes, I copy."

The other guys from the riding class trickled in, and soon everyone knew what had happened. Moe told them, "If I have to get up and leave in the middle, it's to speak to the police."

Alanna smiled at the group and they went around the room again, getting reacquainted. Hans talked a little about Iraq. Each of them shared a little of themselves. Moe tried to skip over herself like Alanna did, but the men weren't having it. Matthew, the man from the Coast Guard, said, "Tell us about Texas. I mean, we know you can barrel race and probably rope a calf. You said ye lived near Houston. I've got some friends in the U.S. Coast Guard. Isn't that where Harvey hit? Hurricane Harvey, yeah, it was Houston, right?"

Seany watched as Moe went stark white. Holy shit. He was a self-centered bastard. She cleared her throat and said, "Yes. I live outside the city in a farming suburb. We didn't get as much flooding." Then she moved on.

He looked at Alanna who gave nothing away. Which told him she knew something. It seemed like the U.S. was always having some sort of hurricane, and to his shame, he didn't really follow the weather outside of Ireland. Moe looked at him, her face like a calm lough. It was a lie. He knew it, and she knew he knew it. The shutters went down, and it sent an irrational surge of anger through him.

* * *

"I SHOULDN'T GO AWAY. Moira needs the support." Moe had given a witness statement about what they suspected had happened in the barn.

Seany's jaw was tight. "If you say so."

"What does that mean? She almost lost several horses. This could have been much worse, Seany. Maybe you don't care about these horses, but I do."

He didn't even get angry. He cocked his head in disbelief. "I can't believe you just said that to me."

She shut her eyes, remembering the huge fight with Mason when Harvey had hit the gulf coast. She swallowed. "I'm sorry. You're right. That wasn't fair."

"What was your dream about this morning?"

"That came out of nowhere. I don't remember."

"You're lying. I'll let it go for now, because we are both tired and on edge. I'm still in my clothes from yesterday. Moira wants you to go. She's worried you're working too much. Let's just clear our heads for a bit, and when my ride is over, we'll talk."

* * *

SEANY AND HANS urged their horses at a slow pace, keeping right behind Devlin as they went through the path toward the park trails. "This is gorgeous," Hans said.

Seany said, "Just wait until we get up ahead. It's something to see."

Devlin smiled as he looked back. "We'll take our time, head up into the hills. Get ready to be dazzled, lads."

The trees parted, opening up to the first sight of Connemara National Park. The breath shot out of Hans. The sun was shining through a patch of clouds like a beam shot out of heaven. It lit up the mossy green hills and sparkled off the lough. Devlin pointed, "Look there. The park ponies!" The park had been gifted a herd of Connemaras, even though it was a domesticated breed. The park made sure to care for them while leaving them in their natural habitat. Hans said, "It reminds me of the Shackleford Banks horses in North Carolina. They've survived hurricanes and climate change and man encroaching on their home with boats and beach houses. They watched the lighthouse for over a hundred years. People go by to get a glimpse of them, but it's their island. It's humbling, really."

Seany's throat was thick with emotion, remembering their boat trip to see those horses during the weeks he'd stayed in North Carolina. When he'd met Maureen. It was indeed humbling. He leaned forward, rubbing Storm's sleek, silvery neck. He crooned to the beast, warming his hand on the horse flesh. There was something soothing and primal about traveling by pony. Nothing artificial or fuel propelled. And although he hated to admit it, not having Maureen here helped him tune into the environment and the sensations. He wasn't letting his mind and heart be distracted from why he was really here. He felt the horse rumble some sort of communication, and he said, "It is beautiful, Storm. Thanks for the ride." He could have sworn Devlin was smiling, even though he didn't see his face.

* * *

THEY BRUSHED OUT THEIR HORSES, and Seany smoothed a hand over Storm as he did it. He mumbled to him, "It was a good ride. Ye got me back just before the rain." The rain was a good thing. It had been a dry year for Ireland, especially here. He remembered Moira mentioning it.

Hans was making similar small talk with his Hercules. Then he said, "How is the new station working out? Alanna said you're working the paramedic side until you are cleared for duty."

He thought about it. "I like the men. The chief is a straight shooter. My direct partner's name is Joseph. He's a great medic. They're lucky to have him. We've been busy. It's a populated city, even though it's not as big as Dublin. We had a carbon monoxide poisoning call."

Hans froze, but Seany said, "The only casualty was the hamster. They got out in time. They were sick to varying degrees but all alive."

"Hamster, huh? Sort of the canary in the mine effect?"

Seany nodded as he brushed Storm's forelock. "Exactly." He paused for a minute. "We just had an attempted suicide at the college." He said it softly, like a dragon he didn't want to wake. The problem was, the dragon was in him. "He tried to hang himself. I mean…he did hang himself. We got a pulse. He's intubated in the ICU. The machines are keeping his heart going, but he's dead. His parents don't want to let him go, but he's already gone, I think."

"Jesus, I'm sorry you had to see that."

"Always a minute late." Seany mumbled it and was surprised when Storm pushed his nose under his arm. He absently stroked him, the horse rubbing against him. "What would make a kid so young just give up?"

Hans thought about it. "There is a sad amount of suicide in the military. The young ones? I think they haven't learned no matter how awful things seem in the moment, it's just a bump in the road. Sometimes it's a really, big, fucking bump. I know all about that. And about not wanting to go on when you've lost someone. Sometimes it's suicide. Sometimes it is just shutting down. Branna's mother did it. She didn't exactly drown herself. She just failed to get into the life raft." A metaphor, but it worked.

Seany looked up to see Alanna and Moe watching them, their hearts in their eyes. His hands were on either side of Storm's neck, his forehead pressed against him. Storm gave a deep, non-threatening grumble, then he pushed his velvety nose under Seany's chin. It made Seany want to break down and cry like a sissy.

* * *

BALOR WAS OFF. He'd been uncooperative going back into his stall when it started raining. He'd been jumpy ever since last night. She'd noticed something before, and now she saw it again. War Hammer was hanging out at Balor's door. They didn't often let War Hammer loose, but the rain would keep him inside. So, today he was roaming free and visiting with the class. When Balor started getting agitated again, he went by his stall and lifted his nose to the larger pony. "War Hammer, come here." It was Rory who said it, and he moved the mini horse away. Balor started fussing again. Moe went to his stall to check for any signs he was sick. Nothing. But the situation last night had upset him. The blood, especially. She wondered again about his past. She said, "Rory, bring War Hammer back here."

Rory did as she asked, and she opened Balor's door. "I'm just going to try something." Balor was in the big stall which was meant for a mother and foal set. They had another empty one where they'd put Sadie and her foal. Moe had an idea. If people could seek comfort and emotional support from an animal, why couldn't another animal do it?

When she came in with the small horse, Balor shifted nervously. "It's okay, big guy. I brought you a friend."

War Hammer was a simple creature. He ate, he played, he slept. He was used to being touched a lot. And he seemed absolutely uncowed in the face of his giant counterpart. She backed up, watching for any signs of aggression or agitation. Then she eased the door shut. She put her chin on her arms while she watched inside the stall. Balor sniffed the diminutive intruder, but he wasn't agitated anymore. War Hammer often liked to stop at Balor's door, and a suspicion developed they'd be a good match.

"I'll be damned," a voice said from behind her. Moira smiled. "Balor is getting equine therapy." The whole group laughed as Moe realized they'd all been watching. "Well done, Moe. Very well done. Now, let's get these last two horses put away so you can get on your way."

"On my way? I thought it would be better if..."

"And I told you that you aren't to step foot in this barn until Wednesday morning. So, go have fun. You've got a two-night holiday. Galway, the Bahamas, Venice, wherever."

Alanna clapped her hand. "Forget all of those cities. You are coming to Doolin!"

* * *

JOSH WOKE on the sofa to knocking on the door. He was half asleep when he yelled. "Did you forget your key again, you dumbass!" Then he heard the rumbles of female laughter. "Oh, shit. Sorry! I'm coming!"

He jumped, made sure he had pants on, then combed his fingers through his hair. He opened the door to two young women, pretty as a picture. "Mary, Madeline, come in. Sorry."

He picked up the scattered mail, his laptop, and his textbooks, making the table smooth. Mary said, "Stop cleaning, you dolt. You need to get your shoes on." He looked at Mary. She shrugged. "Seany called. The ferry isn't running, and you aren't working at the pie shop until half four tomorrow. There's a piss-up in Doolin tonight and you're goin'."

Madeline wasn't as vocal. She came out of his room with his coat, a pair of boxers being spun around on his toothbrush, and said, "You can borrow the rest. Get your ass in the car, lad. You're sleeping at Aoife and David's. It's all arranged."

A thrill shot down Josh's spine and hit him straight in the ass. A good look at Madeline did that to him. "Well, I guess I'm outnumbered." He grabbed his keys and followed as he watched Madeline Nagle get into his passenger side. This was exactly what he needed.

* * *

MOE THOUGHT she'd seen a good part of Ireland when she'd been here a couple of months ago. She'd driven from Dublin to Connemara and back, and the drive had been breathtaking. But she now understood why they called this particular area *The Wild Atlantic Way.* Seany had taken the coastal roads, giving her the best views of the rocky coves and sandy beaches on the Irish west coast. The small villages were charming. Small houses, old ruins, and sprays of sea water pushing up toward the sky. It was cold and windy, yet she still felt the need to open the window and let the sea air permeate her body and soul. She loved the old churches, and ruins which sparked the imagination. Even an old stone silo took on an air of mystery. Was it a silo, or a tower where some young maiden had been held captive? Or a watch tower, looking for ships attacking from the sea? Seany knew some of the areas, but not all. He took her through the Burren, and she wrote notes on her map and took photos, so she could look up the places on the internet. "It's so beautiful, Seany. I really needed this."

He smiled sadly at her, "I did too. Sometimes the cure for life is going home."

CHAPTER 23

Doolin, Co. Clare

Guests were spread all over the town, divided into households depending on how many spare beds they had, and how comfortable the sofa was. Alanna and Aidan had their three children at the family homestead, because Sean and Sorcha could help with the newborn. Tadgh, Charlie, and little William were staying with Granny Aoife and Grandda David, as was Josh. Hans was staying at his old house with Caitlyn and Patrick and their three little ones. Liam and Izzy were staying at Brigid's, which left Seany and his guest.

Moe stood in the driveway, stunned. "It's so perfect. A real Irish cottage."

Seany laughed. "And what do you think you're staying in at Moira's?"

"I know it's a cottage, but this is the real deal. It's like the Quiet Man without the thatch!"

"Did I ever tell you about how Michael and Branna met?"

Moe cocked her head, "I don't think so."

As if on cue, Branna ran out the front door and launched herself into Seany's arms. "You're here! Finally!" She turned. "And Moe is here!" She grabbed Moe and hugged her before she had a chance to say hello.

"It's nice to meet you," Moe said with a girlish giggle. "I've heard so much about the family from Alanna and Seany. I can't believe I'm actually here with you."

"Well, you are. Just in time, since we've added a wing. Come in and meet the kids and I'll show you our guest area. It'll eventually be Halley's room, but she shares with her brother. The baby is still in with us."

"Michael, they're here!" Branna yelled.

Moe sucked in a breath before she could help it. There truly was nothing hotter than a guy with a baby. Seany mumbled, "Did he really have to come out shirtless?" Moe hid a smile.

Michael smiled, "Sorry. I was just coming in from a run when this lad started crying. Excuse the sweat? I'll spare you a hug. We're glad to have you with us. We're going to fill the pub tonight."

Seany leaned in. "It's the off season and a weekday, so we'll have a bit of space."

"I'm supposed to tell you Cora wants to see you before you go back up the coast," Michael said. Then past him came two blurred figures, like rockets headed straight for Seany. "And these are the twins."

Moe smiled, "They are beautiful. All three of them." And it was no lie. The boy and girl looked so much alike; it was staggering. Black, wavy hair like thick waves of silk. And dusty blue eyes much like Seany's, but with a ring of green at the center. The baby, Ian, had tufts of sandy hair like his father, but dark blue eyes, like the stormy sea. She saw those eyes had come from his mother.

Branna said, "Halley, Brian, say hello like a proper lady and gentleman."

Brian said, "Hello, Uncle Seany. Mam said you got burned in the fire. Can I see?"

"Brian!" Branna was horrified.

Seany smiled, peeling off his jacket. "It's okay, sister. It's good to be curious. It shows they care. Now, here it is." He held out his arm, and they both stared over it. "This is why you should never play with fire.

It hurt something fierce. And you know what they did? They put dead fish on me while I was sleeping!" He said it so dramatically, Moe had to hide her smile.

Halley gasped, wrinkling her nose. "Uncle, that's disgusting!"

"It was, love. But later they peeled them off, and it really did help."

Brian said, "I want to be a swimmer, like Da. I don't think I'd like getting burned. I'd rather drown and get eaten by the fish than have someone put dead fishes on me while I was sleeping. A boy at school threw a dead fish at Halley while we were on a field trip. I pushed him in the surf. Ye should have given the doctor a kick up the arse, Uncle."

Moe covered her mouth, trying not to laugh. She made the mistake of looking at Michael. That's when she lost it. Branna shook her head at the three adults. "You three are not helping." But she smirked, trying to keep her own giggles at bay. "He got put in time out on the bus for that little show of backbone."

Seany leaned down, "Ye protected your sister, Brian. Good for you."

Halley crossed her arms over her chest, and she looked so much like Michael in that moment, Seany had to stop himself from laughing again. "I don't need protection. I coulda taken care of the little sod myself."

"Halley! Jesus, Joseph, and Mary. If she isn't related to Brigid Murphy, I don't know who is. Don't say arse, and don't say sod. You both know better. And remind me to have a talk with your Aunt Brigid."

Michael smiled and winked at Moe, "That would be my twin. It's a thing in this family."

But Halley was still looking at his arm. She put her hand to the red, marred skin. "Does it hurt you, Uncle?"

"Sometimes it does. It's not as bad as it was. And some hurts you can't see. Nerves mending. It's like electricity trying to fire off and it hurts in prickles and bursts. It's hard to explain."

She leaned down and kissed his burns, causing Seany to blink rapidly. She raised her head and smiled. "There, now. All better."

Seany swallowed hard, his eyes misting. "Thank you, Halley. It's much better."

They took Moe's bag into the guest room. Seany whispered. "I'll sleep on the sofa bed. I don't want to make you feel awkward, okay? It's not that I wouldn't love to be in here with you, but..."

"I get it. It's too soon and your family might feel weird."

He threw his head back and laughed. "No, my family would feel elated. I've never brought a woman home, and they'd try to trap you into marrying me. I'd have to admit to them I asked you, and you turned me down."

"You didn't really ask. I mean, you did, but you didn't want to get married." She went into the bathroom and left her toiletry bag on the sink. He watched her, and the relief which should have come from her giving him a pass didn't come.

"I'd like to take you to the cliffs tomorrow. We can get up early and do some sightseeing."

She smiled broadly. "I'd love that. I have looked at pictures of them, but I've heard they are much different when you can take the whole scene in at once."

"It is different. Pictures? You've been looking up Doolin?" he cocked his head, his eyes narrowing.

She scrunched up her face, embarrassed. She admitted, "I pulled your street up on Google Earth."

He smiled, "When? When we were kids?" She didn't answer and he moved close. "When, Maureen?"

"Six weeks ago."

He raised a brow. "You wanted to visit?"

"I didn't expect to. I didn't expect anything. I guess I hoped, but then I thought you'd hate me or something. I don't know what I thought." She shook her head, embarrassed.

He thought about it for a minute, then something occurred to him. "You said you were on the pill. When we were together, you said it, but you were a virgin. When did you go on it?"

She turned away, digging in her bag. She heard the door close. He came up behind her. "You said you had a boyfriend before. How long ago? Did you go on the pill for him?"

"No, of course not. I was with Mason three years ago. Just not like that, I told you. I mean, obviously I wasn't." But she didn't answer the question.

Mason, he thought. He wanted to hunt him down and beat the hell out of him. She'd mentioned she wasn't completely ignorant on how to relieve a man. Had she relieved Mason? Had he had his mouth on her? The thought made him mental. But she hadn't gone on the pill for Mason. "When?"

"Why does it matter?" she snapped. He turned her and made her look at him. Her cheeks were pink.

"It's none of my business, but I still want to know. If you'd be willing to tell me, I'd like to know. Maybe because it's like pulling teeth getting any answers out of you."

She sighed, "It isn't any of your business, but I went on the pill when I got back to Texas. After I visited you in the hospital."

"Did you come back here for some fling? Was I your European hook up before you got back to your life in Texas?"

She bristled. "You don't know anything! You don't know what you're talking about!" Her eyes started to burn, but she wouldn't cry. No way.

"You said that before. Make me understand! Why wait so long to take a lover? Why me?"

She spat the words defensively. "Because it was supposed to be you! It was always supposed to be you! Is that what you want to hear? That I couldn't carry on a relationship because no one was ever going to measure up? Screw you, Seany! Of course you don't understand. Forget it! You don't have to worry about why I started taking birth control because I don't even want you anymore!"

He pulled her up against him. "Liar," he growled. Then he kissed her. They kissed until they were both breathless. Then he pulled away, just an inch. "You do want me. And I you, mo chuisle. Not tonight. Not in this bed. But you'll have me. All of me. Then you'll think twice before you leave again." It sounded like a warning.

They were interrupted by multiple fists on the door. "Uncle Seany! Daddy said not to bother you, but I wanted you to see my new trains!" They could hear Michael yelling for him to get away from the door.

Seany laughed against her mouth. He kissed her again, lazy and sweet. He licked her upper lip, then nibbled her bottom one. "I want inside ye, Maureen. Deep and slow. I want to feel you come while you're under me and I'm buried inside you." Her breath stuttered, and a little moan escaped her. "I want you to take me hard and wild, astride me like your damn saddle. I want to slide into you from behind and cover your body while I sink into you. While I come hard and feel you explode around me." She was rubbing her nipples against him. "I'll make it so you never scream another man's name. Do you hear me? You were right. It was always supposed to be me."

* * *

MICHAEL LAUGHED when they emerged from the bedroom. He gave Branna a knowing look. "I'll help you with the drinks, love. Seany, beer?" Seany nodded. "And Moe, we've got everything. We don't drink a lot, but my wife loves buying the stuff."

Branna jabbed an elbow. "I never know what I'll be in the mood for. Maureen, are you a liquor drinker, martinis, margaritas, or beer and wine?"

"What are you having?"

Branna grinned, "I'm not driving tonight, so I thought a French 75 sounded good. Ever had one?" Moe shook her head. "Trust me, it's divine."

"Will I sound like a pussy if I take one of those instead of a beer?" Seany said. He looked at Michael. "What? I like Prosecco. I'm a modern man."

Michael snorted, "Make it four." He went to the kitchen with Branna, and as they turned their backs to the couch, she mouthed *Oh my God!* He leaned in, whispering in his wife's ear. "Do you remember those days? Pulling my shirt tail out so my family couldn't see my hard-on?"

She shivered from his breath on her ear. "And my mussed hair and pink cheeks?"

"The good news is the two fiends will be making sure he doesn't get laid tonight instead of me. Ian better sleep through the night."

"All night? Are you sure we need that long?" She had challenge in her eyes.

"Don't poke the beast, Hellcat. We won't make it to Gus's tonight." His grin was wicked.

Seany said from behind them, "Are you going to make my drink, brother, or talk dirty in your wife's ear all night?"

Michael took the lemon, gin, and other ingredients, mumbling about cock-blocking little brothers.

* * *

Brigid burst through the door of Michael and Branna's cottage. "I can't believe you are having cocktail hour without us!"

"Hello Brigid. Do you want a mocktail?" Branna said.

"Ooh, yes. Something juicy in a fancy glass."

"Finn, French 75?"

Finn snorted, "No, I brought my bollocks with me today. Thanks. I'll just have a beer." Michael and Seany didn't meet his eye. "What? Oh, God. Don't tell me they've infected you two with these craft cocktail recipes."

Michael shrugged, "What? We like Prosecco. We're modern men." Seany snorted at the repeat. "But Branna, love, add the ginger liqueur to mine. I'm very manly and I like some spice."

"Mine too, sister. For better ballcock health." Seany said, causing Maureen and Branna to laugh. Brigid just smacked Finn. "I'll get the unsophisticated eejit a beer."

Seany smiled as he watched his family interact with Moe. She was shy at first but began to open up. He thought it must be when she realized they weren't going to judge her for the actions of a confused sixteen-year-old girl.

Moe said, "So, Seany said it was a really interesting story when you two met, Branna. I mean, I know the whole story of what happened with Aidan and Alanna, but how did you two meet?"

Brigid was jumping up and down in her seat, her drink sloshing on Finn. "I want to tell it!"

Michael put a hand up. "Oh no you don't. I'll tell it. I don't trust your account to be historically accurate. Gender bias and all that."

Branna said, "Ha! Look who's talking. I'll tell it. It all started when I bought this cottage fair and square." Michael pinched her in the ribs, and she squeaked. But she wasn't going to be swayed. Moe warmed as she took in the adoring looks, despite their obvious dispute over the finer nuances of their meeting. Branna finally said, "We'll both tell it."

So, they did. The battle over a cottage, the attraction, the fighting, the wounds and baggage of their pasts, the love and the pain. Moe found herself close to tears. She'd never known Branna's father had been killed in the Second Battle of Fallujah. It was quite something really, that three of them were Marine Corps daughters. "So, you're just another Marine Corps brat like me and Alanna."

Branna smiled. "These O'Brien men like tough women, despite their protests."

"My brothers are the envy of the county. They've all found their mates, and they are strong, beautiful, smart women." She squeezed Finn's hand. "And I found my mate. Come what may."

"Mate? You make it sound so...primal," Moe said. They didn't look at her. They all looked at Seany.

Michael cleared his throat. "It's a story for another time, I think. A bit of family lore." And Moe knew there was something important she was missing. Something they weren't ready to tell her. She guessed that was okay. At least no one blamed her for the teenage heartbreak she'd inflicted on the younger O'Brien. She looked at Seany and was taken aback by the intensity of his gaze. She was definitely missing something.

* * *

Gus O'Connor's Pub-Doolin, Co. Clare

Moe looked around the old pub, smiling at the huge family. There were some tourists as well, but by far, the crowd was local. After the cocktail Branna had made her, she had the warm fuzzies. The pub had a fireplace, old pictures, and other mementos decorating the place. Dark wood trim and well worn wooden tables.

She slowly and methodically met most of the O'Brien clan. Even the grandparents were there. They'd hired some local girls to watch all of the children except the two newborns, who were in attendance for a time. "As it gets later," Charlie had explained, "Brigid will take the babies home. She can't drink because she is pregnant, so we are exploiting her."

"You all have a lot of babies. And an uncommon number of American women."

Charlie smiled and pointed to her husband. "If you could have that specimen of a man lying bare assed in your bed every night, would you go back to America?"

Moe smirked. "I see your point." Tadgh was sexy as hell. He had long hair, for a cop, likely due to his undercover work. She remembered, years ago, running her fingers through Seany's long hair. Now it was cut short to uniform standards. It made him look more like Aidan and his father. All of the O'Brien men, including their grandfather, were devastatingly handsome. The women were just as beautiful. Every one of them. She felt awkward and too plain to be in the mix.

She played with the condensation on her pint glass. "I don't feel like I belong here. It's silly, really, to even feel awkward about it. I really don't belong here. I mean, look at all of you. You're in these perfect marriages."

"Ha!" Charlie said. "Every single couple here had to claw their way to happiness. Don't let this domestic bliss fool you. But you could, Moe. Belong here, I mean." Moe looked into her warm, amber eyes. She really liked this woman.

"Seany is a force of nature. It scares me. I feel like I could be collateral damage."

"You have to decide whether the payoff is worth the risk, girl. I can tell you, from where I'm standing, that is an absofuckinglutely." Moe laughed as Charlie raised her glass. "A toast to the O'Briens. As families go, you could do worse, but you couldn't do any better."

Moe looked up as Seany joined the musicians. Her heart thumped in her chest as he started to strum his guitar. Seany's father played the mandolin. Tadgh was on another guitar. Patrick was playing what Seany had called a bouzouki. Sorcha was playing her fiddle and Liam was playing the large Irish drum which used a wooden piece for striking. When Seany started singing with his cousin Tadgh, Moe felt an absurd urge to cry. Charlie reached across the table, taking her hand. Then Branna joined them. She saw their hands clasped and added her own to the top.

Branna said, "I'm glad you're here, Moe. It's long past time you came for him." Moe felt the urge to argue. It wasn't why she'd come. Argue that they were young and still finding their way in the world. She needed to graduate. It was everything that had been preached through the phone by her mother. Everything she'd heard a hundred times, or so it seemed. She said none of it. She just watched him. Alanna joined them at the table, and Hans stopped by for a quick kiss from all of the ladies. "I have to head back this weekend. I miss Doc and my kids." He kissed Alanna on the head, "My other kids, I mean. I was wondering if I could join you on one more ride on Wednesday?"

"That would be amazing. I wish it wasn't such a long drive for you," Moe said.

Hans laughed. "I've driven longer and in much less scenic places. After living here with Mary, I found I miss this island. And she's going to be so jealous. I feel like calling her on FaceTime from Gus's just to rub it in. That's terrible to admit."

Alanna smiled, "Do it! She gives as good as she gets!"

He pulled out his cell phone and, sure enough, Doc Mary answered. It was midday in Manaus, and Mary was in the cafeteria. She scowled as Alanna and Hans lifted their pints. Alanna was left with the foam of her Guinness making a mustache. Mary said, "You two think you're so clever." She held up a little ball of something. "Look what I have, Hans."

"Ah, lawdy. Gabriela's cheese bread. You're killing me, Doc! Oh, hey, look who's on stage!"

He turned the phone so the musicians were seen behind him. "Liam is coming back this spring. So is Izzy. And we've started campaigning to get Sorcha and Sean there as well. Put in a good word for them with Reverend Mother Faith and we'll work it from this end!"

"Brilliant!" Doc Mary said with genuine enthusiasm. "The boys are asking about you. I keep telling them you're coming back soon. We all miss you, love."

Hans blushed because an entire table of women were watching. "I miss you too, baby."

After he rang off, Moe began interrogating him about the mission in Brazil. They all talked about it, the women envying their family who'd been able to go. And then they told her about little Estela. Caitlyn had made her way over at that point, along with Izzy, and the women crammed around the table as Hans bowed out of the conversation. They told her about how Izzy and Liam had met. About the tragic loss of Eve, Liam's first love, and his journey back to the world of the living. About how Izzy had been his salvation. Moe smiled as she listened. All of these women had their stories to tell. Caitlyn with her journey to motherhood, and even some small details about the matriarch and patriarch of the O'Brien clan. How they'd met their own challenges during the Troubles in Northern Ireland.

"What about Aoife and David? How did they meet?" Moe asked, devouring this rich and wonderful family lore.

"That's one story we've still yet to hear. Someday, we will get the whole of it." Caitlyn's green eyes shone with mischief. "Can ye imagine what David looked like as a young lad?" She fanned herself. "Aoife was a real stunner to be sure."

Seany saw the hens all gathered around Maureen and he cringed to think what they were saying to her. But it pleased him just as much. She fit right in with his crazy bunch of sisters-in-law. All with their own personalities. All with their own stories before the time they'd met his brothers. And even more interesting, the time during which they'd fallen in love with his brothers. A pang of affection hit him so deeply when he looked at them, lovely and vibrant. They'd each added something irreplaceable to the family and to his life. Even Finn, with his dark good looks and knowing eyes. He looked over the pub as he played, then at his father and brothers who shared the stage with him. His grief and pain were like dead space which separated him from them all. He'd always been the baby. The spoiled little brother. The apple of all their eyes. Now he was something different. Apart. And he didn't know how to get it all back.

* * *

Moe broke her two-drink rule by ordering another pint of Smithwick's. She turned to find Madeline Nagle next to her. "Hi Maddie. When did you get here?"

"About an hour ago. You've been swarmed by those O'Brien women. You're like a new exhibit at the zoo!"

She laughed. "I think they're just friendly."

Madeline snorted. "They'll have you married before the week is out." Seany had said something similar, but she assumed it was a joke. "I'm only half kidding. And good for them. They'd be lucky to add you to their ranks."

"Seany and I are a little young for that kind of talk."

Josh came up next to them. "Young for what kind of talk? Madeline, are you talking dirty again?"

Madeline punched him, "Shut your gob. And we were talking about marriage. Well, she wasn't. Don't get your boxers in a bunch. I was talking about these O'Briens. They'll want to keep her. And I disagree, Moe. You aren't too young. It's a flaw in our generation."

"Go on?" Moe said, and she noticed that Josh was all ears as well.

"We want to have it all. In a specific order, of course. Don't get married until you've slept with a few blokes. Don't marry until you've gotten your degree and accumulated the debt to go with it. Get married, but don't have kids until you're rid of the debt. Don't have too many kids. Don't have zero kids. Don't have your first until you've established your career. It's all a load of shite. We've forgotten one important truth. Marriage and children are a byproduct of love, not careful planning. It has its own timeline. Children are a blessing, not a burden. We've overcomplicated everything with crushing expectations and these damn rules. Just keep an open mind, Moe. And keep your heart open. Anything done out of love can't be wrong."

"You're talking about love, though. Seany hasn't seen me in over six years. We are practically strangers."

"The heart knows its mate," Madeline said softly but firmly. That was the second time someone had used the word mate tonight. She really didn't understand.

* * *

MOE WAS STARING out of the car window dreamily as Michael drove them all back to the cottage. "Did you enjoy yourself?" Seany said from next to her in the backseat.

She smiled, the wind of the open window blowing her hair into her face. "I did. I really did. That place is good fun. And your family is really something. All of the wives are so welcoming, and your brothers are…"

He leaned in, scowling, although he had a grin in there somewhere. "Are what?"

Hot, gorgeous, talented, built like Gods, beautiful just like you. "Really nice guys," she shrugged. He narrowed his eyes. He raked his eyes over her for the hundredth time tonight. She was wearing a pretty navy blue sweater, a pair of jeans, and her nicer boots. He thought about having those boots up on each shoulder while he'd pleasured her with his mouth. Tasted her warm, liquid desire. He watched her cheeks turn pink as she read the heat and arousal on his face. He was going to find some way to get her alone before she had to go back to work.

* * *

MOE WOKE to the smell of coffee. She padded through the house in the early light of morning. Branna was up, beginning breakfast and sipping from her coffee cup. She stopped and stared at the sight in the living room. Branna's sofa bed was not large. Maybe the equivalent of a standard double bed. Seany was asleep, but he had two six-year-olds on either side of him. He had Halley in one arm, so she wouldn't roll off, and Brian tucked under the other.

Branna giggled softly into her cup. "They have a longstanding tradition of sneaking out of their beds and sleeping with their uncles, aunts, and older cousins. No one is safe or exempt. And they work in pairs."

She slid onto a stool by the butcher block. "It's sweet. I love my aunts and uncles, too."

Branna asked, "Do you come from a big family? Seany said you have a brother and sister."

"Yes, Emmie and Sammy. Both younger. My parents are both one of four. Big ole Texas family on both sides. My paternal grandparents have a cattle ranch not too far from ours. My mother's parents are farmers. My one uncle is starting to take things over. Wheat, corn, and sorghum."

"Wow, real ranchers and farmers. Did you know Izzy comes from Arizona farmers? Well...orchards, but that's still farming, right? Apricots and apples, I think. Maybe almonds, too? Anyway, I moved around so much, we never had more than a small row of potted tomato plants. I guess you understand, to a degree. It's nice you had somewhere to land, once the military life was over."

Moe took her hand, and it caused Branna's brows to raise. "I'm sorry you didn't. Have somewhere to go, I mean. I'm glad you found such a wonderful place, after all."

Branna's eyes misted. "Me too, sister. It wasn't easy. But a lot of really beautiful things are easy to get. You just have to want it enough to fight for it."

* * *

Moe climbed the stairs to the tourist hub of the Cliffs of Moher, so excited she could barely stand it. "Wait, woman. It's not a race!" Seany was laughing behind her, and she knew damn well he could keep up with her.

"Quit staring at my butt and get up here," she said saucily.

He threw his head back and laughed as he caught up to her. "Guilty as charged. And no. I won't quit looking at your ass. Especially in those jeans. You've filled out magnificently, little Moe." She smirked at that.

"Show me your tower, Prince O'Brien."

"Christ, don't remind me. Some brilliant jackass decided it would be a good idea to paint over the stone. I mean, hundreds of years old and suddenly some committee decides to paint the fecking thing. I think they should have consulted us. It is O'Brien Tower, after all."

She got to the top, surpassed the visitor center, and ran up to the railing. It was cloudy, with patches of sun here and there. The rain had been almost nonexistent in the time she'd been here. She gazed over the dramatic landscape. "It's beautiful, Seany. Just...wow." She said it with a sigh, and he cupped a hand on her shoulder, pulling her close. "Better than Google Earth?"

She smiled. "You aren't going to let me live that down, are you?"

"Nope. Ye needed to throw me a bone, given the grinder you've put my pride through."

"Please, you likely got over it quickly enough," she said dryly.

"Papering over a broken heart is not the same as getting over it, Maureen." When he talked like that, soft and deep, with that lilt and the way her name rolled off his tongue, she felt it all over. She burrowed against him.

"So, what's on the agenda today, since I don't need to shop for a coat?" she said. She was wearing one of Caitlyn's coats. Most of the O'Brien women were too petite. Well, except for Izzy, who lived in Dublin, and had offered to mail her some sweaters.

"I'd love to take you onto the small island, but the ferry is only running out of Galway. The Doolin ferries will start in a month or so. Then I'll take you to Inis Oírr. Tadgh's mother is from there, and it's where you'll see Castle O'Brien."

"You can't swing a cat in any direction without hitting an old O'Brien stronghold. Are you making this up?"

He looked scandalized. "I'm not. This is the clan seat, girl. Best mind your manners. I'll start making you call me *My Lord*."

She tried to elbow him in the ribs, and he said in her ear, "And I think there is something in the old laws about plundering the village maidens."

"Not my village, and too late. You already plundered." He pinched her and she squealed, drawing the eyes of an older couple who just shook their heads and smiled as they walked on. He said huskily, "Not even close to a proper plundering, lass. Not even close."

* * *

MOE LEFT the room when her mother called, wanting to talk freely without any background noise. Her mother missed her terribly. She understood. She missed her family too. Being around the O'Briens was wonderful, but it didn't mean she didn't love them. Her mom was crying now. "You're going to leave me someday. It's payback. I left my mother and married a Marine."

"Mom, you're talking like a lunatic. I'm not going anywhere. This is an internship. I'll be back before you know it." It was only right after the words were out of her mouth that she looked up and saw Seany.

His face was tight. "Branna wanted to know if you'd like a sandwich."

"Seany," but he was out the door. "Mom, I have to go. Not now, Momma! Goodbye." She followed him out into the living room and Branna turned with a loaf of bread in her hand to see both the looks on their faces.

"The sandwiches can wait," she said awkwardly. "Michael, let's take the kids for a walk before lunch."

And just like that the house was empty. Seany said, "Don't explain. I get it. You have a life back in Texas. You've got a horse and overbearing parents and Mason."

"Stop it. Let me explain."

"You don't need to explain. You came here for an internship. Maybe a fling to shed that long overdue virginity. I get it, Moe. This is temporary. It was always going to be temporary."

"That's not true. Stop putting words in my mouth!" She hissed. "Haven't you ever said something to calm a hysterical mother? Even if it was complete and utter bullshit?"

He had his hands on his hips, angry and hurt. "I don't know what to believe. It doesn't matter. Of course you'll go."

She flinched a little, and he closed his eyes, running his fingers through his hair. "I'm sorry. I didn't mean to eavesdrop. And I don't know what the hell I'm saying right now."

"I don't know what I'm doing, Seany. I thought I'd finally gotten over you. I tried. I did. I dated, I buried myself in schoolwork. I was a good sister and daughter. But it was like this ache that never really left me. And then I saw that internship. It gnawed at me, and I tried to dismiss it. Then I would look it up on a map and figure out how far it was from your hometown. Then I'd feel like a fool and start looking around home for a position."

He shook his head, "Wait, what are you talking about? You mean before Alanna called you?"

Her eyes welled up with tears. She nodded. "Yes. I was looking at this internship before you were hurt. And then she called, and I came. I saw you." The tears started falling. "I saw you and my heart could barely stand it." He pulled her into his arms as she continued to cry. "It was real for me. I know people think that teenagers are too young to feel something so deeply. That it's just hormones or something. But it was real for me, Seany. I felt it. I still do."

He kissed her face, all over, drying her tears with his lips. "It was real for me too, Maureen. If I could erase all of those other women, I would. If I could have offered you something even remotely as beautiful as you offered me, I would have. All we have is now, mo chuisle. And I want to try. Please, mo chroí. Promise me you'll try."

CHAPTER 24

Galway City, Co. Galway

Moe walked around the city center while Seany went to his physical therapy session. She bought some fun souvenirs for her family because this shopping was leaps and bounds better than anything in Letterfrack. She also bought a hoodie that said Galway Girl. Completely touristy, but to hell with anyone who got judgy. Today she was a tourist. When Seany picked her up, he was smiling. "I'm cleared for duty early. After this weekend, I'm back with the fire brigade."

"Well, now we have to celebrate. Good thing I got this!" She pulled out a bottle of sparkling wine from her bag.

"Maureen Rogers. If I didn't know better, I'd swear you were trying to seduce me."

"I doubt I will be very successful with your roommate at home."

"Josh works this evening. He won't be home until at least ten." His eyes burned, and there was no humor in them.

"Well then, I guess that gives me a little time to get this chilled." She smiled so sweetly that it almost stopped his heart. That pale skin, those grey-blue eyes, and that Mona Lisa smile.

When they got to the cottage, she smiled. "It's cute. You're so close to the water. I'll bet that makes things easy for Josh. With the Lifeboat duty, I mean. I still can't believe that story you told me about Cora and the little boy."

"Aye, and Maddie."

"He loves her. Or he's almost there." Seany seemed surprised. She just shrugged. "I've seen enough of love between two people to know. And she feels the same."

"You think? I mean, I know she's not immune to him. He draws lasses like flies to honey. He rarely indulges, mostly because of the way he feels about her. The last woman he was seeing was a real nutter."

He told her about Justine as they made an easy dinner. "That's terrible. Is that why he's growing his hair out? I saw the scar before. I didn't ask, because it wasn't my business, but it never occurred to me that he'd been assaulted."

"Yeah, he has a bad history with family violence. That's all I'll say on it. Mostly because he doesn't talk about it a lot. But I swear, I've never been so close to strangling a woman."

Moe shook her head. She said, "Why would he be with someone like that? Maddie is right there in front of him."

Seany smiled sadly. "I think Josh thinks Maddie is too good for him. His father really did a number on him. Alanna said that abused kids can have PTSD just like soldiers or..."

"First responders," she said softly.

"Anyway, that's the why of it. I think Justine was his attempt at papering over the heartbreak." She understood, remembering his own confession.

"Men are idiots."

He chuckled, "I suppose we are. But with Josh it's more. The scary thing about him taking up with Justine is that he excused the behavior. It's what he knows. And how sad is that? His time with us has helped, but the first seventeen years he was living with a violent drunk. It sticks."

After devouring a couple of grilled cheese sandwiches, Seany took out two champagne glasses. Maureen said, "Champagne flutes? Hmm, how many women have you brought here? Because Justine doesn't sound like the champagne type."

"She wasn't. And to answer your other question, none. I haven't had another woman here."

He popped the cork and poured them both a portion. They clinked glasses. "To here and now," she said.

"Slainte," he whispered. After a sip, he took both their glasses and set them on the table. Then he pulled her close and kissed her. She moaned as she tasted the cold wine on his tongue. He cupped her head, threading his hands in her hair. His mouth hovered, stealing sips, holding her away from him. Her breath hitched in her throat. He spoke low and soft, lovers words that he knew she couldn't understand. Then he kissed her deeply, stealing her breath and giving it back to her until she could barely stand. She ran a hand under his shirt, smoothing her palm over his abs chest. His cock was so hard it was painful.

She peeled his shirt off and he had hers off in another second. A pale pink bra with lace cups this time. He lifted her, spreading her thighs to wrap around his waist. He smoothed his hands over her back, then drew her straps down so he could nibble the flesh between her neck and shoulder. He shed her bra and they both cried out as they came chest to chest with nothing between them. "I need ye, a mhuirnín."

She was never going to get tired of hearing him croon endearments to her in Irish. The fact that he seemed unaware he was doing it, and that it was always when he was aroused, sent her own hormones soaring. She was really going to have to ask Maddie what they meant. She'd be too embarrassed to ask Moira. He spread her body out on the bed, then thought of something. She propped up on her elbows and laughed as he brought in the two glasses, the bottle, and the candle they'd lit for dinner. "I'm not prepared to let you out of this room for a while," he said with a rakish grin. He closed the door and came to lean over her. He kissed her until her heart was pounding, her chest pumping. She was back on his pillow now, and she watched with heavy lids as he dipped a finger in the cold wine. He circled her nipple and her head fell back. Then his warm mouth replaced the finger and she scissored her legs, squirming under his mouth. He dipped again, running his finger down her abdomen to the top of her jeans. "I need to taste you again. I can't stop thinking about it." He licked where he'd left the wine, covering her belly with wet kisses. He unfastened her jeans and she was so aroused, it didn't occur to her to be bashful. Just the thought of what he'd done to her in the barn loft had her wet and hot. She watched, eyes huge as he took a sip of wine into his mouth, then put his cold tongue right on her sex. No teasing. No drawing out the moment. She bowed off the mattress as cold flesh met hot. He pulled her tight to his face and moaned against her core.

Seany looked up as Maureen moaned and arched in the candlelight. Her belly flexed as she started the slow and delicious climb to her climax. He spread his palms on her thighs and opened her wide, feeling her hips rock. He varied his intensity, keeping her on the brink. Then he put both hands over her breasts, lightly pinching her pink nipples. She put one hand in his hair as she gripped the headboard with the other. "Come for me." He growled the words as he cupped his mouth over her sex, sending her reeling into a bone bending orgasm. She screamed when she came, and it was fucking perfect. She'd always been on the timid side as a girl, and to see that the woman was anything but timid in bed was a revelation. He slid his fingers into her, sending her right up to her peak again. He could feel her sex contracting, and the thought of her milking his cock like that had him ripping his own jeans off.

He stood, naked and aroused before her. She was limp with satisfaction, but her eyes raked over his body and he saw her arch herself instinctively. It was raw and primitive, but he needed her to understand. "This time, I won't stop." He leaned down, pressing her into the pillow with the heat of his stare. "But you better mean it, Maureen. I won't have you retreating from me again."

"I mean it. I meant it the first time. And I'm not going anywhere."

He never looked away as he worked himself against her slick

entrance. "Tell me if I hurt you, love. We've got time." He inched his way in slowly, watching her face and letting her get used to his size as he slowly filled her. Then he was seated fully, their bodies fused at the hips. She was breathing hard, her mouth pink, her eyes hazy with desire. "You're inside me." She ran a hand over his cheek. Her eyes glittered in the candlelight. He propped up on his elbows, rubbing his lips softly over her mouth.

He swallowed hard, as if overcome for a moment by emotion. He said, "I did wake up for you. I heard you, Maureen. I didn't want to come back, but I heard you and I felt you. I came back for you, mo ghra." Her eyes welled with tears as he started to move. He threw his head back, moaning as he filled her. She wrapped her legs around his hips and watched him in the throes of love making. He was breathtaking, like a fallen angel, too beautiful to look at for long. He was thick and long, filling her so completely. She'd never imagined what this sort of stinging possession could feel like. Something deep in her body answered him and she met his thrusts as she started to fall off the edge again. He sensed her surrender and he lifted her hips with one arm as he leaned with the other. He was so deep. She bucked as she started to come so hard that she saw stars. She heard him go with her, letting out a deep groan as he spilled himself inside her.

They clutched each other, tangled limbs and sweat. She felt him shaking, or maybe it was her. "You're mine, mo ghra. And I'm yours. It's enough for now. The knowing is enough."

* * *

THE NEXT COUPLE OF HOURS, Moe was lost in another world. The pleasure was all consuming. The emotional connection tangled their minds together until they were one being. Their bodies stayed joined in a dance of rolling and straining, seeking and finding. There were times for speaking, and other times when they were robbed of speech. But the intimacy she'd felt over the last couple of hours was devastating.

Seany couldn't make himself let go of the connection. He should let her rest. She'd come to him a virgin. But every time he touched her, her body would call to him. She was so open, with trust and such mutual yearning, that he just kept loving her and worshipping her. Now he felt himself growing hard again as he kissed the soft skin of her shoulder and neck. She was across his chest and he felt her body respond, a wave of motion traveling through her so that she rubbed her nipples against his chest. "Come to me, Maureen." He pulled her fully over him, pressing her upright. She understood what he wanted.

She looked unsure, so he took her hips in his hands and poised her right over his cock. She pressed down and he looked at the place where they were joining and sucked back an orgasm. She was slick and warm and so tight, he moaned at the feel of her, and of the sight of their joining. "I want to feel you come like this. I want to see your face." He filled her to the base of his cock and she arched, exposing her neck and making her breasts high and beautiful. Her tight stomach began to flex as she found a rhythm. The noises she made as she rode him, the look of complete abandon as she rolled her head and put her hair across her face...perfection. The epitome of female desire. He ran his hands up her body and cupped her breasts, thumbing the nipples as she increased her pace. He felt the beginning of her climax and lifted his hips, thrusting deep inside to hit her right in that spot deep in her womb.

Her voice was strained as she said, "Seany, come with me."

"I want to watch you. Let yourself go." He rolled his hips in rhythm with her, rambling in his native tongue the erotic words that somehow didn't come to him in English. It seemed to make her lose control, not being able to deny herself the release any longer. He watched her come, her body flush as she strained and contracted around him. It was exquisite.

* * *

Maureen woke slowly, sensing the heat and comfort of another body. Of Seany's body. This night had been worth waiting for, and she forgave him for stopping that initial, hasty coupling. She opened her eyes to find him rubbing a finger over an old photograph. She said, "Good morning. What do you have there?"

He showed it to her. It was a photo of her on the beach in North Carolina. She kept a similar photo in her nightstand drawer at home in Texas. The only difference was that hers was a selfie, and he was in it. It had been the same day, though. Seany's copy was folded back on each side, cropping out the scenery and just picturing her. Like he'd tried to make it smaller. "I remember this day. It was a good day. Sad, though. It was the day before you went home to Ireland. Where did you dig this up?"

"It fell out of my uniform, the night of the warehouse fire. The paramedics had to cut my clothes off." She looked confused. He said, "I kept it with me. It was a sort of…good luck charm."

"You kept that photo inside your uniform?" The significance of this wasn't wasted on her. Military men did the same thing. "After all this time?" Her voice was hoarse.

"Aye, I did. Right next to my heart," he said as he placed the photo over his heart. "I told you, Maureen. It was real for me, too.

JOSH WAS UP AS WELL, training with the Royal Lifeboat just after dawn. He sent them both off with coffee and toast. Moe kissed him on the cheek, which made him wiggle his eyebrows at Seany. Seany said, "That's enough. She's taken."

Maureen called Moira, and she told her to take her time. The ride with Hans and Seany was at eleven. No more suspicious business had happened at the ranch since she left, which was a relief. The Guards had agreed to do a drive by when they could, as well as the rangers on the edge of the property that bordered the park lands. Since they had a little extra time, Seany took the alternative path through the Moycullen Bogs. It was a foggy, damp morning, which made the drive through the bogs eerie and a little exciting. "What if we found a bog body? I read a mystery novel where they found a bog body in England."

"I'll see what I can do," Seany said with a smirk. "But you've got bogland in Connemara National Park as well. It's been dry this year, though, so it may not seem so ominous."

They stopped in Clifden to have a hot breakfast, not quite ready to break the spell they'd been under. The two nights had been a sort of getaway for them both. "After the ride, I've got to head back. I work tomorrow. But I'd like to see you Saturday night. You've got Sunday off, right?"

"I do. I'd like that."

"How would you feel about taking an overnight holiday up to Westport and Achill Island? It's the off season, so it won't be very exciting, but I can book a night in a guest house or get a cottage for the night."

"You don't have to do that. I mean, it sounds like heaven, but…"

He smiled, "It's settled. The seafood is good up there. Pack warm clothes. I'll be able to get you around six if you think you'll be ready to go. We can be there in less than an hour.

* * *

Letterfrack, Co. Galway

The peace of the day was short lived. While Maureen mucked stalls in the outside stables, a Garda vehicle pulled into the drive. She'd thought at first that it was a follow up to the incidents they'd had recently. When Moira's voice was raised so that she could hear it from the arena, she ran to see what the problem was.

"A bloody competency hearing? Who on earth ordered this? I have a right to know."

The officer was young, and he squirmed under the intensity of Moira's gaze. "I don't know, madame. I'm just following orders to deliver this paperwork. The domestic court information is on the first page."

"What's going on here, Moira?" Seany was there now, right on Moe's heels.

Moira said, "Someone has called for a competency hearing. I have to accept that piece of shite in the envelope and call the clerk at domestic and family court."

Maureen said, "This is a mistake. I don't know a sharper woman anywhere than Moira. Officer, what exactly is your job today? Surely you aren't here to take her anywhere?"

"It's my understanding that it was the original request to have her..." He cleared his throat, "Taken into care. But the county judge overruled it and replaced that order with this one."

"And that would be Judge Kierny? Yes, I know him well. He's a fair man. So, someone wants to have me committed, eh? Based on my advancing years, no doubt. Well, I'm going to take one guess who's behind this and put a barn boot up his arse."

"Hugo, that little shit." Moe's words seemed to strengthen Moira's resolve. She took the paper from the officer's hands.

"I'll be calling the clerk directly. Then I'll be calling a lawyer. Free of charge, as it were, because he's on my non-profit board. If my dear Hugo thinks he's going to go through the back door to get my ranch and my money, I'll make the little piss artist rue the day he dropped out of his mother's bum."

The officer smirked. "Good luck with the aforementioned piss artist, madame."

As he left, Seany followed him to his car, no doubt introducing himself and making the man familiar with not only the guards in his own family, but the officer that was currently taking therapeutic riding lessons in the Monday class. He also told him about the strange "accidents" which were happening at the ranch, and the danger it posed to the horses and staff.

"Aye, I pulled up the watch order and saw that there had been mischief happening. Tell her to get a good lawyer, and I'll do what I can to double the watch. Someone wants things to fall apart here, and I don't know why. It's a good thing she's doing here. We all think so. And no one, including Judge Kierney, could ever suppose that woman to be mentally diminished. I'll write up a statement to that fact. It might be a good idea to have the lads in your class do the same."

Seany shook hands with him, giving him a goodbye in the Irish. He returned the sentiment and went on his way.

"Moira, I'd like you to do a video conference interview with my cousin Tadgh. He's in Dublin on the Special Detectives Unit, and I really think he can help. Sometimes you forget small things that might be relevant. Can you do that? Maybe we can get to the bottom of all this and he can call his colleagues in the area."

"Of course. Thank you, lad. Now, it looks like our Marine has just come down the road. Go enjoy your ride and don't think on it. Just send him my number and I'll do the rest. And I've got to go call that judge." She stopped, asking one more question. "Would you call him? Hugo, I mean."

Seany answered, "No. Catch the little fecker unaware. And Moira, the gloves need to come off. Family or not. His behavior is harassment at best, destruction of property and animal cruelty at worst. If he's responsible for all of these things, he's clearly got a screw loose."

Her eyes misted. "He's blood. I tried to have a relationship with him. My cousin would be ashamed if she were still alive. He's just like his father. It makes me wonder if he's a part of this. I wouldn't put it past him."

"Okay, when you talk to Tadgh, give him the father's name as well. And let's not forget, there is a woman involved in this. A woman made those calls before your open house."

She rubbed her forehead. "Aye, I know. I'll call him right after I speak with the judge and get this damn case dismissed."

CHAPTER 25

The mountains, the forest, and the sea render men savage; they develop the fierce, but yet do not destroy the human...Victor Hugo

The day was fine, and the air was fresh. They went along the path leading to the parklands and beyond. Seany said, "Tell us about your boys, Hans. We've met Estela and Genoveva in the flesh. We've heard some interesting tales as well, but I'd like to know more about the other children." Seany had heard a little about all of the children at St. Clare's, of course, but not from Hans.

So, Hans told them. At one time, they'd had over twenty children at the orfanato. When Genoveva and Estela had come to Ireland, it left a hole in the hearts of all the children. "I'm not going to lie. I broke down like a sissy when I watched them all say goodbye. The teenagers took it hard, because they'd grown up together. The saddest part is that there is always another child. We just got a six-year-old girl named Caskata. It means *like a waterfall.* Pretty, skinny little thing. And we got a baby boy. I'm hoping he'll get adopted, but the sisters will take good care of him if he doesn't. Now, my boys, they're something else. They assign the teenagers to me for mentoring, because chances are no one is ever coming for them. There is a grim future for some of these kids when they age out. So, I'm working with Henrico and Emilio because they want to go into the military. We've already talked to the Army and Navy recruiters. We don't want them getting sucked into mining. It's dangerous. They have a lot of precious gemstones in Brazil and the mining companies are no better than slave traders. My other boy is Cristiano. He's a smart, little guy. Small for his age and blind as a bat without his glasses, so I don't think he'll be able to go into the military. My Mary adores him, so we're bound and determined to get him into a good school when he ages out. If we have to sponsor him and bring him here, we'll do it. He wants to be a doctor, like Mary. He follows her around like a pup, and he's got his own stethoscope now."

He went on as they rode, everyone interested to hear about the sisters and the resident doctors and nurses. "You don't want me yammering on all day, do you? We should be taking in the scenery."

"Aye, we'll likely bring them this route again with the other group." Devlin said. "This is fascinating. Truly. It's a wonderful thing you're doing. So, Sean, this all started with your brother Liam?"

"Yes, that's a long story, but it started with him. Then my sister-in-law and my brother Patrick spent some time there. That's when they adopted wee Estela. She's a lovely, sweet child. An answer to their prayers. You'll likely meet them all when the family comes for a ride."

"To be sure. We know they can all play and sing. I'm looking forward to a ride out with the O'Briens," Devlin said.

"My brother Liam and his wife Izzy will go back this spring. They'll be gone a little over three months. They're trying to talk my parents into a thirty-day trip. My mother is a midwife. They go into the indigenous tribal lands, deep in the forest, as well as on the outskirts of the city to offer medical treatment to the people living in the Manaus slums. Mobile clinics on a riverboat and a bus or something. Vaccination clinics as well. And the mission has a full hospital with a surgical O.R., thanks to Izzy. Those nuns must be quite something."

Hans laughed. "Oh, yes. They are tough and smart and completely devoted to every aspect of that charity mission. The school, the orphanage, and the hospital. And to each other, of course. I never imagined I'd find a place for myself that gave me just as much fulfillment as being in the Marine Corps. Yet here I am. Remarried and living on the Amazon with a bunch of nuns and orphans."

Michele had stayed silent for a while. "So, what do you do besides the transitions services for the older kids?"

He gave her a sideways glance. "Well, unofficially, I'm security. We've had trouble in spades. Drug cartels, animal attacks, and some other problems. Illegal loggers started a fire that took out one of the indigenous villages. So, with all of the unsavory elements encroaching on St. Clare's little bubble, they knew the time had come for some security measures. They hired a retired Army man, Paolo. He started as Izzy's interpreter and it kind of evolved. He's an amazing asset. I work with him to guard the doctors when they are in the city or out in the bush. We also guard the mission. Brazil is as dangerous as it is beautiful. We also handle physical education for the older kids. Sister Maria works with the little ones on the soccer field. That nun is something to see. But we do Cross-Fit with older ones and a bit of mixed martial arts." He narrowed his eyes at her. "Are you looking to volunteer? Because I can tell you that right now, I hate that they're down a man. If Paolo or I need a break or get called home, it would be nice to have some back up."

Michele shrugged. She said, "I'll think about it. I'm not a fan of bugs, but I can tolerate almost anything," she said. She nodded to herself. "When this internship is over, I'll think about it."

They left the valley and ascended up into the rocky, green hills that were so famous in Ireland. Devlin stopped at the summit of one hill and said, "Look over there. You can see the sea from here. You're lucky it cleared up for us or we'd be standing in mist." They could see the dark blue sea and it was stunning. In the other directions were mossy patches of bog land, other summits, and the sparkling streams that fed the land and animals.

Moe looked around at the breathtaking views and thought about all the places she'd lived. Every one of the places had given her something that she wouldn't trade for anything. Texas was home, yes. But it hadn't always been. She wasn't attached to it the way her father was. Home was a state of mind. A stage in life. It wasn't a static existence for her. Never had been. She sniffed deeply of the air. "What is that smell?"

Devlin answered, "That's the heather. You should see it in the summer when it's in bloom. Rolling hills of pink and purple hues. And the smell…." He sighed. "It's heavenly. When we get back to our own lands, and out of the park, I'll show you where the heather grows. You can take some dried bunches and burn it in your hearth in the cabin."

She blushed. "I haven't used the fireplace yet. I didn't have any wood."

Devlin smacked his head, "That would be my fault. Ye should have said something. I know it's heated, but having a fire is what makes it a home. Heather and firewood. And I'll try to find some turf for you, just so you can get the experience."

Moe laughed, "That sounds perfect." They continued on the trail, finding a small plateau where Devlin said they would stop for a late lunch. It was a lovely spot that overlooked the mountain range and the valley from where they'd come.

Michele said, "Moira packed enough to feed an army. We have an assortment of finger sandwiches on homemade bread, some sort of cookies, and bottles of water." She started passing the food around. Everyone had a tomato, cheese, and watercress sandwich, a curry chicken salad sandwich, and egg salad with rocket, for which Michele and Moe needed an explanation. Rocket was the European word for arugula.

They ate in comfortable silence for a time, just listening to the sounds of nature around them. The wildlife was mostly birds. At one point, Devlin froze as a little black bird seemed to stop and watch the group. He pointed to it and Seany looked. Devlin said, "Do you have a watch?" The women and Hans watched in fascination as Seany looked at his smart watch, turned to the bird, and said, "The time is twelve fifty-five." The bird cocked its head, then seemed to lose interest. It hopped off into a nearby bush, but the sense of unease was palpable between the two Irishman. "What was all of that about?" Hans was the first to voice what the three of them were thinking.

Seany answered, "It's a solitary magpie. They don't normally travel alone. When you see a lone magpie, it's an omen of bad luck to come. You can avoid the poor luck if you tell the bird the time." Moe looked at him and Devlin to see if there was any sign they were kidding. Apparently not. They accepted this bit of superstition as completely reasonable.

Devlin continued, "If you don't have the time, then you should salute the bird before he flies off and you lose your chance."

Seany just winked at her. "You think we jest, but it's the God's honest truth. Why tempt fate?"

* * *

Galway City, Co. Galway

Seany covered his last shift with the advanced paramedic unit and realized a small part of him was going to miss the work. The fire services side hadn't seen much action other than an occasional motor car accident or false alarm at the college. So, it surprised him when they received a call of a kitchen fire on the outskirts of town. The hotel was an old one, according to Joseph. They arrived just behind the two engines. An employee of the hotel was motioning for the guests to get farther back.

Smoke was pouring out of the building, but it looked as though the fire hadn't spread to any other floors. Seany's heart was pounding, and he felt the prick of perspiration all over his body, despite the cool temperatures. He pushed on, following behind Joseph as he spoke to what seemed to be the night manager. "There is a gas leak in the kitchen! That old feckin' stove just went up in flames, then boom. I think the cook is still in there!"

Seany almost found himself running into the building, but Joseph put a hand on his arm. "Not yet, Tiger. One more shift."

Seany shook himself, "Too right. Is anyone else hurt?"

The man took him over to a kitchen staff member. The boy's hair was singed on one side, and there were first degree burns on his neck, ear, and part of his face. Joseph said, "Let's get him in the NHS ambulance. He may have smoke inhalation as well."

"My boss, the head cook, was trying to turn the gas main off. He's still in there!" The boy started another round of coughing. The blood was pounding in Seany's ears at this point. He watched the fire team take the hose through the front of the building. Right as they were coming in, two men were coming out. Or, more accurately, one man was dragging another out. "Jesus Christ."

Seany barely remembered the sequence of events. He was on autopilot. Doing everything right. But in his mind, he was screaming. The smell of burnt flesh, the shaking, the frantic eyes begging to die. Joseph was a champ. He spoke to the guy the whole time. "You're going to be okay. Your staff is okay. We're going to get you to the hospital." Seany heard the helicopter in the distance. Galway couldn't handle this. He had to go to St. James where the National Burn Unit was located. It was where he and McBride had been treated.

He found his voice, finally. "It's all right, brother. You're going to the best. I spent some time in there, and I know. Be easy. You're going to be in good hands."

"My wife…" the guy croaked, and a picture of Kamala jumped to the front of his brain.

He said, "The Guards have already called her and told her where to go."

He seemed to ease a bit. Seany looked him over, wanting to stand and run. His burns weren't as bad as McBride's had been. Mostly second and some fourth. He hadn't had any synthetics on. His chef's clothing was cotton, and he'd had a chef's tie-on cap over his hair. The worst of it was to his arm. He'd actually managed to get the gas main off before the entire kitchen had exploded, and the hotel had gone up in flames. He would live, Seany thought. He was young and strong. The helicopter landed, and he helped the life flight medics get him loaded. It wasn't until he got back into the passenger seat of the ambulance two hours later that he started to shake uncontrollably. If

Joseph noticed, he didn't say. At least not right away. Later, toward the end of the shift, they had a moment to themselves.

Joe said, "That had to be hard on you. The burn victim, I mean."

Seany said, "I'm fine. Did I act like I wasn't?" He knew the guy was trying to be supportive, and he hated the tone of his own words.

"No, you acted like a pro. You kept it together the entire time and afterward. The kind of shit you went through in Dublin has driven men to retire. Caused men a lot older and more experienced than you to quit and find another career. I'm saying, you prick, that if I'd been in your shoes tonight, I might have fallen apart. You didn't. You're ready to go back, but if you ever decide you like this unit, I'd be proud for you to return and be my partner."

Something trembled deep in Seany's throat. "Damn it. I didn't think I needed to hear that, but I did. Thanks, Joe."

* * *

Letterfrack, Co. Galway

Maureen looked at the time and a thrill went through her. She couldn't wait to see him. The thought of going into one of the coastal villages and staying in a B&B was so romantic. She'd spent her late nights researching Achill Island and Westport. Just as she was finishing up drying her hair, he knocked. "Come in."

He came in and she had a jolt of fear go through her. He looked like hell. Like he hadn't slept. She went to him and hugged him. He held her close and she felt something relax in him. "Rough shift?"

"Nah, I'll do. I never sleep well on station." *Liar,* he thought. But he didn't want to talk about that young chef getting flighted out of Galway. "Are ye ready?"

"Yep! I've been watching the time for three days!" He kissed her soundly on the mouth.

"I thought on our way out I could stop and see Storm," he said nonchalantly. "Unless he's all tucked in for the night." He shrugged, like it was no big deal. But she had a sneaking suspicion that it was.

That he needed something from Storm that he wasn't going to let himself need from anyone else.

"Of course. He'd like that, I think."

They drove the short distance to the stables and Rory was finishing up trimming one of the mares. "Come to see your buddy, eh? He's just had a nice trim and a brush down."

Moe motioned Seany over to Balor's stall first. She pointed. "Well, would you look at those two. Two peas in a pod. I thought horses sleep standing up?"

"They do both. Normally a horse Balor's size really couldn't lay down in the stall or he could get cast. Meaning he'd be pressed to the wall in a weird position and couldn't get himself back up. They can sleep laying down, but not for a long period of time. They can doze or nap standing up because their legs lock in place. It's all about the anatomy of the pony. If he got stuck laying down, it would eventually kill him because it would be like crushing his organs. Normally he'd only lay down while out in the pasture. He can do it in here because he's in a double stall and there is less chance of him getting wedged. Mini-horses are kind of the opposite. They lay down in their stall where they feel safe. Horses are complicated. Speaking of which, the reason War Hammer is in there with him is because he seems to lend some kind of comfort to that big oaf. I've heard of it before. Sometimes horse owners use goats for the same purpose. Aren't they sweet?"

"Yes, it is sort of sweet. Now, where's my lad. Storm, did you miss me?" Storm had responded to Seany's voice as soon as they'd come into the barn. He went into the stall and picked up a brush. "I know you've already been brushed, but indulge me. How have you been getting on without me? Did ye get up the nerve to ask Skadi for a date?"

The horse nuzzled him, and Moe's throat tightened as she saw Seany sway toward the contact, closing his eyes. He whispered, "I missed you, too."

* * *

SEANY WAS STUPIDLY EXCITED about the two-night stay he had planned. He'd originally had it in mind to take her to Westport and do a drive onto Achill Island. As he'd searched the internet, he struck on another idea and before he knew it, he was pulling the trigger on a full-blown romantic getaway. He remembered all the times his brothers had swept their women off for a little quality time without the children. O'Brien men were hopeless saps underneath all their brawn.

Moe said, "I thought this was a coastal town?"

"Yes, it's in Mayo. We are taking the inland route. It's safer at night." He lied so easily, he was almost ashamed of himself. He kept her distracted with questions about what they'd been doing over the last couple of days.

"The new speech and occupational therapist came to work for the first day of training. They really are sharp women. Moira's interviewing some physical therapists who agreed to do some volunteer time with the hippotherapy candidates. We have a couple of kids with cerebral palsy. They came yesterday and the new OT and I worked with them and War Hammer, since he's more decorative. They got to use body paint on him and we put bows in his mane."

Seany said, "He's lucky Balor let him back in the stall." Moe smacked him. "I'm just saying."

"He got a bath after the boys left. Michele worked with the speech therapist on ways to incorporate speech therapy into the horse lessons. Michele is really amazing. Leaps and bounds past me in experience."

"I doubt that. Ye were on a horse before you were weaned."

"Yeah, maybe. But she has great instincts. Not just with the horses, but with people. Kids and adults. She even thought about how to use our horses to reach out to the elderly community. Like dementia, stroke, and Alzheimer's patients. I doubt many of them could ride, but the older, gentler horses could still be with them. They could brush them and pet them. I don't know. It's just so exciting being here at the beginning. To see the potential good this non-profit could do. Apparently, Moira has people willing to come twice a week and get a hotel in between. One family is willing to drive from Waterford County."

"It's a good thing you're doing. Truly, Maureen. A far cry from Broadway. Do you still do the music mash-ups and choreography?"

She smiled, "Sometimes I play around. I think you'd understand more than some. I mean, you love your music. You're really talented. But it's for fun and for family. You didn't want to do it as a career. I actually tried for a semester. That was all it took. It wasn't where my heart was. I went and toured the equine center and, while I was there, they were doing a student-led therapy class. It was with autistic children. It just...whammy. Yeah," she nodded her head. "That's the only way I can describe it. Whammy. I never looked back."

He did understand. He'd never considered studying music like his sister. He'd considered the Garda, but there was something about the fire and rescue services that called to him. They'd been talking for about twenty minutes when she said, "Hey, I haven't seen a lick of water. And we are going east, not north. Are you sure you're going the right way?"

He didn't smile. Or at least he tried to suppress it. She narrowed her eyes, nonetheless. "We aren't going to Westport, are we?"

"I don't know what you're on about. This is just the scenic route. They're doing work on the coastal route."

"Seany O'Brien. I do believe you've kidnapped me."

CHAPTER 26

(Enter ghost) Hamlet Act 1, Scene 4...William Shakespeare

Cong, Co. Mayo

It wasn't until they'd left the country road and pulled onto a private drive that Seany made her close her eyes. He wasn't sure if there was a sign beforehand that would give away the surprise. He wasn't even going to think about the price tag on this little diversion from the original plan. It was the off season, after all, and he'd booked a package deal with a wine tasting and meals included. He was driving a hand-me-down car, he shared a shoe box cottage with Josh, and his furnishings were all family donations. What the hell else did he have to spend his salary on? And Moe was worth it. She'd told him about the youth hostel she'd stayed in while visiting him in the hospital. Some Dublin hovel with twenty kids to a communal lav. She deserved this. Maybe he did, too.

The lighted drive came into view and then the massive castle. "Okay, love. Open your eyes." He rolled to a stop to let it sink in.

When she opened her eyes she sucked in a scream before it could escape. Then she froze, mouth agape. "Is that a castle?"

"Ashford Castle. 13th century, probably haunted, and ours for the next two nights." She leapt across the front seat and threw her arms around him. Then she pulled away. "This is too much! We can't do this! There is no way we can stay here!" Just as she said it, a gentleman in full livery approached their car. "Mr. O'Brien?"

"Yes, sir. O'Brien party of two." He laughed at the look on her face. "We can stay here and we are. It's done, hen. So wrap your pretty head around it. We've got a wine pairing dinner in forty minutes."

"There is food? I mean, of course there is. Look at this place. Oh, Seany. It's too much."

"I think it's just enough." He said the words so softly and reverently, it made her tear up. "Don't start that, girl. We've got to get changed and into the formal dining room. I for one could use a glass of wine."

Her face blanched. "I don't have anything nice enough to wear in a castle. I packed nice clothes, but you told me to pack warm. You should have warned me!"

He dodged a smack. "Be nice or you'll sleep in the car, you little harpy." He dodged another blow and was almost laughing too hard to tell her. "Maddie took care of it. Caitlyn has enough clothes to clothe a major city, and she passes half of it down to her sisters. I have a few selections and some shoes she seemed to think would fit. I have this handled, love. Stop trying to kill me."

She kissed him hard on the mouth. "You are really something, you know that?"

"Let's get parked and find our room in this monstrosity before we run out of time."

* * *

THE ROOM WAS old world opulent. Dripping with gorgeous art, antiques, a tapestry, and lush fabrics. "I feel like a princess." She fell back on the feathery soft bed as Seany started to unzip the large garment bag and remove his suit and tie. He had one nice, dark blue suit, and this was the third time he'd ever worn it. He hoped it still fit. Then he removed three dresses from the bag. They had two nice dinners to attend, so that left a spare. She jumped up and looked at the dresses. "Whoa. Caitlyn has good taste."

"And she gave me these, whatever the hell they are." He handed her several strange looking packages.

She snatched them out of his hand, blushing. He raised a brow. She sighed. "They are sticky bras. It's a way to wear strappy or strapless dresses and shirts without having the girls coming out all over the place." She held them up one at a time, giving him a lesson in ta-ta support. "We have the bunny shaped, petal shaped, silicone lifters, wing shaped, and these which just kind of cover the pink bits."

Seany shook his head. "Just one more reason I'm glad not to be a woman. Jesus wept."

She took the en suite bathroom while he changed in the bedroom. He was done in no time, she took a little longer. Luckily, she'd already showered. When she came out of the bathroom, the sight of her stole his breath. *Thank you, Maddie.* She looked delicious. He felt like locking the door and canceling dinner. "Wow." He motioned for her to twirl. *Double wow.*

She was in a red silk slip dress. Thin straps that told him exactly why she'd needed the little sticky things. And slide on heels that might have been a hair too big if they'd had a back to them. She was wearing a little bit of mascara and red tinted lip gloss. "You are so beautiful. Ye almost stop my heart, Maureen." There was no girl left in this moment. She was all woman.

* * *

THEY WERE the youngest at the chef's table. The dinner was hosted in the wine cellar and was both old world eerie and decadent with sconces, sparkling crystal, rich hardwoods, and ancient stone walls. Given the off-season status, it was less of a crowd. Although, they were still relatively full compared to many of the coastal bed and breakfasts. Not everyone that stayed did the decadent Chef's Wine Pairing Dinner, however. So, it was a cozy, intimate setting. The older couples were dazzled by Maureen. One of the couples was local, and she told them all about the reinvention of Moira's Connemara ponies breeding ranch. "She retired from breeding and showing her stock and has gone the non-profit direction instead." She said, "They are looking for more board members. At least one. I'm sure you're very busy, but if you are looking for a way to serve the community, we sure could use some local blood in those chairs. Think about it."

"I remember Moira. She's one tough cookie. She's also very well respected and has impeccable taste in interns." The whole table rumbled with humor. She blushed under the praise.

The Chef told them a little bit about the castle. It had many owners in its history. One of the most notable in modern history was when the Guinness family used it as a summer home. It offered everything from falconry school to archery, skeet, and fishing on the lough. Some of the people at the table were doing those extra activities. When they asked Seany, Maureen answered. "This was a last minute surprise. All I want to do tomorrow is creep around this entire castle and then go for a hike. I have simple tastes, I'm afraid."

Seany squeezed her hand under the table. "Aye, and Maureen is an honest to God cowgirl from Texas, so if you want to learn to shoot someone with a six-shooter from the back of a horse in full gallop, she's available from four to six tomorrow." This got everyone at the table laughing, and he just gave Moe a wink.

The dinner was outstanding, served in the style of George V's table. It was course after course of foraged and fresh, mixed with dried elements from the summer harvest. The lamb was from Achill, the dried mushrooms used for the soup had been foraged in early autumn. The wild hake on crab risotto was a sublime starter from a local fisherman in Westport. They were served a roasted kohlrabi salad, baby root vegetables in dill butter, and apple sorbet. All which were made mostly from what they grew in the castle gardens. They kept certain items in the root cellar, just like they had hundreds of years ago. The wine pairings were the perfect accompaniment. A German ice wine ended the evening, and everyone clapped for the chef.

"Now, if you are tired from all the wine, you can retire to those lovely rooms. However, we have a special treat tonight. Our CEO has agreed to let Paul, our in-house steward, guide the bravest of you on a ghost tour of the castle."

Moe squeaked and Seany chuckled, "I think we're in for the tour."

* * *

THE ANGLO-NORMAN CASTLE was built on the perimeter of a monastic site in 1228. Moe had never been inside something so old. When she said as much, Seany told her about Newgrange and the passage tomb which predated the Egyptian pyramids. The entire place wasn't original. Some wings had been added during the Victorian Age. But all in all, it was a sprawling, awe inspiring piece of architecture. The castle's many rooms had been transformed into the type of hotel that left nothing to be desired. Cozy lounges, a library, spa services, a wine cellar to die for, several places to eat, and beautiful gardens that they could tour tomorrow. For now, the steward took them around, talking about the ghost legends that had followed the castle through history. A lone monk in the gardens. A lady in white in the tower. There seemed to always be a lady in white in residence in any place that claimed to be haunted.

It wasn't until they went into an unoccupied master suite that the true tale began. It was decorated with seventeenth century antiques and draped in the finest silks that money could buy. Even the headboard was upholstered and then draped in lush fabrics. The room overlooked a turret and must cost a fortune to rent for the night.

Seany walked by a chest of drawers and stopped, cocking his head. The steward narrowed his eyes. "Is something amiss, lad?"

He shook himself. "No, just a draft, I think." He took Moe's hand, taking a few steps forward, but there it was again. Not a draft, but a chill that went to his bones. And sorrow so overwhelming, it swelled inside him. He paled, and pulled Moe close. "I'm feeling a bit off. Maybe it was the wine."

"It wasn't the wine. You felt him, didn't you?"

Seany cringed inwardly. This was so hokey. "I didn't feel anything."

"Oh, no? Well, come then. Stand by this window sash just two steps forward and tell me that you feel nothing."

The older guests were looking at him with such hope and thrill on their faces, he could hardly refuse. When he stepped forward, the hair stood up on his arms. He felt it again. That wave of sorrow that crushed him to his very bones. He rubbed his head. He couldn't help it. He backed up until he felt Moe's hand on his back. "What the hell is that?"

"It's the dark man. He's seen by some, although not many. Usually children or sensitives. He haunts this bedroom with his black mood and his heart filled with sorrow. The Baron of these lands lost his wife in the child bed, we believe in the mid-1600s. Both she and the child perished. She went into labor before her time, and the midwife was off delivering another child. By the time they found her and brought her to the castle proper, the man's wife had delivered a stillborn son and shortly thereafter followed him in death. He ordered the midwife banished from the estates, although it wasn't her fault. He paced this room for weeks, only leaving to bury his family. Some say he died from a broken heart. Others say he poisoned himself with hemlock."

Seany cursed under his breath. One of the women in the group asked, "And what about this ability to feel him. Can we all sense him if we stand in that spot?"

"You're all welcome to try. I doubt young Mr. O'Brien is keen for another go."

"No thank you. Twice was enough," Seany said. Trying to sound lighter than he was. The thought of his sister-in-law bleeding out in the ambulance when she lost her third child was suddenly fresh in his mind.

The man continued. "He doesn't brush up against everyone, mind you. He feeds off of sorrow. He thirsts for a fellow tortured soul. Misery, in this instance, loves company."

They all looked at Seany uneasily. "Well, on that pleasant note, I'll meet you all in the hall. Hopefully the old Baron isn't game for a stroll." Which made the group all chuckle collectively, and the somber mood was broken.

* * *

MOE DIDN'T LEAVE the room with him. It seemed like he needed a minute, and she wouldn't embarrass him by hovering. The other people on the tour took turns going to the area of the room where Seany had been. The only other person that felt the same chilling presence was an older man from Somerset, who had been in some military crisis in Nigeria back in the sixties and also in some campaign in the Suez Canal area. She remembered him talking about it at dinner. He had a military bearing, and as he stood where Seany had been, she saw the same haunted look in his eyes.

Seany was resting comfortably, reading a book in an ornate wood and velvet chair. He put the old book down on the table where he'd found it, then stood and greeted her with a dazzling smile. "Any other victims?"

"Just one. I'll tell you later. Ready to head up to the room?" she said innocently. It was ten o'clock after all.

He leaned in and said, "I thought you'd never ask."

* * *

THE BEST PART of the evening had just begun. When Moe walked into the gorgeous, luxurious, old world style room, she still couldn't believe he'd done all this. She knew how much he wanted her. His physical passions were strong and his eyes were hungry. Always hungry for her. He'd never told her he loved her. It didn't matter. They'd only been back together a short time. And really, she hadn't said it to him either. Of course he didn't love her. But maybe with time…

He came up behind her and whispered against her neck. "You're thinking really loudly, love."

She arched as he ran his hands around and over her body. She hooked her arm around and put a hand in his hair as he rubbed against her bottom. Then she felt his hands running up her thighs, taking the soft, thin silk of her dress up an inch at a time. "I want you,

Maureen. I want to touch you." She tipped her hips, fusing their bodies. He groaned as he slipped a hand over her taut belly and slowly into the waist of her panties. Her hips jerked when he made contact. "You're ready, mo chuisle. So ready." He used the pad of his middle finger to rub circles right at the center of her passion. "I want to feel you come just like this." His words were rough and edgy. He brought her swiftly to the brink of a soaring climax, and she slid herself against his palm. She ought to be embarrassed, given her shy nature, but the pleasure he coaxed from her body was almost too much to bear. She fell into oblivion, her body in the throes of surrender.

"Seany, I can't…stand." The words were shaky and hoarse, and before she could register what was happening she was turned in his arms. He pushed her back against the door of the hotel room and pinned her, legs off the ground and hooked into the crook of each of his arms. At some point he'd unfastened his trousers and he impaled her with one slick thrust. Her hair was in her face and she was limp as he moved slowly and deliberately. He smoothed her hair back with one hand, and she finally met his eyes. He slid in again and she throbbed around him as she started to climb toward another orgasm. His face was so close, taking in her features with reverence and adoration. His eyes burned for her and her throat convulsed as she bit back a sob. She loved him. She didn't know how she was going to live through it if they had to part again. His face registered something, then he was carrying her slowly to that beautiful bed. She was limp, holding on tight to his neck as she was speared on his hard cock. He laid her back gently. He removed his suit coat, his tie, then slowly he unbuttoned his shirt as he stood between her split thighs…still seated deep inside her body. Then, as if to torture her, he slid out of her body, pulled her ass forward until it was hanging off the bed, and got on his knees.

When Seany's tongue touched her hot, wet core, he almost lost control and spilled on the floor below her. But he was going to wait. He was going to kill himself with the want and the need. He drank in the orgasms he'd given her, slick and warm like honey. Tonight he would bind her to him. He'd possess her. He'd consume her very soul so that she would never, ever think about leaving him again. *Mine.*

* * *

IT WAS MORNING, she knew. The light came into the sheers under the heavy draperies. He was inside her again. How had she lived without this? Without him? He was behind her and had thrown one of her legs back and over his hip so he could take her from behind. They were on their sides and his hand was between her legs. A dual assault that had her ready to come in seconds. Then she was on her stomach as he cocked one of her legs, slid his hands under her to cup her breasts as he thrust hard and deep. She tilted her hips up to get more. "Don't stop!"

Seany felt her clamp down so hard around him that he grabbed the headboard and bore down on her until she screamed, gripping him so tightly he saw stars when he came. He shouted, suddenly glad that they didn't have anyone in the room next to them. She was going to be the death of him.

CHAPTER 27

He woke in the night, and the moonlight shone through the open draperies, bathing Maureen with a white, soft light. Her hair was spread on the pillow and she looked peaceful, flat on her belly with her face tipped up toward him. He envied her that peace. He studied the lines of her face, more defined now than in the photos he'd looked over so many times. He'd thought he had her memorized, but he was wrong. She'd only grown more beautiful. The lines of her body were still long and lean, but the willowy grace of her had been honed into a strong, sensual creature. The girl was still there, of course. Especially as she slept, and a pang of affection hit him so hard, he felt his throat constrict and his eyes prickle with the warning of tears. His Maureen. His Moe. She'd come to him at a time when he'd abandoned all hope, and things were irrevocably changed. He placed a light kiss on her shoulder, then settled into her as sleep found him once more.

* * *

The night had been unforgettable. Moe woke and stretched as she heard Seany stirring in the room. "Good morning." She smiled as she stretched, feeling aches in peculiar places. "We didn't miss breakfast, I hope."

He leaned over the bed and took her mouth with thorough attention. "No, we've still got more than an hour. It's sunny out, so we can hike around the lough today. As long as I get you home by nine tomorrow morning, Moira won't have my hide."

She smiled and asked, "Did she know where you were taking me?"

"She did. As a matter of fact, she knows the new owners. I think she may have called them, because I suddenly got some sort of first responder discount."

She leaned on her elbow, giving him a chiding look. "This really is wonderful, but I feel guilty. It's beautiful, but…"

"Don't say it. You're worth it. We needed this. I needed it, too. There are some kayaks down by the lough that are for guest use. We can walk and tour the gardens, we can go out on the water, whatever you like."

Moe didn't think kayaking was a good way for him to be resting his shoulder on his off days, so she said, "I'd love to just walk around. Then maybe we can grab a couple of those chaise lounges and read in that old library."

"Perfect plan. Now, move that pretty bum of yours or we really are going to miss breakfast." But he sat next to her, feeling a wave of tenderness that seemed to override the lust he always felt in her presence. "Last night was the most beautiful of my life. I needed this. I needed you. I forgot everything for a little while but us. And escaping into you was a gift I can't hope to ever deserve."

"Are you going to tell me what happened on your last shift?" He stiffened and she wished she could take the words back. She'd promised she wouldn't push.

"Let's get ready. I'm starved. We burned a lot of calories last night."

"Seany, I know I said I wouldn't push. But that was about the fire in Dublin. Can't you share your work with me? I just want to help."

"That goes both ways," he said, brow raised. His tone was harsher than it had been a minute ago.

"What do you mean?" she asked. But she knew.

Seany narrowed his eyes. "You told me that I didn't understand anything. That I didn't know what your life had been like. So, tell me. Tell me about your family, about why you broke it off with Mason. And about the hurricane. I can tell you were affected by it. So like I said, you show me yours and I'll show you mine."

She tucked her hair behind her ears nervously. "I just want to enjoy today. I don't want our time here to be dragged down. I'm sorry I asked."

"Sorry you asked, or sorry you got the tables turned on you?"

Her face tightened. "I don't know. Maybe both."

"Okay," he said softly. At least she'd been honest. "I won't push you and you'll extend the same courtesy to me."

The conversation stung, given the intimacies they'd shared last night. But sex wasn't love. She knew this, even given her inexperience. But it still stung. He kept his hurts to himself, which sat there between them like a wall.

She showered quickly, braiding her hair and putting a sweater and jeans under her borrowed coat. She grabbed gloves and a hat for later, as well as her phone. "We can just leave from breakfast. I don't want to waste a minute."

He pulled her close, brushing his lips across hers. "I'm sorry. This relationship thing is new to me. I can't share things that I haven't sorted out in my own head. I do know that you have stories you need to tell, and that it's important for me to hear them. But I'll wait. For now, Princess, let's go enjoy this castle."

* * *

THE SUMPTUOUS BREAKFAST served in the George V dining room was spectacular. They enjoyed a buffet of cold breakfast items accompanied by a full Irish breakfast. Moe was stuffed to bursting. "I should be embarrassed that I ate all of that, but ranch girls like to eat."

Seany smiled at that. "Oh, I don't know if it has as much to do with the ranch or farm. I remember your slender, fifteen-year-old self murdering a cheeseburger meal and then stealing some of my chips."

She blushed. "I don't remember that. So much for picking at a salad and pretending you don't eat. Isn't that what fifteen year old girls are supposed to do on a date? I told you I was out of my league the first week we met."

"You weren't. You were enchanting. I hadn't dated a lot up until then, but I never understood the false front put up by the girls I did take for a meal. Picking at some leaves while they were eyeing the sticky toffee pudding at the next table. What's the point of it? Do they think we want them to starve?"

"It goes back to those Victorian days when the woman wouldn't act like she was hungry, because she was being watched. The critical eyes of her peers. Being hungry and eating until you weren't hungry was considered unladylike."

"Not in my country's history. If your woman was wan and skinny, they thought you were not enough of a man to keep her fed. That must be some sort of English thing." She rewarded the remark with a snatch of her hand, stealing one of his half pastries. "Eat your fill, love. You'll need your strength today and tonight."

They stretched out a map of the estate on the table, once the staff had cleared their dishes. "We'll stay out until tea time. It's a nice affair, and I don't want you to miss it. So, here is a path around the lough. We can do that, or we can do this other route through the gardens and into the forest."

"I like this tower and look here, this is a walled garden that we can tour before heading into the forest. I like the idea of the forest. And there is this Pigeon Hole cave. What do you think?"

"I think you can lead, and I'll follow. It sounds like a good day's hike."

They headed off in the direction of the stone tunnel, donning more casual, practical attire. Seany watched her face more than the scenery. This was her element. Nature brought out the spirit in his beloved Maureen. As gorgeous as she'd been last night, this was when she was at her most beautiful. Knits and denim. No make-up. Her nose and cheeks pink from the cold. She loved the gardens, even in the stark, sparseness of late winter. "I bet this is something to see in full bloom."

"Maybe we'll come back before your time is up." Seany said it, and the words almost caught in his throat.

She shrugged. "I like that it's the off season. It seems like our own private piece of heaven. Every season has beauty." Their solitude was interrupted by a man leading one of the middle-aged couples from dinner last night on a ride through the forest's bridle trails. "We should stop and see the horses before dinner."

"Do you want to ride?" he asked.

"Nah, I can do that with Skadi. I just love stables. I love the smell and the noises, and there is something about the warmth of horse flesh and breath. It's soothing." She spoke with a light air, but the truth was that he was easily discussing her departure this summer like he was talking about the weather. She couldn't blame him, really. It was inevitable. It wasn't like she could stay. Could she? Josh was on a student visa. Maybe she could go to grad school or something. But it wasn't possible. Her college fund was gone. They'd spent it on her undergraduate studies, and she had siblings to think about. When this was over, she'd have to go home and join the workforce. She couldn't stay here indefinitely. It didn't work like that. Ireland had strict immigration laws.

She came back from those thoughts to realize that they were deep into the forest that surrounded the castle. "I wonder what this was like in the thirteenth century. It was probably less pristine. I bet there were cottages where tradesmen and tenant farmers lived and worked, before it became this family estate and they added the extra wings."

Seany said, "Some of Ireland's greatest treasures are made of slowly decaying stone and wood. The Neolithic passage tombs and ruined castles. The ring forts and dolmens and old watch towers. It's like our O'Brien Tower. Sometimes when you try to improve or rebuild something, you cause it to lose what was so wonderful about it."

Moe remembered his disgust with the changes they'd made to the tower. The newly painted stone had indeed lost something. She'd seen pictures of the tower before they'd painted it. She smiled and said, "Our rooms might not be so comfortable if they hadn't, I suppose."

"True enough. And speaking of old things, just ahead is the Guinness Tower ruin. After we see that, we can find the cave you were talking about."

They took photos, stopped and admired the soaring trees. Even saw some wildlife. Mostly rabbits and birds. Seany took her hand, putting it to his mouth and kissing the top of it. "It's beautiful out again today. It's uncommon to have so little rain."

"Yes, I noticed. It's only rained once the whole time I've been here. I expected a lot more."

"Aye, it's good for sightseeing. Hopefully the spring will bring the rain for the farmers, though. And the bogs. It's easier to catch fire if there is no rain. Like your California and Montana fires. Water is our friend."

Moe mumbled the words, so he barely heard her. *Not always.* He led her to a clearing, and they sat on some large rocks, just taking in the sun. "Do you trust me, Maureen?"

"You know I do."

He hesitated; afraid he'd spoil the mood. But it was so rare in life to get this kind of privacy. No electronics or other people. No distractions. "Something happened to you. I don't know when or what exactly, but something did happen. I'd hear it now, if you'll trust me enough."

She didn't pretend not to understand. She just stared into the tall, blowing grass. Dry from winter wind and lack of rain. "I'll tell you, Seany. Just not today. It's not a story for today."

He wanted to shake her. To scream at her and call her a hypocrite. But he knew that in this, she needed time. "Okay, then let's talk about your life after we parted. The good parts, I mean. Your dad is doing better?"

She seemed to relax. "He is. And Emmie and Sammy are growing like weeds. Sammy is in the second grade. Em is finishing up the sixth grade. She turns twelve next month and I was going to try to find something to send her. You should see her. She looks just like my mother. They both ride. We have to put Sammy up on the saddle with an adult if we go out of the arena. My dad is in the market for a fourth and even fifth horse so that we can all ride together. It's expensive, though. My mom was able to go back to work. Daddy is the stay-at-home parent. He was medically retired and he's the one who goes to the school events and cares for sick children. His seizures are better now. It's rare for him to have one anymore."

"And what about you? What were the last two years of school like, before college? Were you the prom queen? Did you date the quarterback?" He nudged her, half teasing.

"I didn't go to prom. I didn't go anywhere. I helped with my siblings. I cooked. I studied. I got a scholarship for my grades."

Seany asked, "Why didn't you go to prom? Did you date at all?" He really didn't want to know. Why was he asking?

"I didn't date anyone for the rest of high school. I just...couldn't." She closed her eyes. "Like I said before. It took something from me when I ended things with you. It kind of hollowed me out for a time."

"And after a time?"

"Why do you want to know?" she asked, suddenly irritated.

"You said you had a boyfriend. Why did it end?" He wasn't sure what he thought he was going to accomplish with this line of questioning, but he couldn't seem to stop himself.

"It ended for a lot of reasons. The easy answer is that I didn't feel for him the same way he felt about me."

"And how did he feel about you?" Seany already hated the guy.

She lifted one shoulder. "He said he loved me. He was older. A veteran who had served in the Army. We were freshmen at the same time, but he'd done a tour in the military first. He'd been to Iraq. We had some things in common. He was a veterinary medicine student specializing in large animals. So, for a while, our common interests were enough to keep a relationship going, but I didn't love him. I wouldn't love him, is how he would put it. So, I ended it. I let him go find someone who could return his affections in the way he needed it. I still see him around campus, sometimes."

"And has he moved on?" he asked. Why did he need to know this? It was torture.

"No. I mean, I don't know. Last time I saw him, he was..." she paused, not sure how to word it.

"Trying to rekindle things?" he asked. Irritation creeping into his tone. She just nodded.

She said, "So, that was my failed attempt at an adult relationship. There were a few dates before that. A couple of performing arts students from that first semester. We didn't click."

"Knowing you now, I can see why. You grew into something more than that girl who liked to do mash-ups and hang out in the theater."

"I did. I mean, I still love that kind of stuff. I like plays and musicals. I play around with my computer software when I have time. I just..." She wasn't sure how to explain it. "I needed it then. And I was good at it. But it wasn't one of those interests that was ever going to turn into a career. If my dad had stayed in the military, and we hadn't gone back to Texas, maybe I would have tried something different. But when we took our family and our horses and settled into the life we have now...I guess something just finally clicked. I was happiest when I was on horseback or in the barn. It's what gives me purpose."

"I understand," he said.

She knew he did. He'd always been a musician. Had been weaned on the music she saw his family perform. But what he got from being a first responder was similar to what she got from working with horses. A higher purpose.

They traveled back a different way, running into the game keeper walking two enormous wolfhounds. Moe had never seen one in the flesh and she was amazed at the size of the gentle beasts. By the time they reached the large stone archway where the portcullis had been, it was almost tea time. "I want to change into something a little nicer and wash up. Everyone seems to dress up for the gatherings."

"Yes, my granny would have a fit if she saw me walk into a formal tea wearing hiking boots and denims." When they walked back into the room, there was a note from the hotel manager and a half-size bottle of French wine. They changed quickly, but their eyes never left each other as they stripped and then put new clothes on. There was something oddly intimate about changing clothes in front of each other with no sex involved. If Seany's hot gaze was anything to go by, there would be time enough later.

After tea in the beautiful Connaught Room of the castle, they went to the old library. Amidst the leather bound books and first editions, Moe found a book of poetry by William B. Yeats. She read it aloud as she laid in Seany's lap. He didn't try to coax her back to the room or pull her behind the shelves. He just played with her hair and listened. It wasn't until later that she realized she'd fallen asleep.

Seany reclined in the chaise lounge with Maureen's head in his lap. And for once, the lust that boiled in him was silent and still. Instead, he felt such a deep affection that it almost had him tearing up. She looked so pretty, curled up in his jumper and a pair of leggings. They'd turned in the preppy tea attire for something comfortable, and had meant to walk out to the estate stables. But for right now, he was just comfortable listening to her read to him. Before long, her voice silenced. Her breathing slowed to a steady, deep rhythm and he knew she was asleep. So, he took the book from her, let her rest, and continued reading where she'd left off. It was one of the most peaceful moments of his life, other than riding through the mountains on Storm's back.

They had to rise early, because Maureen had a job to do and he had his riding class around lunchtime. He couldn't ride on Wednesday, because it was the first day of his big return to the fire brigade. Maureen tensed then stirred, opening her eyes with a start. "Easy, love. It's okay." And then he felt it. A slight tremble. He laid a palm on her chest and her heart was pounding. "What is it? Another nightmare?"

"Another?" she asked. Then remembered him waking her in the cottage. "Oh, it's nothing. Sometimes I have weird dreams. Especially if I'm sleeping somewhere unfamiliar."

She untangled her limbs from the chaise lounge, sitting up and rearranging her braid. "Is there still time to visit the stables?"

He watched her for a minute, and he thought of Josh. His roommate had nightmares occasionally. Seany knew it had something to do with the abusive household he'd grown up in. He hoped to God that something awful hadn't happened to Maureen. Alanna had nightmares for months after she'd been kidnapped. Our demons came to call when we slept. He dreamt about that warehouse fire several times a week. "Are you okay? You're sure you don't want to talk about your dream?"

She said lightly, "I barely remember it. I'm going to run and get my barn boots. I really do want to see the stables." Seany watched her go and wondered which one of them would bridge that last bit of distance between them.

CHAPTER 28

"And once the storm is over, you won't remember how you made it through, how you managed to survive. You won't even be sure whether the storm is really over. But one thing is certain. When you come out of the storm, you won't be the same person who walked in. That's what this storm's all about." ...Haruki Murakami, Kafka on the Shore

Letterfrack, Co. Galway

It had been a beautiful two nights, but the holiday ended as they the inevitably do. They'd risen early, been served a hasty but amazing breakfast, and headed back toward Moe's temporary home. They arrived just in time to change into riding clothes, and headed to the barn.

Alanna was there with the baby, and Seany held him and slowly rocked him as Alanna led the group. They had all been sad to hear that Hans had to leave, but understood about the work he did in Brazil. Michele was there this week, both as an intern and as a veteran. She talked about her time in Iraq, and the men listened with respect and understanding as she spoke about the day a roadside bomb hit the vehicle in front of hers. He watched as Moe reached a hand to her and squeezed it. Women were so much better at this in a lot of ways. Matthew, the soldier, cleared his throat. Then he started to talk about the nightmares that had plagued him over the last few months. The starving children in particular. He dreamed that it was his daughter who was emaciated and hollow cheeked. He dreamed of the sick and dying, and the horrific symptoms of Ebola. Seany kissed Keegan's soft head, suddenly irrationally scared of the world in which he would grow up.

He knew deep down that he should say something. Share the utter horror the hotel's kitchen fire had brought forth in his mind. The remembering. The eyes full of terror and pain as they'd treated that chef. Just like McBride, but his partner had been worse. So much worse.

He just…couldn't. He looked up and saw her watching him. Waiting for him to pipe up and share something. But he wasn't going to let anyone tell him how to grieve. He saw the disappointment in her eyes, but who the hell was she to lecture him or judge him, even if it was just with a look? He raised his chin, meeting her eyes. They were just about done when she shocked the hell out of him.

One of them had to flinch first. The bile rose up in her throat just thinking about it, but she knew that in this instance, it was her move. After all, what he'd endured was so much worse, and she needed a show of good faith. She said, "I know we are ready to get on the horses, but I…" she looked at Seany, then at Alanna. "I have a confession to make. You've all been so brave to talk about everything. You inspire me with your strength, and I figured it was about time I stopped being a coward."

If Alanna was surprised, she didn't show it. Moe looked at her, then at Michele, and finally at Moira. She drew strength from these women, like she always had from her mother. "I have nightmares. Not every night, but more often than I would like to admit. You know I live in Texas, in a small farming town outside of Houston. One of you asked me about," she cleared her throat and looked at Alanna again.

Alanna nodded, so she continued. "You asked me about Hurricane Harvey. Magnolia wasn't hit quite as hard, luckily. We had no power and some flooding, but it wasn't as bad as what you may have heard about. The problem was that my family was inside Houston when it happened. I stayed back to take care of our animals. My father's seizures were pretty bad then. The Veteran's Administration was in downtown Houston. He had to go in for tests before they renewed his meds. It was over a two day period, so they planned to stay two nights with friends. They had my baby brother and little sister with them." Her voice was a little shaky, but she went on. "They thought they'd be out before the hurricane hit, and my dad really needed those meds. The V.A. in America has waitlists, and he wouldn't be able to get another appointment for months." She waved a hand in dismissal. "I'm babbling. I don't really talk about this much. Sorry." Alanna squeezed her hand and told her to take her time.

"My parents were staying in Memorial, an area of Houston that is down the road from the Addicks Reservoir." Seany watched as Alanna covered her mouth in horror and Michele cursed under her breath. He hated that he didn't really know anything about where Moe was living. Maureen started to tear up. "Yeah, that probably doesn't mean anything to y'all but it's two reservoirs, like your loughs, but they hold reserves of rain water. They filled during the hurricane and flooded everything. Just...everything. And it blocked all of the roads so no one could get out, and I couldn't drive in. At one point, my family and our friends were on the top floor of the house. No power. Barely enough water..."

She choked on a sob. "My mother nursed the baby, and my father gave a lot of his share of the rations to her and my little sister. They were on the west side of the city, so they thought they were safe. No one thought the reservoir would jump its banks. They didn't tell me how bad it was. They called me from their cell phones while they still had enough battery. They hadn't flooded yet. Or not completely. The roads out of the city were flooded, but the neighborhood wasn't totally underwater. During that time, a few of us from the college took trailered boats and horse trailers. We'd heard about a farm closer to Houston that had flooded pretty badly. The farmer was older, and his son and daughter-in-law were out of town. He couldn't get the horses out of the barn. The water just kept coming."

She squeezed Alanna's hand. "We went as far as we could. Then the two guys with boats put them in the water and drove us in. We saddled what horses we could and rode the others on bare back with just a bridle. We got them to dry land to a farm a couple of miles up the road, on high ground. The place was for sale, no horses in residence, so we broke the lock on the stable and put the horses in there. It's the only thing we could do. Then the university sent trailers to retrieve them, and they housed them in our equine center."

She swallowed hard, trying to find the words. "During the rescue, there was a foal trapped in the stall with his mother. She'd birthed it under stress when the hurricane hit the coastline. She tried to keep his head above water, but…" She shook her head. "It was dead before we got there."

She looked at Seany, "I didn't know how much it bothered me until we delivered Sadie's foal. That was the first nightmare I'd had since I'd been in Ireland."

"What about your family," Kyle asked the question everyone wanted to know.

"I couldn't get in contact with them. Cell towers were down or overwhelmed. So, I gassed up a friend's flat-bottomed fishing boat and headed into the city. A lot of people did it. They just knew that there were too many people stranded. The first responders couldn't do it alone. Hell, some of the first responders were stranded. Houston has a weird highway system. People tried to evacuate. But once it bottle-necked, everyone was stuck. The city was in gridlock as the storm slammed into the coastline. It's why my parents stayed put. Anyway, I had another couple people with me. One guy owned the boat. We mapped out a few different ways, in case we couldn't get through. We towed a small zodiac with two kayaks strapped to it. We wanted to try to help as many people as we could."

Seany listened in horror at Maureen's account of Hurricane Harvey. The hair stood up on his arms.

Moe told them the rest. They'd found a man floating dead in the water. They'd had to leave him, but they put his body up on top of a submerged car so that he could be recovered. Then they emailed in the coordinates to the Houston Police Department because the lines were busy. When they made it to the home where her parents were stranded, they loaded her family onto the boat, and put the other family in the zodiac. One followed the other, and they picked up another couple with a dog and towed them alongside each boat on the kayaks.

Moe fought the panic that the memories always brought forth. She could close her eyes right now and picture her mother with the baby strapped to her chest. Sweaty, dehydrated, and a little bit shell shocked.

"Once we got everyone to dry land, my grandparents were waiting to take everyone to their ranch. They had a generator and had been going back and forth to our place to feed the horses. We gassed up and went back out with just the two boats. The other retired Marine, whose house was destroyed, started coming out with us. We stayed together, rescued two families at a time from Memorial and Cypress North, because that's as far as we dared to go in the city. The coastal part of the city got hit hard, and those people were cut off. Once the hurricane passed, boats and Coast Guard ships came in from the gulf side to get them help and supplies."

She wiped her nose, not remembering who'd given her a tissue. "It was awful. So many lives were destroyed. 103 dead either directly or indirectly, but that was just the start of it. *Homeless, jobless, hopeless.* That was a sign I saw when we would go into the city to help with the clean up and to bring in supplies. It's such a populated city. There were just too many people. That hurricane hit, then followed up with historic rainfall, all while the city was in gridlock with nowhere for the people to go. They were trapped for days and days. When I picked up my parents, after the worst of it had passed and we could get to them, they were living on the second floor with a bathroom that didn't flush or have clean running water. They'd use buckets of storm water from the bottom floor to flush the toilet. They could feel the house shifting under the pressure of the incoming floodwaters. They were nearly out of supplies because the water came up so fast that they lost some stuff. The men were dehydrated because they wouldn't take the bottled water from the women and kids. My dad had four seizures, so he couldn't help get them out of there. He was neurologically destroyed and should have been in a hospital. He was out of meds because he never made it to the damn doctor appointments. That was after two and a half days. Other people were cut off for three times that long."

She said sadly, "When I dream, sometimes it's about that dead foal. Other times it's about the dead man we put up on the car roof. Sometimes my little sister and baby brother are floating by me, their eyes lifeless. I wake up screaming when that happens. Sometimes it's my mother." *Sometimes it was Seany.* She closed her eyes, shaking her head. "It's so stupid! They're fine. They all survived. My baby brother doesn't even remember it!" She was hiccupping on her sobs and Michele had her arm around her.

Seany stood, finally snapping out of the trance he'd been in. He handed the baby to Alanna and took Moe into his arms. He rubbed her back and crooned to her softly in her ear. Then the other men came around them, all patting her and offering her comfort. "I'm sorry. I shouldn't be breaking down like this. This isn't about me."

"Well, now. I suppose we'll forgive you for today. Next Monday, it's all about me again," Owen said with a chiding tone. Moe laughed, and if it held a bit of hysteria in its delivery, no one decided to notice.

* * *

THE RIDE WAS GLORIOUS. Moe let the warm sun soak into her face. "It feels good to get something that awful off your chest, doesn't it?" Michele said as she rode next to her.

Devlin was at the rear of the pack. The men were so happy to be off the leash and out into the wild, beautiful park land. Moe gave a self-deprecating smile. "I feel sort of silly. I'm not normally a crier, but Ireland seems to bring it out in me."

Alanna was on her other side. "Falling in love with an O'Brien man will do it to you as well," she said with a pitying look. Moe instinctively looked around her to make sure Seany hadn't heard the exchange.

Michele smirked and continued, "It was good for them. Especially that stubborn, bonehead you spent the last two nights with. Bless his heart. He's a tough nut to crack. We'll do it, though. It takes time. And he's maybe too close, you know? I mean, it just happened a couple of months ago. Give him time."

"That's exactly what he said. And maybe I decided to crack today because I wasn't practicing what I preach. The nightmares are back. I guess I just figured it was time to fess up."

"Well, you did good. You aren't their therapist. That's her job" she motioned to Alanna. "It's good to show them a little heart."

Moe gave her a crooked smile. "Thanks, Michele."

Michele said under her breath, "Incoming. Hot fireman gaining on us."

Seany noticed that the two women immediately broke rank from either side of Maureen, and he was grateful for it. He came alongside Skadi and Moe, Skadi snorting as Storm brushed against her. "I'm sorry, Maureen. I'm so sorry you were carrying that around with you. I should have asked the right questions."

"You did ask the right questions. I dodged all of them, Seany. I don't like talking about it. And I should talk about it to someone. My mother doesn't know about the nightmares. No one does. No one but you. You've been there twice. It's not your fault I didn't walk through that open door. I suppose I'm as stubborn as you are."

"You are stubborn. I'm familiar with that particular breed of woman. My mother and sister are prime examples. Once we're done here, I'd like to talk. Maybe just take a walk around your lough and talk through the rest of it."

"The rest?"

"I did the math, Maureen. You were with that Mason fellow during that time. I'd like to hear it all, if you'll trust me enough to tell it."

* * *

THEY WALKED HAND IN HAND, the air growing cooler as the sun dipped low in the sky. "Mason was living near the college when we were seeing each other. He was renting a small house. He had a nice place. A backyard and a dog. Really cozy. He also had a bass boat. I doubt they have those here. It's a small boat that only fits a couple people. It's for fishing in shallow water, like lakes and rivers. I called him when we heard about the trapped horses. He came to my farm, and imagine my surprise when his boat wasn't attached to the back of his pickup."

Seany cursed under his breath. "Please don't tell me he loved his boat that much."

She shook her head, "It wasn't that. He just...he wouldn't go because it was to save animals. He tried to get me to stay behind. He wasn't going to *be a party to this lunacy,* is how he put it. I had to be crazy to head toward that hurricane and flooding. It was too dangerous and the best thing that old rancher could do for those horses was to go out into the stables and euthanize them. With all of the chaos going on, human lives mattered more."

"He was worried about your safety. I can't say that I don't understand. Part of me wants to throttle you for going into the city in the middle of all that."

She turned to him. "And if it had been your parents? Or Brigid, stranded with her babies and Cora?"

"I'm not saying I disagree with what you did. I'd have done the same. Just because you're a woman, doesn't mean you are held to a different standard. You went after your family when you thought you had a good chance of getting to them. You mapped it out. While you waited for the worst of it to pass, you went and helped someone who needed you right then. People first, yes, but you were in a unique position to make a difference for that man and his horses. You didn't run half-cocked into either situation."

His words of praise made her tear up again. This. This is why no other man had ever compared to Sean O'Brien, Jr. Her throat ached with the visions of the past and of the future. Summer was going to come too soon.

Seany pulled her to him and rubbed a hand gently on her back. "I'm so proud of you, Maureen. You are a true hero. And coming from me, that's high praise. Given my family, I don't throw that word around lightly." He hugged her tightly. "Mason was scared for you. He took a pretty harsh approach to the problem. I mean, to be a future veterinarian, I'm shocked he could be so callous about the lives of those horses. He likely isn't a bad sort. Maybe he even regrets it. As a matter of fact, I'd wager he greatly regrets it. Especially in light of your success. Did he offer to go into the city for your parents, at least?"

"After the shutdown with the horse rescue, I didn't ask. It was the final nail in the coffin, not the first. We'd been having problems."

"Do you mind if I ask why?"

"Sometimes people ask a question when they aren't ready for the answer." She left it at that, but he wasn't going to let it go.

"What was the question?"

She leaned back to look at his face, trying to decide whether to answer. "That's a conversation for another day. If ever." And she pulled away, taking his hand to continue their walk. She stopped by the side of the lough, not able to stop the steady flow of tears once they'd started. She squatted at a spot where a brook emptied into the large lake. She flipped her braid over her shoulder so that it ran down her back. Then she splashed the cold, fresh water over her face. She dried her face with the edge of her shirt and looked out over the beautiful landscape. Even in the deep sleep of winter, it was breathtaking. Trees and moss and dried heather covering the land in waves. The water was impossibly clear, with stones nestled in a small amount of sediment she'd stirred. The entire natural canvas was reflected in the cold stillness of the lough. Rolling hills, regal trees, and the blue sky with its hazy, slim clouds. The slight breeze coated her damp skin like a benediction, earthy and altogether smelling of the slowing decay of winter leaves and fresh water. She reckoned this is what heaven looked like.

She wiped the last remnants of her tears away and stood to take Seany's hand again. She was grateful he'd given her that moment. He hadn't hovered. He'd just stood back, knowing that his presence and his soothing silence was all she needed. "It's beautiful here. Your country is so very beautiful, Seany. I don't have to tell you that. It stirs something in me." *Like you do.*

Seany's chest tightened. The idea of her staying here in Ireland. Of her staying with him...He was too afraid to hope.

* * *

Moe made her way to the main house, starving for some simple homestyle cooking. She took in the house anew, her heart warming at the sight of the simple dwelling. The stir of horses behind her, the trees and shrubs, and the remnants of a summer garden. Light through curtained windows and woodsmoke swirling out of the stone chimney. It was as beautiful as its owner. A friendly voice greeted her. "So, how was the Ashford? I'm jealous, by the way. I've been there for tea, but never for a two-night stay." Moira ladled hot stew into broad bowls and handed them to Moe. Moe put them around the table as the rest of the staff started to come into the kitchen.

"It was heavenly. Everything about it. The food, the wine, the romantic gardens and lush forests. I saw their stables. Talk about high tech. Oh! And I met some people who knew you. I told them you were looking for another board member. Maybe they'll call." She told Moira the name.

"Oh, yes. Wonderful people. Maybe I'll call them and put the pressure onto Haddie. She's retired and she loves horses."

"Talking about the short holiday with the hot fireman?" Michele said with a wink. Rory and Devlin exchanged glances. "Sorry, boys. We'll press for details later. Eat your stew."

Moira sat and took a sip of her tea. "You'll all be happy to know I had the competency inquiry dropped. I've also talked to Seany's cousin, the detective with the Dublin Garda, Tadgh O'Brien. I remembered something after he took me through the night of the open house."

They all leaned in expectantly. Moira continued after a bite of stew, "There was an older woman, maybe a few years younger than me. She signed up for a newsletter, but the account was no good. I thought she'd just written it down sloppily and I'd read it wrong. Anyway, she left her pen on the table. Corey and Jameson Natural Resource Corporation. It didn't ring a bell, but the detective started pulling the thread. Three years ago, another mineral company approached me at a horse show. Then they showed up here. They made an offer for the mineral rights to my land. When I refused, they came at me with a bigger offer. They wanted to buy the entire parcel outright. They said they would help me relocate or liquidate my stock to breeders in the area. After all, I had to be looking at starting my pensioner years. They could make me comfortable. Beyond comfortable." She shrugged, "I didn't need the money, so I told them to sod off."

"So, this was Corey and Jameson?" Devlin asked.

"No. I'll get to that. It was around that time that Hugo started coming around. Started trying to take an interest in my affairs, my business. He hit the ceiling when I told him about my idea for a non-profit. It was just an idea at the time. I didn't even know where to start. I think he was hoping I'd moved on from the idea. I never thought the two things were related, but now I don't know."

"So, you said Corey and Jameson wasn't the same company as three years ago?" Devlin asked.

Moira said, "No. The name was Jameson Mining. Apparently, I'm sitting on a prime spot for mineral mining, if they're correct. They are specifically interested in gold mining in this area. They've been trying to get a prospecting license approved by the government. The locals are against it, of course. The mineral companies can't touch National Park land, but they'd love to get their hands on this place. Even if I was going to sell, which I'm not, there is no way in hell I'd sell it for mining. Jameson Mining is under the umbrella of the Corey and Jameson Natural Resources Corporation."

"Those sons of bitches," Devlin cursed.

Moira smirked and said, "Too right. I think the woman who left the pen is probably responsible for the phone calls to cancel our food and music. And she may even be responsible for the attempt to poison the horses. If not, she was working with someone."

"What does this have to do with Hugo?" Maureen asked.

"He's always nosing into my finances. Worrying about me wasting money. I don't know if he's directly involved in these incidents, because he's not going to gain by forcing me to go under. I just think maybe he's been talking to these people. Maybe they are getting more aggressive to get me gone sooner. Then they'll cut that little prat out of the bargain."

"Let's think about the horses. Something has been bugging me." Devlin rubbed a thumb over his lips. "They didn't touch any of the valuable horses. War Hammer, the mule, Balor who is unsellable for a profit because he's got a bad reputation, Skadi can't be bred because of her blue eyes and the same with Clarence."

"What about Sadie? She's breeding. She's worth a pretty penny as well as that foal she was carrying…"

Devlin interrupted. "To an untrained eye, she could look overweight and old. She has the white speckling around her eyes. Someone who didn't know anything about horses might have seen a horse who needed put out to pasture. Someone like our prat, Hugo."

"We also don't know when those flowers were dropped. Skadi, War Hammer, and Balor were all part of the show. It could have ruined the whole showcase. We just happened to keep all of them outside all day. Except for Sadie because she's breeding."

"Listen, I'm going to call Hugo and tell him I want to see him. I was thinking about wearing a digital recorder."

"I hate that idea. Let me count the ways I hate that bloody idea." Devlin was rubbing his face, trying to stay calm.

"I will not let some greedy relative or some greedy corporation ruin what I'm trying to do here. That Garda officer is going to get a phone call from Detective O'Brien tomorrow."

Moe took her hand. "You aren't alone, Moira. No one is going to ruin this wonderful thing you've started. And no one is going to do one more thing to hurt or endanger our horses."

Moe was surprised to see the misting of tears. "You're the family God should have given me." She shook herself, getting the tears under control. "Instead of that little sod, Hugo."

They all laughed then. The gravity of the situation easing a bit. Later, Moe texted Seany, telling him what was happening. Then, asking him to talk to his cousin to make sure that he was aware of Moira's plan. She didn't like the idea any more than Devlin did.

* * *

Galway City, Co. Galway

Seany was twitchy. He thought perhaps it had something to do with it being his first shift with the fire brigade. The first night had been uneventful, only involving a false alarm at one of the college dormitories. Undoubtedly a drunk freshman. Now he was loading the dishwasher, the guys having eaten an early dinner. He was surprised when Finn showed up, wanting to speak with him. Finn put up his hands, "Brigid's fine. So are the kids." The tension left his body.

"What brings you here, brother?" Finn worked in Ennis, so this wasn't in the neighborhood. "Not that I don't welcome a visit. It's been a dreadfully boring first shift. I'm not complaining, mind you."

They met in the common room of the building, Finn seeming a little nervous. "I just needed to stop and see you. Cora had a dream… and so did I."

Seany raised his brows. Finn hadn't talked much about it since the family found out exactly where Cora had gotten her gift. "Okay. That's rarely a good thing." After all, Finn had smelled smoke the night the warehouse fire happened.

"I smelled turf. It was strong. And I smelled dried heather, like you smell on the bog. When I woke, I was sweating like the heat of the sun was consuming me. I was drenched and I'd thrown off the covers. I can't really say any more than that. But Cora was very clear. She had a feeling of dread and she heard horses…screaming. They were screaming." The hair stood up on Seany's forearms. "And she was met by a young woman named Abigail. Does that name mean anything to you? It wasn't clear, Seany. Sometimes that's how it works. But we both picked up on something. Just…be careful. And tell your Maureen the same."

"Tell me about this Abigail?"

"Cora said she was young. Like just out of school. She came to her through dark clouds. Dark heavy clouds. She told Cora to listen for the storm."

Seany's shoulders have an involuntary shudder. "There has been some trouble at the riding center. The guards have been involved. If you get anything clearer, please call me night or day. I'll ask Maureen, but Abigail doesn't ring a bell and I've met everyone there. I'm sorry you had to come all the way out here."

"It's alright," Finn said. "I wanted to come check on you in person. Brigid said you took the lass to the Ashford Castle. This must be love for that tariff."

He didn't address the speculation. "It was really something special. You should take Brigid there after the baby comes. We had fun. Although, you might want to skip the ghost tour. "

"Why is that?" Finn asked as he narrowed his gaze.

"Just trust me, Finn. The man in black is nothing to mess around with. If I reacted so strongly to it, you will definitely not want any part of it."

"The man in black, eh? Well, I'll take your word on it then." He hugged his brother-in-law. "Take care, brother. We almost lost ye once."

CHAPTER 29

Faeries, come take me out of this dull world, for I would ride with you upon the wind, Run on the top of the disheveled tide, And dance upon the mountains like a flame." ...William Butler Yeats, The Land of Heart's Desire

Letterfrack, Co. Galway

Moe rang Seany, getting his voicemail. She texted him, telling him the information she'd found out from Moira. He was going to come and do a private ride on Saturday, and she was so excited to see him. Even one night away from him had her tossing and turning. Her phone rang and she was surprised to see that it was from her mother. It was four o'clock in the morning in Texas.

"I just couldn't sleep, baby. I've been thinking about you. My mother's senses are going into overdrive. Is everything okay?"

She was not going to tell her mother what had been going on here. She wasn't going to leave, and it would cause her mother useless worry. "I helped deliver a foal. We've been doing great things with the equine therapy. I wish you could see this place. It's like heaven. It borders Connemara National Park."

"And how are things with you and Seany? Daddy said you two butted heads at first. Is all that sorted out?"

"Yes, it is. Things are good. Really good." That's all she said, and her mother paused.

"Can I assume that your feelings haven't changed for him, despite all of this time?"

"Of course they've changed, Momma. We aren't fifteen anymore. We're both in uncharted territory."

"Reeeeally?"

Moe laughed and said, "Would you stop. Behave yourself. We are not going there." But she suddenly had questions, and almost wished she had the guts to ask them. "I miss you, Momma. But I'm okay. No matter what happens, I'm okay."

"I'm proud of you, angel. I'm sorry I didn't support this at first. You sound really happy."

Moe said, "I am. And I love the work. I really do. I feel like it matters. The men are getting a lot out of it. Even Seany, despite how stubborn he is. He's back on the fire brigade this week. After losing his partner, I think he's going to need this therapy."

"And he's going to need you," her mother said. "Don't let him push you away. Daddy tried that crap with me, and you know how far that got him."

"Mom…I talked about Harvey." The phone was silent for a while. "I talked to the group and then Seany. And it occurred to me that isn't fair to you. You're my biggest supporter. You and Dad, and I didn't talk to you."

"What do you mean, honey?"

"I mean, I didn't tell you some stuff. At first because I knew you wouldn't want me continuing with the rescues. You had to stay back with the kids and Daddy. It was so chaotic, and Daddy was in a bad way. And I just had to keep going back and helping. I had to. But I didn't tell you after…about the things I saw." Her voice croaked as the tears started to fall. "And I never told you about the nightmares."

Her mother's voice shook as she tried to keep her composure. "Well, then. I guess it's time I quit assuming you're the strongest woman in the world and start listening. Tell me all of it, if you're ready. I'm up for the day and I've got nothing but time, baby girl."

* * *

MOE WIPED her face after ringing off with her mother. She heard Moira come into the barn. "What is it, lass? Is everything okay with your mammy?"

She took Moe in her arms and Moe melted into the contact. "Just a long overdue mother-daughter chat. About a lot of things. I told her about Harvey. I mean, she lived through it too, but she didn't know what I lived through. She didn't know a lot. So, we talked. I love my mother, but sometimes I keep things from her because she's had so much to deal with. I just didn't want to add to it."

"You're a good daughter. But a mother wants to be needed, even when their girl grows up. I'd give anything to have one more chat with Abigail."

"I'm sorry, Moira. That's the only thing I know to say and it's woefully insufficient."

"Well, I tried to coax Hugo over here, but apparently he's too busy traveling. Apparently, he's in London gambling with his father. The reason I know this is because that's all his father does. He taught him everything he needed to know about pissing his life savings away."

"I'm not going to lie, Moira. That may be for the best. Let the police keep working on this. You have way more now than you did before. And you gave them a good description of the woman that was at the open house."

Moira nodded absently. "Aye, I know. I'm just not one to sit idle and wait for things to happen."

"Believe me, I know. Look, Devlin, Michele, and I were talking. We are going to set up a cot in the barn and take shifts. Devlin brought a cricket bat from his brother's house."

"You are going to sleep in the barn?" Moira shouted. "No, Maureen. That's not necessary."

"I think it is. They're targeting the horses. They are trying to break you by hurting the horses and making it look like an accident. Rory is in as well. It's decided, Moira. You may as well submit and keep the snacks coming."

She put her hands on her hips, ready to argue, but Moe said, "I know, I know. Your home, your rules, but we want to do this. Please, let us do this." Just as she said it, Rory pulled into the drive. He came out with his farrier equipment and a folding cot slung over one shoulder. Moe said, "Speak of the devil. He's taking the first shift, then me tomorrow. We drew straws."

Rory went by, pecked Moira on the cheek and said, "Sorry, pet. You're outnumbered."

* * *

Galway City, Co. Galway

It was the last night of Seany's shift, and he was glad to see it end. As much as he loved his job, there were shifts that seemed to go on forever, regardless of the station. They'd gone to a motor car crash, minor injuries with petrol spilled onto the roadway. He went to his cot and slid his shoes off, then took off his uniform shirt. He always slept with one eye open during work, but he did need to get some rest. He'd checked over his uniform twice, then gone to say hello to Joseph, who was working on the paramedic unit tonight.

The guys on his shift were good guys, and it was going to take time to settle in. No one asked him about McBride or the warehouse fire, but he saw the speculation and the glances at his burns. He wondered if they were refraining because they'd been told not to ask about it. He was glad. He wasn't ready to talk with ease about losing McBride. Being like this, here in the station, he missed his old partner with a burning ache in his chest.

He checked his phone and saw that Maureen had called. "Hey, sorry I missed you. How's my horse doing?"

He heard the smile in her voice. "He's just fine. Handsome as ever. Skadi is in season, now, so we've had to move her to the end of the barn. Cassanova and Storm are giving Balor the bad eye. Boys will be boys."

"And poor Skadi will be left unsatisfied," Seany said.

He heard the horses in the background. "You're in the barn late. Are you sure everything is okay?"

Moe said, "Just fine. Your cousin has been a lot of help with the local Garda. I'll explain everything when you get here. I've got a kids' group coming tomorrow. Michele is taking the lead. She's great with kids. So, I'll see you Saturday at ten?"

"I'll be there bright and early." Seany's intent was to get some work done, go to bed early, and get up before dawn so he could see Moe for a few hours before their ride. "I can't wait, love. I miss you."

* * *

RORY GAVE Moe a sideways glance as he finished setting up a sleeping nook in the barn. Michele was checking the horses again before heading to the house. Rory said, "He doesn't know about you sleeping in the barn on watch duty tomorrow? Why so secretive?"

"It's not a secret. I just didn't think to tell him."

Michele laughed. "Smart girl. I know the type. Overprotective alpha males are sexy as hell and a complete pain in the ass."

Moe smirked, suppressing a laugh. "I'll tell him when he comes. No use borrowing trouble, right? I didn't tell my mother either. She'd likely get on a plane."

Rory asked, "Do you really think Hugo is behind this?"

She said, "I don't know, Rory. But someone is trying to shut her down and they are willing to use these horses to do it. Now, I'll be five minutes away. If you need anything, you can call me."

He smirked, showing her the hoof pick and the cricket bat he had on hand. "I've got this handled."

* * *

FURBOGH, Co. Galway

Seany woke the next morning at two-thirty, having retired early. He went into the kitchen to start the kettle when he saw Josh passed out on the couch. Josh stirred, a book on his chest, then went back to sleep. Seany saw a letter on the counter, and he picked it up. *Irish Naturalisation and Immigration Service* was bold on the heading. Jesus wept. He shouldn't read it, but he was damn well going to. He scanned the document, a prickling on the back of his neck. They apparently wanted to reverify proof of his student status. Odd, because he'd shown proof in the fall. It hadn't been a year yet. He returned the letter, sure that it was going to be fine. Josh was a student. He'd been told that his internship with the Coimisinéirí Soilse na hÉireann counted as part of his schooling. Most college programs had internships. And wasn't Moe here doing the same?

He looked at his sleeping roommate and his chest tightened. It would be like having the government come and demand one of his brothers move out of the country. He couldn't fathom it. Then he thought about Moe. She'd have to leave once the internship was up, wouldn't she? She was on a student visa. Some exchange program with her school and some school in Dublin. He didn't even know which one. But the point was, she wasn't here as a tourist. She was here on a student visa that had an expiration date. What in the hell was he going to do when she left?

* * *

Letterfrack, Co. Galway

Seany arrived just after four in the morning, hoping to catch Maureen asleep. He didn't. As he pulled into the small parking space off the access road, his headlights illuminated her sitting on a blanket on the shore of the lough. It was still dark, so he got out of the car and went to sit at her side. "Hello, love. You're up early."

She smiled. "This isn't early for farmers and ranchers. I would have been up in an hour anyway. I had trouble sleeping."

"More bad dreams?" he asked softly.

Moe looked out over the lough. The moon was low in the sky,

sparkling over the crystal lake. The stars had started to fade. Twilight would start in about an hour, slowly easing them into daylight over the course of two hours. It was so different from Texas where the sun blazed, not glowed. They sat in the dark, and she knew she had to answer his question. "You talked to your cousin?"

"I did. He told me everything that's happened and what he found out about the mineral company. Is that what's causing your sleep to be disturbed?"

"Yes, partly. I did have nightmares. They were strange. You know the kind that morph and don't make any sense once you wake?"

He did know. He still had nightmares about the warehouse fire. But in McBride's place, it had been Aidan. Another time, he and Kamala had both been trying to pull him off that ledge. "I know the type. Yes." He needed to tell her about what Finn had revealed. But she was talking, and he didn't want to distract her just yet.

"I dreamed that I was in the boat again, going to rescue those horses. But when I got there, it was this stable instead of the one in Houston. The rain just kept coming, but I had to get Skadi out. And Balor. All of them. I had to get them out before the water got too high." He hugged her, wanting to comfort her. But something came over her. A need so powerful, and something only he could give her. She tipped her face up to his mouth, and he kissed her so gently that it almost made her weep. She pulled his head down and deepened the kiss, and he moaned in her mouth. They started with the coats and the clothes came off quickly and furiously. It was cold. She could see her breath, but she wanted him skin to skin. Soon they were down to socks and nothing else and the early morning air made her nipples tighten. She thought he'd mount her, but he pulled her astride him. "Take me, lass. Let me bear some of this for you."

She could barely see him, except for the night sky reflecting off his eyes and a small bit of light from her cottage. He didn't ask again. He took her hips and positioned himself at her core. He practically growled at her. "Fuck me. You need this. Take from me!"

She sat on his cock with one push, taking the whole of him to her body. They both cried out, the burning heat where they were joined in such contrast to the cold air. "That's it." He sounded like he'd run a marathon. But his body grew liquid, like being inside her had soothed him and he could finally take a deep breath.

Their eyes had adjusted to the low light, and she saw his face more clearly. Moe's head slumped on her shoulders, feeling the same soothing relief. "Maureen," The words were thick with his accent, and heat bloomed on her skin as her name left his mouth. "Come down to me, love. I'd have another kiss from you."

Her hair shrouded them both as he cupped a hand around the back of her neck. She was so beautiful. He just watched her love him with her body. Until she flopped down, like her bones had been removed. Then he started to move again. "You're mine, Maureen Rogers. I let ye go once, but I'll be damned if I'll do it again. This time, ye'll have a fight on your hands." He couldn't hold back anymore. He took her hips in hand and came into her with a fury.

* * *

Moe felt the chilled morning air come into her in slow degrees. She was sprawled across him. Astride him, actually, wearing only her socks.

She raised up her head and he saw the tears in her eyes and wondered what kind of tears they were. "Good morning," she said with a sweet little smile.

He took her face in his hands and her heart thumped as she saw the intensity in his blue eyes. "I meant what I said. I'm no boy to meekly settle for my lot."

She touched his face, saying nothing, but giving him a nod of understanding. Moe was moved by his words, but she noticed that the three most important words had been absent from his eloquent speech. And in their absence, she was too much of a coward to reveal the full extent of her love for him. And she did love him most desperately.

* * *

Seany visited with Storm, who for once seemed genuinely glad to see him. "You look like you've been to the groomer, lad. You're extra shiny this morning." The horse nudged him under the chin, and he laughed. "My shift was boring. No action to speak of. The only fire I've been to was as a paramedic, but it was dreadful."

Moe looked at Michele and she was actually tearing up. The bad ass Marine was getting weepy listening to Seany pour his heart out to Storm. She didn't want to make too much noise, not wanting Seany to stop. Maybe this was the only way he had of telling her what he'd been through.

Seany said, "Aye, he was burned pretty badly. It was hard to witness…and it made me think of Nelson. McBride, I mean. Remember I told you about him. Anyway, it kind of brought it back. Burns are very painful. I hope you never find out. The pain I saw in his eyes…it stuck with me."

Now Moe was crying. It was interrupted by Devlin coming in. "Morning everyone. Moe, I thought I'd go on the ride with you today."

Moe smiled after she'd turned away and wiped the tears. "Yes, of course. Could you show us more of the park?"

"I can. Moira's packed everyone a hearty lunch and snacks. I'm going to take you deep into the forest. I think you'll like this spot."

Moira came in just then. "I'm breaking in the new trainer today. The one filling in for Penelope. You can all go if you like. We'll keep the horses close to home today, given the happenings. Michele, it would do you good, yes?"

"Yes, Ma'am. Thank you!" Michele started getting a gorgeous blood bay named Scarlet out of her stall.

Seany walked into the tack room to get his bridle and saddle and he froze. There was a cot pushed against the wall. Moe came in behind him. "What's this?" he asked.

She told him about the night watch they'd organized. "That's why I can't come with you today. I'll drive down tomorrow to see you. Tonight is my shift."

Seany shook his head. "You're sleeping inside the stables so that you're HERE if someone breaks in and tries to hurt the horses?"

Her brows furrowed. He didn't look happy, and she had to admit she wasn't surprised. She had a jarhead for a father, and she knew that look. "Yes," she said calmly. "We have a cricket bat and a hoof pick for protection." She said the last with a chipper, light tone. It didn't help.

"The hell you are. You are not sleeping here waiting for some fiend to break in and do mischief. Have you all lost your minds?" Michele had walked into the doorway and raised her brows, turning and walking right back out.

"This is my work. My domain, buddy. Don't get high handed with me Sean O'Brien, Jr. or I will use that cricket bat on you! And don't embarrass me…" she whispered that part. "This is where I work. We all made this decision as a team. Back off with the caveman shit. I'm more exposed in that cabin, isolated from everyone, than I am in this barn."

He ground his molars. "I don't like it. I'm staying here if you are."

"We are rotating, Seany. You can't be here every four days. I'm not completely ignorant in self-defense. Relax, and I will meet you at your home tomorrow. Now get your tack and get in there. You are my student. And I already have an overprotective father." She grabbed her tack and marched out with her chin up, and he was ready to rope her like a calf and drag her back to Galway. But a small part of him respected her pluck. She really had evolved from that shy fifteen-year-old. And as infuriating as she was, it was kind of arousing to have her hand him his ass. Cricket bat indeed.

* * *

Connemara National Park, Co. Galway

Devlin nodded to Michele, because she'd asked about the dry surface of the land and bog areas. "Yes, it should be wetter. We've had an uncommonly dry winter. Nice for some, but it makes the fire risk higher."

Michele groaned. "I know all about that. Colorado is officially out of its drought, but it was rough for a couple of years when I first got there. There were fires in the foothills that I could see from my house."

"Do you miss the Marines?" Devlin asked her.

"Yes. Every day. And every day I'm glad I'm not in anymore. It's a confusing condition." She smiled. "I loved being a Marine. I'm proud of my life so far. I've seen and done extraordinary things. I've led men. I've helped get water to villages that didn't have a clean water source. I've buried friends. It's been as hard as it's been beautiful. But this..." She raised her arms around her. "This isn't too bad for an old banged up Marine. I love what I do and where I'm going. I'm hoping to become a full-time trainer at the non-profit back home. They do great work there, just like you do here. Although, you may have them beat with the quality of these ponies. Many of our horses are donated or borrowed. You have champion bloodlines here. Frankly, I'm shocked she'd take them out of the high life."

"Moira would no more sell off these horses than someone would sell their children. She wants this to succeed. And the breed is perfect for this type of work."

"Agreed," Michele said as she patted her horse's neck.

Maureen came alongside her. "I'm surprised some jarhead didn't sweep you off your feet."

"They did. Several of them. I just got right back up on those feet and snuck out the back door when they started talking about getting married."

Seany was the one who threw back his head and laughed. "Oh, you just wait, lovely Michele. You're a handful to be sure. You like things your way. But love comes for us all in the end. At least, that's what my family believes. And there are hundreds of years of family history to back it up."

Moe shivered in her saddle, because it almost sounded like a warning.

* * *

THEY TIED the horses at a strategic area, and Moe could hear the rushing water. "It's just a short walk up that path. It's worth the stop," Devlin said.

Moe walked behind the men, Michele at her side. Michele said, "Oh, the view is mighty fine in these parts." And to Moe's surprise, she wasn't looking at Seany's spectacular ass. That was to say, she wasn't only looking at Seany's ass. She was looking at Devlin's. The completely single, completely adorable, slim and fit Devlin with the dimples and green eyes. "Why Michele, you little vixen."

"Shush, or I'll throw you in that creek. I'm just looking. It can't hurt to look."

Moe gave a husky laugh. "It can't hurt to hit that, either."

Michele gave her a murderous glare, but there was an emerging smile underneath it all. The path opened up and Moe gasped. A beautiful waterfall was nestled among large, mossy rocks. It smelled like fresh, clean water and stone and something altogether earthy. The rushing water blew the tendrils of hair that were loose around her face. She didn't notice at first that Seany was watching her. She turned to him and his smile stole her breath.

Devlin immediately went to work, spreading out the thick wool blankets. His large satchel held enough food for ten people. They ate every bit. Jam sandwiches, cheese, stuffed olives and fruity cookies.

Moe patted her stomach. "Skadi is going to buck me off for these extra pounds. Thank you, Devlin. It was a perfect picnic spot." And in that moment, she and Michele weren't interns. Seany wasn't a student, and Devlin wasn't the head groom. They were four friends eating and talking and spending an absolutely perfect day together.

CHAPTER 30

Furbogh, Co. Galway

Maureen left from Letterfrack early, so that she could spend her day off with Seany. Instead of going out and about, they'd decided to stay home. Josh had a rare night off, and they invited Maddie and Mary over for board games. Maureen showed them how to make Mexican hot chocolate and prepared a feast of Tex-Mex with what she could pull together from what she considered a sparse grocery store. It wasn't, really. But Americans, especially Texans, loved their chile con queso and brisket tacos, and it was slim pickings for ingredients in Galway. She made do with some Old El Paso brand cheater ingredients from the imported section of the SuperValue.

Now the non-Texans were gathered around the cheesy, warm dip like a pack of hungry wolves. Mary said, "I'd take a bath in this stuff. It's gorgeous altogether."

"If you took a bath in this, you wouldn't be gorgeous altogether," Josh said. "You'd be all cheesy and slimy."

Mary grinned after swallowing a mouthful of cheese. "It would be worth it. Moe, ye've got to call my mam and tell her how you made this."

Madeline smiled at that. She said, "You know, you could make it yourself. You are twenty years old, for the love of God. Try cooking for a change."

Mary looked at her like she was daft. "No way. Why do you think I live at home? I've got enough to do with my class load this term."

They continued a rowdy game of *What the Meme,* but then settled into an evening of just catching up. Madeline offered to help Josh with the dishes. "How is the semester going for you, Madeline?" Josh asked.

Maddie loved when he used her full name with his midwestern American accent. And she watched the muscles of his forearms twist as he washed the large bowl in his hands. She said, "It's going pretty well. I'm only taking two classes because I'm working on my final presentation for Humanities and Celtic Studies. I got the two departments to allow me to do a joint project. I've studied classics in languages, arts, literature, and philosophy. I took an archaeology class as well. My project is about how technology has eroded the humanities and the Irish people. We have better access now than ever, but it's my opinion that technology has taken something from the human condition. Eroded relationships, distracted us from true creativity, altered how we learn, and changed our brains so that we require constant stimulation in order to feel normal. This semester was about gathering data, then next semester is going to be more experimental. I was going to try finding students who were willing to unplug for two months, but the colleges and workplaces are so computerized now, I can't see how it's possible. Using older people is kind of cheating, because they aren't as dependent, and half their lives were lived before we had all of these screens. I'm still trying to sort it all out, actually." She looked up and blushed. "Christ. Ye were probably looking for an "everything is great" answer and I'm goin' on, boring you to death."

Josh smiled, "Not at all. I mean, I know I'm not the sharpest tool in the shed, but I can follow along."

"Don't talk about yourself that way, Josh. You're very smart. If I had to read half of those books," she pointed to his stack of textbooks, "I'd flunk out of school. At least when you graduate, you'll have a skill. I'm starting to question the wisdom of my majors."

"Don't you talk about yourself that way," he said. And she grinned because he'd just turned the tables on her. "I understand what you're saying. When I went through high school, most kids had a phone and a laptop or at least a tablet at home. I had to go to the library to do my work because we didn't have internet in our shitty rental. The teachers would say, *Okay everyone, get out your phones...*then ramble off something we were supposed to look up. Then the inevitable, *Josh, just find someone who can share their phone.* The only phone I had was a flip phone that Charlie got me. I had to keep it hidden from my...."

He stopped, as if he'd revealed more than he wanted to. "Anyway, I remember that as soon as the phones came out, the kids would start texting or getting on YouTube or Snapchat and the teacher would be fighting to regain control of the class. I get it. You're right. Sometimes when I'm looking up at those old lighthouses, so isolated from everything and everyone, I wonder what life was like for the old keepers. Before things went automated. They didn't have a TV. They had books. They had candles. They had to make do with a certain amount of supplies until more came. They couldn't Amazon Prime whatever they needed in two days. It was simpler, but I doubt it was less. It sounds like a nice way to live." He looked at her, and her intense gaze made him blush. He could get lost in her deep, grey-green eyes.

"You understand, then. You really understand."

"That said, there are some things that are certainly better. Medicine for one. And I hate to think what would have happened if I hadn't had modern communications when those ferries collided, and they called the Coast Guard and RNLI. "

"They'd have called everyone on the home line. Go back a few hundred years, they may have gone to the cliffs and lit a signal fire. One could argue that if those ferry captains weren't so dependent on technology, maybe that crash wouldn't have happened."

"Forget humanities. You should have gone to law school," he said with a nudge.

Moe watched Maddie and Josh and noticed that Seany and Mary were stealing glances at them as well. She looked at Mary. Mary just shook her head. "Utter fools, the both of them." Which drew a chuckle from Seany and a sly grin from Moe.

Madeline dried the last dish. "We'd better head out. Thanks for the invitation, lads. And the food was wonderful, Maureen. A real treat, to be sure." The women hugged, then Seany pulled both the girls in with each arm. "Kiss my nieces and nephew for me. I'll try to get down to see them soon. That little Estela owes me a rematch for Snakes and Ladders. The girl slaughtered me last time."

Madeline went to Josh, meeting his eyes before she hugged him goodbye. "Goodbye, *mo ghile mear.*" A name she'd given him after he'd pulled her out of the sea, when she was convinced she'd die alone. Josh had asked Seany to translate for him, too shy to ask her. My gallant hero, or more correctly…my gallant darling. It moved through his body, a liquid heat of desire as the words rolled off her tongue. Josh sank into the embrace, letting himself have a small moment to hold her. He wrapped his hands around her waist and rested his head on her shoulder. Then it was over. Brief and heartbreaking for the other three to witness.

* * *

Letterfrack, Co. Galway

The ride was cracking good fun. The meeting had been quick, since they wanted to give the men a lot of time in the saddle. This time, Alanna went along. Penelope was visiting with her newborn baby girl, and so she and Moira watched the two infants while Alanna went on the ride. Before the ride, she'd fed him again, even though she'd only fed him an hour earlier. "He'd be on there all day and night if I let him," she said as she handed him off to Moira.

"Abigail was like that, too," Moira said wistfully. Alanna froze, looking at Seany and then back at Moira.

Seany's face blanched, "Um, Moira…could we talk to you about something after the ride? It's a bit of a long story, so I don't want to hold up the group."

Now they were on the long and winding trail through the park, with a clear day in front of them. They went on a ride that Devlin had mapped out in order to show them an old mine. "This area is rich in minerals. When they made it a park forty years ago, it was closed off to automobile traffic. So, the best way to see this park is either on horseback or hiking. Moira's land backs up to the park, which makes us very lucky to know her."

"What did they mine?"

"Gold, silver, the green marble you see in the shops, and there is also mining for zinc and lead. That's the biggest thing now. They've been mining in Ireland since the Bronze Age. We just have to be careful. Some things can't be replaced. You can only rob the land for so long before there will be nothing left to take."

"Yes, like the turf cutting," Owen said. "Some people are dead set against it, since we don't need it for burning anymore."

"Exactly right," Devlin said. "Now, we're going upwards so let the horses follow at their own pace. They know these trails better than all of us. They won't lead you astray."

Alanna's eyes were everywhere. Seany stayed close to her, knowing Aidan would want her to be well looked after. "This is so beautiful. I hope you're glad I tricked you into it."

Seany gave her a sideways glance. "It's much better than dealing with you headshrinkers."

"Hey!" Alanna said, just as her horse let off a loud stink bomb. "See, he agrees with me. You're ungrateful."

Storm snorted, shaking his head. "If I didn't know better, I'd swear she planned that," Seany said as he gave his horse a pat.

After the tour of the mine, which just involved walking around outside of it since it wasn't safe to go inside, they all headed back to the ranch. As they came into the barn from the dirt road that ran alongside the pasture, Moe squealed. "Sadie!"

Moira said over the din, "It seems it is newborn day at the ranch.

Once you've all tended your horses, you can meet the latest addition to the family."

The big, tough military men and first responders were gaga over Sadie's new filly. "Her name is Tempest, after her father."

"Her father?" Michele asked.

Moira waited to see if anyone would figure it out. "Well I'll be damned." Seany said softly. He walked over to Storm's stall. He put his head out and Seany took his large, beautiful face in his hands. He kissed his soft muzzle. "Congratulations, Da. She's a beauty."

"Do you think they know? I mean, they don't procreate the old-fashioned way," Kyle said.

"He knows," Seany said. "See the way his ears turn toward her and how he sniffs the air? Could you bring her closer?"

Moira walked her over and motioned for Seany to open the stall. Storm nickered at his little, gangly daughter, then nuzzled and licked her. A collective *awe* came out of the group. Moira said with a smile, "Yes, it seems he does know."

Moe was still sniffling from the outburst of emotion that she'd experienced when seeing Sadie and her new baby girl. Something healed in her during those first moments that she hadn't known was broken.

It had to do with flood waters and a stillbirth foal. Her nightmares were haunted with those few days, when the worst of Harvey was at her doorstep. But seeing Tempest with Sadie, both hale and hearty, was like a balm on that old wound. She couldn't wait to tell her parents. Alanna was speaking to the men when she heard her call another meeting. They'd cut the beginning session off early because she wanted to regroup after the ride.

They all sat in the usual spots, and Alanna started the conversation. Talking about how beautiful the ride had been. How in tune with nature it had made her feel. Then she put a question to them. *How do you feel this experience has helped you?* They went around the group. When it came to Seany, he wasn't sure what to say.

Owen was the one to say what was on everyone's mind. "Well,

seeing how ye've not really shared anything like the rest of us, it would be hard to tell."

Seany bristled and Moe tensed. Alanna didn't seem surprised, but she said nothing. "What do you mean? I'm here, I told you why. I got injured in a warehouse fire."

Owen sighed. "So, you got hurt and they sent you to therapy? I'm not buying it. Something is missing in that story. And while we've all learned to talk about our struggles, you're tight lipped as a nun every single Monday. So, maybe you haven't gotten anything out of it."

Seany looked at Moe and she gave him an encouraging look. He shot out of his chair, "I'm not doing this."

Alanna said calmly, "Please don't leave, Seany. You don't have to share if you aren't ready."

Seany looked around at the judgmental faces of the other men. Devlin and Michele stayed neutral, of course. They were professional. He saw the disappointment on Maureen's face, though. And it pissed him off. Maybe they were right, but he wasn't going to be bullied into this little show and tell. "I have to talk to Moira before I go. You can all carry on without me since I'm not adding anything to the conversation."

"You're putting words in my mouth, Sean." Owen wasn't confrontational at all. It would have been easier if he had been. "Only you know how much you haven't shared. You wouldn't be so defensive if there wasn't some truth in it. But I'll back off. Maybe I shoulda held my tongue."

"No, you're entitled to say what's on your mind. I've got to go talk to Moira. I'll see you all before you leave."

* * *

WHEN THEY SAT down at the table, Seany explained to Moira about Finn and Cora's gifts. "Just stick with me. I promise this is going somewhere. My brother-in-law came to see me at the firehouse. He and Cora both have visions through a dreamscape. Each in different ways, but it came to them both. There is always a reason. Usually involving someone close to them. One time, Finn smelled smoke just as he was drifting off. It was so strong; it woke him and he thought the house was on fire. That was the night of the warehouse fire." He watched Moira rub her chill bumps away with her hands. "Cora dreams of places and sometimes people. Sometimes people who have passed on have messages for her. It's usually some sort of warning."

"And what does this have to do with me, lad?"

"I didn't put it together at first. The name didn't mean anything to me until Maureen said something."

"What name? I'm not following." Moira's face had gone pale.

"I'm not so sure about that, Moira. I see it in your eyes. I don't mean to upset you, love. Truly. But it's important that you hear it. I didn't recognize the name because you never told me your daughter's name. Abigail had a message, and I think it may have been for you."

* * *

THE OTHER MEN were leaving in their cars when Seany and Moira came outside. Alanna was loading up the baby, and he kissed her and the child before seeing them off. Moe stood to the side, quiet and serious. Now it was just them standing alone in the area between the house and the barn.

"You said you wouldn't push." His voice was tight and defensive.

"And I haven't." Moe calmly stood with her hands in her pockets, and he was reminded of the day she'd had a standoff with Balor.

"You stood there and let him hijack the entire meeting. And your mouth may not have agreed with him, but I saw it in your face. The others did as well."

She narrowed her eyes. "What exactly did he say that was incorrect?"

"He all but called me a liar," he bit out.

"He didn't say that. He said you were holding out. You are. So again, what did he say that was incorrect?"

Christ, he hated this. Hated that she was judging him. She didn't know shit about what he'd been through. She broke character, however, and said, "Does what I do here mean so little to you?"

"That's a load of bollocks and you know it. I've done everything you've asked. I've bromanced that feckin' pony. I talked to him. I took care of him."

"You'll talk to him, but no one else. Not even me."

His heart was racing. He didn't want to think about McBride. He'd enjoyed the distraction of his new job, his new romance. Why did she have to push?

"What happened with the fire in Galway?" she asked.

"It was nothing. A kitchen fire," he lied.

Moe shook her head. Maybe because they'd been so intimate, she'd expected more. Maybe because she'd shared with him and the group. "I thought we'd come further than this. My mistake."

"It is your mistake. Just because we're seeing each other doesn't give you full access to my pain. It's my choice who I share it with." His words were like a slap.

"You'll have to forgive my naivety and inexperience. I thought this," she motioned between them, "was more than just seeing each other. Thank you for the clarification, Sean." She turned and he tried to speak. She held up a hand. "You've said enough. Too bad it was all the wrong things." She turned toward her cottage and walked briskly, before he could see her tears. And the worst part was...he let her go.

CHAPTER 31

London, England

Hugo wiped the sweat on his brow as his father rambled. He was drunk and he often slipped into a sort of mania with the lubricant of vodka martinis. "Your aunt is even worse than your blasted mother. She tossed her husband aside without a backward glance. He didn't get a dime of her inheritance, the hopeless sod."

"But you're sure that we're going to see some sort of benefit from this? I mean, if she sells outright..."

"Don't worry on that account." But Hugo was worried. When the mineral company had approached him about a potential deal, he'd thought it was a great opportunity. All he had to do was insert himself in her financial matters, convince her to abandon the non-profit idea, and sell for a nice retirement. If she wouldn't sell, he'd sell when he inherited. Surely the old girl wouldn't live more than another five years. But she had stubbornly refused to give him a clue on the contents of her will or about the sum of her holdings. If she dumped the lot into a non-profit, he'd get nothing. The non-profit would outlive her. But he didn't like the tactics the mineral company had used.

"Listen, dear boy. They've got the whole thing sorted out. They're convinced that they've bribed the right people in the Irish government. That prospector license will go through for the area outside the park. They'll hold off, of course. We don't want the property value to skyrocket due to mineral rights. Or God forbid, someone sells the land without including the mineral rights. Just leave it all up to Mr. Corey. He and his partner are certain she's going to want to unload that property. She'll sell the horses off and retire, just like she should have five years ago. Then you can go to work coaxing your way back into the estate."

"But you're sure about her safety? I mean, who gives a bloody shite about those horrid beasts, but I don't want her coming to harm. What exactly do they have planned?"

"Something that won't blow back on any of us," his father said. Somehow that didn't make Hugo feel any better.

* * *

Lady Day Festival-Clifden, Co. Galway

Moe loved the way the Irish celebrated the changing of the seasons. The cross-quarter and quarter days surrounded religious feast days as well as the old, more pagan days that followed the harvest and changing seasons. Spring was a time of rebirth. Of fertility. The Vernal Equinox and Lady Day were celebrated together. Moira explained it all in such a wonderful storytelling voice that Moe had been enthralled on the way to the festival. Lady Day was the traditional day for hiring farm laborers for the coming growing season. It coincided with the feast of the Archangel Gabriel's annunciation to the Virgin Mary that she would be the mother of Jesus Christ.

As Moe walked around the festival, there were religious icons mixed with more pagan looking Celtic wares. There were people selling plants and seeds, and others were selling baby animals like chickens, kid goats, pigs, lambs, and rabbits. There was a stand that sold baked goods like fresh bread and churned butter. She bought some of those items to take back to their booth, which they'd set up in order to promote the riding center.

She walked through the stalls, letting her mind wander to Seany. She'd spoken to her father last night, and he'd helped her gain some perspective. When men were close to the most painful parts, they sometimes lashed out. He didn't know the whole of it, though. *Just because we're seeing each other...* Well, she shouldn't be surprised. She'd come here wanting something that may have been a fantasy. And she'd let things get physical pretty damned fast. The words that spilled from his lips during their love making weren't the same words that came out of his mouth outside the bedroom. She didn't have enough experience with relationships to understand the difference. The truth was, she had a couple months left before she'd have to leave. After he'd realized that he'd taken her virginity, he asked her to marry him. Out of guilt, of course. Thank God she hadn't said yes. She loved him, despite his unwillingness to fully give himself to her. But maybe, just maybe, that wasn't going to be enough.

She was almost done with her tour of the vendor area when she came to a booth that made her stop in her tracks. Jameson and Corey Mineral Company had a booth that was passing out pamphlets. She went up to the booth and there was an older woman, a little bit younger than Moira, that handed her a pamphlet. *Vote Yes for Mining in Galway. Create New Jobs. Support Responsible Mining.* Moe's blood ran cold. She'd seen this woman at their open house. She was almost sure of it. She walked away, took out her phone, and pretended to apply more sunscreen from her bag while she took a selfie with the woman in the background.

She went back to their booth where there were about twenty kids waiting in line to pet War Hammer. "Moira, can I talk to you quickly?"

"That was a fast break. You've got another fifteen minutes," Moira said.

"Yes, I know. But I need to show you something." Moe pulled her phone out of her bag and showed Moira the last picture she'd taken.

She expanded the photo in the left corner where she managed to get a full face shot of the woman running the booth.

"Who exactly am I looking at?" Moira said.

"Does she look familiar at all to you?" Moe asked.

"A bit, I suppose. Yes, I feel like I've seen her before. Who is she?"

"If I tell you, you have to promise that you won't go over there." Moe looked as stern as she could under Moira's intense gaze. "Promise me, Moira."

Moira crossed herself. "I swear it."

"She's at a booth for Jameson and Corey Mineral Company. They are passing out literature to vote yes for mining in Galway." She waited for the explosion. Moira just narrowed her eyes at her.

"That was a rotten thing to do, extracting that promise from me!" But Moira wasn't angry with her. She was livid with the woman that was more than likely the one who'd poisoned Sadie.

"Okay, what now Nancy Drew?" Moira said pissily.

"Now I forward this photo to Detective Tadgh O'Brien. He'll get it in the right hands. The Galway City Garda Station's detective unit took the case over and he's making sure they are treating us as a priority." She texted the number Seany had given her, sending a note and the photo. "Done. Now, let's leave this to the police and get on with the festival. There is nothing we can do. No one saw her do it. Although, I'd love to snatch the old bitch bald-headed for trying to hurt my Skadi."

Moira grinned, "Old bitch, eh? I should take offense at that, but I'm inclined to agree. She canceled my feckin' food truck as well, I'd wager."

"Speaking of food trucks, I think your Boxy and Bangers truck is here. You want some?" Moe asked.

Rory heard her and choked on his laughter. "It's boxty, lass. Not Boxy."

"Whatever. You know what I mean. What is a boxty?"

"It's a sort of potato pancake and sometimes it's stuffed with things. Bangers, as you've already discovered, are sausages."

"Sounds like a lot of fat and carbs. Count me in," said Michele, who had been listening to the entire exchange. "Oh, and Devlin called. He and the new guy are keeping busy training with Chancellor and Gandolf. They are putting them through the jumping course to see if they can get Gandolf to be a little more obedient." Gandolf was the young dominant white who liked to play in the mud. "Then they are going to give Cass and Hercules a workout. He also wanted me to tell you that Tempest and Sadie are doing great. Tempest is playing with the older colt. He's got some pictures for the website."

Moira smiled. "I hate to sell them. I mean, the buyer for the dun colt seems to be having financing issues, so he may be staying with us. But that breeder from Maam Cross wants Tempest for breeding. He's willing to pay big."

"Do we have the resources to keep them both?" Moe asked.

"Aye, of course. I don't need the money. I just keep thinking about the way Storm and Sadie both seemed to…" She shrugged, the words escaping her.

"Love her," Moe said.

Rory said, "Take the money." Michele elbowed him.

Michele said, "They are great breeding stock. And their parents are really good, even-tempered horses. Someday they could be great assets to our therapy team. But the decision is yours. Did you have a contract? Did you take payment for her?"

"No, I didn't. He was wanting a colt so he could stud him, but he'd take a mare. It was verbal. We've done business before. I guess I could talk to him. After what happened to Sadie, I just hate the idea of separating them. Caul births are considered to be good luck in humans and horses. It's a rare thing." She sighed, looking at Moe, then Michele, then War Hammer. "I think we should keep them both."

Moe squealed and threw her arms around her. "I'm going to text Seany. He was devastated for Storm and Sadie when I told him that Tempest had a buyer." She took out her phone. "Then I'm going to go get us all some boxy." Then a pang of hurt assaulted her. She really wasn't on speaking terms with him right now. Still, he'd be happy. She just wasn't going to be the one to break the silence. He'd hurt her pretty deliberately and she wasn't in the mood to be gracious.

"It's boxty!" Rory yelled, laughing at her back. It broke through her self-pitying train of thought.

Moira shook her head. "Christ, I'm getting soft in my old age. I wouldn't have thought twice about selling that foal ten years ago."

"You're doing the right thing," Michele said. "That filly is special. I feel it when I look at her."

* * *

MOE WATCHED Balor in the arena and had to smile. He was doing well. He really was. And he was also turning into a terrible flirt. Skadi was still confined because she was at the end of a fertile cycle. Balor, Cass, and Clarence were all sniffing around, so to speak. The urge to mate was ingrained in all animals. She took a picture of Tempest and Sadie. Storm was also separated, because he'd been showing signs of aggression when the foal was loose in the arena. Not wanting the other horses to get too close. But horses were herd animals, and the other mares doted on both of the young ones. He was also keen to have a go at Skadi. Double threat. So, he was in the penalty box…just like his favorite rider.

When she finally made it back to the cottage, she was exhausted. She just wanted to put her feet up in front of a glowing fire. She lit the turf that Devlin left for her. It was a silly gesture, but she knew he was doing it so she that could experience an old-fashioned fire. She put the dried heather over the burning embers, and the smoky, sweet scent was pleasant as it permeated the air around her. She changed into her pajamas and sat in front of the fire with a cup of tea, picking up the novel she'd started last week. She didn't have a TV or internet, and she couldn't say she missed it. Her phone worked, and she'd started an international plan before she came. She just enjoyed unplugging and relaxing.

She hadn't meant to fall asleep on the sofa, but she woke in the middle of the night, still smelling the heather and smoky peat that had long gone out in her hearth. She went to the bedroom, and climbed into bed. Her phone was charging on the nightstand. She checked her messages and found one. *I'm sorry. Please come to me on Saturday night. I'm a complete bastard.*

She paused over the phone, not sure how to respond. So, she didn't. She heard another text come in a minute later.

You said it was a conversation for another time. What was the question Mason asked? You said sometimes people ask questions when they aren't ready to hear the answer? What was the question?

Shit. She thought about it for a moment, then said to hell with it and replied. *He asked me if I'd ever been in love.*

Her phone rang instantly, but she was tired and hurting. She wasn't in a particularly giving mood. She let the call go to voicemail.

* * *

Glasnevin Cemetery, Dublin

Seany swallowed hard as he approached. The headstone was in place now. It hadn't been when he'd been here last. *Nelson McBride. Loving Husband and Father. Devoted friend.* The Dublin Fire Brigade crest and their firehouse ID was carved on the other side of the stone. *Fallen while in service to our city.* There were fresh flowers, and he knew who they were from. Yellow tulips were the first flowers he'd ever gotten Kamala. He got them for her on their anniversary every year because they'd been married in early spring. He pictured her here on the first wedding anniversary that she'd had to spend alone. Sometime very recently, if the condition of the flowers were any indication.

He pictured sweet, smiling Kamala laying across this mound of earth, weeping at everything she'd lost. That vision was more than Seany could take. The tears came for the first time since he'd seen his partner lying in that hospital bed. Tears that he'd shed when he thought that Nelson would still pull through. He hadn't cried since. Not really. He was stunned to realize it. Once they started, he couldn't stop. He cried until he shook, kneeling in the grass at the grave of his dear friend. "I'm so sorry. God, please forgive me. I couldn't save you and it's killing me, mo cara. It's eating me alive." He heaved in great, wracking sobs until his face was flushed and soaking wet. He didn't even realize he wasn't alone until he felt a hand on his back. He looked up into the teary eyes of his partner's only love. She dropped down next to him and took him in her arms. "You go ahead and get it out, Junior. It's about time you got it all out."

They cried together until Seany's head hurt and he was completely exhausted. She lifted his chin. "I'm glad you came, Junior. I thought I was going to have to drink this alone." She held up a bottle of Prosecco. "It's our anniversary. I forgot it in the car and went back for it."

They popped the top on the bottle, unconcerned about the fact that it wasn't even noon. They drank straight from the bottle, passing it back and forth, and pouring some on the ground periodically. "He'd have liked this," Kamala smiled at Seany. She swiped fresh tears from her cheeks. "He'd have liked the tears, too. He told me that if he got killed in the line of duty, he expected me to bawl like a baby for at least two years."

Seany laughed, a bit of Prosecco dripping off his chin. "That is so like him."

"So, Junior. Do you need some time to yourself, or did you want to tell us both?"

"Tell you what? Why do you think I wanted to tell him anything?"

She smiled. "I sent you off, half-cocked, to fall into bed with that old flame of yours. Obviously you've stepped in it and you needed advice."

He narrowed his eyes at her. "You don't know so much," he said.

"I know enough. Nelson stepped in it a few times in those early years. I made him work for it."

"Aye, she didn't return my last text, even though I said I was sorry."

"What happened? We want to hear it all, except the juicy parts. I'm not ready for that. You can get him alone for that part." She said this all while motioning to Nelson's stone as if it were a three-way conversation. He knew her. She used humor to mask her pain. Right now, she wanted to focus on someone else's problems. So, he told her.

Kamala wiped the tears off her cheeks. She waved away his concern. "I'm okay. So that's it, then. You couldn't talk about him. You couldn't talk about what happened that day."

Seany closed his eyes as if to protect them both from it. "Yes."

"Well, Junior. This is a good start. You can start by telling her about this. About today. This was hard, and she deserves the opportunity to love you through this." Love him through it. That was it. That's what his parents did. They loved each other through the hard stuff. Kamala was right.

CHAPTER 32

Tomorrow was Maureen's day off. She'd thought about going to Galway tonight, but she'd stopped herself. He'd hurt her. She couldn't go to him. She fought with herself about it and decided that she had to protect herself. If he wanted to be with her...if he wanted to make this really work, then he'd have to put in just as much effort as she had. After all, she'd crossed an ocean for him. And that was no exaggeration. As happy as she was that she'd taken this position, she'd initially come here to see if there was anything still between herself and Seany. Or if time had caused what they'd felt to wither and die. She wouldn't trade this time in Ireland for anything. She could easily see herself staying here. Her father had told her that this was her time to go out and find her adventure. And she'd found it in the unlikely hills and valleys of Connemara. In the calm, liquid gaze of remarkable ponies. She hadn't just fallen in love with Seany O'Brien all over again. She'd fallen in love with this place. But if Seany wasn't as invested as she was, she'd have to eventually leave it all behind.

"Maureen," Michele said for the third time.

She shook herself. "Sorry, wool gathering."

Michele shook her head. "He must have really screwed up by the looks of that long face."

"I don't know about that. It's just...hard. Whatever I felt for him six years ago, it's nothing like what I feel now. I just don't know if it's going to be enough. There are a lot of obstacles."

"Obstacles were meant to be climbed and cleared, sister friend. I'm single and in my forties, so I'm not a wealth of useful advice. But he cares, Moe. A lot. The stuff with his injuries, that's something different."

"It's not just that he was injured. His partner died. He tried to save him, and he died of his wounds."

Michele whistled under her breath. "Damn. I knew it was something more, but God damn." She shook her head. "Believe me. After a career in the military, I can tell you dying is easier than being the one who survived. I saw all sorts of men who couldn't forgive themselves for being the ones who survived."

"Yep. And I've given him a lot of room on that front. I just...need this ball to be in his court. Is that wrong?"

"Given what went down at the meeting, I'd say no. It is definitely his move."

"We had a fight after the meeting. He told me that just because we were seeing each other, it didn't give me full access to his pain. He got to choose who he shared it with. Obviously that someone isn't me."

Michele winced. "What a shit. Yeah, I would say it's definitely time for some grade-A ass kissing."

* * *

Moe woke to the smell of soft heather and peat. She thought she'd put the fire out, but the smell was unmistakable. She woke to see a slight haze in the room that stung her eyes. She jumped up to check the fireplace, but it was clean and cold. She hadn't made a fire tonight. And now, as she looked around the room, there was no haze of smoke. She must have been dreaming.

* * *

Seany's cell went off just before midnight. "O'Brien," he answered.

"All hands on deck. There's a forest fire in Connemara!"

He recognized the voice. A Lieutenant that worked the opposite shift. Seany's guts dropped into his shoes. "Where in the park?" he asked.

"It started in one of the western bogs. No rain for weeks, so it lit up like a match. They're not sure what started it. Just get your ass into the station. We need everyone. The retained staff have all been called in to cover the city. We're all going into the park. I need you here in twenty minutes. Can you do that?"

"Yes, I'm leaving now," Seany said as he grabbed his keys and wallet. He rang off and his heart was pounding as he explained what was going on to Josh.

Josh said, "Jesus, I didn't think forest fires happened here. It's so wet."

"Not for the last couple months. That bog turf burns like hell during dry spells. Can you call my parents and tell them where I am? They'd want to know."

He was at the station within fifteen minutes. "O'Brien, you're with McConnelly's team. You're on the hose if you think your shoulder is up to it."

"Tip top, Chief." He was surprised to see the Chief suiting up as well.

"No one say a word. I'm going. Protocol can kiss my ass." Usually someone as high ranking as he stayed on the sidelines in a command capacity. "This was probably some eejit doing an illegal controlled burn on the border of the park. It happens. If that was it, I'm going to gut the fecker with my favorite axe." Then they loaded up without another word and headed toward Connemara.

There were no public roads in the park. You couldn't drive through it. But the park services had their access in key points, and this is how the tankers got close to the fire. The park was close enough to the coast to get a fair bit of wind, which wasn't going to work in their favor. They'd be able to draw water from the river for the hoses, after their tank ran dry, but they needed the air support above to really have a chance at quelling this fire. It was hot, the turf burning quickly and spreading to the trees and shrubbery. Seany tried to get a read on where they were in the park, then he saw the skyline more clearly as the moon came out of the clouds. "Jesus, McConnelly, how far are we from Letterfrack? There is a ranch located right on the park border."

"Closer than you're going to want to hear about. Focus, O'Brien. If it leaves the park, then we'll deal with it."

Seany could hear the air crew over the radio. "We have full involvement in three areas along the west side of the park."

Once they were fully suited, they began the ground assault. It was like nothing Seany had ever seen before. Like an ocean of heat and rage. Colors assaulted his eyes through his mask. Licking tendrils of orange, yellow, white, and the space between. That black void where the air was all gone. The skeletons of trees were not like the burning frames of buildings and the creaking floor joists that could give way and end life as you knew it. But for the first time since that warehouse fire, he was completely engaged. No fear, only focus. The thought that this fire could leave the borders of the park was a thought he pushed out of his mind as he watched the backs of the men around him. He heard the plane overhead just as it dropped water along a strip of forest about a thousand meters in front of them. It helped, but this fire was not letting up anytime soon.

MAUREEN WOKE to the shrill of her telephone. "Hello?" She croaked the words, because her throat was hoarse and raw. It was back. That subtle layer of cloudy smoke. This time, she knew she wasn't dreaming.

"Maureen, it's Josh. You need to wake everyone up at the ranch. There is a forest fire in the park lands adjacent to the riding center. Seany got called in about an hour ago. I'm watching it on the news. It hasn't left the park, but they are fighting it from the ground and the air." Just as he said it, she could hear the planes zooming overhead. She threw her clothes on and was out the door in a minute.

* * *

THEY WERE TRYING to use the land formations to their advantage because they couldn't get the heavy equipment inside the park fast enough to dig ditches. They came at the fire from two sides. They couldn't get trucks at the eastern tip, so the planes would have to work on it. Seany heard over the radio that they were deploying the Irish Army's fire brigades, but it was going to take them a little longer to get here. The planes were going back around to the ocean to gather up more water. He'd seen them train before, and it was amazing to watch them come in low, skim the water until the tank was full, and head back to the fire. They used them in the States all the time, as the western states were plagued with catastrophic fires almost every year. He suddenly wished they had their own fleet of planes. If they did, this fire would be out already, no doubt. They'd run their trucks dry, but were able to use one truck to draw from the river, feeding water to the other trucks.

The men were working tirelessly for a couple of hours, and he knew these men were the best he could hope for when taking on a blaze like this. Everyone was already exhausted and overheated, but they pressed on, knowing it was going to be a long fight. The Irish Air Corps provided support from the air, and the Coast Guard was ready and waiting to fight from the sea if the fire went within range of their ships. Connemara was on a peninsula, so he felt certain they could keep this contained. But what he didn't know was how much of the park it was going to take. He also didn't know how close it was going to get to Moira's horse ranch. He wished to God he'd called Maureen. He should have made her listen. As if from some sort of divine power, the unspeakable came over the communications.

"We've got a bordering residence burning. The Clifden Retained

Station is spread thin, but they're on their way. It's a horse ranch near the Bunnaboghee Lough."

Lt. McConnelly came over the radio. "O'Brien, isn't that the ranch where you go for the riding thing?" Seany couldn't breathe. They all knew his American lass, as they called her, was living on the ranch as an intern.

"It is. I need to go, Lieutenant!"

"The hell you do, O'Brien." Suddenly McConnelly was next to him. "I can't spare you." Just as he said it, the Army Fire Brigade showed up behind them. Seany's eyes met his, the challenge evident. "Oh, for fuck's sake. Take one of the full tanks and go. Take Chief Braddock and Boyle with you. The Chief is making me nervous."

"I heard that, you insubordinate sod." Chief Braddock came next to Seany. "Let's go, lad. We've got to get this hose pulled in before we do anything."

* * *

Moe came within view of the stables and house and let out a scream. "Moira! Michele!" She ran toward the house just as Michele burst through the back door with Moira slung over her back. Moe got out her phone and called 999. "We have a fire at the Burke Riding Center in Letterfrack! One seventy-year-old female and one forty year old female suffering from smoke inhalation. The house is burning fast! Please!"

Moe was relieved to hear that the planes had seen the ranch fire from the air and already called it in. "Please, tell them to hurry. The horse stable is at risk. It's not far from the house."

Just as she said it, Devlin came peeling in with his tires smoking, and Rory was riding shotgun. "Is everyone out?" Devlin's eyes were wild as he took a headcount.

Michele said through fits of coughing, "Storm woke me up. He was going crazy. I smelled smoke and came out of the stable to find smoke and flames shooting out of the roof of the house." She spoke as she laid Moira out on the ground. She was coughing and gasping, her face a mixture of red and sooty black.

"It's all over the news. There is a forest fire in the park. Let's get the horses out of that barn!" Devlin barked. Moira was already trying to get up, her body looking so frail in her flannel pajamas. "Moira, you need to sit and wait for the ambulance.

She shouted, "They started the fire right under my bedroom window! I've lost my house. I won't lose my ponies!" She suddenly bent and vomited, and Michele smoothed her hair back.

Michele said softly but firmly, "We'll take care of the horses, Moira. You need to sit. Please, sit here so we can concentrate on something else."

That's when they looked and saw smoke coming from the back of the barn. In a flash of black clothing and a white face showing in the moonlight, a man ran from the area behind the barn. Devlin ran after him. The son of a bitch was no match for Devlin in a full fury. He tackled him. "What the hell did you do!" his voice boomed. He punched the man in the face, then did it again.

Moe yelled, "Devlin! The horses!"

Devlin yelled to Rory. "Tie that piece of shite up before I beat the wee mongrel to death!" His accent was so thick that Moe could barely understand him. She understood it. Those horses were like family. And Michele…Moe grabbed her just before they ran in the barn.

"You could have burned up in there with the horses," she sobbed. But there was no time to linger. She kissed her friend on the forehead and they ran.

They came into the barn just as the fire started to creep up the back entrance where they would have let them loose into the arena. Devlin yelled over the crackling wood, "Take them out the front! Toward the lough!" There was a small pasture next to the lough, behind Moe's cottage. "Moira! Get out of here!" Moira was behind them, practically coughing up a lung as she slid her barn boots on her feet. She ignored him, going for a stable door.

They took three horses out, Moe using the mounting block to get onto one of the horses while Michele and Devlin bridled all three. Then she rode seatless as she led a horse on each side down the road to the lough. Moira, not willing to stay put, rode another mare alongside her, then stayed at the lough to help on that end. When Moe ran back, Michele had bridled Clarence and went in for more tack. Devlin brought out two more horses, and Moe jumped on Clarence to lead them away. She rode him back to find Skadi and Franklin waiting. Michele passed off another horse to Rory just as the fire truck pulled in from the road. It was a small truck from Clifden, not the Galway City truck Moe had been hoping for. Seany was likely deep inside the park, unable to break away. But no sooner had she thought it, than a large tanker pulled in and Seany jumped out. He didn't even speak to her. He just went to work on the hoses, not bothering with his equipment. He had his pants and suspenders over a t-shirt, and he was covered in sweat. He must have been out in the park and shed his coat for the ride over. His thick arms worked proficiently, and the sight of him made her want to weep.

Seany yelled to the other men. "I'm going to help get the horses out, Chief."

Braddock yelled, "Get your fecking helmet on, at least!"

The house was more than half consumed now, and the Clifden truck was working to control it. The wind was blowing embers toward the barn. She watched in horror as the hay on the floor of the barn caught on fire while flames on the barn structure continued to spread. Then she heard one of the horses scream. She jumped off Clarence's back and ran into the burning barn. Seany yelled after her, but Devlin ran in next.

"Jesus Christ, Chief! Take the hose around back with Boyle!" It didn't occur to him that bossing his chief around wasn't prudent. He ran into the barn, hearing one of the horses scream either out of fear or pain. And that woman of his ran into the burning stables without hesitation. He ran in behind her and saw she was trying to control Balor.

"Devlin, take him! I need to get Sadie and Tempest!" she screamed.

Seany yelled, "Get the hell out of here, both of you!" He could hear the hose open up on the side of the barn, but they wouldn't go full blast with people on the other side of the wall. Both the stubborn goats ignored him. Then he heard it again, and new it was Storm. He was kicking the wall of his stall. The smoke was so thick near him, but Seany saw it. The glow of the hay catching just at his hind legs. Storm screamed and it sent a bolt of fear through Seany. *Not again.*

He almost ripped the hinges off the stall door. He grabbed the blanket off Storm's back as he bolted past him. He ran behind him just as he reared up, and he put out the flames that were burning up the horse's tail and searing his back leg. The smell of burning hair and singed skin made Seany ill, but he didn't have time to think on it. "Storm! Easy, boy. I'm here, laddie." He jumped on the mount block and grabbed a handful of mane as Storm bolted out of the barn behind his little daughter. Seany hung on for dear life as he followed Moe on Sadie's back, heading for the lough. Moira was trying to keep the horses calm. Seany said, "Moira! Storm is burned. Have a look, if he'll let you get near him."

Moira murmured to the horse like only a true, lifelong horse whisperer could. Storm's skin shifted in waves, like a shimmer. His pain receptors firing off. Anxiety and adrenaline warring in his body just as much as in the humans who'd come to rescue him. But Seany couldn't stay with him. He ran back to the fire, passing Maureen. "Keep your ass out of that stable!" He pointed at her.

"Not until the last horse is out!" she screamed. But as they ran up, Devlin was riding Hercules out, and Michele was bringing out Chancellor and Galileo. Rory came out with three more. War Hammer and Balor were on one side and Frida was on the other. They were being led to the lough by Rory's steady hand. War Hammer wasn't on a tether. He just padded along next to Balor like he was out for a Sunday stroll. That's when the heavens opened up, and it began to rain. The relief washed over Moe like a balm. She started to cry as she looked around. All of them were accounted for and safe.

Seany checked the water level in the tank, then radioed to Chief Braddock. "Everyone is out!" As soon as he said it, they let the hose go full force, splintering the charred wood. Then the rain started and he whooped out loud. Finally, something was going to go their way. It would help with the forest fire, at least.

* * *

MOIRA CAME DOWN THE ROAD, having left Devlin and Rory to mind the horses. She watched as the remnants of her house hissed under the assault of the hoses and the blessed rain. Then she looked at her stables. She covered her mouth as the sobs racked her body. The entire north wall was ruined, which made the roof unstable. It was, for now, completely unsound. They'd likely have to demolish the whole barn.

Moe looked around. Seany was gone now, back into the fray. She'd seen him briefly, getting the rest of his uniform back on, but he was gone, now. An older man came from around the barn and said to Moira, "It's almost out, Mrs. Burke. I'm so sorry."

Michele's tears were quieter. Just a look of despair and two streams coming down her blackened face. Moe took Moira by the shoulders. "Look at me, Moira. Everyone is safe. The horses are all safe. The rest can be rebuilt. Do you hear me? Everyone is safe."

She looked shell shocked. "This is what Abigail was trying to say. Something about dark, heavy clouds. And to listen for the storm." She paused and amended, "Listen for Storm."

Michele said, "Storm is the one that woke me." Her throat worked, a sob ready to escape, and then quelled. No doubt from years of disciplined restraint. Moe respected her so much.

Then she thought about what they'd said. Storm…the hair stood up on the back of Moe's neck. Cora's dream. And Finn…he smelled burning peat and heather. She'd woken up twice to the smell of burning peat and heather.

Moira walked to Michele. Then Devlin, Rory, and Moe. They circled her and moved in for a big hug. Michele looked like she didn't know what to do with all of the love.

"You saved Moira," Devlin croaked. "Oh God, lass. We could have lost her. And you. You could have burned alive in that barn." It was as emotional as anyone had ever seen him. His eyes glistened with unshed tears.

Moira pulled Michele to her. "Some people were just born to be heroes. Thank you, love." She unleashed another round of raspy coughs.

Michele was trying to keep her composure. It wasn't in her nature to cry like a girl. But there wasn't any possible way to hold back the tide of tears, given the circumstances and all of this mushy shit coming her way. Then she shook herself. "I didn't do anything any of you wouldn't have done. Now we need to get her to the hospital." They all smirked at one another. Their praise was making her feel awkward. She swiped at her tears, giving them a crooked smile.

Moe decided to change the subject, letting Michele off the hook, so to speak. "How's the fight going inside the park, Chief Braddock?" If he was surprised she knew his name, he didn't show it.

"We're winning, and that's something. It's burned up about twenty acres, but they've got it contained. A small fire, in the big picture. And this rain is just what we needed. It's going to help the whole area." Then he looked over in the grass, just past the Clifden fire engine. "Who the hell is that?"

They all looked over at the man Rory had hog tied under a tree. Moe said, "I suspect that's the man who set this fire."

"You mean this was arson? This wasn't from the park?" he barked out.

Moira answered, "It's very possible he set both fires. But this was the big prize. Ruining me or killing me." Her words were bitter. "You better call the guards, Chief Braddock. The detectives can fill you in on the rest."

* * *

MOE WATCHED as both fires slowly died out. Then she looked for him. She'd been frantic when Josh told her about Seany fighting a forest fire. Then she hadn't had time to think at all. Now all she wanted to do was see him. He'd been like an avenging angel, riding out of that barn barebacked on Storm, clinging to his mane. "Is Storm okay, Moira?" Her plucky boss was currently in the back of an ambulance, sputtering about not needing medical care. This was as good a distraction as any.

Moira said, "He has a nasty stripe across his left leg. It'll likely scar, but he'll be fine. The vet is on the way to check them all for smoke inhalation. She's probably already there." She looked back at Maureen. "I'll be staying next door in the other unit, once I beg for some clean sheets from you." Her voice was a raspy whisper, and it broke Moe's heart.

Moe said, "Of course. And Michele can bunk in with me. What about the horses?"

"The veterinarian staff is putting a call out to all of the local horse stables." She was racked by a fit of coughing, and the EMTs put an oxygen source across her nose and face. When she stopped the coughing, she said, "The trailers are all okay. That's probably what we should do next. Get as many trailered as we can and get them out of the night air. Storm will have to go to the clinic. I think the foals should go as well. The doctor will have to assess the rest."

Moe heard the water shut off, then she watched for him to appear from the back side of the barn. Then she saw them, carrying lengths of hose past the fencing. She didn't think, she just ran.

Seany saw her and dropped the hose. He undid his chin strap and dropped his helmet just as she tackled him. He smelled like sweat and smoke, but she just started to kiss him, sobbing against his mouth. "You foolish, idiotic, stubborn woman!" He said between kisses. "You scared me half to death!" He kissed her again. "You're such a pain in the ass!"

"Just shut up and hold me! You can yell at me later!" They were both blackened by smoke, which ran down their faces as it mingled with the rain.

He didn't notice. He covered her mouth with his. "I should have come to you last night. I shouldn't have left things like that. I love you, Moe. I've always loved you."

"I love you, too. I never stopped. I swear to you. I never, for even one day forgot you, " Moe's voice was desperate, and her tears started anew. "And I'm not going anywhere. I won't run this time. I love you, Seany."

Chief Braddock smacked the young, probationary fireman who had come with them on the back. "That is love, lad. That is true love." And if he had a tear in his eye, the others in attendance pretended not to notice.

Michele and Moira were both examined by the EMTs, despite their protests. Michele was released, but Moira was taken to Galway. At her age, they weren't prepared to let that cough go untreated. Everyone else worked to the point of exhaustion, letting the tragedy and horror of this night wash away with the rain.

* * *

SEANY HELPED both with his tank and the Clifden crew's. They were told to head back to Galway, as the Army Fire Brigades were helping on the ground. The Garda patrol officers showed up, as well as the detective who had been communicating with Tadgh. They'd get to the bottom of it all. And no doubt it had ties to that mineral company as well as Moira's nephew.

He couldn't leave until he checked on Storm. They were loading him in the vet's trailer as he walked Moe and Michele to the cottage. Moira was going to stay with Devlin in his spare room, after the hospital checked her over. Devlin had insisted on it, leaving the two sides of the cottage to the girls.

Seany approached Storm, his coat off and wearing only his t-shirt and suspenders. The sweat had dried on his skin, and the early morning air was chilly before sunrise.

He pressed his head to Storm's, and the horse actually began licking him and fluttering his gums over his forehead. "Wow, kisses. This takes our bromance up a notch." The horse put his muzzle under Seany's chin, rooting upward. Seany laughed. "Okay, okay. I love you, too, buddy. I love you, too." He walked around to see the angry burn across his left leg. Obviously, some burning debris had dropped into his stall from the primary fire, burning him and starting the hay ablaze. His long, flowing tale was singed almost completely off, but it was the angry pink skin that broke his heart. The horse had been utterly flawless. Regal in his breathtaking beauty. "You earned that scar, just as I did." He held up his arm where the thick stripe of scar tissue showed above his wrist. "See. I was flawlessly beautiful once as well."

Moe laughed beside him. "Modest, too. You both are so modest. Not at all cocky or sure of yourselves." She pulled Seany by the neck to meet her mouth. "And you're both heroes."

He cocked his head, so she told him about what Moira had said. And about Michele telling them that Storm had been the one to wake her.

"Listen for the storm." He looked at the beautiful horse, "Listen for Storm." He hugged the pony's neck, and Storm curled his head around to rest it behind Seany's. The horse equivalent of a hug.

They loaded Storm and Tempest in the same trailer, and the other foal and War Hammer in the other. The rest were being farmed out to neighbors. Then the men returned to their fire stations, and then finally home to their beds.

* * *

THE NEWS of the Burke Therapeutic Riding Center burning to the ground spread rapidly through the local community as well as the equine community. Help with the clean-up and donations began pouring in long before the noonday sun. The thought of an entire herd of award-winning Connemaras being wiped out by arson had the whole equine world in an uproar.

Moira slept the entire next day. Devlin relayed the message by phone, not wanting to leave her. She woke periodically, sobbing and calling for her daughter.

Michele and Rory helped Moe try to salvage what they could from the stables. The tack room had water and smoke damage, but the tack was mostly usable. Most of the structure would need to be rebuilt, if not all of it. It was all going to depend on the insurance company. As Moira's livelihood, lost wages for the staff, and boarding expenses for the horses were going to be costly. The insurance adjuster assured Michele that the claim would be expedited. After all, it was a local insurance company, and they took care of their own.

Moe said, "Must be nice. After hurricane Harvey, it took years to finish all the claims. People are still rebuilding."

Michele shook her head. "That's disgusting."

"Yep, it is." She pushed her rake, "So...some internship, eh?" She shoveled the charred hay out of the stalls as she and Michele broke into hysterics. They were holding their sides, laughing with arms slung over each other. And then they weren't. Laughter turned to tears and they were crying. Emotions were high and confused. They just stood in the rubble, thinking of how they'd almost lost Moira and all of these beautiful horses, and they wept. Rory came in and found them, tear-stained faces, backs up against a stall door. He sat down with them, handing them both a bottle of cold water.

Rory said, "If I didn't say it before, well done Michele. Moira might be dead if you hadn't gotten her out. She's like me own gran." His voice broke. "And ye both kicked some serious ass getting the horses to safety. If you two hadn't been here, we would have lost half the herd as well." He let that sink in. "The Garda called Moira. The man confessed, as if we needed it. He was hired by Corey and Jameson, just as we thought. Hugo is conveniently with his father in London, but they've been called in for interviews. The London police have already gone to the father's flat. Apparently he's a known gamer, big debts. I won't be surprised if the old sod gave Hugo a nudge."

"Those greedy sons of bitches," Michele cursed. They looked up to see Seany's car pull into the drive. "Time for you to take a break, girlfriend."

When Moe walked into Seany's arms, she saw Michele behind him mouthing, *Make-up sex!* And pointing toward the cottage. She giggled like a school-girl when Seany winked at her, then slung Moe over his shoulder like a caveman. Carrying her off in that direction.

Michele looked at Rory. He shook his head, "If I'd known it was that easy, I'd have tried it years ago."

"The whole hot fireman vibe he's got going doesn't hurt."

Rory feigned insult. "What? There's no hot farrier romance novels out there? I can be a leading man!" Which had them both laughing as they headed over to Devlin's for a tea break.

* * *

He took her hard and fast against the front door. That was the start of it. She had her t-shirt rucked up, her bra unclasped, one leg out of her jeans, and her panties shredded. He was still buried inside her, their breath mingling as he stared into her eyes. "Marry me," he said smoothly. She just smiled, pulling him in for another kiss. She'd felt the intensity and darkness in him, and when he'd spilled himself inside her, he couldn't hide the shaking. He'd likely regret asking in the heat of the moment. Emotions were too high.

She took his face in her palms. "Talk to me. Please. I know you're thinking about that night. About that loss. It's natural that this would bring it all back. Please, talk to me."

He stiffened, separating himself from her and pulling down her long shirt before he took another step back. She just dropped her hands, letting go. "I'm sorry, Seany. I'm sorry I can't be what you need."

He furrowed his brows, looking straight into her. "You're exactly what I need."

"Sex doesn't cure everything, Seany. I'll be there in that way for you whenever you need it. If you need the closeness or the connection or even just oblivion, but it's not everything. It's not enough to build a life…a marriage."

He ran his hands through his hair, suddenly angry. He buttoned his jeans, not looking at her. But she saw it in the lines of his face. Angry was okay, though. It was something. "What do you want to hear, Maureen? You want me to tell you the whole awful tale? You want the details?"

"I want you to tell me the parts that hurt you and won't release you. I want to bear some of it for you, Seany. I am not fragile. I can do this for you. I can hear the awful thoughts that you can't tell anyone else. You can trust me with your pain." She was so calm, he almost resented it. The reserve that was so much a part of her, but that he'd never master.

He leaned in, "You think you want to hear it, but you don't. And I don't want you to hear it. I don't want this blackness in my mind to touch you."

She put her arms out. "It is already touching me. It's a wall between us. If that's okay with you, then by all means, Seany, keep it to yourself!" Her calm demeanor slipped just a bit, and he exploded.

"I watched his face while he cooked alive!" He screamed the words at her, and it opened up a chasm inside him. "I held onto him, frozen because it was ripping my arm off! We were suspended in that awful, fucking nightmare! It was an eternity before we got a foothold. I couldn't let go, even though the pain was unbearable. All while I looked into his eyes and saw straight into hell. He knew he'd die. He spoke about his wife. He thought he'd die that day, but instead we watched him linger in a hospital bed!"

His voice broke and the tears streamed down his face. "Aw God. I wanted to let go. Just for a split second I wanted my pain to stop, but the bigger part of me would rather fall into that hole with him and die than to let him go. Then I had to watch him slowly die on the ventilator. Kamala had to watch. He knew he wasn't leaving that hospital. I looked at his kids and heard his mother's sobs. I pictured my mother standing there in her place. I felt so guilty that it was like being slowly poisoned!"

He was sobbing on his words now, and he realized he was on his knees. Moe was in front of him, holding his hands. "I wished I was there in his place...but during another split second of pure selfishness, I was grateful that my mother wasn't burying a son. And I hate myself for it!"

A tremor went through his whole body and he met her eyes. "I loved him. He taught me and took care of me like any one of my brothers would have, and I failed him. I felt the life leave him. I felt him go cold when his breathing stopped. I can't get it out of my head! I felt him go cold!" His voice was frantic, and he knew he was babbling, but she was right there with him. Letting him get it all out. Being the rock he needed.

Maureen held his hands, kissed them both on the tops. She said, "I'm so sorry. I can't take this pain away, but I can love you through it if you'll let me." Her throat ached with the effort of holding in her grief for him. Because this wasn't about her. Then he just started to sob. She held him… and he cried until he couldn't cry anymore. She kissed his eyes, then his cheeks which were hot and dry. Finally, when he'd exhausted himself, he found her mouth. He whimpered as he kissed her and she surrendered herself to him, letting him take everything he needed.

He undressed her slowly, taking care with her. Then he undressed himself while she watched, a hazy arousal evident on her face, but something deeper. A love so evident that he knew he could fall into her and she would give him everything. He lowered himself next to her, moving the tendrils of hair that were scattered around her beautiful face. She smiled so sweetly that it broke his heart. "When I heard this place was on fire, I damn near dropped dead on the spot. All I could think was that I might lose you. I hadn't even told you I loved you." He kissed her eyes, trying to dry her tears. The ones she shed for his pain. He put his forehead against hers. "I went to his grave yesterday. I went to tell him about you. I just…lost it. I miss him, Moe. I miss him everyday."

She touched his face. "Oh, Seany. My love. I'm so sorry you're hurting. I can't even imagine this sort of loss." His tears fell on her neck, and her own ran into the hairline at her temples. She raised her mouth to his, kissing him softly. He looked at her, more serious this time. "Marry me," he said as he slid into her body. He palmed her ass and raised her hips to meet his. "Marry me, Maureen." But she couldn't speak. His rawness was too much. The vulnerability he shared with her, even as he took her body, left her speechless. She arched and sobbed as she climaxed, feeling his pace quicken and deepen. She couldn't stop the sobs any more than she could stop the catastrophic release as it rolled through her body.

They fell asleep for a time, him still inside her. When she woke, he'd covered her with a blanket and was making some tea. She rolled out of bed, groggy from the stress and the sex and the tears that seemed to come so easily to her now. She slid his shirt over her head and walked to the galley kitchen. She sat and he pushed a cup of tea in front of her. "You're staring, Seany." He was so beautiful. Shirtless with low slung jeans, he was long and lean, with sculpted muscles and a face that stopped her heart. And those blue eyes, always those eyes that saw right into her.

He was staring. He knew it. He didn't stop, even as she blushed under his intensity. "Look at me, love." When she finally did, he reached over and cupped her chin. "I love you, mo chroí. My heart," he translated. "Marry me, Maureen. Marry me and live here with me in Ireland." He thought about Josh and the uncertainty of his future. The threat that he could be sent back to America. That's not why he wanted to marry her, but the thought of her leaving again was inconceivable. "I know I have no right to ask it of you, but I'm asking it just the same. I can't let you go, love. You're my mate. That means something in my family. It means everything. I knew it when I was fifteen years old, and I knew it when I woke up in the hospital." He leaned in and kissed her, soft and sweet. "And I know it now. Once an O'Brien finds his mate, it's forever." He came around the counter and took her in his arms, kissing the hell out of her before she could argue or answer. "Tell me you'll have me, i gcónaí." *Always.* "Say yes, a chuisle." More kisses.

Her tears came again. Her voice was rough from sleep and the smoke exposure and all sorts of emotions that were assaulting her. But the biggest one was fear. Fear of having to leave the only man she'd ever loved. A man who'd suffered terribly and laid himself out before her. A true partner. She nodded her head. "Yes, Seany. I'll marry you. It can't be right away, but yes."

He frowned, but the corner of his mouth tipped up in humor.

"How long are you going to make me wait, woman? We're an impatient lot."

"I have to see this through. There is so much that needs to be done. She'll have to furlough the speech and occupational therapists until we can get the stable rebuilt. The kids' program will have to be delayed. It's so sad. She needs me here, boots on the ground. Then I need to go home. I have to tell my parents in person. I want to go home and let them see how happy I am."

Seany smiled, kissing the tip of her nose. "Then we'll go tell them together. I'd like an autumn wedding."

"Or a Christmas one," she said. She laughed when he frowned. "There is no rush, Seany. I'm not going anywhere."

More seriously he said, "Would you mind living here? I mean, you're it for me. If you put your foot down, I could try to be happy in Texas." He shook himself. "No, that's not right. I would be happy in Texas. I'd be happy as long as we were together."

She warmed at the magnitude of that gesture. "I love Ireland, Seany. And I know your roots in this place go deep. I've lived many places. I'm adaptable. I wouldn't take you from here. We'll make a life here with your family. My parents will understand."

His body relaxed, and she understood what it had cost him to make such an offer. "I love you for the willingness, though. It means everything to me."

Seany put an arm around her waist, almost spilling her tea. "I love you, a stór. I am a complete lovesick eejit." He kissed her giggling mouth, feeling whole for the first time since he'd said goodbye to her in a small, North Carolina airport.

CHAPTER 33

I've often said there's nothing better for the inside of a man than the outside of a horse...Ronald Reagan

Letterfrack, Co. Galway

In the end, Corey and Jameson lost their campaign to gain a prospector's license to mine in Letterfrack. There was a swift investigation into the fires. The points of origin for the forest and bog areas showed the same accelerant had been used. The can of petrol had been dropped behind the barn after it had been used to start the fire on Moira's house. They'd escalated their pursuit of Moira's lands with an attempt to burn her alive in her own home. And kill all the horses, putting an end to any dreams of a riding center.

After the investigation led to several arrest warrants, Mr. Jameson fled to South America with his wife and aging mother. Mr. Corey, however, was taken into custody along with the arsonist he'd hired. England would extradite Hugo's father, who plotted behind his son's back to have Moira's place burned down with her in it. The mineral company executives had agreed to pay off his outstanding debts and were going to cut Hugo completely out of the deal. Apparently, Hugo was a prat, but he wasn't a murderer.

Poisoning the horses, however, had been his idea. They'd suspected as much. After all, the mineral company only wanted the land. The fact that Hugo had targeted what he felt were the less valuable animals had been what tipped off the detective in charge. If someone had wanted to ruin Moira, they'd have killed off the entire herd. Hugo wanted those valuable bits of horseflesh still sellable if he inherited the estate. He'd admitted as much, caving under the stress of the arrest and interrogation. In order to escape charges of conspiracy to commit animal cruelty and being held accountable for fraudulently filing an incompetency case against Moira, he gave them everything he knew about Corey and Jameson, including his father's involvement. He'd learned his lack of loyalty from his sire, after all. And he'd been pretty angry that they'd done a side deal behind his back. Even more angry than he'd been at the attempt on his cousin's life. After all, he was a morally corrupt sod.

It only took a couple days to get all parties involved to turn on each other in pursuit of a plea agreement. The rest would get no bargains, however. The scorched, scarred land of Ireland's beloved Connemara National Park would serve as a reminder to the Irish Government not to offer any leniency.

Seany had to go back to work, but Moe was surprised to see a car pull up and Seany's mother, sister, and niece get out. Cora ran to her. She enveloped the girl in a tight embrace. Cora said, "I'm sorry, Maureen. I'm so sorry." To Moe's horror, the child was crying.

"Sorry for what, angel? You've done nothing to be sorry for, honey."

Cora said, "I didn't get enough. I should have tried harder. I might have done more or given you more information."

"Now you listen to me, Cora Murphy. No one is responsible for this but the men who started this fire. They were greedy, awful people. You are a good girl. And you are so smart and brave. Don't you be sorry for a moment."

"That's right." They both turned to see Moira standing there. "Come child. Let's walk a while, and I'll tell you about my Abigail."

Moe watched them walk down the path to the lough. Brigid and Sorcha each hugged her in turn. "Thank you for bringing her all the way up here. I think she needed to come. And maybe we can take her to the neighbors to see a couple of the horses."

"How is Storm?" Brigid asked, worry lining her face. She turned to her mother. "Storm was the horse Seany rode...and the one he saved."

Moe said, "I think they saved each other. Storm got through to Seany when no one else could." Moe found herself tearing up again.

Sorcha took Moe's face in her hands. "You love my son." It wasn't a question. Moe nodded anyway. "Well then, let me tell you a story. It's an old tale about this branch of the O'Brien clan." They walked the path to the lough, and she told Moe about the enduring legend of the O'Briens. Each male in the bloodline had a fated mate. Once he found her, he'd love her and only her until death.

"So that's what he meant." She said the words softly, but the two women registered her meaning. Seany had chosen her. They simultaneously burst into tears. They looked so much alike, Moe thought. They even cried the same. They pulled her in for a hug.

She wasn't going to tell them about the engagement. Seany wanted to tell them together. Moira was going to give her a week off to spend in County Clare, letting the family get to know her and show her where Seany grew up. That was as far as she could plan for now. She looked back at the charred remains of Moira's dream. She would rebuild. And Maureen was going to be here to help her do it.

* * *

THEY MET at the lough away from the trauma of the charred buildings. All of them, in a circle of chairs with Alanna there to guide them through their last meeting. It had been postponed a week, due to the overwhelming amount of work the staff at Burke Therapeutic Riding Center had to do.

"I'm sorry we had to end this way, but Moira has invited you all back once they are up and running again. She's going to make time in the schedule for y'all to have a reunion ride. They should have the bridle trails cleared, and you'll be happy to know that they contained the fire in the park. There is still plenty of beautiful countryside to explore."

The men were angry, as they had a right to be. They were attached to this place, to the horses, and to the staff. They were doubly sad to hear that this was Alanna's last day. "I'll find a replacement, but my life is in Belfast. Let's just say I had a personal interest in this first class." She winked at her brother-in-law. Seany looked at her with such love in his eyes, it caused her to tear up.

They went around the circle, talking about the tragedy at the equine center and about their own continued recovery. When it was Seany's turn, he took a deep breath. "I know I haven't been very forthcoming up until now."

He smiled at Owen when he said, "You don't say?" Laughter rumbled through the group.

So, he talked. He spilled it all out, about the fire and about the partner that he'd loved like a brother. "The night I was injured, it was a warehouse fire in the Liberties. There was an explosion. My partner and I were clearing rooms on the third floor when the floor collapsed under us. I caught my partner by the arm…" He put his head in his hands, sucking air. Trying to fight the assault of images that ran through his brain. Glimpses of McBride's eyes while he hung on for dear life. His eyes in the hospital. He'd known he wasn't going to walk away from that fire. *I'm sorry to put this on you, Junior. Tell my wife I love her.*

Owen came next to him, putting a hand on his back. The group moved in, offering their support. "Take your time, brother. We're not goin' anywhere."

* * *

AFTER THE EMOTIONAL SESSION, the men went on their way. But Seany drove to a neighbor's stable, where he knew he'd find a few of Moira's ponies. He greeted Sadie and Tempest, smoothing his hands over the soft, downy hair of the foal that would someday be replaced with a sleek, shiny coat like her father's. Tempest was playful and affectionate, and he wondered if she'd grow into the cool, majestic demeanor of her father or keep the softer nature of her mother.

He walked to Storm who'd poked his head out of the stall upon hearing Seany's voice. "Hello, mo cara. How's the leg?" He opened the stall door, knowing that Maureen was speaking to the stable manager and he had some privacy. He closed himself in with his devoted friend. He rubbed his neck, feeling the connection rise up between them. Storm put his muzzle under Seany's chin. "I've got some good news. The stable is already under construction. You're going to be spoiled. And they installed a sprinkler system in case of a fire. A better heating system for winter. An indoor shower. A proper equine spa."

The horse chuffed, his thick tail whipping a fly away as his sturdy rump shifted. Sadly, his tail was much shorter because the flames had burned the hair a good twelve inches. Seany said to him, "I'm getting married. I don't have to tell you who the lucky girl is. You're half in love with her yourself. You're always flirting. I just wanted you to know that I'm not going anywhere, my friend. You've been there for me, even when I thought I didn't need you." Seany's eyes filled with tears. "I was scared when I heard about the fire. Scared of losing her. But I was scared of losing you, too. I couldn't bear to lose another partner." He rubbed his face over the horse's warm neck, his tears dampening the hair. "I'm so glad you're okay. That you're all okay. And we will get through this together."

* * *

DEVLIN, Michele, and Maureen found Moira after a half hour of looking. She was astride Sadie. Devlin had retrieved the ATV from the outbuilding. The women tailgated as he drove the estate. The horses were housed at neighboring farms, so the ATV was the quickest option, and it was in one of the only buildings that hadn't burned. He turned the engine off and they all dismounted, far out into the furthest pastureland of her property. He said, "Well, now. You're giving Mam a day out without her foal." His tone was light, but the worry lines etched his handsome face. She slid off Sadie's back like a woman half her age. They sat together on some large, flat rocks that had been moved there for a resting spot.

Moira said, "I've been to see my solicitor. The insurance will cover almost everything, so no worries about that. I've had a sit down with him about my estate, should something happen to me. It's long overdue. I just didn't have anyone, so..."

She shook herself. Devlin said, "Moira, there's time for all that. You're still in shock."

She raised her chin. "I am more clear headed than I've been in a long time. I could have died in that fire. Then where would we be? I was sitting here trying to figure out how to tell you everything, so I guess now is as good a time as any." She played with a blade of grass as she spoke, "I've left the horses to the non-profit for as long as it stays afloat. In the event of my death, you will take over as the Chairman of the Board, Devlin. No one else will do. You'll take care of my horses and my staff."

She turned to him and put both hands on his face. "You were the son I wish I'd had. I lost Abigail so young. I never thought I'd stay alone, but that's what happened. I stayed alone without any more children, and I made peace with that life. Then this scruffy haired lad came into my barn and took root in my heart for the better part of fifteen years."

Moe felt Michele take her hand, a shudder going through her. There wasn't a dry eye in the group, but the show of emotion from Michele really did her in.

Moira wiped away Devlin's single tear. "You are my soul heir, my lad. It's not like I'm going to give it all to that piss artist nephew of mine. He'll be cooling in the gaol for a few months at least. After the fire, I thought a lot about this place and my life here in Connemara. It occurred to me that I didn't have no one. I had you." She looked around. "I have all of you. And Rory and Penelope. And my beautiful herd of ponies. Who better to leave it to than my dear Devlin?"

His face showed pain. Like the thought of Moira not living forever was on his mind, rather than the generous inheritance he'd gain. "I can't, Moira. I don't…"

She shushed him like a schoolboy. "It's done, pet. I'm not going anywhere anytime soon, but when I do, you'll be taken care of. And you will take care of everyone else. If I didn't believe that, I wouldn't have done it. Now, let an old woman have a little peace and quiet. Take the single one out for a nice meal."

Michele blushed. That hard ass Marine actually blushed. So did Devlin. But he met Moira's eyes and nodded, then he looked at Michele. Moe had seen the growing fondness he had for Michele and wondered if she returned the sentiment. She was a little older than he was, but she was fierce and full of spirit. What did a few years matter? Things were going to get very interesting around the barn.

* * *

Furbogh, Co. Galway

Seany took her to a secluded place in the wilderness surrounding his home. It wasn't Connemara, but it was pretty, nonetheless. They'd begun with a light picnic, and now he was moving inside her. The crushed heather underneath their blanket was earthy and floral, mixed with the soap and shampoo that always lingered on her skin. She was looking up at him, the overcast day causing her grey eyes to deepen. The rain started softly. Finally, the rain had come to soothe the dry bogs and forests and had continued regularly since the night of the fire. Ireland needed its rain. He smoothed his hand across her wet palm, entangling their fingers. "Give me your mouth, Maureen."

Maureen felt the tension in her womb as her name rolled off his tongue. He kissed her then, deep and lingering. Their bodies slid as the rain soaked them. The blessed rain that would give her spring and summer in her new home.

Seany looked down at his mate, full of love and passion and depths that always eluded him. Challenged him. He hadn't been ready for this great love when he'd brushed up against it as a lad. He was ready now.

She'd be his wife, and suddenly the years they had before them solidified in his mind. He saw travel, adventures, laughter, fights...there'd always be fights. But there would be the making up. And there would be children. Perhaps a son with his father's eyes and his mother's auburn hair. Maybe a little girl with serious grey eyes and a Mullen temper. What a combination that would be. But there was time. She was his now, and he was hers. And they wouldn't be parted again.

* * *

AFTER THEY RETURNED from their picnic and changed into dry clothes, they headed south to Doolin. Moe had eventually called her parents and told them about the fire. And for once, she didn't find herself sugarcoating the details of her ordeal. She didn't need to protect her family. She needed to let them in. *You sound happy, baby. And I'm guessing that's not just about the job?* Her father sighed sadly. *You went and grew up on me, didn't you? And you're in love. I hope to God he deserves you. You traveled an awfully long way to find your happy ending.*

She'd said, *He does love me, Daddy. No one has ever loved me as much as he does. He's a good man, and you're going to love him.*

Now they were headed to a big family dinner, and Moe was a little nervous. Seany parked in the lane where his parents lived, as the drive was full of his families' cars. As he came through the door, he was hailed as the Connemara hero. He just shook his head. That was the thing about family. He'd never convince them that he hadn't taken on that fire alone and came out victorious. "I wasn't the only hero. Our Maureen ran into a burning barn wearing significantly less protective gear." He weaved the tale, Maureen riding bareback with another horse tethered on each side. They were riveted, and his brothers were all just a little bit in love with her. *Our Maureen.* Those two simple words were such a gift to her, because they didn't bat an eye. They thought she was their own. They knew she belonged.

Sean approached his namesake and youngest son, his eyes gleaming with joy. Seany was surprised when he took him in his arms like a child. He put his large palm on Seany's neck, and Seany fought the urge to start crying like a boy. His father smelled his hair, then said, "You're back, my lad, and you're whole." His voice was rough with emotion.

"I'm okay, Da. Or at least…I'm going to be."

His father pulled him tighter. "Every one of my children has their own scent. As strong and unique as your personalities. When you have your own children, you'll see. And that scent takes you back to simpler times. Times when I could protect you from the world. Heal your wounds with a bandage and a kiss. It's not so easy now."

Seany tightened his arms around his da. "You're doing great, Da. Don't ever doubt it."

Seany looked at Moe and a sheen of tears misted her eyes. Then the embrace was over, and his da went to Moe.

Seany's father took Moe's hand in both of his. She was mesmerized by him. By his handsome face and the direct blue gaze that was just like his son's. Both sons really, because Seany and Aidan both mirrored what he had undoubtedly looked like during different phases of his life. All of the other kids looked like a combination of the two parents, but Aidan and Seany were all O'Brien. He said roughly, "The men in this family are drawn to strong women." He looked around, his voice thick with emotion. He looked at all of his sons' wives, and at Finn. "You're all fierce in your own way."

Moe watched as Tadgh kissed his wife Charlie between the eyes. Michael just watched Branna, his eyes so full of love. Liam, lean and intense looking, watched his wife with a more predatory gaze. Like he would enjoy getting her alone. Aidan cradled his newest child, Alanna tired and sunken into his shoulder for comfort. Caitlyn and Patrick were covered in children of various ages. Finn was resting his chin on Brigid's head, her body pulled tight against him as he held her around the waist. The whole family was full of happy marriages. Sean said, "And he loves you, dear girl. He's always loved you. We've been waiting for you."

She squeezed Sean Sr.'s hand, quelling the urge to burst into tears. She'd dreamed of this day. "Well, then. It's a good thing I agreed to marry him." There was a moment of stunned silence.

Seany approached her from behind and whispered in her ear, and she heard the grin behind the words. "I thought we were going to tell them after dinner." But no one was looking at him. Their jaws were collectively dropped.

Brigid smacked her hands together. "Hot damn! Pay up, everyone! I said by the first week in April. You all owe me a tenner."

Seany didn't know why he was surprised. "You started a betting pool?"

Brigid grinned, looking at her grandfather. "I did no such thing. Grandda David started a betting pool. And now he has to pay up." Seany laughed as Granny Aoife gave him a smack on the shoulder.

Moe smiled at the exchange. David just laughed, looking at his son. "They remind me of you when you brought this one home," he said, pointing at Sorcha. "Although, I haven't heard him threaten to throw her down and…"

"Da! We don't need to share that story in mixed company," Sean said. Laughter rumbled through the room. Sorcha's laughter was the loudest. Such love, Moe thought. Just like her own family. They were all going to get along so well. Her father was going to fit right in. And her mother would love these fierce, strong women.

She shrugged, giving them that Mona Lisa smile. Its subtle beauty working its own special brand of magic. She settled her gray eyes on Sorcha, then Izzy. "We thought maybe the late autumn or early winter, when everyone is back from Brazil. We are going to tell my parents in June. We want to do it in person. But we wouldn't have the wedding without you all. And like I told Seany…this time I'm not going anywhere. I'm in it for good."

There was a collective whoop as Liam picked Moe up and spun her around. "Welcome to the family, love. I knew from the moment he turned toward the sound of your voice and opened his eyes, that you were the key to everything."

* * *

Glasnevin Cemetery, Dublin, Ireland

Moe knelt at the graveside of Seany's partner, and the knot in her throat was so painful she couldn't stop the tears. Seany was on the other side, pulling at a sprout of weeds, as if to busy himself. He said, "You always said that I needed a good woman. I just wanted you to meet her." He said the words as if his friend was in front of him.

There were two small flat rocks on the gravestone. One painted to look like a bug and one that he thought was supposed to look like a car. The boys' initials were on the bottom. A carefully crafted gift to leave their da. He took each one between his thumb and fingers, rubbing the artwork. Then he placed them back where they'd left them. The hot tears welled and dropped into the grass. His chest lurched and he sucked down a sob. But instead of the cool air of spring curling around him, he felt strong, lean arms wrap around his shoulders. She held him, cooing to him like a child as he silently wept.

"I'm sorry this happened to you, my love. But you'll never bear it alone again. You have a wonderful family, you have me, and you have Storm." She kissed his face, wiping his tears before she planted a soft kiss on his mouth. "We're together now. And this time, it's for good."

EPILOGUE

Josh finished his laundry before heading to meet his mentor. He hadn't been able to go to Doolin with Seany and Maureen. Work and school had to consume his every waking hour right now.

Seany was happy, and Josh was happy for him. Seany had been through a lot, and he'd been a friend to Josh when he hadn't known one single person his age in Ireland. That first year, when he'd separated himself from his parents, he'd had to find his way in unfamiliar surroundings. The new normal was safety, and he'd never had that before. Hadn't understood how life could be when you had good parents. Charlie and Tadgh had given him a loving family and a safe home, but Seany had given him friendship. An easy, fun relationship at a time when nothing else seemed easy.

Things were going to change, though. Seany had assured him that the wedding was six to eight months off, at the very least. And if they had to relocate, he and Moe wanted Josh to live with them. Get a bigger place and share expenses. He wasn't sure what he was going to do. They'd be newlyweds, and he didn't want to deny them their privacy because Seany felt obligated to include him in their plans. He could move back in with Tadgh and Charlie. They'd give him the spare room. But he hated the idea of leaving the west coast. He loved the Wild Atlantic Way. Loved being able to drive into Doolin for the weekend or have lunch with Katie. The closest thing to a matriarch that he and Charlie had. And then there was Madeline. He closed his eyes, an ache rolling through his chest. Without Seany and Maureen as a buffer, how would he see her?

Josh tried to focus on his trip today. They were taking a boat to an old lighthouse up north toward Donegal. He picked up the letter that had come from immigration again. He'd read it probably twenty times, reading into the simple request. Something was wrong, and Justine was behind this. He knew it deep down. She'd warned him more than once that she could make trouble for him. After all, her last boyfriend had worked for immigration, or so she'd bragged. He thought about his last conversation with the old keeper who was training him.

Genuine fear crept up his spine and prickled under his skin. What the hell was he going to do? This was his home. He was an O'Brien. It's the only time he'd ever really belonged. He couldn't leave his family behind.

ACKNOWLEDGMENTS

I always worry about using the internet as a primary source. When I can, I try to find a book on my subject matter or a credible professional website. I've used everything from the FBI website to old maps I bought at an estate sale. For this book, I found a used copy of *The Connemara Pony* by Sonia Kelly. That said, I'm no expert. I rode more when I lived in Colorado, but I don't have horses. I do love them, however. I love being in the saddle. The Rocky Mountains are most majestic when seen from the back of a horse. I often interchanged the word horse and pony in this book, but Connemaras are actually considered ponies. That's not an age thing. They are the largest of the pony breeds, averaging about fourteen hands. The native Irish ponies have been bred with Spanish horses, and even thoroughbreds and quarter horses over the years to refine the breed, but they are still some of Ireland's most interesting and beautiful natives. It's been a pleasure learning about them, and I'm so happy that Maureen Rogers decided to do her internship in Connemara. It was long past time she came to claim her O'Brien man.

The making of the book was a different experience from the others. Coming off spine surgery, Dark Irish was such a challenge for me. My body and mind were tired and suffering. I thought things were picking up as I prepared to start book seven, but then the whole world changed. COVID 19 changed our lives in a very big way. My husband was teaching from home. My kids were learning from home. My son is autistic, so I actively homeschooled him through the remainder of the year instead of just overseeing his distance learning.

My father's health began fading fast in January of 2020. Despite that fact, I never thought he wouldn't pull through. He'd cheated death so many times. He was so tough throughout the various health scares over the last three decades. But then I was holding his hand, singing to him as he drifted away. It was the most brutal moment of my life. Every morning I wake up and for a second, I don't remember. Then I do. So, my mind and heart are battered. My house is full instead of empty during the day. So, writing Book 7 was challenging, and it took a lot longer to get done. Despite all that, I am proud of it. It came together nicely with some help from my team of beta readers and copy editor.

I hope you enjoy this long-awaited reunion. Seany has been a favorite from the beginning. And we remember the day they met, when Moe's father, Mike Rogers, had a seizure behind the wheel while driving at Camp Lejeune. That was the day Seany first laid eyes on his mate. I hope it was worth the wait.

I always like to give artistic credit to my favorite songs. You know me. I can't go visit the O'Briens without a trad session breaking out. The song *Hills of Connemara* is one of my favorites and is written by Sean McCarthy.

I'd like to thank my friend Michele Kane, who is a retired Marine Officer and riding instructor and a whole lot of other things when she's needed. I'd like to thank the entire staff and team of volunteers at Hearts & Horses as well. H&H is a non-profit in Loveland, Colorado that provides therapeutic riding lessons to adults with disabilities, at risk youth, children with developmental delays or autism, and wounded warriors from the Colorado community. My son, George, took riding lessons while working with a trained occupational therapist. He rode Rebel, a sweet appaloosa who sadly died the next year from a twisted gut. My husband went through the veteran's program and rode a beautiful, strong-willed Irish Sport horse named Zulu. Zulu matched Bob's stubbornness blow-for-blow. Zulu is still helping new riders at Hearts & Horses and is still too pretty for his own good. If you shop on Amazon Smile, consider designating your charity points to Hearts & Horses, Inc. in Loveland, Colorado. Rest in Peace, Rebel. You made a sweet little boy speak and laugh and finally submit to wearing a helmet.

www.staceylreynolds.weebly.com

Printed in the USA
CPSIA information can be obtained
at www.ICGtesting.com
LVHW052120300724
786897LV00015B/1135